Untouched

MAISEY YATES

BERKLEY ROMANCE
New York

BERKLEY ROMANCE
Published by Berkley
An imprint of Penguin Random House LLC
penguinrandomhouse.com

Copyright © 2014 by Maisey Yates
Excerpt from *Unbroken* copyright © 2014 by Maisey Yates
Penguin Random House supports copyright. Copyright fuels creativity, encourages
diverse voices, promotes free speech, and creates a vibrant culture. Thank you for buying
an authorized edition of this book and for complying with copyright laws by not
reproducing, scanning, or distributing any part of it in any form without permission.
You are supporting writers and allowing Penguin Random House to continue to
publish books for every reader.

BERKLEY and the BERKLEY & B colophon are registered trademarks of
Penguin Random House LLC.

ISBN: 9780593819968

Intermix eBook edition / January 2014
Berkley Romance mass-market edition / October 2024

Printed in the United States of America
1   3   5   7   9   10   8   6   4   2

Book design by Kristin del Rosario

CHAPTER

One

It wasn't like she even wanted any of this for herself.

Lark Mitchell looked around the completely unconventional wedding being thrown in her yard and fought the urge to cry.

Which was dumb as rocks, because there was no reason to cry. Seriously, the bride was wearing a black wedding dress. It was ridiculous. And, okay, the bride was also marrying the man Lark had spent the better part of two years completely fixated on, but that was no reason to cry.

It wasn't like she *loved* Tyler. And in the year since he'd started dating Alexa, his new wife, and moved to New York, Lark had completely gotten over him.

No, this wasn't heartbreak. She was just in the throes of that left-behind kind of melancholy that she was more familiar with than she'd like to be.

She'd felt that way when most of her friends had gone off to college and she'd stayed in Silver Creek to help out on the ranch. She'd felt it all through high school when other girls had gotten dates and she'd gotten the chance to tutor cute boys in English.

Just this sort of achy feeling that other people were going somewhere while she stood in the same place.

Or, in this instance, sat in the same place. At one of the florid tables placed around the lawn. This little wedding had come to Elk Haven Stables because Tyler was once a ranch hand, and because the bride in black was best friends with Lark's sister-in-law, Kelsey.

Lark adored Kelsey, but she could honestly do without Alexa.

Which might be sour grapes. Maybe.

But damn, woman, marry a dude your own age. Tyler was in her own demographic, and he hadn't known her in high school, which helped, because as awkward as she was now . . . high school had been a biotch.

"Hey, sweetie."

Lark looked up and saw Kelsey holding baby Maddy on her hip and looking down at her with overly sympathetic blue eyes. "Hi," Lark said.

"Are you okay?"

"What? Yeah. I'm . . . so okay. Why wouldn't I be okay? I had a crush on this guy for like two seconds, a year ago. I never even kissed him."

"I remember how much you liked him."

"Thanks, Kels, but I'm a grown-up, as much as Cole doesn't like to acknowledge it. I've moved on. I have another man in my life now."

Because she was sure three rounds of cybersex six months ago with a guy she'd never met counted as having someone in her life. And if not, it at least bolstered her lie. She needed the lie. It was so much better than admitting she was pathetic. And that she spent most days in her room doing tech support for various and sundry people while eating Pop-Tarts and streaming *Doctor Who* through an online subscription service.

Yeah. Saying she was involved was better than admitting that.

"Oh. Do you? Because Cole"—Kelsey narrowed her eyes—"Cole doesn't know."

"No. And it's okay if it stays that way." The idea of her brother finding the transcripts from those little chats she'd had with Aaron_234 was ever-so-slightly awful.

Almost as bad as admitting that the closest she'd ever come to sex was a heavy-breathing conversation. Over the Net. Where you couldn't even hear the heavy breathing.

The very thought made her cringe at her own lameness. It was advanced geekiness of the highest order.

At least she excelled at something.

"I'm not going to keep secrets from Cole," Kelsey said, sitting down at the table. "I mean, I won't lie to him if he asks."

"He shouldn't ask. It's not his business." Of course, Cole wouldn't see it that way. To Cole, everything in her life was his business. Thankfully, Kelsey and Maddy had deflected some of that, but then there was Cade. Cade, who was the more wicked brother. The irresponsible one. The one who should be cool with her doing whatever and finding her way in life by making a few mistakes.

But Cade was even worse than Cole, in his way. The hypocrite. She always figured it was because while Cole guessed at what debauchery was out there in life, Cade had been there, done that and bought the souvenir shot glass.

She'd considered ordering the shot glass online, so to speak. But she'd never done a damn thing. So all her brothers' overprotective posturing was for naught, the poor dears.

Although Cole had nearly torn Tyler a new one when he'd suspected they might have slept together. Alas, no such luck.

She'd love to have a mistake that sexy in her past.

All she had was a greasy keyboard and a vague, stale sense of shame, which lingered a lot longer than a self-induced orgasm.

"Yes, well, you don't want to keep your boyfriend from us, do you?"

"He's not my boyfriend. He's not. I exaggerated a little. It's not like that."

"Oh, so . . . is he someone in town, or . . . ?"

"He's on the computer. He's not . . . I haven't talked to him in a while." Like they'd ever really chatted about anything significant. It was more like a straight shot to "What are you wearing?"

"Oh . . . okay."

"But the bottom line is that I'm fine. With this. Right now. Alexa and Tyler are welcome to their wedded bliss. I'm not in the space to pursue wedded bliss. I have other things to do." *Like sit on your ass and shoot zombies?*

No. Real plans. To travel someday. To have adventures. Maybe a meaningless fling here and there. In Paris? Paris seemed like a good place for a meaningless fling. Silver Creek certainly wasn't. She knew all the idiots here.

Worse, they knew her. They knew her as a bucktoothed nerd who would do your calculus while you did the cheerleader. It was a poor set of assumptions with which to begin a relationship, so she just never tried.

It was better than doing the guy who was doing the cheerleader. Doing math was way less painful. Keeping it virtual was a lot less painful.

Otherwise you ended up watching the only guy you'd ever really thought you might have a shot with marrying another woman. Not that that was what was happening. Because she didn't love Tyler, damn it.

But if she had married him, she wouldn't have done it in a black dress. She was a gamer geek with limited social skills, but even she knew major life events were the time to drop your freak flag a little bit. Wear some lace. A pair of pumps. Ditch the Converse All Stars for a couple of hours.

Not that anyone had asked her, of course.

"I'm glad; I was a little worried about you."

Worry for Lark's well-being was apparently a virulent contagion at Elk Haven Stables. Cade and Cole had a bad case of it, and Cole had clearly infected his wife.

"No need to worry. I'm golden. I'm not in a picket-fence place right now."

"Yeah, neither was I," Kelsey said, shifting Maddy in her arms and looking pointedly at the little bundle of joy.

"Unless you can get knocked up driving by sperm banks now, I'm not going to be in your situation anytime soon."

Kelsey laughed, the motion jiggling Maddy and making her giggle. "Yeah, steer clear of those clinics, or you might find yourself shackled to an obnoxious alpha cowboy for the rest of your life."

"Already am, Kels. Two of them. We're related, which means I can't just ditch them. I'm not marrying a cowboy." She looked back at Tyler. "I'm sick of cowboys, in fact. I'll find someone metropolitan who knows that high fashion isn't a bigger belt buckle and your Sunday go-to-meetin' clothes."

"Nothing wrong with wanting something different," Kelsey said. "I guess Cole is my something different, so I can see the attraction to something you aren't used to. I still rent out my house in Portland. If you ever want to go try something a little more urban . . ."

For some reason, the idea made Lark's throat feel tight. "Uh . . . maybe another time. Cole is just getting all his social media stuff going for the ranch, and you know he needs close help with that. He's death to computers." All true enough, but in reality, she could do most tech help remotely.

She would leave someday. Just not today. Or next week. Or next month. But that was fine.

"Well, that's true," Kelsey said. "But I'm not tech-illiterate, so I can help him a little. I do work on my computer, so I'm pretty familiar with everyday glitches."

"But who would optimize your blog?" Lark asked. "It's just starting to get huge."

"True. The modern world is a wonderful thing."

Kelsey was a health and wellness columnist, and she still had her column published in papers across the country, but since moving to the ranch, she'd started doing a lot of humorous posts about acclimating to life in the sticks, and thanks to her already established audience, it had become an instant hit.

And Lark was in charge of design and management of the website and its community.

Which was nice. It was nice to feel important. Nice to be needed.

"So you're really okay?"

"Yes," Lark said. "Stop giving me your wounded puppy eyes—I'm fine."

"Great. I'll be back in a minute, I have to go grab Cole."

"Neat," Lark said, reaching down beside her chair and pulling her phone out of her purse. She was itchy to check her email, because it had been a couple of hours and she hated the feeling of being disconnected.

She keyed in her PIN and unlocked the screen, her email client immediately loading about fifty messages.

She opened up the app and scrolled through the new mail. She had another one from Longhorn Properties. She'd been negotiating with the hiring manager, Mark, for a few days now. She hadn't told anyone in her family about the offer, because she knew her brothers would get all proprietary and think they had to do it all for her.

Like she wasn't smart enough to handle her own job opportunities in her own field. And yes, she worked for the family by and large, but she'd also done websites for several local businesses and had become the go-to IT tech for Silver Creek residents.

This would be her biggest deal by far. And the first time she'd be signing a contract for a job. But she was ready for the challenge.

She'd be setting up computers, servers, firewalls and web filters at a ranch for troubled boys, and then doing a little bit of tech training too. It was a big undertaking, especially with everything she already did at Elk Haven, but honestly, she could use something to mix up her life.

Something that wouldn't take her too far from the safety of her bedroom.

She had a little bit of a complex. She could admit that.

But she'd lost her mother so early, and then her father. Cole, Cade, the ranch—they might drive her nuts, but they were all she had. All she knew. Life felt horribly insecure outside of that. Terribly fragile.

Life was safe in video games. When you had armor and you could collect health right from the ground. Along with an AK-47 to take care of anyone or anything that might threaten you.

She skimmed the email and typed in a hasty reply, asking for more details on time frame and payment, then hit SEND.

"Is that thing welded to your hand?"

Cade walked over to her table and sat on the edge of it, his friend Amber in tow. Amber gave her an apologetic look. She would be annoyed with Cade silently, but Lark knew if push came to shove, Amber's allegiance was with Lark's obnoxious brother.

That was one relationship she had no desire to ever figure out.

"Nope, detachable." She tossed the phone down into her purse. "Unlike your stupid face, which you're sadly stuck with."

"Very few people have a problem with my face."

"Oh, dear, the tone of this conversation is lowering already," Amber said.

He turned to Amber. "Women really like my face."

Amber's forehead wrinkled, her brows drawing together. "Do they?"

"If not my face, they like my . . ."

"No!" This came from both Amber and Lark in unison.

"My personality," Cade said. "Sick people. You are sick people."

"Yeah, we all believe that was going to be the next word out of your mouth, Cadence," she said, using a name she'd assigned to Cade in childhood to piss him off.

Her brother hopped down from the edge of the table, wincing when his foot made contact with the grass. He froze, a pained expression on his face as he waited for what Lark assumed was a wave of pain to pass through him.

"Hey," she said. "I didn't think your leg was bothering you as much now."

"It's not," he said.

"Lies. Dirty lies. What's up?"

Cade gave her a hard look. But she knew he'd tell her, because he knew she had no problem harassing him until he did. "Nothing," he said, his tone hard. "It's nothing new. Just the same shit. It's like there's this nice little highway of pain that goes from my knee up to my spine. Not any worse."

Just not any better. Not really.

She hated that. Hated that Cade couldn't ride anymore. Hated that he hurt all the time. That day had scared years off of her life. She'd been convinced, when they'd gotten the call about Cade's fall, that he was going to die too.

That she was really destined to lose everyone she loved. All of her family. That she would be left alone.

She blinked and tried to pull her mind back into the present. Cade wasn't dead. He might be surly, and he might have a limp, and he couldn't compete in the circuit, but he wasn't dead. She really appreciated that, since as much as he drove her crazy, she needed him.

"Well, glad it's not any worse."

"Me too."

"So, want to get hammered?" she asked, not that she made a practice of getting hammered—but it seemed like it might be a good idea.

"Hell yeah," he said. "And Cole bought a lot of booze. His wedding gift to the newlyweds."

Amber's lips twitched. "You're going to get hammered drinking champagne? Because Cole bought champagne. For the toast."

"I have a talent where alcohol is concerned."

"I know," Amber said dryly. "I've held your hair, so to speak, while you puked off a hangover or ten."

Lark made a face. "Sick. I've never had a hangover."

Cade shrugged. "That's because you live timid. I don't."

"And you're all busted up to prove it," she said, knowing Cade would rather joke about his condition than say anything weighty about it.

"But I've lived. Bless me, Father, for I have sinned. Indeed."

"STFU, jackass," Lark said.

He put his hand on her forehead. "You're starting to speak lolcats. Get off the computer once in a while."

"You don't even know what lolcats is."

"Something to do with cats and cheeseburgers. Amber texts me crap like that all the time."

"At least she tries to modernize you," Lark said, shaking her head.

"How did this become a commentary on me? At least I come out into the light every day."

"Look," Lark said, holding her—admittedly pale—arm out in a shaft of sunlight. "I don't even sparkle!"

"Suspicious. I'm suspicious. Seriously," Cade said, "I worry about you, in your cave all the time. You've got to live life, Lark, or it's going to pass you by."

"Are you seriously giving me advice?" she asked. "Name one thing in your life that's organized, or settled, or . . . aspirant."

"Fun, Lark, I have fun. With real people. Outside. Look around you; it's in high-def."

"You're an idiot, and also, I have a life."

"Virtually."

And if that didn't count as having a life she was screwed. She bit the inside of her cheek. "Annnnd?"

"And maybe you should get hungover, is all I'm saying."

"But maybe have enough class not to go drinking all the champagne at a wedding to accomplish it," Amber said, somewhat pointedly.

Yeah, if Lark did that here, she really would look lovelorn and pathetic.

"Then I'll hold off. Anyway, you don't know everything about me, Cade."

"Beg to differ."

"You don't."

"If I checked your browser history I would."

"Nuh-uh." No one touched her computer but her, but even so, she didn't leave certain things lying around on it. Secret shame was secret.

"Witty comeback," he said. "Witty indeed. Why don't you go talk to someone? Meet a guy."

"Right. Meet a guy. Cole would be interrogating him before a full greeting exited my mouth."

Cade shrugged. "You take the good with the bad."

"You're both mostly bad," she said, not meaning it at all.

Amber rolled her eyes. "Have fun," she said to Lark. "And catch up with us later maybe? You can help me haul his drunken ass to his room."

"I say we leave him on the lawn."

"Fair enough," Amber said, turning and following Cade down to the table laden with drinks.

Lark bent back down and took her phone from her bag, trying not to think too much about her brother and his comments. Look what "living" had gotten him. And anyway, a hangover was hardly her definition of living.

She didn't have to drink herself into a stupor to feel like she'd reached the heights.

She opened up her mail app and saw another one from Longhorn HR. She opened up the message.

The money offer had doubled, and the length of the contract was for six weeks, with the possibility of extension. And attached was the contract, to be returned as soon as possible.

She knew exactly what her answer was.

She fired off a quick reply and the promise to email the signed contract over that night.

There. It wasn't much. It was a local contract, and she would still be able to live at home while she fulfilled it. But it was something. A decision made on her own. A step toward meaningful independence.

She put her phone back into her bag and stood up, taking a deep breath. Then she headed over toward where the bride and groom were standing, by the cake.

She was going to offer her congratulations and sincerest well wishes. She wasn't feeling quite so left behind anymore.

Quinn Parker was mean when he was pissed. Okay, he was mean most of the time, but especially when he was pissed.

And he was currently pretty pissed.

"You don't have anything?" Quinn asked Sam, his right-hand man and basically the only person who could put up with his shit.

"Nothing concrete. It's pretty tough to prove you didn't do something, Quinn, barring a confession from someone else."

"Beat a confession out of someone else."

"Who?"

"I don't know." Quinn rested his elbows on the granite countertop and stared across the bar at the empty living area. The cabin was almost completely done now. Though "cabin" seemed like a misleading word for the place.

Five thousand square feet. Huge kitchen, a dining room big enough to seat twenty. A living room made for the same number. And a section of private living space for himself.

The rest of the grounds had a kitchen that stood alone, along with outdoor dining. Classrooms. And cabins that were much more like actual cabins. Small and rustic. Just right for boys who needed to get their heads on straight.

His new role as philanthropist didn't sit too well with him. Especially because a few local news outlets were wanting to do a piece on the ranch, and that was the last thing Quinn wanted.

Because if they started looking at his present, they'd look into his past too. And that was a minefield. It would start with his family background and move on to his arrest record, straight down to being barred from the Rodeo Association.

No way in hell was he issuing an invitation for someone to open that Pandora's box.

But he could just keep hanging up on reporters. The important thing was the ranch. And messing with Cade Mitchell's head.

"I was thinking Cade was the guy we might nail, in truth."

"Really?"

"Yeah, really. I don't know. You think he's as injured as he said he was?"

"He got trampled pretty good. I saw the video."

"Yeah, he got the hell beat out of him, that's for sure."

It had been an ugly sight. Quinn had been there, watching from the gates, when Cade had taken a fall off his horse, who had been spooked beyond reason, stomping and bucking. And unfortunately, Cade had been trapped beneath the animal at the time.

It was the worst injury he'd seen in his years on the circuit. It had left everyone there with a sick feeling in the pit of their stomachs.

But Quinn's sick feeling had stayed. Because when the spike was found beneath the horse's saddle, and when inquiries were made, Cade had pointed his finger at Quinn.

True, he'd never liked the bastard. Cade was the golden boy on the circuit. Mr. Good Time. Every buckle bunny was on him after events, every sponsor was after him for an endorsement. And all that was fine, because Quinn attracted

his own women. The all-American good-time boy was nice
for some. But some women liked dark and dangerous, and
he wasn't above catering to that. And as for endorsements,
he frankly had a fortune on his hands now that his father
was dead.

The man commonly billed as his father anyway. Though
Quinn, and everyone else in his family, knew differently.
Whether they'd ever speak it out loud or not.

He didn't need any of what Cade Mitchell had, no matter
what anyone thought. And while Quinn had never been a
particularly nice son of a bitch, even he had his limits. If
Cade had taken a swing at him in a bar fight, Quinn would
have knocked teeth out of his head and made that million-
dollar face a lot less valuable.

Even he had enough . . . pride? Conscience? Something.
He wouldn't just ambush a man, especially when the move
would injure an animal like this one had. The horse was
fine, but it had been reacting to pure, biting pain.

Quinn might not like Cade, but he had no beef with the
horse he was riding.

Bottom line, Quinn was a bastard. Cade knew it, the
Rodeo Association knew it. Hell, the man commonly called
his father knew it too, though he meant "bastard" in the
more traditional sense of the word. Everyone else just thought
he was a prick. But no matter how big of a prick he was, he
wouldn't do what he'd been accused of.

And the accusation had damn well ruined his life. Taken
his credibility, taken the only thing he'd ever cared about.

Barred from competition. For life.

Damn it to hell, he had to fix that. He had to prove it
wasn't his fault. All of his appeals so far had been denied.
Apparently, he needed evidence. He closed his eyes and felt
a cold sweat on his back, the memory of his last hearing
playing through his mind, more terrifying than the times
he'd stood trial in court as a teenager.

I need evidence? Show me your evidence.

This ain't a court a law, Mr. Parker. We don't need

evidence. All these men here, bein' of sound mind, have come to a unanimous decision based on the testimony of Mr. Cade Mitchell.

He opened his eyes again and looked around at the cabin. Things were definitely starting to come together. A whole lot of things.

"I'm going to have a little job for you coming up, Sam," he said.

"Oh, really?" The other man straightened and crossed his arms over his broad chest.

"You and Jill, actually."

Sam's expression tightened. "All right."

"I'm going to send you on an all-expenses-paid vacation to Elk Haven Stables."

"That's the Mitchell ranch, yeah?"

"Yessir. If Cade Mitchell has exaggerated his injuries in any way, it will be pretty clear pretty quick. If I show my face over there, he won't drop his guard."

"I thought you wanted him to know you were here."

"I do. And he will. But he doesn't need to know you work for me. And on his ranch he's bound to be relaxed. Just for the first week, at least, I want you and Jill there pretending you're on an anniversary trip."

"Won't we need a reservation?"

"You have one. Mark called it in."

"He's a helpful sumbitch, ain't he?"

Sam was obviously irritated with the directive, but Quinn couldn't figure out why. A little all-expenses-paid alone time with his wife should make Sam happy. Although Quinn couldn't see the appeal, personally, since he had no intention of ever having a wife. Though Jill was a nice enough woman. Not his biggest fan, but he did monopolize a lot of her husband's time, and even more of it since Sam had been in Silver Creek helping him get things together.

"Yes, he is. He's also arranged a contract for me that will prove very useful indeed."

"Aw, shit, man, what did you do?" The lines on Sam's face looked more drawn.

"You say that like you think I did something bad, buddy. I think I'm offended."

"Did you?"

"Depends on your perspective."

Sam shook his head and pulled his cell phone out of the front pocket of his shirt. "I'll have to call Jill and see if she's up for this. Otherwise it'll be me staying in that cabin by myself, looking like a nut job."

"Mark might be willing to come down and stay with you."

Sam flipped him off on his way out of the room, grumbling as he dialed his wife.

Quinn braced himself on the counter, palms flat on the granite surface. Yeah, he was pretty sure Sam would think what he'd done was a very bad thing.

Cade would think so too.

And that made Quinn feel nothing but good. Because Lark Mitchell had signed a contract to come and work for him for the next six weeks.

It was a good thing to keep your enemies close. But it was better to keep their little sisters closer.

Because there was nothing on God's green earth that would piss Cade off more than having Lark in close proximity to Quinn. Like sending your lamb to bunk with a wolf.

Quinn smiled and pushed off from the counter. Oh, yeah, if Cade Mitchell had secrets, Quinn would find them. If Cade had a weakness, Quinn would damn well exploit it.

Quinn Parker was mean when he was pissed. And Cade had sure as hell pissed him off.

"Die, zombie bastards! Die!" Lark took another sip of her Rockstar and set it back down on her desk, clicking her mouse button furiously and unleashing a hellish rain of shotgun fire on the army of undead monsters schlepping their way across her computer screen.

Today she was starting her new job, and she was determined to start it right. Some people chanted little mantras about their personal success and being good enough and smart enough. Lark just wanted to blow the hell out of Nazi zombies.

And of course she'd had an energy drink, the breakfast of gaming champions. She was ready to take on her new job as head tech goddess of the Longhorn Ranch, part of the Longhorn Properties family.

She fought the urge to crush her can against her head like a frat boy. Mainly she resisted because she'd tried it once and had succeeded only in smacking herself in the head, but also, she was self-conscious enough to know what a douche move that was.

She pushed away from her desk, the chair rolling smoothly across the floor, then she stood up, brushing her hands over her black pants and black top. It was her most professional outfit: a button-up shirt and some dress pants. She looked a little like she was ready to wait tables at the local diner, but hey, she was used to working at home and rocking jeans and T-shirts.

But this was a real job with a contract, and she wasn't doing that. She walked out of her bedroom and into the hallway that overlooked the main living area of the house.

Crossbeams made from logs ran across the vaulted ceiling, and a panel of windows took up the whole far wall, giving a view of the family ranch. Their legacy. The only thing they had left of their parents.

Lark took a deep breath and continued on down the stairs. She still felt the sadness of losing them like a weight on her chest. She'd grown used to it resting there; she didn't think it had ever gotten any lighter.

It was hard for her to remember her mom, which was its own kind of pain. But their dad? She remembered everything. The way he smelled, the way he laughed, the way he talked. He was gruff, but he was loving. And sometimes she wanted to ask him a question, or just tell him about her day, so badly that the realization she couldn't was like having a hole punched in her chest.

Even after six years. It seemed so much longer and so much shorter at the same time.

Cole walked out of the kitchen just as she descended into the living area. "Hi," she said.

"Where are you headed?"

"Um . . . I have a job to go to."

"An interview?"

"No, like an actual job. I got the job already."

"You what?"

"I got the job already."

"When?"

"Like a month ago," she mumbled, looking down at her black shoes.

"And you didn't . . . tell us?"

"Well . . . here's the thing, Cole . . ."

"Who are you working for?"

"Longhorn Properties? They just bought a ranch out here for—"

"Well, who the hell is that? That name is supposed to mean something to me? How do you even know it's legitimate?"

"Google-Fu."

"What?"

"I have mad Google skills, which, in this case, means I typed it into a search engine and got information," she said dryly. "And this is why I didn't tell you."

"Because you could Google it you didn't tell me? How the hell am I supposed to check this . . . company, guy, whatever, out?"

"Not because I could Google it, Cole; because you're an overprotective nut job who would dress me in a roll of bubble wrap before I went anywhere if you could. Because you think it's your job to check this out for me, when I can do it for myself."

"And?"

"Legit. Cattle ranch in Texas, dairy up north. Lots of things that are dusty and involve farm implements. I have no reason to fear what I'm walking into."

"But I . . . I . . ."

"I know. I know. But, Cole, why don't you channel some

of your overprotective angst into imagining how you'll deal with Maddy's first dates, huh?"

"Since he's never had to deal with one of yours." Cade walked out of the kitchen eating a bowl of cereal. "Because you've never had one." He continued on by and out the front door. She shot a dirty sneer at his retreating figure and then turned back to Cole.

"Worry about him," she said. "He needs . . . something. Focus, direction. He's just a snarly, sarcastic buttmonkey, and he's starting to piss me off. He's around all the time."

"He does live here."

"And I don't really think he should."

"It's the family ranch. You live here."

"But you don't share control," she said. "I don't want it. I want a cave filled with computers. I don't want to ride the range, or whatever. Cade, on the other hand, would probably appreciate a little more control."

"Like I'd give it to him."

"My point exactly. Anyway, since you and Cade clearly have things to talk about . . ." She turned and headed for the door.

"Nice try. We'll talk about this later."

She turned back to face him. "I love you, Cole. You've been the best big brother ever. You took care of me . . . You've just always taken care of me. After Mom died. And then even more after Dad died. But you have Kelsey and you have Maddy. And I'm twenty-two. I don't need you to be so . . . on all the time."

He shifted uncomfortably, pushing his hat back on his head. "I know."

"Do you?"

"Yes. But I love you," he said, "and your safety and well-being are really important to me. Just because I have Kelsey . . . it doesn't change that. I love my wife, but you're my sister. And you'll always be . . . that little girl who blew her nose on my T-shirt when she cried."

"Oh . . . Cole . . ." She let out a breath. "I really do appreciate that. And I love you too. But . . . you have to let me do stuff for myself. We'll consider this in baby steps. Starting with a ranch that's a fifteen-minute drive away."

"Please tell your employer you have two brothers who own many guns between them."

"I will." She wouldn't. But she didn't really think Cole wanted her to. Well . . . he probably did, but he would know she wouldn't.

"And next time tell me what you're up to. Not to get permission or anything; just because I like knowing what's up with you."

"Okay."

"Kelsey says you might have someone in your life?" he asked, his voice getting a little nervous.

"Turncoat," Lark muttered.

"I have ways of making her talk."

Lark made a face. "I bet. Okay, really, really I'm going to work now, and no, I'm not telling you anything about the absence or presence of my love life. And in return, you don't need to tell me about yours. Really. I'm good."

He arched a brow. "Go."

"Am." She turned and walked out of the house, clomping down the steps and jogging across the graveled driveway area toward where she parked her little car.

Black, with crank windows and a tape deck. The thing was older than she was, and she loved it. The fabric on the ceiling had started to bow in, and she'd put it back up with tacks she'd shaped into constellations. It also had a sketchy heating system, which meant she had to drive with gloves and a scarf sometimes.

Cole hated it. He wanted to buy her something else. Something safe. She had a feeling he'd buy her a tank if he could.

But she liked her car, which she'd bought with her own money six years ago, and she wasn't going to let Cole have a say in it. Just like he didn't get a say over where she worked.

She knew some of it was her own fault. She liked the security she got living on the ranch, living with Cole and

Cade. Being surrounded by family. But she needed her freedom too.

It was a little contradictory, and she knew it. She laughed a little bit while she turned the key in the ignition and shifted into first. "Why can't he just read my mind and make sure things are exactly how I want them?" she asked the empty car interior.

She let out a breath. With any luck, her new job would help her get the little bit of distance she needed, and a little more respect from both of her brothers.

She knew what she was doing. They just had to trust her.

"Hello?" Lark poked her head into the empty living area of the massive house. There was no furniture yet, and her voice echoed off the honey-colored logs that made up the walls of the structure.

The air smelled sweet. Like sawdust and lingering smoke from recent cuts made into wood. Everything was clean, ready to be moved into. Except there was nobody around.

She waffled in the entryway, not sure if she should go in or wait at the threshold. It was a house, so normally she would wait. But it was a not-yet-moved-into house, which made it feel different. More like public domain.

"Can I help you?"

She turned around and her stomach took a free fall into her toes. Standing there, shirtless and in snug, low-slung jeans, his chest covered in sweat and dirt, was the single most beautiful man she'd ever seen in her life.

No, "beautiful" was the wrong word. He wasn't beautiful. That implied softness. There was no softness there. His angular face, shaded by the brim of his black cowboy hat, was all hard-cut lines. Sharp cheekbones, a square jaw.

Rock-solid pecs and defined abs, partly concealed by a bit of dark chest hair over golden-brown skin. No, there was nothing soft about him.

And on him, the big belt buckle, the kind she'd been so disdainful of previously, seemed to fit. Seemed to draw her eyes down to a very interesting place on his body.

Ahem.

Her eyes drifted to his shoulder next, to the intricate design that was inked there, spreading down his biceps. A black-and-white outline of a warhorse, shrouded partly in what might have been the dust kicked up by its hooves.

Well, frick. There went her whole "not interested in looking at boring old cowboys" line. Because he was most definitely a cowboy. And she was most definitely looking.

And then she looked back at his face again and a feeling of familiarity trickled through her. A spark of recognition, and she wasn't sure why. Wasn't sure from where.

He started to walk toward her, removing his hat as he did, and the feeling that she should know him intensified.

"I'm here about the job," she said. "Lark Mitchell."

Something flickered in his dark eyes. Surprise? Maybe he hadn't realized how young she was.

He looked her over, his expression assessing, then he wiped his hands on his jeans and extended one for a handshake. "Then I'm your new boss. Quinn Parker. Nice to meet you."

And suddenly all of the pieces locked into place.

Quinn Parker.

From the circuit.

She'd seen his picture in graphics on TV during televised events. She'd even seen him ride. And she'd rooted hard against him, her allegiance of course with Cade.

Quinn Parker. The asshole who was responsible for her brother being unable to ride. For his limp. For his pain.

His constant, barely tolerable pain.

Rage washed through her, a torrent of boiling water that started in her chest and rolled outward, flooding her face with heat.

"Quinn . . . Parker?" she bit out.

He flashed her a smile, teeth bright white against his tan skin. "You've heard of me?"

"Yeah, your name came up a few times when my brother was recovering in a hospital bed, so badly broken doctors weren't sure he'd ever walk without assistance again. So yeah, I've heard of you. And now I'll be leaving."

She slammed the door to the house and started to walk away, shaking with rage.

"I don't think you'll be leaving," he said, his tone easy, with a thread of steel running through the words.

"And why is that? Are you going to hold me hostage?" She crossed her arms and cocked out her hip, then realized that he might very well intend to hold her hostage. She didn't know how crazy the bastard was. By all accounts, he'd sabotaged her brother's ride and critically injured him, ending his career, all for a little prize money.

That was its own brand of crazy, and she realized she honestly didn't know what else he might do.

"Hardly, but you sort of put yourself in a hostage situation, if you want to call it that."

"Meaning?"

"You signed a contract for this job."

"I was misled."

"How?"

"I . . . You . . . I didn't know it was you."

"It's not me. Well, I own Longhorn, so it is. But I also have investors, etcetera, so it's not only me. And the contract you signed was with Longhorn. There's nothing misleading about that."

"But you knew it was me," she said. "I didn't know it was you."

"I needed someone here in Silver Creek to help me get this operation going, and you were the only name that came up. I could have brought someone in, but that would have been pointless."

"I can't even look at you, much less work with you."

"You better get used to both, honey, because whether you

like the idea of working for me or not, you signed the contract. Six weeks, and unless I somehow don't fulfill my end of the bargain, which is to pay you for your work, which I will do, you have no right to renege on it."

"But I . . . I don't . . ."

"And the fines for reneging on the contract are hefty. Or do you not remember that section of the contract you signed only a month ago?"

Yes. She remembered. And she'd ignored it and blithely signed anyway. Because she could get out of the contract if there was misconduct or a failure to pay, so she'd felt safe signing it. Had felt like there was no way it could go wrong.

Well, it had gone wrong. It had gone wrong in the shape of a tattooed bastard who had ruined her brother's life.

"I can't work for you."

"You can't work for me? Because you think I ruined your brother's career. Well, as much as I know I should just save my breath, I'll tell you right now, I didn't touch your brother's damned horse."

"He says you did."

"Knew I should have saved my breath. Regardless, I didn't. And you can't get out of our agreement, so you might as well just go ahead and believe my version. At least for the next six weeks."

"I can't do that," she said. "And you deliberately concealed your identity. Do you deny that?"

"Hell no. I'm a shady bastard. I didn't cause Cade's accident, but I didn't say I was an angel."

"I can't believe this." Cade would be so pissed. And Cole . . . Cole would think this just confirmed that he needed to be the one in charge of her decision-making.

She thought back to the way she'd felt at the wedding, how she'd felt like she was finally moving forward. Like she was finally getting somewhere with her life and her career. And now she just wanted to laugh hollowly at the bitter irony of it all.

She'd made the choice to step out, and she'd made a big-ass mistake.

"You'll hardly see me," he said. "I have actual ranch work to do, and I'm not overly concerned with the computer stuff. That's your domain, not mine."

"It's a conflict of interest," she said.

He smiled—slow, dangerous and damned if it wasn't a little bit . . . seductive. It made her stomach feel tight. Made her feel like she couldn't breathe. "What do you think I'll do to you? You think the Big Bad Wolf is going to eat you?"

"I'm not some limp fairy-tale character. If you try to touch me, I'll mace your ass, do you get it?" she asked, not feeling half the confidence she was attempting to exude. No, inside she felt like Jell-O.

He chuckled, a low, rolling sound that stoked the heat inside of her. The angry heat. It was angry heat. That was all it was. She couldn't feel anything else for the man who'd been responsible for Cade's injuries, and no matter what Quinn said, she knew he was.

Cade was certain, the Rodeo Association was certain. So much so that they'd banned Quinn from competing for life. Cade had been triumphant over that. An eye for an eye. He couldn't ride in competition anymore because of his physical limitations. And now? Now Quinn couldn't either.

"You're welcome to try," he said.

She frowned. He wasn't taking her threats very seriously. Maybe she should mace him and get herself fired.

"And now you're thinking of ways to get yourself fired," he said, crossing his broad arms over his chest. "I'm not going to do that. Too easy. Don't forget, I knew who you were."

"So what? You're just here to poke the hornet's nest?"

"Hell no. I'm here to get this ranch started, to give these boys a new start on life. I want the best thing for them, and that means the best computer system, since we will be continuing some schooling here, even over the summer. You were the best this town had to offer, and I hired you. For good money. Not only that, once the project gets rolling, you're going to be able to get some good publicity for yourself. You could end up with a serious business on your hands. A little independence."

How did he know she wanted that? How? What voodoo magic did this guy possess?

"At what cost?" she asked.

"A lot less than if you walk away from the contract."

Either way she was screwed. If she confessed the situation she'd landed herself in, any respect she'd hoped to earn by landing the job would be nullified. But if she took it she would be shaking hands with the devil, and she wasn't all that excited about the possibility.

"This ranch, this is really for what you said?" she asked. "For troubled youth?"

"You read the press release, didn't you? My hiring manager was supposed to send you all the info."

"While leaving your name out, right?"

He shrugged. "Yeah."

"Well, yes, he sent it to me."

"It's real. I have fifteen boys showing up in two weeks to start getting on the road to rehabilitation. They've all been in different types of trouble. A couple of them are going to require the presence of their parole officers. Some of them haven't made it that far down the road yet, and I aim to redirect them."

"Isn't this a little bit like a sick person offering antibiotics to everyone but himself?" she asked.

He arched a dark brow. "Maybe I've reformed."

She didn't think so. The man exuded darkness. Danger. From his muscles to the ink on his skin, there was nothing safe or reformed about him.

"I sort of doubt it," she said.

"Either way, I'm getting this ranch going, and then I'm leaving."

"Where are you going to go?"

He shrugged. "Back to Texas, maybe."

"You don't sound like you're from Texas."

"Shucks," he drawled. "I don't?"

"No."

"Well, I'm not, but it's currently the place I call home." A muscle ticked in his jaw. "I used to live on the road, but for some reason, I don't seem to anymore. Could be because I can't do my damned job anymore because a pissed-off injured jackass pointed his finger at the first person he could think of."

His words hit Lark hard, anger burning hotter in her. "Oh, really? Is that how you see it?"

"Yeah, honey, that's how I see it. If there's one thing I know, it's this. Cade will never be a hundred percent certain of who did this to him. Without a confession or video evidence, which there isn't at this point, he'll never know for sure. But I know for a fact what I did and didn't do. I'm the only one who knows for sure if I'm guilty or innocent. And I'm innocent." Something changed in his eyes, a cold hardness there she hadn't seen before. "In this instance anyway."

"Your word against Cade's," she said.

"Or not, because he could be wrong. Granted, I could be lying, but again, I'm the only one with certainty. I'm also the one that's either going to pay you thousands of dollars or fine you thousands of dollars, and trust me, I would love to watch Cade Mitchell have to write me a check to bail his baby sister out of trouble, so at this point, it's up to you and I can't lose. You can, though. So think about it real carefully."

Lark bit her lip, holding back an angry flood of words until she was sure she could speak without spitting. "Where are the computers?"

Quinn walked in front of Lark on the narrow path that led to the building where the computers were housed. By and large, the boys would be doing online courses throughout the year, and they'd set up the entire classroom in a large building at the edge of the property.

Longhorn Ranch was laid out a lot like a camp. There was a lake on the property, and Quinn was having docks installed. He'd also ordered canoes, of all things. By the woods they had an obstacle course. Something to run off any excess energy. And something to make them do for hours at a time if the little bastards copped too much attitude.

Lord knew he wished someone would have done it for him.

It had surprised him how much he'd enjoyed getting the place ready. No one could ever accuse him of being nurturing. But when it came to knowing what a bunch of punks needed to get their asses in shape—that, he knew.

Because he'd been there. He'd been that kid that might have gone off the rails if he hadn't been given focus. When he'd been forced to work for his food, well, then he'd learned real quick that he had to focus. That he had to stop being so amused with his own badassedness and get his act together or he'd damn well starve.

And then he'd found the rodeo. He'd had incentive to do right for real then. He'd started as one of the guys who opened the gates, doing hard labor for no glory. But eventually, he'd saved up, purchased his permit and won the required events to become a card holder.

That had meant the world to him. It was something he carried in his wallet still. Thirteen years on. It was faded, it was old, but it was his. Something he'd earned. Something he'd never imagined would be taken away from him.

But it had been. For no reason other than that Cade Mitchell hated his guts and he'd been a convenient target for the other man to point a finger at. Either because of anger or to keep people from looking too closely at him.

All Quinn knew was that he wouldn't let it stand. He would get absolution by any means necessary. He'd had one place in life he'd fit. And no, he hadn't had a hell of a lot of friends, and clearly the board wasn't a crew of his biggest fans, but he'd had his place.

Not anymore.

With any luck, Sam would find some evidence to knock Mitchell on his ass. Failing that . . . failing that, there was the girl.

He'd been surprised when he'd seen her standing there. Surprised by how attractive she was. Oh, she wasn't a bleached blonde with a plastic rack and a belly-baring top, which was a type he often ended up in bed with, since they were the kind of women who hung out looking to pick up cowboys of ill repute.

Lark had a kind of . . . natural beauty to her. Something fresh and almost sweet. A softness—and it wasn't just in her enticing figure. Though she looked soft in that way too. Not in a negative way, but like a woman should be. Full breasts that were the gift of God and not of a surgeon's hand. A trim waist and rounded hips.

Soft, pale skin. Glossy brown hair.

Everywhere a man touched her, he would be reminded that she was a woman.

Yes, her beauty had been a shock.

"Through here," he said, pushing open a door that led to one of the large outbuildings. It was more rough-hewn in looks than the main house. Wood left natural, unfinished. There were chairs in the front room, and desks, and through the entryway, into the back, there was a big room with tables that were, for now, empty. And the wall was lined with boxes. Computer boxes. "And this is where you can start."

"Nothing is even plugged in," she said.

He shrugged. "Yeah, I figured you could handle most of it. It is what you're being paid to do, after all. Get everything set up. Start with opening the boxes."

She gave him an evil glare. "Really? Seems outside of my jurisdiction."

"Until you form a union, I'm not going to worry much about that."

"I could use the boxes to make some protest signs."

"I think going on strike might be considered a violation of your contract, in which case, I'll be knocking on your brother's door and asking him to help settle up your debts."

"Okay," she said, hands planted on shapely hips. "Let's get one thing straight here and now. This is between you and me."

He almost laughed. Of course it wasn't between the two of them. It never had been. He would have hired the guy who'd set up his ranch in Texas if he hadn't seen an opportunity to get a foothold in Cade's world via his much-doted-on sister.

Now, he wasn't exactly sure what he was going to do with

her, but the fact that he had her, at his mercy in many ways, for the next six weeks was enough for now.

"Sure," he said, instead of voicing the truth. "But if that's the case, it cuts both ways. This is between you and me, and Cade has nothing to do with it."

"That's not . . . I can't . . ."

"Then I can't."

"If I default on the contract, Cole and Cade have nothing to do with it. I don't want you showing up at their door and making my problems their problems."

"You strike me as the kind of girl who hasn't had very many problems, honey. And I bet the ones you have had were taken care of by Daddy or by your brothers."

"Oh, you think that?" she asked, one delicate brow arching. "You don't have anything but hair under that hat, do you, cowboy?"

"Don't tell me your brothers wouldn't jump to protect you if you needed it."

"Sure they would. But you have no idea what I've been through. Don't make assumptions."

"Is that any way to talk to your boss?"

"You gonna fire me? Because then you can't hold anything over my head."

"Nope. Not going to fire you."

"What do you want?" she asked. "Because no matter what you say, I don't believe any of this has to do with me being awesome at tech and you wanting to pick up someone local. I don't even think it's a coincidence you're here."

"It doesn't concern you, because as you just pointed out, what happens here is between you and me, and no one else. Why I'm here? Not your damn business."

Her dark brown eyes assessed him, her brows drawn tightly together. She didn't trust him. She was smart. And he was going to have to work hard to get past that. Because she shouldn't trust him.

But it was in his best interest that she did.

"Fine. I'm just going to be your tech monkey. *Oooh ooh ah ah.* Get me a freaking box cutter and I'll get to work."

He walked over to the counter that lined the back of the room and rifled through a box that was sitting on top of it, digging for her requested item. He walked over to where she was standing and held out the cutter, the blade not extended.

She took it from him and pressed the button, pushing the blade up. Then she bent down and sliced the top of the first box. "All-in-one," she said. "Sweet. Unless you need to pull one apart to repair it. Easy to set up, though, so I won't complain."

"Maybe I should return them and get something that will challenge you."

"Don't you have horses to shoe? Cattle to prod? Lives to ruin?"

"Am I ruining yours a little by standing here? If so, I think I might just hang out."

"No. I find your presence therapeutic. You're a living, breathing, shirtless Zen fountain."

"Then maybe I'll stay."

She shot him a deadly glare and took the cutter to the top of the next box. "This is going to be really boring."

He shrugged, giving her ass a once-over when she bent down to dig through the box. No, this wasn't boring at all. He didn't want to think about how long it had been since he'd gotten laid. He'd had too much on his mind lately to even think about that.

"Suit yourself. This might take you a while—if you want to stay for dinner, you're welcome to. I have a chef, and he'll be cooking for everyone in the mess hall."

"Mess hall? Is this a boot camp?"

"Something like it." He tipped his hat. "See you at dinner."

"No, you won't!" she called after him as he exited the room and the building. Right when he went out into the warm, dusty afternoon, his phone buzzed in his pocket. He looked at the screen and hit the ACCEPT button. "What's up, Sam?"

"Jill agreed. So when are the reservations for?"

"Tomorrow."

Sam swore. "Thanks, Quinn, might have given us some notice."

"Why? She's gonna be pissed about a vacation?"

"This isn't a vacation so much as espionage for my boss. Who she thinks is kind of a dick."

"Jill doesn't like me?"

"Not much."

"Well. All right, then. Anyway, she can just relax and enjoy. I just need you to keep your eyes open for anything I might be able to use to build a case against him." He looked back over his shoulder. "Look, Lark is here, so that means you can't be. You can't be associated with me, and neither can Jill. Not until after the week is up."

"I'm not comfortable with this giddy-up spy ring thing you have going on. That's not what I do, man."

"No, you and I travel the circuit. We're rodeo men, Sam, unless I stay barred. For life. Then I'm not anymore." He took a deep breath. "You could go back. Find someone else you can assist on the circuit."

"You know I won't."

"Then you have to be part of the giddy-up spy ring. I'll get you a deputy badge if you want."

"I'm flipping you off."

"Not as powerful when I can't see your middle finger."

"Just trust me. It's up there."

"I do."

"So, Lark is there. And what exactly do you plan on doing with her?"

"What do you think?" Quinn asked. He genuinely wanted to know. It might give him some ideas.

"Are you going to seduce her?"

An uncomfortable rush of heat assaulted him, his stomach tightening. "No."

"I thought—"

"You think I'm a bigger jackass than I am, Sam."

"No, I think you're angry, and you're just on this side of desperate, Quinn, and at this point, I wouldn't put much past you. I don't blame you, but I will remind you, she's about four years older than my own daughter, which means that as much as I like you . . . if you're going to use her? Hell, bro, you won't have to worry about the Mitchell brothers kicking your ass. I'll do it for them."

"Noted," Quinn said, gritting his teeth. He didn't like Sam's assessment of his character or his state of mind. He wasn't above making Cade think he might seduce the other man's sister; he wasn't even above manipulating her emotional loyalty just to screw with Cade. But he sure as hell wouldn't do anything as sick as screwing her just to screw Mitchell.

Even he had his limits.

"Good. Well, I'd better tell my wife to go and pack her things."

"Great, I hope you enjoy it."

"A week alone with Jill in a tiny cabin? The jury's out."

"What's going on with you two?" He'd always seen Jill and Sam as solid. Sam had been married ever since he'd met the guy fourteen years earlier. But the tone had definitely been changing over the past few years. He talked about her less.

He smiled less in general.

"Nothing," Sam said. "That's the thing. All right, buddy, talk to you later."

"Yep." Quinn hung up the phone and took another look at the outbuilding. And he thought about the woman inside. Yeah, she was hot. And in other circumstances . . . hey, maybe they could have tangled the sheets. But he had a hard line, and that was it.

He wasn't mixing sex and revenge.

It was time to forget about Lark and her curves and think about how he was going to clear his name—and make sure Cade Mitchell paid for all of the false accusations.

Vengeance was best executed with singular focus.

CHAPTER

Four

Lark finished getting the last computer plugged in and online, then stood up straight, surveying her work. Not bad. You know, except that she was working for Beelzebub himself and the cost would undoubtedly be her eternal soul—but other than that, it was good work.

She let out a breath and pulled her purse off the counter, digging around for her keys before heading outside. It was nearly dark. She'd been too absorbed in her work to notice how late it had gotten.

That meant avoiding that dinner invite might be stickier than she'd imagined. Oh, except no. She might be working for the devil, but she didn't have to eat his food. There was some kind of epic biblical metaphor in there somewhere, she was sure of it.

She just needed to get home and get in front of her computer and try to decompress from this insane day.

She walked back up the bark-covered path and toward the main house, then paused in the open space where her car was parked. Did she have to clock out or . . . was she good since she was contracted for a specific amount? Oh, *grrr*. She didn't know. Which meant tracking Quinn down again.

She didn't want to track him down. Unless it was to punch him in the face.

She sighed and headed toward the building he'd mentioned was the kitchen, then stood by the front door for a minute before raising her hand to knock.

A woman answered the door, in her late thirties, dressed in a very plain T-shirt and jeans. Was she Quinn's girlfriend? She didn't look flashy enough to be Quinn's girlfriend. Because if he was anything like Cade had been back in his rodeo days, he went for girls who went through a can of hair spray and a pallet of blush every week. Big hair, big lips, big boobs. Men like him took a Texas mentality to the women they went after. Everything bigger. Of course, they had those little waists that practically looked corseted, so not *everything* bigger.

This woman didn't have that look at all, but she was answering the door.

And why should she care if the woman was Quinn's girlfriend? It didn't matter.

"Hi," Lark said. "I just need to speak to Quinn for a moment?"

"He just sat down to eat."

"Oh, well . . . it's urgent. I was working on the computers, and . . ."

"Come in and eat."

She looked past the woman at the door and saw Quinn, along with about twenty other people, sitting at a long table with big wooden bowls set in a line across it. Pasta, salad and bread seemed to be what was on the menu, and Lark's stomach growled, a reminder she hadn't stopped for lunch.

"I should go. Home. Which was . . . actually what I—"

"Fifteen minutes to eat; it'll round out the hour. Now come on in," Quinn said.

Lark stepped inside reluctantly, feeling like she was violating some kind of sacred blood covenant with Cade by breaking bread with his mortal enemy. But . . . the bread was already cut, so there would be no literal breaking of bread. Just chewing of it. And she was hungry.

"Fine. For a minute."

She came in and smiled at everyone, realizing belatedly that she probably seemed like an ungrateful Bitchy McNasty, since she was, in their eyes, turning down a free meal offered by their boss, who seemed to repel none of them.

"I mean"—she smiled wider—"thank you so much, Mr. Parker, I would love to."

The quality of his smile changed, and she could tell he really enjoyed her having to call him Mr. Parker. Having to be nice.

She could just announce what a horrible person he was to everyone in the room, but something stopped her.

I'm the only one who knows for sure . . .

She hated that. Hated that his words had managed to take root somewhere inside of her. Hated that it all made her pause.

So instead of saying anything, she sat down at the far end of the table from him and started to fill her plate up with food.

Quinn made introductions around the table. The woman who'd answered the door was Sandy, a woman hired on to teach the boys. Everyone there was a teacher of some kind, specially trained to handle difficult children.

"Coke?" he asked.

She arched her brow. "Coke, huh?"

"Not a drop of anything harder on the premises," he said. "We have a lot of boys coming here who have a tendency to get in some serious trouble. I'm not bringing trouble to the grounds." He picked up his glass and took a sip of what looked like water, then set it back on the table. "Plus, I'm an asshole when I'm drunk, so it's good to keep it away from me too."

Her lips twitched. She was tempted to ask if he'd been drunk the day he'd screwed up her brother's life, but again, she held back.

"Yes, I'll have a Coke. Diet if you have it."

"That we do have. Diet pairs nicely with pasta."

She laughed reluctantly, and everyone at the table chuckled. After that she kept quiet and listened to everyone else talk. About the plans for the ranch, the boys who would be coming soon, how the teachers were going to handle particular situations.

She had to hand it to Quinn. He'd brought on a team of serious experts, and he himself was clearly pretty well-researched in ways to handle troubled youth. She hadn't thought for a second about the implications of having beer on the premises, but everything Quinn was doing with the property was exceptionally cautious.

Damn him. She couldn't fault him on this. Or the project at all. It was shockingly decent for a man who'd supposedly deliberately sabotaged a competitor's ride.

Although there had been no way of knowing the extent of the damage a spike under a saddle might do. The idea had been to shorten Cade's ride, she was certain, not to shorten his career, and nearly his life along with it.

No, she knew that. But it didn't take away the fact that that was what had happened. That Cade's career was over, and that he was in pain every day of his life.

Her spaghetti suddenly tasted like glue.

She put her fork down and stood. "Thanks for dinner," she said. "It was really nice to meet all of you. Really nice. See you tomorrow."

She stood and walked out of the building, knowing she seemed abrupt and weird and maybe even rude, but not caring so much right then.

She started fishing for her car keys, lost somewhere in the bottom of her purse, muttering curses as she did.

"Hey, what the hell?"

She whirled around and saw Quinn standing there. "Oh, what the hell? Sorry, I just realized I was eating with a man who nearly killed my older brother."

Quinn's head jerked to the side like she'd slapped him, the impression of her words as clear on his face as a red handprint. "Killed him?"

"He almost died. Did you not know? He lost almost half

of his blood because that damned horse ripped through all
that muscle and took out an artery in his leg. He broke four
discs in his back and three vertebrae. He's as stiff as a seventy-
year-old man on a cold morning—do you know what that
does to his pride? He won't say that, but it does. It kills him
inside whenever he has to ask for help, or when he can't
finish a day of ranch chores. He hates it when Cole gives
him easier stuff, but can't say no because he knows he has
to take it. That's what you've done to him. That's what you
did. All for a win. Was it worth it? Did the top spot on the
leaderboard feel good? I hope it did, because it was the last
one for you. Fitting, since it was the last one for him too."

"Hey, look, that's shit. I'm sorry if that's how bad off he
is, but I didn't do it. There's no proof now, there was no proof
then."

"Then why are you barred for life?"

"Because, honey, I'm bad blood, or did you not get the
memo?" He stepped out of the pale light coming from the
porch and into the shadow. "I'm not one of them. I never
was, I never will be. Cade Mitchell is, though. Golden boy.
And it's much easier to believe his word than mine."

"What makes you bad blood?" she asked.

"Some people are just born with it. They can never be
good enough. They can never belong. Born to screw up.
Born to take the least honorable path, that's me. It's always
been me. Ask my family about it sometime. I walked onto
the rodeo circuit, a nobody from the East Coast who wasn't
a part of any family anyone had heard of. Dark skin and a
bad attitude. Hell, baby, they didn't want me around. They
never did. This was all very convenient for them, and I am
a popular scapegoat."

"I don't think any of that's true."

"What? You don't think they made any prejudgments
about me? You're wrong there. Whether it is my skin, or my
criminal record—and I do have one, I won't lie—they did.
And I was the most popular guy to hang out to dry."

"That's not why Cade never liked you. He said you were
a mean, arrogant son of a bitch with an attitude problem that

wouldn't quit and . . . well, he said you probably have a . . . a"—her cheeks burned, but she forced the rest out anyway—"a small dick under that big belt buckle. So there."

Quinn chuckled and crossed his arms over his chest. "Well, he's actually right. Except on one score." He leveled his gaze on her, and even in the dark, she could feel the intensity of it. "I'll let you guess which one it is."

Her face burned hotter and her eyes drifted to the point below his waistband, which was, thankfully, obscured by the darkness. She only hoped that lapse, that moment when she'd looked, without thinking of course, had gone unnoticed by him. "I can't think of what it might be."

"Do I seem nice to you?"

"No."

"Humble?"

"Not in the least."

"How's my attitude?"

She swallowed. "Bad."

"Then I think you know the answer."

"Sick. Men are sick," she said.

"You said it, honey, not me. I don't have very much in the way of honor, but I'll defend what I've got."

"Well, congratulations on your penis."

He laughed, and not that kind of superior chuckle, but a real laugh. "Thank you kindly, ma'am. I expect I ought to let you get back home now."

"Yeah. I expect. Look, we'll be able to do this as long as I don't have to deal with you very much. I do like what you're doing here, but I don't like you. I can't. I suppose you understand that."

He nodded once. "Sure. See you tomorrow."

"Right. Well." She waved and turned away from him.

Quinn shoved his hands in his pockets and watched Lark walk back to her car. The conviction in her voice when she'd been talking about Cade had been a surprise. It made him wonder if everything about the injury was true. If it really had been that bad.

But he had to find out for himself. Cade had been so

willing to chuck Quinn under the wagon that it made him suspicious. Blame like that was only useful when you were trying to cover your own ass.

Otherwise why point the finger so vehemently? He would find out for sure and go from there. He knew one thing. He knew that no matter his physical state, he was going to make Cade clear his name.

And if he wouldn't, Quinn wasn't above making the other man's life a little more hellish.

Sure, it was petty. Sure, Cade had already lost a lot. But he'd stripped everything from Quinn for no reason at all. He'd left him with nothing. Because the rodeo had truly been his whole life.

And a man with nothing but time on his hands was a very dangerous thing.

Cade Mitchell would discover that soon enough.

Lark put her car in drive and pulled away from the property, skidding on the gravel, in a hurry to put him behind her.

She had a smart mouth on her. When Cade had talked about his little sister in the circuit, he hadn't mentioned that. He'd made her sound like a girl. Sweet and vulnerable. But she was a woman who packed a punch. A woman with some pretty intense loyalty.

If it came to it, loyalty like that could always be turned. Twisted.

And at the moment, he wasn't feeling like that was too far beneath him.

Hell, very few people seemed to think anything was beneath him. Might as well prove them all right.

"How was work?"

Lark jumped while closing the front door and ended up slamming it a lot harder than necessary. Cole was standing there looking fatherly. So annoying.

"Good," she said. She would leave out the part about Quinn Parker being her boss. It was a big part, but it was the one that made her look stupid and a little like a turncoat, so she was keeping that on the down-low. "I set up an entire computer lab. I'll be working on getting all the right things installed on all the computers over the next week. It's a ranch for troubled youth, so I need to get a lot of safeguards on the computers, and I'm just going to assume the little punks are computer hackers. It will make my life more interesting, and it will keep there from being any breaches in security once things get going."

"No porn on the premises?"

"That's the idea. And no unauthorized contact via computer. Which seems archaic, but these kids have been removed from bad influences by their parents, by and large, so contact through email, text, whatever, that's not happening."

"Smart. Are you sure you're going to be safe over there with a bunch of hooligan-type kids?"

"Hooligans? Really?"

"Riffraff."

She rolled her eyes. "If anyone offers me a cigarette, I'll say no."

"I am kind of serious, though. I want to make sure you're safe."

"I'll be safe. Actually, I met most of the staff tonight. There are cowboys that are going to guide the kids through the ins and outs of ranch work—teachers. One is a survival guide, and he'll be taking them on hikes."

"Sounds . . . good."

"Yes. It does. And legitimate. Nothing sketchy. I did a good job." She wasn't just lying by omission; she was lying like a rug. And she hadn't really intended to do that, but it had kind of come out, and now it was too late to take it back. Anyway, she deserved a little respect from Cole. She was a grown-ass woman and all that.

"I'm sure you did."

"You are not. That's why you were waiting by the door to pounce and ask about my day."

"You are late. You're not getting worked too hard, are you?"

"Nope. I got fed. I ate with the teachers."

"Sounds . . . good," he said again.

"It is."

"What's good?" Cade was standing in the kitchen doorway, a bottle of beer in his hand.

"My job," she said, her face heating. Because she felt like a jerk. Because what had seemed okay a moment ago didn't seem so easily justified with her brother standing there. "It's going well. Everything is legit. Cole was sure I'd done something really stupid."

"I never said that."

"You pretty much did. Because let's be honest, Cole—you think I can't make my own decisions."

"I never said that either."

"But you think it."

He let out a heavy breath. "Lark, I'm sorry, but you're my baby sister—"

"Who is twenty-damn-two, thank you very much."

"And you live at home."

She winced. "And you want that to change?"

"Hell. No. I'm just saying, you're still under my protection, Lark, and I take that very seriously."

"Cole." Cade shook his head. "She's not a kid. You have to ease up."

"I didn't say anything." Cole pushed his hat back on his head and scowled. "If you want to act like I'm a tyrant, then give me a chance to act like a tyrant. Fine, I don't think you know a damn thing about the real world. I said it. So I worry about you now that you think you're just going to go out into it."

"I'm down the street," Lark said. She was angry, angrier probably because she'd effed up and gotten tricked by Quinn. Because in some ways, Cole had been right, and she should have asked for his help, but because she hadn't she was in an impossible situation. "And anyway, I deal with people online all the time for the business. I know how to conduct myself."

"Virtually," Cole said.

"Knock it off, asshole," Cade said, coming to stand beside Lark. She almost laughed. Because Cade had given her a hard time about the same thing not that long ago, but obviously he wouldn't let Cole do it too. And because she didn't deserve to have Cade defending her.

"It's fine." She looked at Cole. "It's fine. Cade, Rockstar me."

Cade rolled his eyes and went back into the kitchen, returning a moment later with her favorite energy drink in hand. She lifted it and smiled. "Thanks. Now I'm going upstairs to recede into my virtual world like the little socially challenged creature I am. Feel free to hang out down here and talk about how incapable I am. I'll be resting up. For that job thing I have that I got on my own and that rocks. Oh, and did I mention that I'm making really good money? Because I am."

She turned and started to head up the stairs.

"Lark."

She turned and looked down at Cole. "What?"

"Sorry. I'm overprotective. I can't turn it off that easily."

She flicked the tab on the can. "Right. I know. Thanks."

"Seriously, don't be mad at me, please. Or I will send in the baby to give you kisses."

"Ohhhh . . . fine," she said. "But I'll take kisses from my niece anytime."

"I knew I would get you." He smiled, a little sheepishly, and some of her annoyance disappeared.

"Yeah, yeah. Fine. I'm going now." She continued up the stairs and into her room, closing the door behind her and pressing her computer's ON button while sinking into her chair.

She knew Cole meant well, but honestly. She wasn't a kid. She put her feet up on her desk and grimaced. Okay, maybe she still acted a little like a kid sometimes. She slowly lowered her feet back to the floor.

But then, there were a lot of people in her particular field who were like her. She was a computer geek, but she also made her money with computers, so it was acceptable. She clicked the icon for her favorite game and started loading up a campaign that was already in progress. Before she was able to transition from the waiting room to the map, there was a knock on her door. "Come in."

The door opened and Cade was there, leaning against the frame. "Hey."

"Hi." She looked down. She didn't really want to talk to Cade right now. It would only stab her conscience. But he was being nice, and she didn't want to be a jerk during the rare moment when he wasn't.

"Sorry about Cole. You know how he gets."

"Yeah, I do."

"And while I tend to express it more by busting your chops, I understand how he feels."

"You?"

"You're our baby sister. I know it was scary as hell for you to lose Mom like we did. And I know it was scarier to lose Dad too. To have no one. You were so young, and . . . and I can't imagine what it felt like being left with just . . . us. But from our point of view? We were all you had and we were just a couple of dumbass guys. Me, a skanky rodeo cowboy, and Cole, with the dysfunctional marriage and do-gooder complex. We weren't fit for you, Lark. And we knew it. And you have no idea how terrifying that is. So we tried to compensate."

"You were hardly ever here."

"I was making good money, and you know it wasn't just for me."

She nodded mutely.

"And Cole . . . Cole stayed married to that witch way longer than he should have because he was trying to do the right thing. Because he was trying to be enough."

"He should have asked me. Because I would have told him to ditch the bitch."

Cade laughed. "Yeah. Thank God he finally did."

"And thank God for Kelsey, who generally keeps Cole's focus off of me."

"The point is, I know Cole is a pain, but I know how he

feels too. You were our responsibility starting at a young age, and sort of like obnoxious parents, it's hard for us to let go."

Lark bit her lip, guilt rolling through her. "Yeah, I know . . . I do know that it's hard. You guys are all I have too. I know how suddenly you can lose family. I know how quickly life can get upended. Something happens and everything changes. That's one reason I've been happy staying here. One reason I haven't wanted to leave. Because I know family is precious, and you guys are all the family I have." Her throat tightened.

She felt like a worm. A gross, slimy, sibling-betraying worm.

Except what choice did she have? If she didn't follow through, she had no doubt that Quinn would show up here, smug and jackassy and demanding payment for the broken deal. She would look like an idiot, and he would get money from her family.

At least this way he wasn't taking money from the Mitchells, and he wasn't giving money to them either. He would have to pay a Mitchell for doing damn fine work. That was something anyway.

"And we love you and stuff, which is where the attitude comes from sometimes."

"Thanks, Cade."

He put his hands in his pockets. "Yeah, well. Don't tell anyone about this little moment of sincerity. It'll damage my rep."

"I won't let anyone know you were decent for five minutes, don't worry."

He winked. "Thanks." Then he straightened and closed her door. She shut her eyes and listened to his footsteps, uneven and heavy thanks to his limp, as he went down the hall.

Yes, she was a worm. But a worm in a binding contract, so there was really nothing she could do about it.

Nothing but finish the job. And she would do it really, really well so Quinn would have nothing to complain about.

When she thought about it, he'd probably expected her to pitch a hissy fit when she found out who he was. Which she had. And he'd probably really like her to quit so he could do his broody, nasty bad-guy thing and come collect money from Cade.

Or at the very least, he'd probably love to find her in breach of contract due to her behavior.

Too bad. He wasn't going to get the chance. Nope.

She might have made a mistake signing the contract, but he'd made a mistake thinking that she would be the easy way to get to Cade. There was a vague woman-in-the-refrigerator air about it all. Too bad for him she wasn't a passive, two-dimensional comic book woman. She was a real woman, and she was going to hold her ground.

She turned back to her computer and clicked into the map, adjusting the scope of her virtual gun and training the sight onto a passing zombie.

Oh, yes. Quinn Parker had underestimated her. She squeezed the virtual trigger and leaned back in her chair.

She wasn't weak. And she would prove it.

When Lark showed up at work the next morning, she was dressed more casually than she'd been the day before. Dark blue jeans and a button-up top that looked like she'd bought it up at the general store.

Plaid with little silver-rimmed, pearl-centered snaps. Interesting. He couldn't help but wonder how easy buttons like that would be to pop open.

Quinn redirected his thoughts and walked over to where Lark was standing, about to go into the computer room.

"Morning."

"Good morning," she said, her eyes dropping to just below his belt, her cheeks turning pink.

Remembering their exchange from last night, no doubt. She was a sharp woman, that was for sure, with an even sharper tongue. He kind of liked it. He was used to women who didn't try to challenge him. Women who were a little tipsy and into feeling his muscles, and then some, back at the hotel. Women who got all breathless and wanted him to be rough and dirty and everything they imagined having a bad boy in their bed would be.

He had a feeling Lark would gut-punch him if he tried anything. And for some reason that made her buttons, and the thought of undoing them, more interesting.

There was something wrong with that. Something wrong with him. Well, that wasn't new news. He'd known there was something wrong with him from day one. So had everyone in his family.

"Yeah, it is. Do you know what you're doing today?"

"Getting everything online and building a porn fence those little bastards won't be able to scale no matter how hot the boob-lust burns."

"Good luck. Teenage boys are highly motivated by topless women. If ever one of them was going to become a hacker, that would be why."

His eyes flickered down to those buttons again. It wasn't only teenage boys who were motivated by breasts.

"It might lead to a job opportunity, because trust me, if they can bypass my security measures, then the future is bright in the computer industry for them."

"You're that good?"

"I'm going to build the Great Firewall. You'll be able to see that sumbitch from space."

"No alcohol. No naked women." He paused. "We really are bringing them into hell for a reboot."

"They need it, don't they?" she asked.

Quinn nodded, trying to get his mind off of those buttons. "Yeah. They do. I wish I'd had a place like this. I might have got my head on straight a little sooner."

"What was it that made you get your head on straight?"

"Jail sucks," he said. "That, and I wanted a career in the rodeo, which you can't do from behind bars. You have to be around to ride. You have to be willing to bust your ass, and when you're busy working hard, you're too tired to get into trouble."

"Oh."

"Yeah, I've made some mistakes in my life, but trust me when I say most of them happened more than a decade ago."

She bit her lip like she was trying to keep words from

punching their way out of her mouth. Then she relaxed a little. "Well, great. Good for you. Good for you . . . I'm going to . . . build the Great Firewall."

"Of course."

She disappeared into the building and he shook his head, turning and heading back toward the house. He had some paperwork to deal with. Having Longhorn turned into a nonprofit meant there were a lot of *I*s to dot and *T*s to cross.

And if his brain was occupied with all of that, then he couldn't obsess about Lark and her buttons. He had way more important things to obsess about. Paperwork, for starters.

And what Sam would be reporting from Elk Haven Stables.

Jill looked around the cabin she would be staying in with her husband for the next week. Courtesy of his dickhead boss. She let out a breath and walked to the far wall of the cabin, then back again. It was a very small space to be sharing with Sam, all things considered.

Like rooming with a stranger. And after twenty-three years, she had no damn idea how that had happened. But she couldn't remember the last time she'd had a conversation with him. Couldn't remember the last time he'd looked at her like he even saw her. It always seemed like he was looking right through her.

The front door opened and Sam walked in, his expression grim. "All checked in."

"Great," she said.

"Yep."

She looked at him and wondered when he'd gotten old. He had new lines around his eyes and gray at his temples. And then she just wondered if she didn't look at him anymore either.

"So, what are your plans for the day besides playing spy games?"

"Nothing. They have horses available. I might go out for a ride. Been a while since I did that."

"You do that for your job."

"Not up in the hills."

"True. Fine."

"Why, what are your plans?"

She shrugged. "Nothing. I don't really have them. I might work."

"Of course."

She let out a long sigh. "Yeah, whatever the hell that means, Sam. We're here doing crazy work for your boss, but I get attitude when I say I'm working?"

"You could ride with me."

"I don't want to," she said. She regretted how shrewish that sounded almost the minute the words came out, but she couldn't back down. She didn't want to back down.

He sighed. "That's fine, Jill. I'll be back around later."

He turned and walked out of the cabin, and Jill let out a long breath. She'd screwed up again. She felt like she only said the wrong thing with him now. Maybe it was just a testament to how difficult it was to talk to a stranger.

She sat down at her computer and logged in. Her throat dried when she saw she had an email from Jake. She clicked it open and skimmed it. It was mainly about work. About the sales threshold for the month and how everything was going so far.

And then she got to the last line.

I'm going to miss the sexiest woman in the office this week.

She squeezed her eyes shut and closed the email program. That was overt, even for Jake. He was a flirt, that was for sure. And she truly, truly had no intention of ever taking him up on any of his subtle offers.

But she couldn't remember the last time anyone had called her sexy. She was a forty-three-year-old woman who'd been with one man. She'd given him her beautiful years and had given birth to two children, with the stretch marks to prove it.

So yeah, she was hardly beating admirers off with a stick. Including her husband, who seemed bored by her at most.

She opened up the email again.

Sexiest woman in the office.

Damn it. What was she doing? She shut her laptop, pushing up off the desk. Forget work. She would just go for a walk. Try to forget her fight with Sam. And try to forget the email from Jake.

"Take a lunch break, Mitchell."

"Busy," Lark responded before turning around, and then when she did, the air got pulled straight from her lungs. Quinn. Not shirtless this time, but in a dirty, tight white T-shirt, the edge of his tattoo extending just past the edge of the sleeve.

He was wearing tan Carhartts, low on his hips, streaked with dirt, a tear in the upper thigh that was just . . . distracting. Could she see a hint of skin there, or was it just frayed pant material? She fought the urge to stare. But it was hard.

What was it about him that was so magnetic? Why couldn't he be a troll?

Evil people should be required to signify said evil in their physical appearance, à la Disney cartoons. At the very least, their laughs should be some sort of sinister cackle.

But Quinn's wasn't. Even when he was being a jerk, his laugh was like a low roll of thunder that rumbled through her body and made her feel like a storm had just blown through.

It was lame. Somehow, when she was with Quinn her brain cells reduced by a third.

"You aren't too busy to eat. I'm not going to let you skulk around grumbling and pretending that I'm a slave driver and unreasonable and trying to kill you. You might want me to be, but I'm not. Lunch. Now."

She let out a breath. "Fine. No need to get all command-ish."

"Apparently there is."

"You aren't the boss of me."

A slow smile curved his lips. "Baby, I absolutely am the boss of you. You signed a contract, remember?"

"Then I ought to sue you for sexual harassment. *Baby*. Good Lord. Next you'll be asking for a martini and your slippers."

"Is that your way of calling me sexist?"

"No. You're sexist. That was my way of calling you sexist."

"Neatly done. Now come on, there's a sandwich waiting for you. And I didn't ask you to make it, so I think that's a strike against your sexism accusations." She made a face. "Everyone else is done already."

Thank God. That might mean he would leave her in peace with her sandwich.

"I haven't eaten though, so I'll join you."

Bastard.

"Neat."

He laughed again, that sort of pleasant laugh that was all deep and . . . sexy. Damn it all, it was sexy. "You're so transparent. I like it."

"What's to like about transparency when someone clearly disdains you?"

"Because you don't like me, but I do unsettle you."

"In that way the villain in a movie unsettles me."

"That's not it." He held the door to the dining room open for her. The long table was empty except for two plates with sandwiches and potato chips, one set at the head of the table, the other just to the left.

"Yes," she said, "yes, it is."

He sat at the head of the table and she fought the urge not to move her plate down farther to put some distance between them. That would be transparent. As was looking below his belt buckle and at the rip in his pants.

She didn't mind if he knew that she didn't like him, but she didn't want him to know that she thought he was hot.

"Okay." He put his elbows on the table and picked his

sandwich up with both hands. "If you say so." He took a bite of the sandwich, and she found herself watching his mouth.

"Were you raised in a barn?" she asked, picking her own sandwich up and keeping her posture straight and her elbows very much not on the table.

"Nope. In a fuckin' mansion."

"Lies," she said.

"Truth."

"What were you, the stable boy?"

"As much as my dad would have liked that? No."

"Uh . . . I thought you were all . . . you know, you seem like . . ."

"Like I'm not from an affluent background."

"Well, yeah. And you said you had a rough . . . time."

"I did. But most of that was my own fault. You know, it's pretty easy to think you're invincible when your parents pay for everything. And I really enjoyed making their lives hell while they footed the bill. Then I left home when I was seventeen and found out that life is a lot harder than I realized."

"You had a family and you just left?"

"Complicated," he said.

"Are your parents still alive?"

"My mother."

"Do you ever see her?"

He swallowed. "No. I haven't talked to anyone at home . . . it's been more than ten years. I didn't go back for my father's funeral."

"That's not complicated at all. That's stupid."

"What?"

"It's stupid. Both my parents are dead. I couldn't talk to them if I wanted to, and you have no idea how much I want to sometimes. But I can't. I never can again. And you can. You could call your mother and talk to her, but you don't. You could see your whole family anytime, and you don't. You missed your own father's funeral."

"My family aren't worth visiting, how about that?"

"I'm sorry, did you not just tell me that you were a

jackass who did everything you could to make their lives hell?"

"Repaying the favor. Don't talk about what you don't know about."

"So tell me about it."

"Why?" he asked.

Why indeed. She shouldn't care. She shouldn't be letting this make her mad, but she was. It was her trigger, and Quinn wasn't the first person to be on the end of one of her blazing "call your mother" rants.

Because she'd been a child when she'd lost her mother, and all through her life, especially when she'd hit puberty and had been stuck in a house with only men, and then only men and her brother's psycho thank-God-now-ex-wife, she'd wanted her mother back so badly her whole body had ached.

And there were all sorts of people who resented their mothers. Resented their caring and their hovering.

She would trade anything to have that.

"Because," she said. "We're both here. We have to eat lunch. We already don't like each other. Some people would promise not to judge. But I will. I'll judge you basically no matter what because I already don't like you. But at least I'm being up front about it."

"Fair enough. Fine. I'm a bastard."

"Yeah, we've met. Tell me something I don't know."

He shook his head. "Nope. You misunderstand me. I'm a bastard. The product of my mother's illicit affair with, of all people, the gardener. At least it wasn't the pool boy. We almost avoid clichés this way."

"And you know that for sure?"

"Everyone does. But no one says it. Let me tell you about my family, since you want to know; and feel free to judge them too, since you're in a judgmental mood." He put his sandwich on the table and leaned back in his chair. "Blond. Fair. Extremely conscious of heritage and blood. Both of my parents—and I say 'parents' in the loosest sense, as my father, the one I was raised with, is not my father—are descendants of America's first families. I'm the youngest. My brothers and sisters are all blond haired and blue eyed, clearly from that fine lineage my father is so proud of." He smiled. "I'm not. Or did you need that spelled out for you?"

She looked at Quinn, at his dark eyes and hair, skin that was a deep olive color. "Just because you don't look like them . . ."

"It's more than that. My father knew from the moment I was born that I wasn't a Parker. To avoid scandal, he gave me his name and he never said a thing, but everyone knew, Lark. Everyone knows. My parents' friends knew. My brothers and sisters knew. It was my brother that told me for sure. Because he knew about the affair. And when he told me that . . . well, there was no more doubting, not even a little bit of it. I'm not a part of my dad's precious brood. Not one of the pureblood wonders who can trace their line to Plymouth Rock. I'm my mom's midlife crisis. The one she had to look at every day until she just decided not to look too closely."

"Quinn . . . I don't . . ."

"Because it's complicated, right?"

Lark swallowed hard. "Yeah. Okay, that's a little complicated."

"I'm sorry your parents are dead, Lark. I'm sorry you didn't have them growing up. But mine were alive, and I didn't have them growing up either. Not the way you should have your parents."

"Quinn . . ." She bit the inside of her cheek and searched for words. For advice. But what advice did she have to give a man who was (a) an asshole and (b) more than a decade older than her? He'd lived more. Seen more. And he'd dealt with things she couldn't even imagine dealing with.

Her parents had been so rock solid. A wonderful couple. Her father had cherished her, and her mother. Quinn's father hadn't really been his father. His mother hadn't liked him because he reminded her of her sins.

And then there was all the living he'd done since leaving home—and she was still in her childhood bedroom. Yeah, anything she said would be laughable. And she wasn't sure why she was even compelled to try.

She wasn't sure why she cared at all. Why it made her chest ache a little bit to think about a boy born knowing he didn't belong, and treated like he didn't every day of his life.

I'm bad blood.

He'd said that to her once. Was that what he thought? Really? That he was born wrong? Born bad, and there was nothing else he could ever be?

"I don't know what to say," she said. "I was going to offer advice, but it would be stupid and trite. I don't have any. But that—it sucks, Quinn. You shouldn't have been treated that way."

"Sins of the father visiting the son. Or in my case, sins of the mother. That's life, Lark. It's my life anyway. You did ask." He leaned back over the table, elbows firmly planted on the surface. "And I've committed more than my share of sins. I'm not paying for hers anymore. And I'd rather not pay for the sins of someone else. Of whoever's responsible for your brother's accident."

"So it's back to that."

"Yep. Because that's the thing that I'm paying for now. I've done a lot of things, but I did my time. I went to jail for driving like a drunk asshole when I was sixteen, and I deserved every moment I spent behind bars for it. Went back again for stealing from a Minute Market later that same year. Just thankful I wasn't tried as an adult either time. I've had more hangovers than I can count, and got the hell kicked out of me by a guy whose wife I was screwing around with. Though that was an accident. Not the screwing. I didn't know she was married. Either way, I've earned a lot of consequences and taken every damn one on the chin. But I am not paying for something I didn't do. I spent too much of my life that way already."

He stood from the table and she stood too, vaguely aware that she'd only taken a couple bites of her sandwich. Not really caring.

"Quinn, I don't even know what to say to that. I don't know you. My brother is one of the best men I know. And

I don't think he would lie, ever, about something like that. He has to know. He has to."

"I don't pretend to be nice, Lark. I don't pretend to be decent. So if I say I didn't do something, trust that I didn't. I could give you my long list of transgressions, and it's long, but that's not on there."

It was hard not to believe him. Now that she felt like she knew him—which was stupid, she didn't, they'd talked for ten minutes—it was hard not to believe he was telling the truth.

Because she genuinely believed that the man standing in front of her would cross his muscular arms across his chest and admit, with defiance, that he'd done it if he had.

She pushed that thought aside and put her hands on her hips. "So, okay, you say it's all legit, so I'm supposed to report back? Is that what all this is about?"

"Maybe," he said. "Maybe I'd take that. But would you give it?"

"No. I'm not going to go tell Cade I believe a stranger's word over his."

"Am I a stranger?"

"Yes."

"We just ate our second meal together. I told you about my childhood. You yelled at me. We're practically a couple." He took a step around his chair and toward her, dark eyes trained on hers. "The only thing I haven't done is kissed you."

"You wouldn't."

"Would I still be a stranger if I kissed you, Lark? Or would you feel like you knew me a little better?"

"You would be punched. In the face. That's what you would be," she said, taking a step back.

"Would I?" He extended his hands and brushed his knuckles over her cheek, the edge of his thumb brushing her bottom lip. "Well, can't say I'm in the mood for that." He dropped his hand. "We'll have to stay strangers, then."

He turned away from her and she pushed her hand, which was shaking, through her hair. "What's your game, Quinn?"

"I'm not playing a game. I want my life back."

And underneath those words, she heard the unspoken threat. That he would do whatever he had to in order to accomplish his end.

Good thing she was so determined not to be his means to that end. Yes, she was. That meant no sympathy, no more talking. And definitely no kissing.

"I don't know, man. Everything looks legitimate from where I'm standing."

Quinn pressed the phone harder to his ear and listened to Sam's voice, coming through the other end, sounding tired and a little bit ragged.

"And by that you mean . . . ?"

"He looks like hell. He looks like a guy who barely walked away from getting trampled on by an angry horse. Which I think he is."

"You've only been there one day. Have you seen him ride?"

"No, but I don't think he can, Quinn."

"But you don't know," Quinn ground out.

"No. But I don't know how I'm supposed to be sure, if me seeing the guy limp around isn't good enough."

"Stay for the week."

Sam hesitated. "All right."

"What's wrong with staying the week?"

"The cabin feels crowded."

Quinn dragged his hand down his face. "Sorry."

"It's fine. It is what it is."

He and Sam weren't the kind of guys who shared feelings. They shared stories about near-death experiences and which horse looked like it was in a killing mood when Quinn was drawing for an animal before competition.

This was outside their zone. Still, some lame-ass rodeo metaphor slipped out of his mouth. "You can't finish the ride if you aren't trying anymore." It got quiet on the other end. "Never mind. I don't know what I'm talking about."

Sam laughed. A humorless sound. "I don't know, Quinn, you might be more right than you think."

"Well, stick it out if you can."

"I can." And Quinn didn't know if they meant the week at Elk Haven or the marriage anymore, but he hoped Sam meant both.

"Great. Call me when you have more news."

"Sure."

Quinn hung up and put the phone on the counter, looking out the window at the wall of pine trees that surrounded the property and the blue mountains that rose up behind them. If Cade was telling the truth, if he was as injured as he claimed, that left Quinn without a scapegoat.

He didn't even have a guess about who else might have done it.

And he sure as hell didn't have evidence.

It was like losing hold of a lifeline out at sea. Watching the damn ship float away. It would have been easier this way. Easier to prove it wasn't him. As it was, there was nothing. Just his word, which didn't seem to be worth a pile of horse shit to anyone.

Hell, he didn't seem to be worth a pile of horse shit to anyone. Not without the rodeo.

Damn.

He put his hands over his face and tried to scrub away the tension in his forehead. He had to figure something out, because the alternative was a life without the circuit, and that was a future he just didn't want to face. It was one he didn't think he could face.

No. There was a way. There had to be a way to make it all work, no matter what Sam found out about Cade.

He put his head in his hands and rested his elbows on the counter.

Were you raised in a barn?

He lifted his head. Lark. Of course. There was a reason she was here. There had been a reason from the moment he'd first realized he could get her in his employ without her realizing it. He hadn't connected all the dots until just that moment.

But it was obvious.

An image flashed through his mind of the way she'd looked when he'd offered to kiss her. Her dark eyes wide, lush lips looking much more tempting than he'd counted on. The entire proposition, which had been meant to goad her, was much more tempting than he'd counted on.

Oh, yes, he knew what he was going to do.

He was going to seduce Lark Mitchell. He was going to make her his. And when she was his, she wouldn't belong to Cade anymore. Oh, he might not sleep with her, but he was going to seduce her.

Because Lark had pointed out something very interesting. They were all each other had. They were family.

Well, he didn't have much of a family. He'd had the rodeo. And Cade had taken that from him as though he had every right to do it. So Quinn would take something of his. Take the most important thing—just like he'd done to him.

It wouldn't be easy, seeing as she hated him. He'd never tried to seduce a woman who hated him before. Frankly, he wasn't sure he'd ever had to seduce a woman before. Back in high school, women had been attracted to his money and the fact that he was a bad boy. In the circuit, it had basically been the same thing. The status of hooking up with the winner of an event, or a chance to slum it with a rough, dirty cowboy. Either way, women pursued him.

But Lark wouldn't be making a move on him anytime soon. No question. She would need pursuing.

The thought ignited something in his veins. A predator's

instinct, maybe. Something old, buried in his DNA. A biological imperative. He'd never given much thought to things like that, but now, with heat, excitement, anticipation, coursing through his veins, he wondered.

Sam could keep an eye out at Elk Haven. Quinn could manage everything just fine here. He hadn't thought he would enjoy revenge quite this much.

Lark made it home for dinner that night, and she tried her very best not to look shell-shocked by her earlier encounter with Quinn. It would only get Cole's hackles up, and then he would start sniffing around, and she did not need that.

But Quinn's offer of a kiss seemed to be on repeat in her mind, and it was making her feel all shaky and melty. She did not like it.

She didn't like that he seemed to have burrowed under her skin, under defenses she hadn't realized were breachable.

What was wrong with her? Maybe she needed to track down Aaron_234 again and they could get their dirty chat on. But then, now that she had the memory of what Quinn was like, in the flesh and very much real, the idea of some illicit lines of text just didn't seem that thrilling.

She sat down at the table next to Kelsey. "Hi," she said.

"Hi. How's the job?"

She hoped her cheeks didn't look as hot as they felt. "Great."

Kelsey arched a brow. "Is there a guy?" she whispered.

"What?" Lark hissed.

"You turned all pink."

"I did not."

"You did."

Luckily, Cole wasn't paying attention to the exchange, because he was feeding Maddy, who was sitting on his lap, with one hand in his dinner plate.

"Fine. There is a guy, a little. But it's just that he's cute. It's not a thing."

"Right," Kelsey said. "I so totally believe you. Except I don't."

"Having a sister is overrated."

"You don't mean that. You love me. I've brought estrogen into this house. It's tripled, thanks to me."

"Fine, but please, don't say anything."

"Cole and I have a cone of trust. I don't keep secrets from him."

"You are the worst. You guess everything and you blab it."

"We won't tell Cade."

Lark grunted. "That's a relief." In way more ways than one.

"Hope we aren't too late."

Lark looked up and saw a couple walk in. Guests, she assumed. In their early forties. The woman was pretty, with light blond hair and blue eyes, and the husband was better-than-average-looking. Probably the kind of guy who looked better now, more distinguished, than he had at twenty. Tall, broad and with chiseled features.

Normally she booked guests, but thanks to the very easy computer program she'd gotten set up, even Cole could do it when he had to. As a result, Lark didn't know the new couple.

"Not at all." Cole smiled and gestured to the big table. "Have a seat."

They ate family style at the ranch. There was a smaller dining table in the kitchen for when privacy was required, but generally, the Mitchells, the employees and the guests all ate at one big long table, sharing in their cook's amazing skills.

Meals were always loud, and Lark sort of liked it that way, because it gave her the ability to talk to Kelsey without her brothers being able to overhear. Of course, Kelsey was a self-confessed rat fink who would give her secrets up to her husband, but she wasn't going to give Kelsey any of her real secrets.

The wife of the couple sat down next to Lark, while the

husband sat across from them, next to one of the ranch hands.

"Jill." The woman extended her hand. "Nice to meet you."

"Lark," she said. "Lark Mitchell. Part owner of Elk Haven Stables."

"Oh, great. It's nice, a family ranch like this."

"Yeah, when it's not claustrophobic," she said, being perfectly honest.

"I'll bet." She smiled, the expression tugging at lines around her eyes.

Kelsey leaned over and introduced herself, and the three of them spent the rest of dinner having innocuous conversation about activities at the ranch. When dessert was served, Kelsey suggested the women move into the living room with coffee and their apple pie.

Lark sort of wanted to go up to her room and hide, because she felt like all of her issues were written clearly all over her face, and if Cade looked at her long enough, or hard enough, he would be able to read exactly what was going on.

Still, she didn't want to say no. Mainly because she would feel like a jerk for bugging off, and she already felt like a jerk.

She settled onto the couch and looked out the windows at the mountain view. It was getting dark outside, the last lines of pink fading over the tops of the hills. A reminder of how much she valued her home. Her family.

"So, Jill," Kelsey said. "Cole and I have been married for about a year. How long have you and Sam been married?"

"Twenty-three years," Jill said, her smile looking a little strained to Lark.

"Wow," Kelsey said. "That's inspiring."

Jill laughed. "Is it?"

"Well, yes, looking at you from this side of a year. Of course, I never expected to end up out here with him anyway, so the whole thing still kind of blows my mind."

"I never really expected to be here either," Jill said,

looking down into her coffee. There was something sad about her, something that even Lark picked up on—and the fine art of social interaction and recognizing nuances of human emotion wasn't really her thing.

"Didn't expect to be where?" Kelsey asked gently.

Jill let out a slow breath. "Just make sure you keep talking to each other, Kelsey. Stay interested. It's funny. You live with someone for so long, they become part of everything you do. And eventually you get so used to them you stop realizing they're there. Until one day you look up from your work, from taking the kids to all their sporting events, or whatever it is you do, and you realize this other person is still there. And that you're not really sure who they are anymore. It sounds crazy, but . . . but it's how it happens." Jill took a sip of coffee. "And I didn't mean to be a drag. I'm sorry."

"You aren't a drag," Kelsey said. She had that look on her face, though. Worried and determined at the same time, which meant her sister-in-law was trying to come up with a solution. Which meant she was dangerous to be around.

Maddy let out an earsplitting wail from the dining room and Kelsey lifted her coffee mug. "I'm going to ignore that." Lark laughed. "What? Cole can deal. He's a good dad like that. I'm eating pie, damn it," Kelsey grumbled.

"So is he," Lark said.

"I'll make it worth his while." She wiggled her eyebrows.

"Spare me," Lark said.

"Oh, right, you're just saying that because he's your brother. But he's my husband, and I think he's foxy, and I like to get it on with him. And since you're all swoony over a guy at work right now, you are in no position to judge. Because you have fallen prey to the weakness."

"Ah, the weakness," Jill said. "I vaguely remember that. There's nothing quite like the first few months of a relationship."

"When you can't keep your hands off each other," Kelsey said.

"I'm not in a relationship. I'm a casual admirer of a pleasing male physique that happens to be in the same vicinity I am for several hours of the day. I don't even like him."

"That doesn't always matter," Jill said, then shrugged. "Well, it doesn't. I didn't like Sam when I first met him, but it didn't stop me from thinking he was hot."

"I wasn't Cole's biggest fan either."

"I'm not looking to marry the guy," Lark said. "I'm not looking to *anything* him. Just looking. A little casual visual objectification while I work. Better than whistling while you work, that's for sure."

Cole came out of the dining room holding Maddy, who was red-faced and indignant. "Hey, I'm about to put the princess to bed." Kelsey stood. "I've got it," Cole said.

Kelsey shook her head. "I'll go up with you. Nice to meet you, Jill," she said.

Jill nodded, and she and Lark both watched the family go upstairs. "I miss those days," Jill said.

"When your kids were little?" Lark asked.

"That. And the beginning of our marriage. I miss new. Or if not new, then just . . . the excitement. Probably like what you feel watching your coworker."

Lark swallowed. "Yeah. Well, he's nice-looking, but I'm not going to act on it."

"Why not?"

"What? Well, because . . . because."

Jill sighed. "Marriage is long, Lark. And there are a lot of good things about it, though I have to admit I'm not in the best place with mine. But . . . there's something special about those early feelings you have for someone. The butterflies. The way they make you feel just by looking at you. I guess . . . I'm just saying making memories for later might not be a bad thing."

"I doubt this particular guy wants to make anything with me. Least of all memories. But . . . I'll keep that in mind."

Sam came out of the dining room then and gave them both a strained smile. "Ready to head back?"

Jill saw his strained smile and raised it with an obviously false one. "Sure."

"All right, then. Good night."

Lark watched the couple leave, then sat for a while, brooding over her pie. She was not going to make a move on Quinn. Sure, he was sexy. She could admit that. But he'd hurt Cade. And she wasn't in any position to allow him to make her doubt that.

Her loyalty was to Cade. No matter how sad Quinn's stories were, and no matter how hot he looked with his shirt off.

End of internal discussion.

Jill got out of the shower and ran a towel over her hair before coming back out into the living area of the cabin.

Sam was sitting in front of her computer, his expression frozen.

"What?" she asked, holding a towel to her body.

"What is this?"

"What?"

"What the hell is this?" He stood up and pointed at her monitor, his dark brows drawn together.

She walked over to where he was standing and saw her email open to the one she'd received from Jake earlier. "Why were you reading my email?"

"I needed to check something online. I wasn't snooping on purpose, but I didn't think opening your laptop could be considered an invasion of privacy, since—and this makes me an ass—I thought we still shared some things."

The sexiest woman in the office.

The words burned into her eyes. They seemed to shout in the small cabin.

"I read more of his emails to you. He says shit like that a lot. And you never told him not to."

"I never encouraged him either. He just says things like that."

"Are you sleeping with him?"

"No!" Her face burned, her heart beating fast, hands shaking. It was like watching a car accident about to happen, one she couldn't stop. One she just had to brace herself for. Knowing that it wouldn't end well. "I would never . . . How could you think I would do that?"

"I'm finding all of this in your inbox and you're asking me how I could think that?"

"You're in my inbox."

"I didn't get into it on purpose, but after I saw that? Hell yeah, I looked. I'm human, damn it, and some other man is calling my wife sexy."

"Well, someone should!" she shouted, shaking, a tear sliding down her face as all of the words she'd been storing up inside her for the past couple of years came flooding out. "How long has it been since you even looked at me, Sam? Really looked? When you want sex, you come home and get into bed with the light off and start grabbing at me. You don't tell me I'm beautiful. You don't say you want me, or that you need me. You don't even look. Lights off, every time. And do you know how long it's been since we had sex?"

"How long?" he asked, his voice scratchy, brittle.

"Four months." She looked down and tried to breathe. "Did you just not notice?"

"I've been gone a lot."

"Yeah."

"I noticed," he said.

"But?" she asked.

"All that stuff you have to say to me? About how I don't see you? About how I don't want you? It's not any better here. When I do get in bed with you, when I kiss you, you roll over and just let it happen. I got tired of feeling like you were just putting up with something."

She knew there was a fair amount of truth to what he was saying. That she was guilty of that. But she couldn't say it. There was too much hurt, and anger, and now shame, piled over it all. And she couldn't dig her way out. Couldn't get to the truth of it yet, not while all of that rested on top of her heart, crushing her.

"That didn't happen overnight. That's what happens when you know your husband doesn't even care that it's you in his bed anymore, as long as someone is there."

"Bullshit," he bit out. "Let me tell you something really honest here, Jill. I've had a hundred chances to cheat on you. I travel a lot with Quinn. The women who come on to him? They have friends. But you know what? I've never done it. Because it does matter who's in my bed. It has to be you. It has to be my wife."

"Why?" she asked, throat dry.

"Because I made vows to you."

"Is that the only reason?"

"Honestly?" He looked away from her.

"Might as well be," she said.

"For the past year or so, yeah." He stood from his position at her computer, and she noticed how tired he looked. How sad. "But sometimes vows are all you have."

"I'm sorry if I don't find that flattering."

"You should. Because it means I'm not saving any emails from anyone calling me sexy. It means I'm not entertaining any ideas of betraying you, no matter how I feel at a given moment."

"But were you planning on ever fixing this, or were you just going to leave it like this?"

He shook his head. "Don't put it on me. Were you planning on fixing it? Or were you just planning on taking compliments from him and hoping it got you through with me?"

"I didn't have a plan. It's not like I was hoarding the email. I just got it. And it . . . it surprised me this time, Sam. What it meant to hear that. Maybe I didn't know how much I needed it."

"Well, maybe you should have figured that out with me."

"I didn't do anything," she said. "I got an email."

"That meant something to you."

"I'm being honest with you about it, Sam. That's all I can

do at this point. I can't take back the fact that it flattered me to hear it. I can't take back the fact that I feel like I'm starving for it. And that I'm not getting it from you." She pressed harder on her towel, clinging to it more tightly. She already felt so naked, she felt like she needed more layers. She wanted to hide—from the vulnerable feelings, from Sam.

How had it gotten so bad that she wanted to hide from the man who had, at one time, known her better than anyone? How had they turned into this?

"I'm going to go get dressed."

She turned and went into the bathroom, taking her pajamas with her, and when she reemerged, Sam was lying on the couch, his boots off, his arm flung over his eyes.

Not talking. Ignoring it. Because that's what they both did. Ignore it, and it will go away.

She wondered if that was what they'd done with their love.

CHAPTER

Seven

Since Quinn's decision to seduce Lark had been made, he found himself appreciating her beauty even more than he had before.

It was definitely not the kind of beauty he was used to being attracted to. Soft, natural. Yet it was so incredibly enticing, maybe because it was so different. And maybe because everything about his plan was wrong.

Yeah, maybe that was it. Maybe it appealed to his bad blood. Seemed like the kind of thing that might light his fire.

He gritted his teeth. Damn, he was a bastard. But then, he'd always known it. Why not embrace it?

He grinned and walked into the computer lab, where Lark was bending over a table, her round, perfect ass on display for him. He wondered if she had any idea just how tempting she was. Or what a position like that made him think of.

Holding on to her hips while he . . .

Blood rushed south of his belt. Yeah, better to redirect his thoughts. He wasn't going to approach her sporting a hard-on. He also had to be able to think, which was hard when the blood was drained out of your brain.

"Do I have to remind you to take a break again?"

Lark lifted her head and turned, one dark eyebrow raised. "You're lucky I could see you in the monitor or I would be mad at you for sneaking up on me."

"I wasn't sneaking up on you."

"You were advancing on me slowly without announcing your presence. Do you have a better definition for 'sneak'?"

"I was just walking in without shoutin' atcha."

"Well, now you're somehow making it sound extra polite. And I don't think anything you do is extra polite." She turned fully, bracing her hands on the table behind her, the motion pushing her breasts forward.

And he was powerless against the need to look. So he did. And he didn't bother *sneaking* it.

She noticed too. Her cheeks started to turn pink, the blush starting at the center and spreading out, suffusing her face with color.

"What's wrong?" he asked.

She narrowed her eyes. "You know."

"Do I?"

"Quinn . . ."

"You've been calling me by my first name like I'm a human and everything."

"I know you're a human. If you were anything else, I wouldn't hold you responsible for your actions."

"I definitely have some animal instincts."

She wrinkled her nose. "You're as bad as my brother."

That was not the comparison he wanted. Brotherly was not the image he was trying to portray. "I remind you of your brother?"

"Not especially. But look, I was basically raised by men, and Cade has no filter. I've heard more male observation on women and sex than anyone wants to hear from a family member, and I'm just . . . I don't find any of it shocking anymore. Or titillating in the least."

He looked down again. "Interesting choice of words."

When he met her eyes again, they were glittering with anger. "Do you need a definition? Because it has nothing to do with what you're thinking."

"Sure it does. You have very titillating . . ."

"No," she said. "No." He smiled, and she did too, the corner of her lip tugging up reluctantly. "Stop. Don't amuse me."

"Why? Because then it's hard for you to hate me?"

"No, I still do. And that makes it all confusing."

"Join the club." He was a liar. He wasn't confused. He knew exactly what he was doing. He knew what coaxing smiles out of her would lead to. He was going to grow attachment between them, affection. At least from her end.

"What are you confused about?"

"Just how interesting I find the woman who hates me." Again, not confusing and not a mystery. Seducing a woman who hated him? Taking all that fire into the bedroom? Oh, no, there was nothing confusing about the appeal of that.

"I don't trust you."

"Good. You shouldn't."

"And here you've been asking me to believe you didn't do anything to Cade."

"Yeah, I didn't. But that doesn't mean you should trust me." There, it was a warning. An honest one. And if she didn't listen, it wasn't his fault.

"Don't worry about that. I won't."

"Great. I hate for people to have expectations of me. Good ones, anyway, because then I might have to rise up and meet them."

"That, you really don't have to worry about. Do you know what I expect from a snake, Quinn?"

"What?"

"I expect him to bite me. Maybe not right now, but someday."

"And you think I'm a snake?"

"You said you had some animal in you. I'm calling it like I see it."

"Good. Keep expecting me to bite you," he said, flashing her a smile. "Might keep you safe."

"Am I in danger?"

"It depends on what you consider danger."

"I have Mace in my purse, so I don't consider you too dangerous."

"I like that even better."

"What?" she asked, eyes narrowed.

"The possibility of you biting me back."

"Well . . . I don't . . . I can't. I would if I had to. Self-defense."

"Oh, really?" He took a step toward her. "So if I leaned in and bit you"—he lifted his hand and traced a line from her neck, just beneath her ear, down to the edge of her shirt collar, with his knuckle—"here. You would have to return the favor?" He kept the motion slow and, frankly, seductive, but the only question was: Which one of them was being seduced by it?

Because she was so soft. Like silk to the touch. And warm—warm enough that he thought if he pulled her against him, she might be able to transfer some of it to him. Not to his skin, but to somewhere deep inside of him. To places that were always cold.

"Retaliation," she said, her voice thin, shaky. Affected. "Not returning favors. Defense of my . . . person."

"I see." He lowered his hand, and her frame folded in on an exhaled breath. "I'd hate to make you feel like you were threatened." He took a step back and watched her face closely. No, he didn't want her to feel threatened at all. He wanted her to feel that same pull he did.

"Good. Good thinking. I'm dangerous when cornered."

"Oh yeah?"

She nodded. "Yep. Like a honey badger."

"Very scary."

She smiled, and it felt like a fist was squeezing his gut tight. "Yeah, yeah. I'm terrifying. At least I am when I play *Zombie Watch*."

"*Zombie Watch*, huh?"

"No matter how fast they shamble, I will find them, and I will destroy them. I'm the one-shot kid."

"I'm assuming this is a computer game?"

"Yes. Do you live under a rock?"

"No. I live outside."

She wrinkled her nose. "Outside is overrated."

"This from a girl who lives on a ranch out in the boonies?"

"Yeah, well, it's not my first choice of setting."

He crossed his arms over his chest. "Really? Where else would you live?"

She lifted a shoulder and planted her hand on one of the chairs that was placed in front of the computer table. "I don't know. It doesn't really matter, because I don't do very much. Out, I mean. I mean . . . my work is on the computer, and my hobby is on the computer, so . . ."

"Honey, you need to get out more."

"Nope."

"Honey badgers don't belong inside," he said, a smile tugging at the corner of his lips. He was enjoying messing with her more than he'd imagined.

"Honey badger don't care," she said, planting her hand on her hip.

"In the great outdoors, I'm less likely to corner you. Less likely to get . . . bitten."

"You seem very concerned with that whole subject."

"It's an interesting thought."

"Yeah, well, I probably won't bite you, so don't concern yourself too much with it."

"It's too late," he said. "I'm concerned. Definitely pondering it."

"Quinn," she said, her tone filled with warning. "I'm going to have to report you to HR."

"I'm pretty much HR around here, and I think I'm fine."

"What do you think I need to do outside, then?"

"Do you ever ride anymore?"

She pursed her lips. "Not much. I used to when I was a kid. I used to ride with . . . I used to ride with my mom."

"And you don't anymore?"

"I told you, me and outside are not so much."

"And I told you that you should try it. In fact, that's part of your job today."

"No. It's not."

"Yes, Lark, it is. You have to go on a ride with me."

She frowned. "What about me says 'great outdoors' to you? I'm fish belly." She held her arm out, which was not fish belly in his opinion but a very enticing, rich cream. "I've never tested this theory, but based on my vampiric habits—nocturnal tendencies, nothing related to the consumption of blood—too much sunlight will reduce me to a pile of ash."

"I doubt it, Lark, I really do."

"But you wouldn't know until it was too late."

"I'm not seriously concerned."

She let out a long breath. "Do I really have to go riding with you?"

"Yes," he said, decisive now. Because that's what he needed. To get her outdoors. To get her alone. And she shouldn't spend all her time alone inside playing zombie games either. Not that he really cared. "You need to get a better feel for the layout of the property. This way we can check out the trails. I'll take you up the ridge that's just through the trees."

"Is that what the kids are calling it these days?"

"I could tell you what adults are calling it these days, but I'd just make you blush again."

And she did. It was damn cute, and he wasn't sure why. He'd never been into women who blushed. Hell, he'd never seen a woman who was capable of it. His sisters had never done anything so gauche; it would have offended their mother's icy reserve. The one she pretended to have anyway.

And the women he'd picked up on the circuit and while he was working ranches? Those women were more likely to make him blush than the reverse.

"Finish up what you're doing in here, then meet me in the stables."

Her lips parted, her teeth still firmly clenched together, the expression not one he could readily identify. "What? What's that?"

"Smiling," she said, not separating her teeth. "I'm so happy to be going out riding."

"That is one fake-ass smile."

"Yuh-huh."

"Great, I'll see you and your false enthusiasm in about an hour."

"Oh, I'll be there. And so will the smile."

"You don't need to bring the smile."

Her "grin" broadened. "Sure I do."

"Fine. See you there." He lifted his hand and slid his thumb along her lower lip. "And this too."

That made her expression falter and sent a kick of adrenaline through his veins. Oh, yeah, this was going well. He ignored the lick of flame that went from his hand up his wrist. Because it didn't matter what he felt. The only thing that mattered was how she felt about him.

And he could tell that he was reeling her in. Just like he'd planned.

Lark grumbled the whole way to the stable. She wasn't thrilled to be meeting Quinn, mainly because she wasn't thrilled to be in proximity with Quinn. Except her body seemed to be on a totally different wavelength than her brain, heart and jackass-o-meter. She knew she didn't like him, she felt she didn't like him and she sensed just why she shouldn't like him.

Just that little uptick in her heart rate when he'd touched her lip had made her feel like she'd betrayed Cade. Made her feel almost as sick as she was excited. There was no excuse for something like that, no excuse for her to respond to him, not when she knew exactly what he was.

And yet.

And yet her heart was beating fast and her legs felt a little Jell-O-y. And her hands were shaking a bit. Almost like she was excited. Excited to be riding horses, which made her sneeze.

Yes. That was it. The horses. Sure, she lived on a ranch, but she never rode. So maybe she was excited to do a thing she was allergic to. It made more sense than being excited about seeing Quinn. That made no sense at all.

None. He was a jerk. He was Cade's enemy. He filled out a pair of work jeans like no one's business.

That last part was off topic. And irrelevant. Enemy. Jerk. That was all that mattered.

She kicked a rock and continued into the cool shade of the stable. Quinn was there already, with two horses tacked and ready to go.

She leaned against the doorframe. "Hi." She also treated him to her non-smile, as promised.

He looked at her and shot her a real smile. Wicked. The kind that made toes tingle. And other things too. The kind of smile she hadn't known existed until she'd met Quinn Parker.

Devilish, sexy bastard!

"Ready to ride, darlin'?"

The invitation brought to mind riding of a completely different kind. The image that flashed through her mind's eye was quick and shockingly graphic. Shrouded in darkness and covers, Quinn's hands on her hips, her legs draped over his hips as he whispered in her ear, low and husky . . . *Ready to ride, darlin'?*

She blinked. Well. She'd never had a full-on, out-of-control sexual fantasy in the middle of the day. And definitely not in front of the guy she was having the fantasy about.

Inconvenient. Also shockingly detailed. She could feel it. His heat, his breath on her neck . . .

Oh boy.

She looked back at Quinn, who was just staring at her like she might be crazy. What was wrong with her? He was evil. There could be no fantasizing about evil men.

"Pshhh. Yeah. I can ride. Let's ride." She cleared her throat, which wasn't blocked at all, she discovered, just incredibly dry. And constricted. Lord, she felt like she'd swallowed a pincushion. She made a weird wheezing sound like a cat working a hairball and tried to adjust her stance, putting her hand on her hip and stumbling slightly.

Wow. She sucked.

"All right, then, cowgirl, saddle up."

"Sure."

She walked over to the horse and hesitated at his side. He was a big bay who looked half asleep. The kind of horse they use at Elk Haven Stables when overweight business execs wanted to come play cowboy.

It was a little insulting. Except it wasn't like she was the world's most accomplished rider. She was hardly a rider at all. When her mother had been alive, they'd done a trail ride every Sunday after church.

And after that she'd stopped. It hadn't felt like the right thing to do, going alone. She'd never loved the riding; she'd just enjoyed spending time with her mom.

She blinked and pushed the memory away. It was hard to think about what it had been like when both of her parents had been alive. She'd been so young that it was hard to remember. Only nine when her mom had died.

Her mother had been so strong. A real kick-butt ranch woman. She'd done it all, and she'd had no fear.

And then she had an accident driving her tractor through mud that was too deep, on ground that was too uneven, because she'd been too stubborn, too certain, for her own good.

Life didn't reward that kind of bravery. That kind of character. Which really sucked.

There was a lot more safety in your bedroom than there was outside, that Lark knew for sure.

And yet here she was, about to ride a horse.

Just do it, Mitchell.

She put her foot in the stirrup and her hands on the saddle horn, launching herself up onto the horse's back. "All right," she said, settling in and gripping the reins. "Let's do this thing."

Quinn laughed and mounted his horse, nudging him gently with his heels and moving ahead of her and out of the barn.

"Wait," she said, urging her horse forward, reacclimating to the rhythm of riding. She'd ridden a few times since her mother's death, just in the arenas at Elk Haven, but nothing regular, and it had probably been three years now since she'd ridden at all.

"We're going to head up this trail," Quinn said, gesturing ahead of them at a path covered in bark. "It'll take us through the trees and up to the ridge. And by that I mean *ridge*—a part of a mountain."

"We're back to needing to give words clear definitions, are we?"

"Hey, you were the one who seemed confused."

"Hardly, but I know how men are."

"Got a string of broken hearts in your past, do you?"

She rolled her eyes, but Quinn was still in front of her and couldn't see it. "Tons. I'm the vamp of Silver Creek. The woman everyone's mother warns them about."

"I can believe it," he said, tossing her a quick look over his shoulder.

She had no idea why, but the casual comment made her feel a little warm all over. "Oh, well . . . thank you. I guess. Except I'm really not so much."

"I believe that too."

"You can't believe both. One is a lie."

"You blush a little bit too pretty to be a vamp."

"I don't blush."

"You blush like a schoolgirl."

She knew she did. She was doing it now. And the more he mentioned it, the more she did it. Her face was burning. "I'm not a girl. I'm a woman."

"I did notice that. And I'm not insulting you. I think a little pink in your cheeks is sexy. I like it, because it tells me you're thinking naughty things."

"I don't think naughty things."

"Ever?"

Ready to ride, darlin'?

"Never," she said. "I'm virtuous. A paragon."

"A virtuous zombie slayer?"

"I blush because I'm shocked. Not because I'm thinking naughty things."

"That's disappointing."

She tightened her grip on the reins. "No, you know what's disappointing? You. Men. Men are shockingly predictable." She said it all with a hint of irony, because yeah, her brothers were like this. They talked about sex because they always thought about sex. Because no matter how much they tried to shield her from the way they'd man-whored around, it had sort of soaked into her consciousness. Because when it was all you thought about, of course it seeped out.

But in terms of personal experience? Yeah, there was basically none. She was Lark Mitchell, terminal nerd, little sister to Cole and Cade Mitchell, who would put a knuckle-shaped imprint on the face of any guy who ever dared touch her.

If they were lucky, the knuckle imprint was all they would get. If they weren't lucky, they might go from stallion to gelding in one easy step.

And the men of Silver Creek knew it.

Even if they didn't, frankly, she'd never bothered to pursue anything. Because it was way the heck easier to just not care. Caring hurt. Always. Caring meant loss.

It was way safer to talk dirty at a guy you met in a gaming forum than to risk rejection in real life. Than to risk real-life feelings.

"Men are predictable, huh?"

"Completely."

"So you know what I'm thinking right now?"

"Something lascivious and inappropriate."

"I'm wounded. I'm thinking about the view," he said, nodding toward the trees that lined the trail that was slowly climbing up the mountainside. "About the way the sun shines through the trees. How deep the green gets, to where it fades to near-black in the shadows. About the way the air smells, like wood and pine and clean. How's that for predictable?"

"Oh . . . um . . ."

"Also, I'm thinking a little bit about how pretty and pink your lips are, and wondering if they taste as sweet as I think they might."

And just like that, every rational thought flooded out of her head. She wanted to say something about how he was completely predictable. And he was full of BS with all his lyrical waxing about the view. And something about misdirection and deception.

But she couldn't think straight enough to form a coherent thought, because her brain was stalled out on the idea of him tasting her lips. Not just kissing them—*tasting*.

Because that thought brought to mind a lot more than just lips against lips. And a lot more, even, than his tongue in her mouth, which she knew was a thing, personal experience or lack thereof notwithstanding. No, this made her think of a slow, sensual act. Of him savoring her flavor as his tongue slid along the line of her mouth.

It made her ache inside. Made her want things she'd never wanted this bad.

Yeah, she knew about desire, and being turned on. That was why she'd pursued virtual methods of relieving herself. But she didn't know this. This deep need for touch. For connection. Not just for the image of a tongue on her skin, but for the feel of it.

Hot, slick, and slow.

She wondered, in that moment, how *he* would taste. How his skin would feel beneath her hands. How hard his muscles would feel. He would be different from her. He would be rough, and she knew that he had body hair.

Gah. Why was that so hot? She'd never fancied herself a male-body-hair fan. But right now, she was fascinated by the memory of his chest hair. By how uniquely masculine it was. And she was suddenly obsessed by the realization that she'd never touched a man's hairy chest.

And that she needed to change that.

Dear Lord, what had he done to her? What was he doing to her? She should hate him. Despise him. And in truth, she sort of did . . . when she remembered that he was Quinn Parker, the man who had ruined her brother's life.

But it was getting harder to remember that he was *that* Quinn Parker. Because the man that she talked to, the man she'd spent time with, didn't seem like that man. There was a disconnect happening there, and she wasn't sure why. Or how to stop it.

The emotional element, the fact that she truly had a hard time disliking him when they were together, was honestly more disturbing than the attraction.

And that was saying a lot, because the attraction was disturbing in the extreme.

"You got quiet," he said.

"I'm ignoring you."

"Why?"

"Because what am I supposed to say to that?"

"You could tell me what a jerk I am. You could tell me how predictable I am. Or, you could tell me that you're a little curious too."

"I'm not," she said. *Lies, all lies.* "Not even a little."

"I bet you're blushing, baby."

"Don't call me baby."

"I bet you're blushing, Ms. Lark Mitchell, because you're thinking about kissing me."

She sniffed. "You forced the image into my head."

"And?"

"And?"

"Did you like it?"

She sputtered. "No."

"That only makes me determined to change your mind."

"You're just looking for an excuse to get bit."

He stopped his horse in the path and turned to the side. "Well, I'd be lying if I said the idea didn't intrigue me."

She pictured it now, just like he'd threatened earlier, the scrape of his teeth on the delicate skin of her neck. And then of course she'd have to bite him back . . . on the lip maybe.

She blinked. "Then lie to me."

"I'm not interested in your biting me at all. I'm even less interested in kissing you."

"Well, good." Then she wondered if the last part was also a lie. She was almost consumed with concern over whether or not it was a lie. Of course she wanted it to be true. She wanted him to not want to kiss her.

Totally. Maybe. Almost.

He turned back to the trail again and forged on, and she urged her horse forward again. The whole rest of the way the beauty was lost on her as she castigated herself for her sick, wayward desires for a man she should want to punch, not smooch. And also she did a fair amount of trying not to look at his broad shoulders and how they tapered down to a narrow waist and . . . and . . . she really tried not to look at his butt.

She could hardly see it—it was sitting on a horse, for heaven's sake.

So she should stop wondering about it.

She bit her own lip and tried to shut her internal hussy up while they kept riding. When they got to the top of the ridge, the landscape broke open, revealing a clearing covered by grass and purple flowers.

It was the silence that struck her first, even before the view. A quiet so profound that it seemed to close in around them. The view hit her next. It was familiar—those same blue mountains she could see from her bedroom window, the same green that filled her vision when she looked out of the big living room windows at Elk Haven.

But outside like this, up on the mountain, it was different. She didn't do things like this. She didn't go outside and explore. She hadn't in forever, and only now did she fully appreciate that the view of it from behind glass wasn't the same as being out in it.

It felt wild, free. And with Quinn right there, it felt a little bit dangerous. Which only made it feel kind of exciting.

Which was annoying.

"It's something, isn't it?" he asked, getting off of the

horse and walking toward the edge of the ridge, planting his
hands on his lean hips.

"Yeah," she said. She dismounted too, with less grace
than he had, and moved to where he was standing. "Pretty
amazing."

"Different than Texas," he said. "And Virginia."

"I've never been . . . anywhere, so I can't compare it to
anything. But I still think it's beautiful."

"Why haven't you been anywhere, Lark?"

She shrugged. "I don't know. Because Cole and Cade
would never have had a chance to take me anywhere.
Because . . . because." *Because I'm too afraid to go anywhere or do anything.*

The realization made a cold feeling settle in the pit of
her stomach.

"You should travel. It's good for you. It was good for me.
If I would have stayed where I started . . . I don't even like
to think about it."

Weird, because, yet again, Quinn seemed to be showing
signs of a conscience, and she'd so firmly convinced herself
he must be a man entirely without one. But he didn't seem
to be. It was that weird disconnect between the Quinn he
was supposed to be—the monster she'd imagined—and the
man she'd met.

"I don't know. Google Earth is a pretty powerful tool for
the borderline agoraphobe."

"You don't seem agoraphobic to me."

She looked down at her hands and flicked a piece of dirt
out from under her thumbnail. "Is there a name for the kind
of person who just wants to feel safe?"

"Human," he said.

She looked back up at him. "Oh, well, sadly life doesn't
come with enough of a guarantee for me. I'm highly suspicious of it in general."

"Life has taken a lot of glee in kicking me in the balls
repeatedly over the years, so I share some of your suspicion.
But sometimes . . . sometimes you have to take a chance,
even if you might get kneed in the groin again."

He turned to her and started walking toward her, his eyes intent on her. Her heart thundered, hard and steady, and breathing suddenly became a laborious and impossible act.

He stopped in front of her and extended his hand, his knuckles brushing softly over the line of her cheekbone. "Sometimes taking a chance is worth it," he said.

"What if it will get you bit?" she asked, the question a strangled whisper.

He leaned in, his lips so close to hers she could feel the heat radiating from his skin. "Then it's most definitely worth it."

She inhaled, starting to say something, but then the firm press of his lips against hers stopped both motions completely. And she was lost. Drowning. He cupped her face with his hand, bracing her, his heat engulfing her as his mouth worked wicked magic on hers.

She opened to him, shuddered as his tongue slid against hers, as need trickled through her body, a slow burn on a hot day that she knew was going to hit just the right spot and explode in a blaze that would be beyond control.

He wrapped his arm around her waist and pulled her hard against his chest, and the burn exploded. She didn't know where to put her hands, so she tangled them in his hair, holding him tight to her as he continued to kiss her, deep, hard and sensual.

She'd never really been kissed before. Not like this. She'd sort of attempted making out with a boy in her advanced calc class in high school. It had not gone well. Braces had clinked together, and there had been an exceptional amount of saliva. And frankly, another person's drool in your mouth had seemed icky at the time.

But this wasn't like that. This was slick, but sexy. His tongue didn't seem invasive; it was inviting, an echo of a much more intimate activity. And it made her ache at the apex of her thighs. Made her feel empty. Desperate to be filled.

She wanted more of him—all of him.

This was different from the computer, that was for sure. Text couldn't touch you. Dirty words might turn you on, but they left you with a certain amount of control.

Quinn was a living, breathing man who had the power to increase pressure at will, decrease pressure, tease her by tracing the outline of her lips with the tip of his tongue, nip her softly, show her exactly why he'd been so preoccupied by biting.

And when she was sure she couldn't take any more, he gave more. And he kept giving more until her legs were shaking, until her breasts ached and she was wet between her thighs. She was so close to coming it was embarrassing.

He hadn't even touched her body except for the hand on her back and the hand still cupping her face. Still, each flick of his tongue sent a lightning bolt through her, igniting the dry tinder and stoking the fire.

She arched against him, desperate for more, for him to take it further.

Taking her cue, he tightened his hold on her and dipped her low. She followed the movement, bending her knees and going down to the grass softly, with Quinn over her, still kissing her.

He was kneeling above her, not pressing against her like she wanted. She wanted to be tangled in him. Wanted every inch of his hard body against hers. She wanted to ride his thigh so that she could ease the ache between hers.

She was so close to falling right over the edge. So close to release she was shaking.

She wanted to put her hands on his skin. Beneath his shirt. She wanted to trace the horse tattoo on his biceps.

And that thought stopped her cold.

Horses. Quinn.

Cade.

Hearing her brother's name in her head was like being dunked in a river.

She wrenched her mouth from his and scrambled away, gasping for breath, getting to her feet as quickly as she could, tripping and stumbling before finally straightening.

She was trembling from the inside out, and she still felt hollow. Unsatisfied. Angry and frightened.

Sick to her stomach.

How had she done that? How had she forgotten? How did she even begin to justify this moment? She felt like everything inside of her had been grabbed by big masculine hands and shaken hard, jumbled up to the point where she couldn't sort any of it out.

One thing she did know, though. Quinn was Cade's enemy. And what she'd done had been nothing short of a betrayal. Of the man who had stepped in and helped support her, in so many ways, when she'd lost her parents.

Her brother, who was part of her last remaining family.

Brothers were always important, family was always important. But she knew it, understood it, better than most. Because she knew what it was to lose it. And she'd lost enough of it through no fault of her own. Had lost enough of it just because life sucked and not because she'd done something to push them away.

If she lost Cade because of her own actions, she could never forgive herself. Ever.

"How dare you?" she asked, the words, unplanned and angry, coming out low and unsteady.

"How dare I what?" he asked. "Kiss a woman who clearly wanted to be kissed?"

"No! Stop. Don't oversimplify it. How dare *you* kiss *me*. Knowing who I am, and who you are. And what you did."

"I didn't do a damn thing to your family, Lark Mitchell. It's a tired refrain, but I'll play it again if I have to."

"Just shut up," she said. "I can't . . . I can't deal with this. Maybe I can work for you, and maybe . . . maybe part of me can even believe you, but I cannot kiss you."

Panic spread through her, at the realization that it was too late, she had kissed him, and mostly at the realization that she couldn't do it again. Ever.

But she wanted to do it again. No matter how bad it was to want it, she did.

"That's a damn shame," he said.

"Why is that?"

"Because I liked kissing you."

She breathed out and put her shaking hands on her hips. "Yeah. Well. Of course you did. Lots of men do." *Lies.* "But you can't. Not again."

He chuckled. "You sure are cute when you're imploding."

"I am not imploding."

"Looks like an implosion from over here."

"Well, I'd invite you to come take a closer look, but I don't want you to get close to me again."

"Afraid you'll kiss me again?"

"Kiss *you*? You kissed me!"

"It's hard to remember the fine details, but it seemed like you were enthusiastic enough."

"*You* did. *You* did it."

"And you didn't kiss me back?"

"Ir-freaking-relevant! I had a natural reaction to a marginally attractive man pressing his lips to mine, but the minute I could think, I didn't want to kiss you. And I never, ever would have started it!"

Lark's face was burning, her entire body quivering.

"You think I'm attractive?" he asked, a smirk spreading across his maddeningly handsome face.

"Marginally."

"Whatever."

"No, not whatever. I don't want your head getting too big for your Stetson."

"Nice of you to worry about me, Lark, but your concern isn't necessary."

She snorted and walked back over to her horse, swinging herself up onto his back with one clumsy motion. "I have work to do. And I don't need you to lead me back down the trail, so why don't you just stay up here and enjoy your view."

"I like the view better when you're here," he said.

She pursed her lips and decided against saying anything else. Instead, she just urged her horse on and left him there. If only she could leave all that pesky desire behind too.

CHAPTER

Eight

Lark drew her knees up to her chest and looked out the window. She was sitting on her bed, sleepless, and pouting like a child. Over her own actions.

Guilt was like a wild animal eating at her. She'd never experienced anything like it before. Not on this level. Vague guilt over doing the wrong things as a child. A little bit of silly, adult guilt over her sexy chat time online.

But not this. Not this intense, unending pain that made her feel heavy, tired and yet unable to sleep.

So she was just sitting there, in bed, wide awake and angry. At Quinn, at herself. Because she still wanted him. She wanted more of what they'd shared, more of the fire and need and lust that burned so hot she was sure it had left scorch marks on the bottoms of her shoes. But it was impossible.

She hated that she wanted it. She hated that she couldn't have it.

She was just unhappy in general.

She scooted to the edge of the bed and planted her feet on the floor, a heavy sigh escaping her lips. She was such a mess. She stood and crossed the room, hesitating at the door before turning the knob and walking out into the hall. There was no one around. Cole's and Cade's doors were firmly closed, and the lights were off downstairs.

She sighed and went down the stairs, not sure why she was doing this instead of playing a video game until she passed out. Maybe because stupid Quinn had made her conscious of the fact that she did so much inside. Maybe because he'd made her hungry for different tastes, different textures. For touch.

At least outside the air would be sweet like hay, and the breeze would blow across her skin. Maybe that would take some of the intense pressure off of her chest. Maybe it would make her feel less restless. Bring her some satisfaction. She doubted it, but it was worth a shot.

She pushed open the front door and walked out onto the porch, breathing in the cool air. Nope. It didn't do a thing to satisfy the ache inside her. Didn't give her the sensory experience she was seeking.

The porch swing creaked, and Lark whipped her head around. There was a pale, person-shaped shadow sitting there that she couldn't place.

"Kelsey?"

"No, sorry. Jill."

"Oh," Lark said.

"I didn't mean to startle you. I was just . . . I'm hiding, so it's best to be quiet when you're hiding, right?"

"Who are you hiding from?" she asked.

She heard the other woman shifting. "My husband, actually."

"Oh." Lark leaned over and flipped a switch by the wall that turned on a string of rope lights that lined the perimeter of the porch. "Sorry, I know you're hiding, but it would be easier if we could see each other."

"That's okay." She smiled—a thin smile, like all the smiles Lark had seen on her face.

"So . . . why are you hiding from your husband?"

"We had a fight. Last night. We've been avoiding each

other all day, and I was in the mood to keep up with the avoidance."

Lark sighed and sat in a chair opposite the porch swing. "I'm trying to hide from me, but unfortunately, it's not really working."

Jill laughed. "Now that you mention it, I think I'd rather hide from me than from Sam, but like you, I'm stuck with me, so it can't happen."

"Why do *you* want to hide from you?"

"You first. I already confessed I'm hiding from my husband of twenty-three years. Next embarrassing confession is all you."

"I kissed a man I shouldn't have kissed," she said, her heart thundering in her ears. "And it can't happen again. But I want it to happen again. I can't stop thinking about him, but I should."

"Why is he a wrong choice? Is he married or dating someone else?"

"No."

"Then what's wrong with him?"

"It's . . . My brothers wouldn't approve. At all. In fact, I can kind of see it ruining my relationship with them, and I don't want that. It's . . . complicated."

"Do you love him?"

"No." Lark shook her head. "No. I just . . . want him. And maybe that's wrong. I don't even like him."

"But you want him?"

"Yes," she said, her face getting hot. "And I've never . . . I don't have experience with this. With men. With wanting men. I don't understand how I can want him when I know I shouldn't. When I know I don't like him."

Jill let out a long sigh. "Love is complicated. It's not magic. Not a thing you just fall into and stay in forever because you felt it once. It's something you have to work at. It's something you have to remind yourself to do, because it's not just a feeling, it's an action. But . . . sex is magic. It can be. Sometimes you meet someone and there's a spark, and it doesn't matter if you like them or even know them. The man you want isn't always the man you should want. Sometimes sex brings people together and sometimes it tears them apart. It's one of the strongest connections two people can have. And when it's not there, it can start . . . breaking down everything else."

Lark got the feeling Jill was mainly talking to herself, but in there, she heard words she needed to hear. Sex was a force that was bigger than reason.

"Is there a man you want that you shouldn't?" Lark asked.

Jill shook her head. "No. There was. About twenty-five years ago. A cowboy. And my mom warned me that he would break my heart. I was eighteen when I met him, and I didn't know him, but I wanted him. With every bit of myself. We had nothing in common. Except that we couldn't bear to be apart."

"You married him though, didn't you?"

She nodded. "Yeah. And that's the moral of that story. Sex can make you fall in love too."

Lark recoiled. "I don't want that."

"That's one of the hazards of good sex."

"Well, maybe he's not any good."

Jill laughed. "Are you actually hoping he's not?"

"I told you, I don't want to fall in love." She bit her lip. "Did you like Sam when you met him? More than just . . . sexually."

Jill nodded slowly. "I didn't at first. Because he was arrogant and dumb, and he drank beer from a Solo cup. But then he smiled at me and things changed. I thought the sun rose and set on that smile. And then . . . well, then I slept with him. My first time, incidentally. And my world felt . . . changed. I thought there had never been a funnier, more gentle man created. Well, then I liked him a lot."

"Well, I don't like . . . the man I kissed. So maybe my odds of falling for him are low."

"Maybe."

The corners of Jill's mouth turned down, the lines that

bracketed her lips deepening. Lark looked down at her hands. "I've never had anyone to talk to this stuff about, so I'm sorry I'm attacking you with my questions."

"That's fine. I have a daughter who's about four years younger than you. And honestly, if she were asking me these questions, I'd put her in a turtleneck and send her to an all-girls school, but . . . but with you maybe I see more of myself. And now . . . after being married as long as I have . . . I'd sort of kill for the chance to have a wild fling. But my fling days are over. My big fling turned into a husband who hogs the covers and thinks 'New sweater?' is a compliment."

"Another point against love."

"I'm sort of the Scrooge of love at the moment." She grimaced. "Bah humbug, and things like that."

"I'm Scroogey re: love too," Lark said. "I'm just . . . in the throes of that magical sexual-attraction thing. Inconvenient."

"Yeah, it can be. Love is a choice; attraction is like getting hit by a train. But you can ignore it if you have to."

"And I have to." Lark paused for a second. "So Sam was your big fling, huh?"

"He was."

"Do you mind telling me what happened? I mean . . . what happened to bring you to hiding on my porch swing near midnight?"

Jill shook her head. "The thing is, it wasn't one thing that happened. I think . . . I think he stopped smiling as much. That smile that used to make me feel like he was holding my heart. And then I stopped looking for ways to make him smile."

"Forgive me, because, frankly, virgin here. But sex made you fall in love, right?"

Jill laughed. "Um, yeah, it was a part of it."

"And . . ."

"And we haven't had it for a while. It's been even longer since we've had magic sex."

"Maybe you need magic sex?"

Jill stood up and stretched. "Maybe. But you don't really want to jump a guy who doesn't seem that interested anymore.

And especially considering how pissed he was at me last night, I'm not getting any anytime soon." She paused. "Thanks."

"For?"

"For asking," she said. "Not very many people want to talk to an old married lady about her problems. My friends back home certainly don't. They just want to pretend they don't see my problems. Because if they did, they might see theirs in there somewhere."

"Thank you for talking to me."

"No problem, Lark. Good night." Jill headed down the porch steps and disappeared into the darkness, and Lark stayed in the chair on the deck.

Sometimes you meet someone and there's a spark, and it doesn't matter if you like them or even know them.

Yep, that's exactly how it was with Quinn. It was that little touch of magic that transcended common sense. Damn man and his magic hands. And lips. And body. That was why. He was just too hot to be real. And she had a bad case of lust.

But unlike Jill had been, she wasn't eighteen. She wasn't naive. Not completely. Sure, she was a virgin, but only physically. She'd really steamed up the computer monitor with Aaron. She knew stuff. Desire and orgasms and stuff.

She hadn't fallen for Aaron. She had, in fact, been quite annoyed with his trying to make small talk when all she'd wanted was a little bit of an illicit thrill. So there. She'd sort of technically already used a man for only sex.

Her brain replayed the day's kiss in her mind, a heady reminder of just how different, how much more intense, a simple kiss had been in comparison to a virtual shag.

She stood and let out her breath in one big gust. Didn't matter. She wasn't going to do anything about it. And she wasn't going to feel guilty either. She was just a victim of the magic of sexual attraction, that was all.

Like Jill had said, she couldn't help that she'd been hit by it, but she didn't have to chase after it. So she wouldn't. She could ignore it. She could keep on working with Quinn like it had never happened.

Maybe. Probably.

Definitely. Because there was no other choice. She was still locked into a contract, and there was no way in hell she was ever, ever, ever kissing him again.

Jill opened the door to the cabin and closed it quietly, just in case Sam was asleep. She flipped on the lamp that was on the desk and started taking her sweater off.

"Hey."

She looked up at the sound of her husband's voice, rough, loud in the silence of the room. He was sitting in the chair by the bed, fully dressed, still in his boots and hat.

"Hi," she said, straightening.

"I have something I need to say to you."

She felt the world tilt under her feet, felt like reality was breaking into little pieces and falling away slowly. And she knew that in a moment there would be nothing left to hold her up, because in that moment, that long moment of silence, she guessed what his next words would be.

He wanted a divorce.

Her worst fear. The reason she'd never confessed how bad it was for her. The real reason she'd never wanted to talk about their problems. For fear he would decide they were just too big. For fear it would make him want to give up.

And it was about to happen.

"What?" she asked, her lips cold.

"You are so fucking sexy."

"What?" She'd never once heard her husband say something like that before. Ever.

"It's the honest truth," he continued. "I don't know how I missed telling you that, every day, from the moment I met you. But I did. One day, honey, I forgot to tell you. And then I just kept on forgetting, and even though I thought it, even though I never thought differently, I didn't tell you. So I'm telling you now, because I've made a damn mess of this. Of our life. And I want to try and clean it up."

"Sam . . ."

He stood up and crossed the room to where she was standing, his slate-gray eyes burning into hers. And she saw not the boy she'd fallen in love with, but the man he'd become. The man she hadn't looked at closely in years.

If she met this man in a bar, she wouldn't be able to say no to him. In that way, she hadn't changed. Not since she was eighteen.

"No, I have to say it. You need to know. You need to know that I regret the distance between us. That when I'm on the road I lie awake at night hard as hell thinking about you, about being in your arms. And being where we've been the past couple of years? With this distance between us even when we're in the same room? It's like an endless hell. To come home to you and still not be with you."

"Y . . . you . . . I didn't know . . . How come you didn't—"

He pulled her up against him and kissed her. Deep and hard. Thorough. The kind of kiss that she'd consigned to a box of memories. It was so full of longing, of regret, of intense, dark need.

And she fought against it. Because they weren't this close anymore. Because it had been so long. Because she didn't know him anymore.

"Kiss me, baby," he said, his voice rough. He cupped her face, tracing the lines around her mouth with his thumbs. "Kiss me like you mean it."

She closed her eyes tight, tears leaking out and rolling down her cheeks, and kissed him back. Kissed him with all the truth he was asking for. With all of her anger and frustration, all of her desire.

And when they parted, she was breathing hard, shaking. "Shouldn't we talk first?"

"We can talk," he said. "We can talk about how beautiful you look. How hard you make me. How much I want to see you naked, suck on those gorgeous breasts of yours."

She blushed. She honest to goodness blushed in front of her husband. "People . . . people like us don't say things like that."

"Maybe that's the problem. Because damn it, woman, you thought I didn't want you. You had to get your compliments from another man. When I'm done, you'll know how much I want you. And his emails won't mean anything."

"Is that what this is about?"

"Hell. Yes. No other man is going to say that stuff to you. Because you're *mine*."

And for some reason, that simple statement, the one that should have offended her, made her want to cling to him and weep. Because he did want her. Still. He wasn't indifferent.

"See what you do to me?" He took her hand and put it against the hard ridge of his cock, and a thrill shot through her.

"I do." She squeezed him, pressed her palm against his heavy length. And then she forgot to be angry, or worry about all the baggage.

"Look at me," he said. And she did. She felt like she was seeing him for the first time in years. His face, changed by the years, lines around his eyes, his expression one of complete hunger and need. For her.

"Always," she said.

"I'm an ass," he said. "And I'm sorry. But otherwise, we're done talking for now."

He swept her up into his arms and carried her to the bed, setting her down in the center of it. He took his hat off and put it on the nightstand, then tugged his shirt up over his head. He was still in great shape, still the kind of man who took her breath away. It was more than abs, though he still had them. It was just him. The raw masculinity, the strength. The kind that came from inside.

And she should tell him. Because what had she done for his ego lately? Nothing. She'd been too wrapped up in her own little world of hurt that she'd refused to share with him. That she'd refused to help him fix.

"You're still the most beautiful man I've ever seen. You made me lose my head when I was eighteen, and you're making me lose my head right now."

He joined her on the bed and pressed his forehead to hers, kissing her on the lips. "You have no idea how happy I am to hear that, baby."

"And I can't remember the last time you called me baby."

"Do you like it?" She nodded. "Good."

He kissed her lips, her neck, his hand working the button on her jeans and drifting down, inside her panties, stroking her slick skin. "Oh . . . Sam."

"That's right. Don't forget that it's me, Jill."

"Sam," she said again, and he increased his pace, stroking her, taking her to heaven. Because he knew just how to touch her, this man who, in some ways, seemed like a stranger, but knew her body better than she did.

"That's right. You're my wife," he said, his voice rough, his hand firm and sure. "Mine."

"Yes," she said.

He stripped their clothes off of them, the desperation in his movements exciting, new. Something she hadn't experienced in years. And it was with her husband. And he'd been here the whole time. She just hadn't seen his desire. And he hadn't seen hers.

He thrust into her, hard. She gasped and he covered her mouth with his, his pace demanding, intense, and she did her very best to match him. Lust, desire, rose up inside of her, along with a feeling of connection, of love, so bittersweet, so filled with imperfection and desperation, so overpowering it made her want to weep.

"Sam," she said, because she didn't know what else to say. She said it over and over again as he moved inside of her, as she kissed his face, his mouth.

"Yes, baby," he said, his voice rough. "Yes."

And for the first time in two years, they were on the same page. They rode the wave together and went over the edge into oblivion.

It was a freaking embarrassment. Quinn Parker was lying awake in bed with the hard-on from hell, and it was all Lark

Mitchell's fault. Lark Mitchell and her clumsy kisses that spoke of a woman who had less experience than he'd initially imagined.

A woman who might be more easily wounded than he'd imagined. A woman who, inexplicably, in spite of her fumbling, seemed to have a power over him he couldn't harness or define.

Damn.

She'd seemed shocked when he'd slipped his tongue between her lips. And then she'd melted into him. Clung to him. Kissed him back with an enthusiasm that was so raw and genuine it had nearly brought him to his knees.

Hell, in the end she *had* brought him to his knees. He'd been ready to strip their clothes off then and there.

He swallowed and cursed his dry throat. Another discomfort to add to the ones he was already struggling with. The woman was a menace. She should come with a list of side effects tattooed to her forehead. Lark Mitchell: known to cause sweating, dizziness, erections lasting longer than four hours and dry mouth.

Even then, he had a feeling he would have ignored them. And he'd be in the same hell he was in now.

After another hour, he gave up and consigned himself to the inevitable. If he couldn't have Lark with him in bed for real, he would have her in his fantasies.

His last hazy thought as he wrapped his hand around his cock, before losing himself completely in arousal, was that this wasn't how it was supposed to be. He wasn't supposed to want her like this.

That wasn't what this kind of seduction was about. It was about giving himself another weapon. Giving himself more power.

But as he shuddered out his release with her name on his lips, he didn't feel like he had more power. He felt wholly unmanned. And so satisfied he would wait until morning to feel any regret.

CHAPTER

Nine

Lark was determined not to seem affected the next time she saw Quinn. Because he didn't deserve her blushes. He didn't deserve her wanton fantasies and desires. And yeah, she had them, but as she'd discussed with Jill, sometimes that sort of thing just happened.

But she was going to make a conscious decision to make sure it didn't keep happening. Because one kiss was enough. More than enough.

Had it only been one kiss? It had seemed like a lot more. Did you count kisses in the number of times a man leaned in? Or did you count it by length of the kiss? Did each thirty seconds roll over into a new one? She had no idea.

But even with her limited knowledge on the subject, she was determined to be cool. Which was why she could have cussed a blue streak when she saw him the next day and felt her face get hotter than blazes.

All intentions of playing it cool were totally not noted and followed by her body. Little slutty betrayer. Her body was in full-on skank mode, and no matter how much she scolded it, it just shook its tushy and kept on with the lurid thoughts.

She hadn't known her inner hussy was so intense.

"Mornin', Lark." Quinn rested his hand on one of the desks, an infuriating grin on his face. Infuriating, because he was doing the playing-it-cool thing, and she was sure she was brighter than a road flare.

"Good morning, Quinn," she said, schooling her voice so that it came out level and calm instead of shaky and filled with all her inner flail.

"And how is your Great Firewall shaping up?"

"Great," she said. *In spite of yesterday's interruptions.* "Things are starting to form. We'll be ready for the boys soon, I think."

"Great. And when you're done with that, it's time to start working on setting up the staff stuff."

"Joy."

"Beyond that, you think you're up for doing basic computer things with the boys?"

"Didn't I tell you I know all about men? Guess what? Teenage boys aren't any different."

"Is that what you think?"

She tapped her temple. "That's what I know."

"Tell me what you know," he said, leaning back against one of the desks.

She put her hand flat on the desk she was nearest to and leaned against it, trying to look casual. She had a feeling she was walking right into a trap, but she was too stubborn to back down. "I told you yesterday that men are predictable. And then you proved to be predictable." *Oh, that's a nice bear trap there, why don't I just walk right into it?*

"I was predictable?" He arched a brow. "Women have called me a lot of things, baby, but predictable isn't one of them. Except for yesterday—you called me that yesterday. But no other women have."

"Maybe because they care about your ego and I don't?"

"Possibly. Continue."

"Well, you went for the obvious. You went for the physical.

That's how men are. It's how they are from the time they're thirteen, and they never change. I was raised by my older brothers, like I said. And that means I've seen a whole lot of that 'male' thing. And I'm neither intimidated by it nor impressed by it."

"But you are turned on by it."

She sputtered, then recovered and tried to affect a casual posture. "Eh . . . pffft. Whatever. Not . . . No."

"I didn't turn you on yesterday when I kissed you?"

"Nuh-uh."

"So you put your tongue in my mouth for fun?"

"Well . . ." She pushed off from the desk and put her hands on her hips, trying to ignore her burning cheeks. "It's not . . . It's a . . . biology . . . thing. And . . . just like men are programmed to look at boobs and go for the kiss, women are programmed to respond to the kiss. And yes, be . . . turned on, if you will, but it's not anything to pitch a tent over, Parker. Nothing flattering."

He chuckled. "You're edging into protesting too much, Mitchell."

"Just don't get all chest beat-y over the fact that I kissed you back for, like, a flipping minute. It's just that natural man-woman thing, and you know full well it can't happen again and why."

"You really want to hate me, don't you?" he asked.

"Well, yeah."

"But you don't."

She turned to face the computer she'd been working on and tapped mindlessly on the keys, ignoring his statement.

"Careful, Lark, I might take your lack of stating you hate me with a fiery passion as a compliment."

"I hate you," she said, fully aware there was no venom in her voice.

"Once more, with feeling."

"I hate you, you jackass. Now can I get back to work?"

"In a minute."

She tapped her fingers on the desk and shot Quinn the evil eye, while trying to keep him out of focus so she wouldn't be assaulted by his good looks. "Is there something I'm not doing to your satisfaction?"

"No, I'm just enjoying talking with you."

"Why? I'm insulting you and generally being a jerk. You should want to leave."

"But I don't. That could be because I'm predictably male and enjoying the way your ass looks when you bend over the desks."

She whipped around to face him fully, her eyes wide. "That's it. Inappropriate times a billion. Not okay. Did I not make it totally and completely clear that you were never, ever to kiss me again?"

"Did I kiss you?"

"No! But you said things. And you know that that's off-limits, because the only reason for you to say anything would be so that you could kiss me again."

"If that's what you think . . ."

"What? You're going to try and say I'm full of myself?"

"No, I was going to say your imagination is sadly lacking if all you think I'm after is a kiss."

Her mouth opened, then snapped back shut. She couldn't think of what to say. "You know?" she said finally. "I am attracted to you. Fine. So I admitted it. Great. I am attracted to you. But I have the decency to keep it to myself, rather than bleeding it all over you."

"Maybe I want it all over me."

"But I don't!" she said. "And you know why."

"Because you think the worst about me."

"Because no matter what you did, my brother would see it as a betrayal if I were with you. And frankly, I don't want to be with a man who might have done the things he thinks you did. Or the man who did the things you freely admit to. So there."

"You have a lot of opinions about who I am."

"Yes. I do."

"Are any of them based in reality?"

"Um . . . yeah. Yeah, they are. You told me you've done bad things. And I believe your assessment of that. So now, in addition to that, I know you tricked me into taking a contract with you. And then not only did you do that, you're one grope away from a sexual harassment lawsuit, and also . . . you're . . . you're . . ."

"What?"

"I don't know. Stuff. I don't like you. I just don't."

His eyes traced her figure, so noticeably she felt it like a physical touch. "You look at me a lot for a woman who doesn't like me."

"Your looks aren't as disagreeable as your disposition," she said, sniffing.

"Nice to know," he said, crossing his arms over his chest. "But I'm disagreeable?"

"Yes. For all of the aforementioned reasons—and plus, we're not compatible."

"Really?"

"Yes."

He shifted and rubbed his chin with his hand. "I'll take a list of reasons why."

"Fine. You . . . you don't look at relationships the same way I do."

"How so?"

"Well, are you even going to pretend you haven't gotten off with every buckle bunny who ever batted her lashes at you?"

"Nope. Not for a second."

"See, there's my point. I don't do sex for the sake of sex." She felt her cheeks burn, because the statement was misleading on many counts. The first being that she'd never had actual sex, the second being that she'd had cybersex simply for the sake of getting off, so she was a fake prude and a hypocrite.

"Really? Never?"

She shook her head, digging her heels right into her lie. "No."

"Really?"

"Yes, really," she said. "Because . . . because I just don't behave that way."

"Why not?"

"Unlike some people, I don't go around looking for rewards via bad behavior, okay?"

A grin turned up the corners of his mouth. "Is that so?" He pushed off from the desk and started to walk away from her, heading toward the exit. Then he paused and turned back to her. "Well, let me know if you're ever looking for a reward for bad behavior. Because if you give me about fifteen minutes . . . I bet I could reward your bad behavior twice. Maybe even three times."

Her face went up in flames. "You think awfully highly of yourself," she said.

He shook his head. "Nope. I'm just sure of the chemistry we have between us."

"Chemistry?"

"You know, like when you put baking soda and vinegar in one of those papier-mâché volcanoes?"

"Yes."

"That's you and me, baby."

"You'd be the vinegar."

"Sure," he said. "But that's beside the point. We're . . ."

"Combustible." She finished his sentence without thinking.

"Glad you agree."

"I . . . I . . ."

He tipped his hat and stepped out the door. "See you later."

"I don't agree!" she shouted, even though he wasn't there anymore. "I was just finishing the thought on your lame metaphor."

She turned back around and faced the computer, grumbling and blushing furiously. Well, this had not gone at all well. Nope. Not well at all.

So much for playing it cool. In her defense, it was too hard to play it cool when the guy was so darn hot.

She blew out an exasperated breath. She just had to get over it. Stick her head in a bucket of ice or whatever she had to do in order to ignore it.

Because ignore it she would. Yes, she would.

*   *   *

It was getting dark when Lark emerged from the computer lab again, and there was no one around. The kitchen was empty, the other parts of the school were empty. The cabins were empty. She could just leave. She didn't have to go and let anyone know she was heading out.

And so she wouldn't. So there. Problem solved.

She walked down the path and toward the parking area and stopped, frozen. There was a tractor parked in front of her car, and a truck parked behind it.

"Awww, man." She grimaced and looked around. There was no one out there. No one around at all. She knew the truck belonged to Kevin, one of the work hands, but she hadn't seen him anywhere.

And she had no idea who was responsible for the big-ass tractor.

She looked around again, feeling helpless and annoyed. She was blocked in, and there was no one readily on hand. And that meant she would be taking a trek to the big house. To see the boss man. Whom she badly wanted to avoid because, gosh darnit, he was driving her insane with his smirks and his knowing looks and his sexy pecs, which she was so freaking aware of, even when he wore a shirt.

That image of him on her first day, half naked with his muscles so very, very there, and his tattoo, so enticing and only serving to enhance the look of his biceps, was burned into her brain, and she couldn't seem to excise it.

No. In fact, it had become a watermark over her vision. So that when she was looking at Quinn, even while fully clothed, that was what she saw. Hell, when she was looking at other things entirely it seemed to be what she saw, and the whole thing was driving her insane.

She was a traitor of the most epic proportions.

She forced all erotic Quinn-based images aside and stalked toward the main house, praying that someone who wasn't Quinn would be around, and that they would be the one to answer the door.

She took a deep breath and knocked, waiting, her stomach tightening more and more. Each passing second injecting her with more adrenaline, more ridiculous nervousness— she wouldn't call it excitement—over who was going to answer the door.

And then the door did swing open, and it was Quinn, shirtless and in low-slung jeans that showed those lines, whatever they were called, the ones that formed into an arrow, pointing right down to a point of extreme interest, the lines that turned smart girls stupid. Yep, those lines. And then, beyond them, abs. That chest.

And she suddenly forgot how to talk when she came to the tattoo again. The tattoo that seemed to be the embodiment of him. A horse. Its mane flowing in the wind, the expression on its face one of terrible fury. It was anger, and wildness. It was Quinn.

And when she looked into his eyes, she saw all of that and more.

"I . . . I'm blocked in," she said finally, wondering how much time had passed between when he'd opened the door and when she'd finally spoken.

He looked her over quickly. "You don't look blocked in."

"Not *me*," she said. "My car. I can't go anywhere because there's a truck parked in my way."

"Whose truck?"

"Kevin's."

"I thought he left a long time ago. After dinner. About the same time as Sandy." A smile crossed his face. "Yeah, I'm betting they not so sneakily left together."

"Argh! Well, what am I supposed to do? What about the tractor?"

He arched a brow. "What tractor?"

"The one that's in front of me. My car is the meat in a hillbilly sandwich. I've got Ford behind me and John Deere in front, and I can't go anywhere."

"I probably have the keys for the tractor."

"Well, can you move it so I can leave?"

"I could." He stood there still, a big wall of muscle, unmoving.

"Well, will you?"

He smiled. "Sure, darlin'. Come on in while I get the keys."

"Darlin', my ass," she muttered as she waited for him to move away from the door, then stepped inside the house.

It was truly a thing of beauty. There was some furniture in it now, a big sectional with slatted wooden details on the side that matched the beams on the walls and the vaulted ceiling.

She stood with her hands behind her while Quinn went down the hall and rummaged around for a while.

"The place looks nice," she said, feeling the need to fill the silence so it wouldn't get all full of awkward.

"Thanks," he called back. "It's starting to shape up anyway." He came back from where he was and into the kitchen. "I won't be living here, not once things get going. I'll be hiring someone to live here full-time. Oversee, caretake. But not just yet."

"It looks like the kind of place you would live," she said.

"You think?" he asked.

He was still shirtless. And it was all distracting.

"Well, yeah. It's rugged and . . . outdoorsy."

His lips quirked up into a half smile. "You think I'm rugged and outdoorsy?"

"It's not a compliment, it's an observation. Stop looking so thrilled with yourself."

"I took it as a compliment. It's a positive observation, so it seems like it counts."

"Doesn't."

"Well, I'm going to go and move the tractor."

"Great. Thanks."

"Wait in the warmth," he said, walking out the front door, shirtless still, leaving her standing there in the entry by herself.

She paced from there into the living area and looked out the windows, mainly seeing her reflection in the glass. She was still feeling weirdly buzzed, like she'd started feeling when she'd knocked on the door.

Or, if she was honest, like she'd been feeling since he kissed her yesterday.

It was just a whole bunch of hard-up virgin nonsense. She'd left it too long. But there was seriously no guy in town she wanted to get freaky with. There had been Tyler. She'd thought she had a chance with him, not for marriage and babies, but at least for sex. And then he'd gone and gotten his stupid head married to another woman.

This was all Tyler's fault.

Okay, kind of a stretch to blame yesterday's ill-advised make-out session on a guy who didn't even live in town anymore, but whatever. It was so much easier than blaming herself.

The front door opened again and Quinn came in. "Won't start."

"What?"

"It won't start. Actually, per the note on the dash, that's why it's there. It needs to be serviced. Sorry."

She flung her hands into the air. "What am I supposed to do?"

"Call your brother to have him come and pick you up?"

"No," she said. "No."

"Have me drop you off?"

She pictured Cade or Cole walking out and catching her with Quinn. "Probably not."

"Your brothers still don't know I'm your boss, do they?"

"No."

"How about this: I'll drop you off, but I'll do it far from the house. Will that work?"

She narrowed her eyes. "Why?"

"As much as I would love to be there when your brother finds out you're working for me, I'm not in the mood to get punched in the face."

Quinn honestly didn't know how he was going to play this. She was trapped. Which made him feel the urge to twirl a mustache he didn't have. He could drive her home and make sure her brother saw them. But that would shatter things a little bit earlier than he intended.

Because she hadn't been seduced yet.

And then there was the option of getting her to stay here. But there was no way to pose that scenario without sounding completely lascivious and generally untrustworthy.

He was both, which also made it difficult to sound like anything else.

"Figure it out, baby. It's either bunking down with me or taking a ride." She lifted her thumb to her lips and started gnawing on the nail. "Third option, you can hitchhike and hope you don't get eaten by wolves," he added, his tone dry.

"Oh . . . wow. The wolves are tempting."

"Oh, really?"

"Less dangerous."

"They have big teeth," he said.

"So do you."

He looked at her, at the slow blush spreading over her pale skin. "All the better to eat you with."

And he pictured it. Tasting her. Spreading her thighs and savoring her flavor, delving deep. He took a step toward her, and he was sure every one of his graphic fantasies was written on his face.

She gasped, which turned into a choke, and gave some validity to that thought. "Yes. The wolves. I think I'll hitchhike. If I get eaten, tell everyone I fought valiantly and kept my dignity."

"You are not hitchhiking," he said. The image of her, out there in the dark all by herself, made him nervous and edgy. It surprised him. Surprised him that it made him feel anything. That he cared at all. But he did. "I'll take you back to your brother's house, and I'll drop you off and make sure he doesn't know it's me. Okay?"

"And how will I get to work in the morning?"

"I can pick you up in the same spot I drop you off at."

"And what will I say happened to my car?"

"The truth. Hillbilly sandwich. Coworkers who are so busy screwing each other they don't realize when they do things like leave their trucks somewhere they might be blocking people in."

"Fine," she said. "But he's going to think it's weird if you don't come in to talk to him, won't he?"

"No, I think it's weird he would need me to. You're a grown woman."

She looked down, then back up. "Yeah, I know."

"You don't have to ask his permission, and you don't need him to meet your employer, right?"

"Right."

"Trust me, he'll like it better than you getting eaten by wolves."

She held up her hand and made a small measurement with her thumb and forefinger. "Marginally, if he knew who was driving me. All right. Let's go. And put a shirt on, for heaven's sake."

"You don't want me to drive you home shirtless?" he asked.

Lark rolled her eyes. "Could you be more redneck?"

"I reckon."

"Oh, go put a shirt on."

Her gaze drifted to his chest. He liked that. She was not very subtle when it came to checking him out, and that made him hot. All over. He was used to women who gave coy glances and looked at him with hooded eyes. All very much a game.

But Lark wasn't playing a game. She didn't want to look at him, but she did. She didn't want him to notice, and yet she was so obvious, so unpracticed, he couldn't help but notice that she was.

He walked into the kitchen and grabbed his black T-shirt from the barstool and shrugged it over his head. When he looked back at her, she was watching him again. And she whipped her head away quickly, as if that would somehow make him think she'd been staring at the front door the whole time.

"All right," he said. "Let's go." He grabbed his keys from

the wall and opened the door, following her outside and leading the way down to where his truck was parked.

Lark didn't wait for him to open the door for her, she just jerked it open herself and climbed in, buckling and staring straight ahead, her hands in her lap, her jaw set.

He got in the driver's side and started the engine. The close confines of the truck affected him a lot more than he'd imagined. He was used to picking up women. At rodeos, bars, whatever. And often he drove them to the hotels where they had their one-night stand, but he didn't remember the cab of his truck ever feeling like this.

Like all the air had been sucked out of it.

The truck was the kind that had a bench seat. He used it for ranch work, and it was older, not like the newer truck he had back in Texas. Until now, he'd missed his more plush ride, with its leather interior and engine that didn't growl like a feral beast. Right now he didn't miss it so much, because right now he was fantasizing about all kinds of ways a bench seat could be used.

It made his palms sweat. Made him hard. Make him shake. What was it about Lark Mitchell that turned him into the horny, insecure high school boy he'd never been?

He'd never been the kind of guy to sweat over a woman. He'd attracted them from the time he'd first started growing facial hair. Women who were older. Who liked a bad attitude and a dirty mouth. Never a woman like Lark, with her air of innocence and sweetness.

Not that she was all sweet. Hell no. She was sweet and tart, which made her way more enticing.

She wasn't pure innocence either. There was an edge of earthiness to her. One that he badly wanted to see more of. He wondered how much of it she'd discovered? Wondered if a man had ever really taken the time to awaken all the passion he knew she had simmering under the surface.

Immediately, he hated any man who'd ever tried and left her unsatisfied. But then, if he'd found out there'd been a man who'd satisfied her completely, he would have hated him too.

He would have cheerfully wrapped his hands around that man's neck and squeezed.

He tightened his grip on the steering wheel in response and maneuvered the truck onto the road.

"So . . . things going well?" she asked. "Things getting . . . set up and stuff?"

"Yes. This is terrible small talk. It's small talk we've already had, in fact," he said.

"Oh. Well, should I say something else?"

"Yeah, why don't you say something real?"

"What do you mean?"

He shrugged his shoulders, his hands still on the wheel. "I don't know. You don't like me, right?" He thought he might check in case it had changed.

"Right."

"So how about this: There's nothing you could say that would ruin our relationship. Because you already know I won't fire you. You don't like me, you don't care if I like you. Seems like we're in a good position to have some honesty between us."

The irony of that statement, considering his plans, wasn't lost on him. And he wasn't sure why he even wanted her to tell him something. To build closeness? As part of the seduction? Maybe, but that wasn't why he'd asked. He had no idea why he'd asked. He just had.

"So what? This is, like, a cone of silence?"

"Yeah, why not? Who would I tell?"

"And why are we doing this?"

"Because it's better than this meaningless, bland garbage. I've had my tongue in your mouth. It seems stupid with that considered."

"What, so I somehow owe you honesty because I acted like an idiot and kissed you?"

"Just thought you might like a chance to say something."

She hesitated. "Fine. I love my brothers. I love my life at Elk Haven and I'm not ready to leave it. Because the world scares me. With that in mind, I know a lot of what I'm going to say next seems hypocritical and ungrateful, but we don't

like each other already, so who cares if you know?" She
tapped her fingers on the window. "I feel like I'm suffocating there sometimes. There are too many ghosts. Cade and
Cole mean well, but I can't do anything without them butt-
ing in. It's a lot of work trying to keep them happy. I spend
so much time trying to keep them happy that I'm not exactly
sure what might make me happy. I do stuff on the computer,
and that's all me. It's secret and it's mine. But that's the only
place I don't . . . I don't worry about what they think."

He chuckled. "That's funny. I spent a long time trying
so hard to piss my family off that I didn't know what I liked
either. I just did things to make them mad because I wanted
the result. A lot more than I wanted what I was doing specifically. Either way, doing things for other people is stupid."

"Life advice, Quinn? Really?"

"Why not? Cone of silence, right? And I'm older than
you. I've done more than you. Probably made a hell of a lot
more mistakes than you, so trust me, living for other people,
no matter the reasoning, isn't the way to live."

"But you did all that because you were mad at them. I do
it because I love them. Because I'm grateful."

"So your entire life has to be one big thank-you?"

"Yes. No. I don't know. I don't know what I'm doing. I
don't know . . . I don't know how to want something else,
but I'm not totally happy with what I'm doing. So how's that
for stupid?"

"Sounds about right."

"What? Stupid?"

"No, just what you said, it sounds like life to me."

"Turn left," she said, and he steered the truck onto a long
dirt driveway. "You make me feel almost normal."

"Well, I don't know how you got that out of the conversation, woman. You're weird as hell."

She laughed so hard she snorted, and that made him
laugh too. Which was the strangest thing of all. The way
that she affected him. That she affected him at all. He wasn't
used to a woman affecting much more than his dick.

He didn't have a lot of friends. He didn't really have any,

apart from Sam, who was paid to stick with him. People in general made him feel very little. Except anger.

But Lark Mitchell made him laugh.

"Can you pull over up here?" she asked.

"Sure." He put his truck in park and left the engine running. "You're sure you can walk from here?"

"It's not far."

"I really would rather if you weren't eaten by wolves."

Lark looked at Quinn in the dark, at the lines of his face, highlighted by the moon, and she tried to stop her heart from speeding up. But it was impossible. She felt . . . She didn't know what she felt. He was now the only man she'd thoroughly kissed. And he was the only person on earth who knew how she felt about life. About her brothers. About what she wanted, or rather, the depth to which she was confused about what she wanted.

It made her feel like a bond was slowly forming between them. More than chemistry. More than anger. And it was unsettling, to say the least.

"Well, unsurprisingly, I don't want me to get eaten by them either."

"All right. I'll pick you up here tomorrow."

"Great."

Except she didn't get out of the truck. Because that bond thing seemed to be holding her there. Seemed to be compelling her to stay. And more than that, it seemed to be compelling her to move closer to him, rather than scrambling for the door.

Her heart was beating so fast and hard she could hear it echoing in her head, the only sound in the truck cab besides the dim rumble of the engine and their breathing, which she didn't think she was imagining was getting heavier with each passing second.

Even as she leaned in closer to him, she questioned her sanity. She asked herself what she was doing. But she kept hearing her own words, over and over again, and they were louder than the warnings.

I spend so much time trying to keep them happy that I'm not exactly sure what might make me happy.

Right now, she was wondering if Quinn's lips against hers might make her happy. And right now, it seemed like that might be more important than anything else. It was so dark in the truck, its engine keeping out the normal night sounds. It felt like something different. Something out of time and reality.

It seemed safe. And incredibly dangerous.

She lifted her hand and touched his face. His skin was warm and rough, thanks to the end-of-day stubble. And right then, she knew what she wanted. Nothing deeper than the physical, nothing longer-term than the next few seconds.

But right then she wanted to kiss Quinn Parker more than she wanted to keep on breathing.

So she did.

The touch of his lips to hers was like fire, burning through her, savaging her, flame streaking along her veins, leaving nothing untouched, nothing spared.

He growled and forked his fingers in her hair, parting her lips with his tongue and delving deep. She opened to him, responded to him, to the desperation in his actions. This was different from the kiss they'd shared on the mountaintop. There was no restraint here. They weren't in the wide-open spaces with the sun shining on them.

They were in the dark. They were in a space only inhabited by them. Close and secluded. It was only them. Their breath. Their lips. His hands roaming over her body now, and hers all over his.

He kissed her neck, down to her collarbone, the press of his mouth on her skin hot, wet, so freaking arousing. She felt completely desperate for more. For everything.

She grabbed the hem of his shirt and tugged it up over his head, letting her hands roam over his bare skin, the hard muscles of his back. He shifted his hands, cupped her breasts, then undid the first button on her top, kissing the exposed wedge of skin.

He continued down, undoing buttons, tasting bare skin, until her shirt was open all the way. He looked at her in the dark, his eyes glittering. She was crossing new lines with him. Doing new things she'd never done. Reaching new heights of intimacy.

And it felt too good to stop. Too good to let nerves take over. Too good to do anything but let him continue on.

He reached his hand around to her back, then cocked his head to the side. "Front clasp," he said. Then he moved his hand back in front of her and with one deft motion, undid the catch on her bra, leaving her truly exposed to him.

She knew who it was. She knew who was making her feel like this. On the edge of losing her sanity, on the edge of climax. It was Quinn Parker. And she knew being with him like this was wrong.

But the wrong made it more exciting. Or maybe it didn't. She wouldn't know. She'd never been in this position before.

He leaned down and kissed her neck, then her collarbone. And down to the curve of her breast. He continued lower, swept the flat of his tongue over her nipple before blowing lightly on her damp skin.

A sharp ache shot through her, coupling with pleasure so intense she couldn't keep herself from making a sound. She sounded like a bad porn, even to herself, but Quinn didn't seem to mind.

Instead, he turned his attention to her other breast, repeating the action there before sucking her nipple deep into his mouth.

She grabbed on to his shoulders, digging her nails into his skin, not caring at all.

He chuckled, his breath hot on her skin. "See, Lark? Being bad can be awfully good. I like you as a bad girl." He flicked open the button of her jeans and lowered the zipper, sliding his hand down beneath the denim, beneath her panties, his fingers sliding through her slick folds. "Oh, yeah, you're definitely a bad girl. And you want me, don't you?"

She could only nod. She was way past words now. Way past logical thought. There was nothing more than burning need, white-hot pleasure and Quinn Parker. Everything else was irrelevant.

He drew his finger upward, working it over her clitoris. She threw her arm over her eyes, not bothering to suppress her sounds of pleasure, not caring about anything but how she felt. How good he made her feel.

Suddenly, he sat up.

"What?" she asked, feeling dizzy, disoriented and so turned on it was painful.

"What I have planned requires more room." He opened the driver's-side door and stepped out of the truck, standing facing her. He pulled her shoes off and let them fall to the ground. Then he reached in and tugged her jeans and underwear down her legs, balling them up and throwing them into the truck behind her.

Then he gripped her hips and pulled her forward, raising her butt off the seat of the truck, his eyes intent on her. So intent that, even with how dark it was, she fought the urge to cover herself up.

"You're so beautiful," he said, his voice rough. "Oh, Lark . . ." He leaned in, pressed a kiss to her inner thigh. "What did I tell you? All the better to eat you with."

A hot flash of embarrassment burned through her, just as his tongue touched her. And then everything went white behind her eyes, a flash of light, of fire, so intense she couldn't breathe through it, couldn't think. Couldn't do anything but feel.

He tasted her, deep, long. She should be horrified. To have him do this, something so intimate, something she'd never even gotten around to fantasizing about. But she wasn't. It felt perfect. Indulgent. Amazing.

His tongue was wet, the slick friction sending crackling flame through her, coiling low in her stomach and settling there, burning steadily. Building. Growing. Threatening to rage out of control.

He shifted his weight, wrapping his arm around her so

that his forearm was supporting her weight, and then he took his other hand and stroked her, gently, just enough to add fuel to the flames.

Then he pushed one finger inside of her. And the fire exploded. She was consumed by it. Burning up, completely and totally. And she welcomed it, bathed in it. Heat and pleasure so far beyond what she'd imagined possible.

She'd had orgasms before, but not like this. She had no control here. She had nothing more than complete and total surrender. And she reveled in it.

Slowly the flames receded. Slowly, she started finding her breath. And then suddenly, it all dropped away.

And she realized she was flat on her back in Quinn Parker's truck, in the middle of her driveway, albeit her secluded driveway, with the door wide open and her legs spread.

And she'd just done a whole lot more than kiss him.

She blinked and then jerked out of his hold, moving into a sitting position and scrambling madly for her jeans.

Shit. She was going to cry. She was going to cry like a little girl who wanted her mommy. Because she felt like one. And she did. She wanted someone to hold her and tell her it was okay, and there was no one to do that.

Because it wasn't okay. It wasn't okay.

With shaking hands she tugged her jeans on, stuffing the panties in her pocket. She stumbled out the passenger's side door and went around to the driver's side. "Shoes," she said, her throat dry.

"Lark . . ."

"Shoes." He bent and picked her shoes up, handing them to her. She jammed her feet into them, her stomach pitching.

"Are you going to walk off all pissed again like I did something horrible to you?" he asked, his voice low, deadly.

"No," she said. "You didn't . . . I did . . . I did it. I . . . I don't know what I'm doing." She wrapped her arms around herself and started walking away from Quinn's truck.

"Lark." She heard the door slam shut behind her. "Lark. Damn it, stop."

She whirled around to face him. "No. I can't. I can't do this with you."

"But you want to," he said, his voice rough.

"So what? *So what?*"

"Doesn't what you want matter?"

"Not in this case, Quinn. No, it doesn't."

"Why not?"

"I don't want to want you!"

"But you do."

"It doesn't matter."

"So what? You get off with me, even though you can't stand me? And now you're going to run off, sick to your stomach because you wanted me, and because you indulged that want? Because I disgust you that much?"

"Yes!" she shouted.

For a second, she thought the moonlight revealed a flash of pain in his eyes. But just as quickly as she saw it, it disappeared again.

He shrugged. "Then you should be even more disgusted with yourself. Because no matter what you think you want, baby, I can make you come. Easy. Think about what that says about you."

"Believe me," she said, wiping at her dry eyes. "I have thought about it. I don't like myself very much right now either."

"Join the club."

"I'm not coming in tomorrow."

"Suit yourself. I'm docking a day's pay off your contract."

She flung her arms wide. "Freaking spiffy, Quinn, do what you have to. Please yourself."

"You don't mean that."

"Sure I do."

"No, you don't. Because pleasing myself involves getting you naked again." He smiled and laughed, but there was nothing happy or humorous about either expression. "I wonder what that says about me?"

He jerked open the door of the truck and then pulled the

passenger door shut before starting the engine. Lark turned
away from him and started walking down the driveway,
toward her house, her entire body numb straight down to
her soul.

When Quinn had been touching her, she'd never felt so
alive. And now that reality had hit, she'd never felt so empty.

Quinn Parker was a very inconvenient paradox. She'd
never had a better reason to hate a man. But there had never
been a man in her life whom she'd craved so much.

CHAPTER
Ten

"Don't you have work today, Lark?" Cade walked into her bedroom with a soda in his hand and sat on the edge of her bed.

"Nope," she said, knocking back her energy drink and grimacing as the fizz burned in her nose. "I took the day off." She set the can back on her desk and exited out of her game.

"Why?"

Because my boss, your sworn enemy, is a dangerous, sexy jackass who went down on me in his pickup truck, if you must know. "Because I needed it."

"Well, shit, does that pass for a good reason to take a day off? Because I feel like I need one."

"Cole would give you one."

"Yeah, if I played cripple, which I won't."

"You're too stubborn for your own good, Cade." The mention of his injuries made her feel even worse, which she hadn't imagined was possible.

How could she want something this much when she knew it was so wrong? So bad?

You're definitely a bad girl.

She blocked out Quinn's husky, sinful voice. The truth was, she wasn't a bad girl. She was a girl whose whole life was in a bedroom in front of the computer. Because living virtually allowed her to feel like she had a life she didn't have.

It allowed her to dabble in sex without risking anything. It let her go on adventures without being in any danger. It let her make choices and do things she would never actually do in real life for fear of the consequences.

Well, last night she'd done something in real life. It had been raw, hot, amazing, far beyond anything she'd ever imagined. And it had been a huge mistake.

How ironic that half of why she never did anything was to preserve her relationship with Cade and Cole, and when she finally did do something, it was the one thing that was almost guaranteed to blow that relationship all to hell.

"Yeah, I probably am. Amber thinks so."

"Really?"

"Yes. She thinks I need to figure out disability or some such bullshit, but I'm not disabled."

"You can't do the job you used to do."

"But I can work."

"You don't make what you did. And . . . and per our financials for the ranch, we're sort of missing that income."

"But when these contracts take off, the horses we're breeding for the circuit . . . all that money will be back. And it's thanks to my connections." He shrugged. "See? Not so disabled. Anyway, I got the world's biggest effing insurance payout, I don't have to make what I did. And I'm not disabled."

No, of course he wasn't. He couldn't hike for long distances, or ride a horse that did anything beyond a kid's birthday party circle, or stand at all for long periods of time, but no. Not disabled. Dumb man and his male pride.

This should remind her why she hated Quinn. But she kept thinking about his claims of being innocent. And for some reason . . . she didn't think he was lying.

"Cade." She didn't know what she was doing or why, but the words were coming out anyway. "The man you think . . . the man you think was responsible for your accident . . . you're sure he did it?"

"It's not even an accident, Lark. He did it on purpose. And I know it was Quinn Parker, trust me. You've never met a meaner son of a bitch."

"Really?" she asked, looking down at her hands. Her whole face was numb. Which was weird because she'd never been overly conscious of her face having feeling, but she felt the absence of it keenly.

"Everyone else was my friend, Lark. Quinn never said more than two words at a time to me, and when he did, they weren't nice words. He was antisocial. He has a criminal record. Hell, nobody liked him. And they barred him from competition, so that says it all, I think."

Her throat tightened. "I guess it does."

Except it made her wonder which was the real Quinn. Actually, she knew what her brother said was probably true. Quinn was the kind of man who could be that way, she was sure about that.

But she also knew why. She knew he'd never felt like he fit. Knew where he'd come from.

She didn't think that made him be the kind of guy who would hurt anyone. Because while she'd seen evidence of the meanness, and of the way he could be hard and blunt, she'd never thought he would hurt her, or anyone else.

"You seem deep in thought, Lark."

"Yeah," she said, looking over at her energy drink can and staring at the logo on it. "I just . . ."

"Is it Tyler?"

"What?" Tyler was like a distant memory. A hurt that seemed to be a part of someone else's life. Quinn was too large in her present; he eclipsed any feelings she'd ever had for anyone else.

"Tyler. I know you liked him, and now he married someone else."

"I just liked him, Cade, that's all. I didn't love him."

"Just checking."

"Well, you don't need to check. I'm fine." She was so not fine, but there was no way she was telling him what was going on either. "I appreciate it. You checking in on me. I know you care, and that's really . . . thank you."

"No problem. This is all we have, right? Each other? So even though Cole is an asshole, we have to stick together."

Yes, they did. And that was the reason she lived the way she did. Because Cole and Cade had sacrificed so much to raise her. Even before her father died, they'd been major influences in her life. They'd driven her to events, especially Cole. Taken care of her. And deep down, she'd always been afraid that if she made things too hard on them, she'd lose them too.

And she didn't want to lose them.

Because if she lost them, what would she have left?

"Yeah," she said, her throat dry. "We do."

"You know if anything's bothering you, you can tell me."

"I know," she said. But she couldn't.

"Great. Well"—he pushed up off of the bed and headed toward the bedroom door—"I have to go work. I can't just blow it off like some people."

"Whatever, man."

She turned back to the computer and didn't move until the door clicked closed behind him. And then she put her forehead on the keyboard and ignored the low-level bumping noises her computer made in protest.

Why was she so determined to ruin everything? Well, not her specifically, but her body. Traitorous traitor.

"Hey, Lark . . . Whoa, hey."

"Does anyone knock anymore?" She rolled her head to the side and saw Cole standing in her open doorway, then she sat up.

"Sorry, Cade said he was just in here."

"Yeah. He was. What?"

"Why are you . . . Face. Keyboard."

"I'm just tired."

"I was wondering if you knew where your car was or if I have to file a police report."

Oh, dangit. "I left it at work. I was blocked in and I got a ride home."

"Who gave you a ride?"

"M-my boss."

Cole arched a brow, crossing his arms across his broad chest. And there was Protective Older Brother Stance Number Three. "Nice of him," he said, his jaw clenched tight.

"Yes, it was nice of him. As he pointed out my alternative was being eaten by wolves."

"And you didn't call me?"

"It was late. I didn't get finished until late, and I didn't want to pull you away from dinner or anything. I respect that you have a life. And I don't have to always be all up in it. Novel concept, right?"

"I see. So why didn't you go into work today?"

"I'm tired."

"Did he hurt you?"

"What?" Cole was like a mother-effing bloodhound. It was hideously annoying.

"Your boss. What's the deal with him? Why is it he gave you a ride back last night, you're all defensive and you didn't go to work today?"

"Nothing, Cole, gosh. My car was blocked in—nonworking tractor and a coworker who left his car. Nothing nefarious." *Except oral sex in the driveway and a huge screaming match after.*

Cole looked at her hard, and she knew her cheeks were turning pink.

"At least respect me enough to know when I don't want to tell you, Cole," she said, her throat tightening. Because she knew she looked upset. She knew she was turning red. She knew she looked like she was hiding something. Because she was.

So she just had to try to appeal to Cole's human side. And hope he'd developed one in the year since he'd met Kelsey.

"Lark, if anyone ever hurts you—"

"It's more complicated than that. And I know you probably get what that means. But please don't ask me, if you think you know, or think you don't, but want to. I'm not ready to talk about it."

A muscle in his jaw jumped and his hand tightened around the doorknob. "Do you remember when I offered to run Tyler out of town because I thought he'd hurt you?"

"A woman doesn't forget the time her brother offered to kick a man's ass for her."

"With that in mind, you know I would gladly inflict violence on any man that hurt you. And a man who is paying you to work for him? I'm sorry, Lark, but I swear, if he touches you, I will end him."

"He hasn't," she said, lying. And she knew she looked like she was lying. But it wasn't Cole's business. She'd asked him, pretty respectfully, to back off.

"Lark . . ."

"Cole, how old am I?"

"Twenty-two," he said.

"So you do know that I'm not a child."

"Lark, it's my job to protect you."

"Not from everything in life, Cole. I have to be allowed to live."

He shook his head. "Living like you mean, that's overrated. People can talk blithely about mistakes and how they made them who they are. But my first marriage? It was hell, Lark. If I could spare you mistakes like that . . ."

"If you hadn't had that first marriage, you wouldn't be having your second one now. With Kelsey. Because without Shawna, you would not have banked your . . . y'know. And if you didn't do that then Kelsey wouldn't have gotten pregnant with Maddy, and you wouldn't have your wife or your daughter. Check. Mate. Ass. Hole." She turned back to her computer. "Now let me make my own mistakes, or not make them, or whatever. I will neither confirm nor deny."

"Lark," he said, his voice rough. "Fine. You're right. It

all worked out for me. But I don't want to see you hurt. Ever."

"You can't cover me in Bubble Wrap, Cole." And the minute she said it, she felt like a hypocrite. Because wasn't that what she did to herself? All the time?

A little virtual Bubble Wrap. To cushion her encounters and relationships. To make everything feel safe and secure.

"I know."

"Well then, stop trying to." That was just as much for herself as it was for him.

He nodded and backed out of her room, closing the door behind him.

"Save me from nosy brothers," she muttered.

And from herself. She felt like she was on the edge of something. A shift, a change. In herself and in everything around her. She didn't like it in the least.

She had spent her life playing it safe, and now her body seemed to be taking matters into its own hands. The simple fact was, when she was with Quinn, things between them exploded.

He was the first thing she'd ever wanted, really, really wanted, that she really couldn't have. The first thing she'd ever wanted that might compromise her little cocoon of safety.

But she didn't love him. She was just addicted to how he made her feel. And no amount of good feeling was worth compromising her family.

No matter how very good it was.

"So, did you see anything?"

"No." Sam shifted his weight and glanced over at Jill, who was standing over by their truck. "Sorry, Quinn. I did keep an eye on Cade, but he seems . . . injured. He never rode more than a couple of feet, he limps, he looks like he has a lot of pain. He's not faking anything."

Quinn ignored the hard rock of disappointment that

settled in his gut, right next to the hard rock of disappointment that had been there since last night. Since Lark had run out on him and left him unsatisfied and craving release.

He shouldn't be disappointed. This wasn't emotional. It was making things right. It would have been simpler if he could just prove Cade was the liar, but then, in truth, it had always been a long shot.

"Fine. So we'll move on."

"What else are you planning?"

He felt like his biggest chance had just slipped through his fingers, but he couldn't leave now. He had the ranch here; the boys were coming next week. And he'd been sure—he realized it now, with a blinding flash of certainty—that Cade had just been lying.

Pointing the finger and collecting the money.

Yes, he'd told himself it was a long shot, but deep down he'd believed it was true. And now Sam was telling him it wasn't.

A heated image flashed through his mind. Lark's thighs spread for him, her hoarse cries of pleasure.

Yes. There was still Lark. There was still revenge. If he couldn't make it right, he'd make it even. Or he'd use Lark to convince Cade to recant.

He ignored the voice in his head that told him Cade's punishment was his limp. Fine, but did it justify his stealing Quinn's career too? Two of the biggest rodeo stars pulled out of commission over one incident.

What had happened to Cade, Quinn would never wish on anyone. But there was no reason for him to be dragged into it. He hadn't done it. He'd paid for someone else's sins all of his life, and he'd be damned if he'd continue.

"I'm not sure."

"That's a load of BS, Quinn. You know what you're planning."

"How about it doesn't concern you," Quinn said.

Sam shook his head. "I like you, Quinn. Love you like a brother, even. But I sure as hell don't trust you half the time."

"But you know I didn't do this."

"Yeah, I know."

Jill pushed away from the truck and walked toward them. "Quinn, I'll be honest. I don't like you a lot of the time, and even I know you didn't do it. But Cade's not lying. He's hurt. He lost his career."

"And so did I," Quinn said. "For no reason except that Mitchell needed to point a finger. And he pointed it at me. He's the one who brought me into it, and so whatever happens . . . it's on his head." He looked between Jill and Sam. "What are your plans now?"

"Do you still need me here?" Sam asked.

"Extend your stay at Elk Haven. I need you back, but not until . . . not for a while. If Lark sees you here, she's not going to be happy."

Jill's expression sharpened. "What does Lark have to do with this?"

"She works for me."

"And?"

He shrugged. "And nothing."

"Quinn . . . If you hurt her, I swear . . ."

"Got to talking to her during your time at the ranch?"

"She's young," Jill said.

"She's a grown woman."

"Tell me you aren't going to involve her in this." Jill crossed her arms and stared him down, pale blue eyes filled with steel.

Quinn looked right back. And lied his ass off. "I won't."

"Good. Fine."

"So you can either go back home for a while, or you can stay at Elk Haven; it's up to you. I'm paying."

"Elk Haven," Sam said. "It's been . . . nice."

"Well, good." Though he was a little nervous about having Jill in Lark's proximity now. Still, with the way Sam was eyeing his wife, like she was a particularly tempting dessert, he was hoping they would be too distracted by each other to mess with what he had going with Lark.

Of course, he'd effectively screwed that up last night.

But it had felt so good. And it had felt an awful lot like self-indulgence. A lot less like revenge or seduction than he'd intended.

She'd been so sweet. So responsive. Right up until the moment she'd freaked the hell out and told him his touch disgusted her. Though that was, in its way, responsiveness. Just not the kind he enjoyed.

He'd enjoyed the kind that had come before it. Slick flesh and sweet sighs of contentment. She'd been so tight around his finger, so sweet on his tongue. He wanted more. He wanted it all.

And he wasn't sure if she was ever going to come back and face him.

Well, he did have her car. Although she might consider the rattletrap an acceptable loss, all things considered. But then, he'd threatened to come to the ranch and collect money right from her brother, and he *would* do it.

Still. Regardless of what had passed between them. Yes, he was attracted to her, but she was a means to an end. Nothing more. If he got the enjoyment of getting off with her as an added bonus to the justice of getting reinstated in the circuit, then fine.

But she wasn't the important thing here. And he had to remember that. Sam was right not to trust him. He wasn't trustworthy. He'd never sought to be. He was bad blood, from the moment he'd been born, and it wasn't going to change now.

There had only ever been one thing good about him. He'd only ever done one thing well. He'd been a damn good rodeo cowboy, and beyond that? He was a bastard. A man whose own mother couldn't love him.

Everyone had known what he was the moment he'd come into the world. He might as well prove them right. He'd shock no one, disappoint no one, and get back to the only place he'd ever fit.

It seemed like it was worth the cost to him.

He pictured Lark's face from last night. Her lips parted with pleasure, and then later, dark eyes filled with confusion as she'd walked away from him like he was standing at the mouth of hell ready to drag her in.

If anything made him question what he was doing, it was her.

Now's hardly the time to grow a conscience, Parker.

No, it was far too late for that. And he'd come too far to go back now.

"Are you coming in to work tomorrow?"

Lark opened her eyes and looked at her bedside clock, her cell phone mashed to her ear. Ten thirty. She didn't usually go to bed this early. And she didn't usually get calls this late. "How did you get this number?"

"It's on your file."

Lark rolled to her side and pushed herself into a sitting position. "Oh, really?"

"Yes, really. Don't act so surprised by the fact that your boss has your number. You're too smart for that."

Well, the thing was that Quinn seemed like something other than her boss. Something other than a client. He seemed like something else altogether. He was, after all, the only man to ever put his tongue in her mouth.

Among other places.

Her whole head got hot just thinking about it.

"I'm not very smart, as evidenced by my behavior over the past few days."

"Such as?" he asked.

"Such as getting in compromising positions with a man I barely know."

"I know you a lot better than the women I usually position myself compromisingly with."

She blinked rapidly. "Case in point of why we shouldn't be doing any of that kind of stuff. To me, you're a stranger. Essentially."

"I feel like I know you pretty well," he said, his voice dipping to a lower register, getting huskier. Sexier.

He sucked the words right out of her brain, and she found herself completely unable to come up with a response to that. Because she was back in that moment. Fire burning through her, pleasure like she'd never imagined existed . . .

She tipped over, pressing her face against her pillow, and made a noise that was halfway between a whimper and a snarl.

"That good, huh, baby?"

Mortification coiled in her belly and curdled like sour milk. She couldn't believe she'd actually betrayed that much. "Don't flatter yourself," she said, her voice muffled by the pillow.

"I don't need to. Your reaction did that for me."

She lifted her head. "Oh, my running away screaming into the night flattered you? You really do have ego issues, my friend."

"I'm your friend now? That means I'm not a stranger."

"Quinn," she growled.

He laughed. "Sorry, Lark."

A silence fell between them, and it wasn't awkward, which was weird. It felt companionable. Comfortable. So strange, because things between them were never comfortable. They were always lightning charged and combustible.

"Apology accepted."

"So can I come and pick you up tomorrow?"

"Yes," she said.

"And do you promise not to pepper spray me?"

"Do you promise not to kiss me?"

"That depends," he said. She heard fabric rustle in the background, and she wondered if he was in bed too. The idea made her feel even warmer than she already was, and she kicked her blankets down to her toes. "What will you be wearing?"

"Nothing exciting," she said. "Jeans and a T-shirt."

"No buttons?"

"No," she said, teeth gritted. Why didn't she hang up? Why didn't she tell him to leave her alone?

You don't want him to.

She ignored the voice in her head that wanted to tell the truth and clung to the misty illusion of *Who knows?*

"Damn," he said, his voice a rough whisper that vibrated through her. "All right, that begs the question . . . what are you wearing right now?"

The question made her feel like she was standing near the fire again. She was unclear about whether it was the heat of arousal or the flames of hell, coming after her for her betrayal. She shouldn't answer. She should hang up.

But she was too curious. Held captive by the possibilities of what might happen next. Of what he might say or do. And with the phone between them, at least he couldn't touch her. It couldn't go further than she was ready for it to go.

And anyway, it might not even go anywhere.

She looked down at her bare legs, then at the upside-down, to her, image of two dinosaurs talking. "A brown T-shirt. With a Stegosaurus and a Tyrannosaurus. And it says, 'Curse your sudden but inevitable betrayal.'" She was really sucky at this dirty-talk thing when she wasn't typing it and getting a chance to screen her words. She really should have lied and gone with lace. She'd lied with Aaron. She'd said she was way hotter than she was. And she'd claimed to own a thong. And claimed to be wearing said thong. She didn't own a thong.

He chuckled. "Sounds like a warning."

"Do you need the warning?"

"I might."

Her stomach tightened. "At least you're honest."

"As insightful and entertaining as your T-shirt is, what else have you got on?"

"Um . . . uh . . ."

"I'll tell you what I'm wearing."

"Okay. Go."

"Black boxers."

Her throat dried. "Is that all?"

"Yes."

The silence worked its way under her skin, made her pulse throb. Her entire body throb. "Oh."

"I'm in bed," he said.

"Me too," she said, her throat so dry it felt like it was lined with sandpaper.

"So now I shared what I was wearing, or mainly not."

"You know about my T-shirt."

"But the rest?"

"Just . . ." What was the sexy thing to call underwear? What was she doing? "Panties."

A throaty purr shivered down the line and reverberated down to her toes. "What kind?"

"They aren't . . ." *Lie, damn you, Lark! Tell him it's a thong. Crotchless. Something.* "They're just cotton. With a Superman *S* on the front."

He chuckled. "I like this."

"Why?"

"Because I know you're telling me the truth. If you'd said something lacy and see-through, I would have called you a liar. But I can picture this."

"Are you picturing it?" she asked.

"Hell yeah."

Her heart was thundering. Her breasts felt heavy, and an ache was centered between her thighs, growing deeper and deeper. "And do you . . . like what you're picturing?"

"I remember how you look naked."

"It was dark."

"Doesn't matter. Your breasts are so perfect. You have the prettiest nipples I've ever seen. So perfect I had to taste them. And your legs . . . long and shapely. That's what I like about you—you're shaped like a woman. Curves in all the right places. Hips a man can grab on to."

"Are you saying my hips are big?" she asked, her throat so tight she could barely force the words out.

"Perfect. I'm saying they're perfect. And do you want me to tell you how sweet you taste?"

"Quinn—"

"It makes me hard just thinking about it."

She moved her hands over the top of her thighs, restless, hot. She should be so mad at him for saying that. "Remember how things got left between us last time?" she asked.

"Yes."

"You were mad at me. I was mad at you."

"That's about right."

"I said your touch disgusted me."

"Yeah, but you're a liar."

She was a liar. "Even so, I said it."

"I'm not touching you now, am I, baby?" But it felt like he was, his words almost as potent as the sweep of his tongue over her flesh had been.

"No."

"So do you want me to hang up, or do you want to hear more about how hot I am for you?"

That was the question. But she could end the call at any time. It wasn't like being with him in person. She had more control here. More distance.

"I'm listening."

"If I were there right now, do you know what I'd do?"

"What?"

"I'd lift your shirt up, not all the way, just enough so I could see your panties. And I'd trace the *S* with my finger."

Unconsciously, she found herself doing exactly what he described, a hiss escaping her teeth as her fingertip drifted over her clitoris.

"Did you just do it, Lark?" he asked, his voice low.

"No," she lied, heat flooding her face.

"Don't lie to me again. Did you?"

"Yes." The word came out a rushed whisper.

"Good. Keep doing that. Do what I would do if I were there." She could tell him no. She should tell him where to stick it. She didn't.

"Okay."

"After I did that, I would push your shirt up the rest of the way so I could see your breasts." He paused. "Did you do it?"

"Not yet."

"Do it," he bit out. "Now."

She put her hands just beneath the hem of her T-shirt and pushed it up over her breasts. "I did it," she said.

"Good. Are your nipples hard?"

"Quinn. Jeez."

"Are they?"

"Yes," she said, flexing her toes, trying to excise some of her restless energy, some of her nerves and arousal.

"Touch them," he said.

"Quinn . . ."

"I would if I were there. I'd tease them. Suck them. Since you can't do that . . . I'll let you off just touching them."

"Generous of you," she said, sliding the tip of one finger over a hardened bud.

"You have no idea how generous I'd be if I were there. I wouldn't just touch you there. I'd put my hands between your legs. Feel how wet you were for me. You're wet, aren't you?"

Arousal pounded through her, an insistent beat. She felt so hungry, for him, for more. And because she knew he would ask her to, she moved her hand from her breast, down beneath the waistband of her underwear.

"Yes," she said, an answer to his question, a confirmation of how good it felt to be touched, even if it was just by herself.

"Remember what I did last night?"

She bit her lip and nodded, then realized he couldn't see her. "Yes."

"Touch yourself like that. In that same rhythm. We both know you like it."

She nodded again, sliding her fingers over her clit, a sharp cry escaping her lips. She wasn't unfamiliar with this act, but having Quinn give the orders, knowing he knew what she was doing, amped it up to a whole new level.

"Do you know what that does to me?" he asked.

"Tell me," she said, her voice shaky. "You touch yourself, Quinn. And tell me about it."

She could hear him moving, could hear the shifting of fabric. "I'm hard for you," he said.

"I wish I knew how you looked," she said, her fingers still working over her own body. "It's not fair. You can picture me, but I can't picture you."

"I'm sure you can use your imagination."

Yes, she could. She knew what naked men looked like. But the thing was, she didn't know what one felt like. So while she could close her eyes and imagine what Quinn might look like naked, she couldn't get a good idea of how it would feel to touch him.

Would he be hot? Smooth? She knew he'd be hard. She'd felt the outline of him through his jeans, but she wanted to know more. She was almost desperate to know more.

But she didn't want to admit the extent of her inexperience. "Of course," she said.

"This is torture," he said, his voice a low growl. "It's not my hand I want."

"You can't come here."

"Why not?"

Her hand stilled. "You know why."

So did she, but she was still turned on, high on her need for release, and it didn't seem to matter very much.

"Because I'm bad for you," he said, the growl in his voice exaggerated.

"Yes," she said, resuming her movements, pleasure streaking through her like flames.

"Oh . . . baby, you have no idea how much I want you."

It was that statement that pushed her over the edge. She cried out, her internal muscles clenching tight, her eyes squeezed shut as Quinn's face, his chest, his abs, flashed through her mind.

A second later, she heard a low grunt on the other end of the phone, and she could only assume that Quinn had gone over the edge with her.

She lay there after that, her arm straight out, away from her head, the phone loose in her fingers, her heart pounding hard, shame, her newfound semi-constant companion, trying to crowd her post-orgasmic bliss.

She put the phone back to her ear and heard Quinn breathing hard on the other end. "So," he said, finally. "I'll pick you up tomorrow?"

"Yeah," she said.

"See you at nine."

The line went quiet and Lark threw her arm over her head. "You suck," she said into the empty room.

She really did suck. She was the *worst*. But right now she felt sleepy. And satisfied. And she didn't want to run from Quinn. The trouble was, he wasn't here.

She rolled over onto her side, pulling her covers up over her shoulders and holding them tight. She wished Quinn were behind her, his strong arms holding her close. She would worry about why she shouldn't want that later.

Right now she just did. Right now she ached for closeness. She buried her face in her pillow and pulled the blankets tighter.

Things would be so much simpler if she could hate Quinn. But she didn't. She couldn't.

She felt like she was being torn in two. And the only way to stop it was to release her hold on one of the things she was clinging to.

Right now, she didn't think she could do that.

"Good mornin'."

"Stuff it, Parker." Lark got in the truck and slammed the door behind her, and Quinn gave her a sideways look. She had her head down, her focus on her hands in her lap. She was angry at him. Again. After he'd given her an orgasm. Again. It took a lot to satisfy this woman.

He opened his mouth to tell her she was starting to seem ungrateful, but something stopped him. Maybe it was the color in her cheeks, the fact that she refused to look at him at all.

The fact that he could almost feel her shame and embarrassment radiating from her. And that had never been a part of the plan in his mind. He hadn't wanted to hurt Cade by shaming Lark, but it seemed like that's what was happening.

He'd imagined her just growing an attachment to him, and him being able to use that, but while she was definitely drawn to him, she didn't appreciate anything about it. She was being dragged kicking and screaming into an attraction she didn't want.

In fairness, he hadn't meant for last night's phone call to go as it had. That had been off script. Then again, so had their time in his pickup. A kiss, maybe, but he hadn't planned on taking things as far as they'd gone.

And last night all he'd wanted to do was call and try to patch things up. Try to get her sweet again.

Good job, asshole.

He hadn't made her like him any more after that. He'd made her come, though, and in his experience that didn't usually make a woman so damn mad.

"What do you think you'll work on today?" he asked, turning the truck around and pulling out of the driveway.

"Don't ask me that."

"Why not?"

"Do you care? Does it mean anything to you at all?"

"Are we talking computers?"

"Yes, we're talking computers. I know the other stuff doesn't mean anything to you."

"Do you?" he asked.

"Yes. Yes, I do. And I don't want to talk about it."

"Then why did you?"

"I thought maybe you were talking about it, so I had to say something," she said.

"Well, I wasn't. I don't have anything to say on the subject, in fact."

"Well. Fine. I don't either. I have work to do."

He spared her another quick glance before looking back at the narrow two-lane road. "Which was what I was asking you about."

"I know. I just don't think you care about the work I do as long as it gets done."

"I actually do care, since I'm paying you."

"Fine. The firewall is operational, and I'm making sure everything is good with the LAN connections. I'm moving on to the office computers now, and I'm going to set up an intranet for your employees—not for the kids—something that will allow them to share information, send email, etcetera."

"I don't know what most of those words meant."

"I didn't figure you did."

"I feel like I've missed the digital age. I do most of my work outside, and that's how I like it. I think if I would have stayed at home I would have had all that touch-screen shit. Would have worn a tie and worked at a desk."

Just thinking about it made him feel like he couldn't breathe. The idea of being trapped behind a desk all day, four walls of an office closing in around him.

"I'm not sure whether I would have been a brilliant businessman or a terrible one."

"Why is that?" she asked.

"Because I didn't know the value of hard work. I felt like I could have whatever I wanted and I didn't really care who I hurt so long as I got what I wanted. The law was also something I wasn't overly concerned with."

"You would have made millions."

"Not worth it."

He looked at her again and caught her peeking at him sideways through the curtain of her dark hair. "Oh, really?"

"Yes. Really. Anyway, I inherited a lot of my dad's money when he kicked it, so why do something I hate when I don't need to do it to get money?"

"You're such a charmer, Quinn."

"Nah, I'm not."

"Nope." She shook her head. "I was being facetious."

"I actually got that. Although for all that you say you don't like me, you don't seem to back it up."

Out of the corner of his eye he saw a flash of movement and he turned, treated to a full view of Lark's middle finger held high. "How's that?" she asked.

"You know what that means, right?"

She curled her lip and shot him a snotty look. "Duh."

"Not exactly a threat, baby, since part of me just wants to say 'Go right ahead.'"

She lowered her hand slowly. "You're so inappropriate."

"No more so than you."

"Lies. And anyway, I said I didn't want to talk about it."

He turned the truck into the driveway that led up to Longhorn. "Hard not to talk about it when it's all I can think about."

"See, that doesn't make any sense to me, Quinn."

"Why not?"

"As we've established, you're a buckle-bunny magnet. And those women are . . . you know . . . uh . . . accomplished in the coital arts."

A laugh burst out of his mouth. "Right."

"So I'm not exactly sure why I, a total nerd who is not, am occupying any portion of your thoughts except the ones that say, 'Dear Lord, that is one awkward hot mess.' I'm naturally suspicious of it."

"Really?"

"Yes. I told you I was wearing Superman underwear and you still gave me a heavy-breathing call, so forgive me if I'm a little confused."

He put the truck in park in front of the main house, but left the engine running. What she was saying . . . all of those thoughts had passed through his mind. Sure, he'd started out wanting to seduce her to screw with Cade, but it had changed. Grown. Until, without any preplanning, he'd ended up talking dirty to a woman who was wearing a T-shirt with dinosaurs on it. She was right—it didn't really make sense.

But damned if he could do anything to change it.

"Maybe it doesn't have anything to do with what you're wearing or how skilled you are," he said, hesitating a little bit, because he wasn't sure where these words, these sincere and gentle words, were coming from. "Maybe it's just you."

Was this part of his plan, or was this real? Was it coming from some deep part of him he hadn't known about? That seemed impossible. He was thirty-four years old; he didn't think he had parts of himself left to discover.

He was a simple bastard. He wanted sex, food, drink, in that order. And he wanted to do the one thing in life he was good at, and God help anyone who stood in his way. He didn't say romantic, sensitive shit. Ever.

He said things like *Take your panties off, darlin'*. And women did. So he'd never had to say anything deeper, because with those simple, crude words he was able to scratch number one off his list. And if after leaving the hotel he could hit a twenty-four-hour drive-through for a cheeseburger and a Coke, he could hit them all in one straight shot.

So what the hell these words were doing coming out of his mouth, and whatever this ache was—in his chest, not just in his balls—he didn't know.

But they had. And they felt a lot like the truth.

He looked at her fully now, her head down, her hair concealing most of her face. "Lark." He reached out and brushed his fingertips against her hair, tucking it behind her ear.

She jerked back. "Don't." He lowered his hand, and a tear slid down her pale cheek, dropping onto his knuckles, the impact of it hard as a metal rod across his bones. "Please, Quinn, just stop this. Please. I have . . . I have Cole and Cade. They're my family. They raised me. I know I complained about it. About feeling smothered sometimes. And I do. It's true. But in the end . . . in the end, they're the only family I have. If I lose them because Cade finds out that . . . that I did this with you . . . Be honest with me . . . what do you want from me?"

His stomach felt like lead, a massive chunk of it sitting on top of other vital organs. And when he spoke his next words, he picked them carefully. Made sure they were honest, unvarnished and cold. Because he realized right then what he had to do.

"I want to fuck you."

She closed her eyes. "Is that all?"

"Yeah."

She shook her head. "Then . . . then please don't touch me again. Because that . . . that isn't worth losing my family. I'm sorry."

Another tear followed the trail of the first one, leaving glimmering tracks on her skin. And he felt like the lowest creature on earth.

It was one thing to go after Cade, but he'd been . . . he didn't know what he'd been doing to involve Lark. She didn't deserve it.

And if he was any kind of man, he had to step back. He had to cut her out of this.

"Tell me you don't want it," he said, his voice rough.

"I don't want it," she whispered. "I can't want it."

"Okay. Then I'm not going to touch you again. I don't want you afraid I'm going to harass you or anything, or stop you from doing your job. And I'm not going to hurt you."

"Possibly it's too late."

"I've also given you . . . what, two orgasms? Can we call it even?"

She laughed, a shaky, watery sound. "Oh my gosh. You're so inappropriate." She looked at him, dark eyes glittering. "You can't be inappropriate like that anymore. You can't say things like that. It has to be like nothing happened between us. Please. I need it to be like nothing happened."

"Whatever you need, darlin'."

"I need you to not say that. No 'darlin''. No 'baby.' No 'honey.'"

"Whatever you need, Lark."

"Why are you being so damn decent?"

"Because it's not fun to see you cry. And whatever I have to do to keep it from happening again . . . I'll do it. I didn't want to hurt you." That was the honest truth. He didn't want to hurt her, even if it was already too late. At least he wouldn't continue hurting her.

"You . . . I mean, it's not a bad hurt."

"No?"

She forced a smile. "Just a flesh wound."

She looked so young right then, with her long hair down around her face and tears in her eyes. And he was struck then by just what a massive son of a bitch he was. She was a nice girl. And he was not a nice man.

She was twelve years younger than him. And that hadn't smacked him in the face until just this moment. The gulf between them was so much bigger than he'd let himself acknowledge. And he was a way bigger ass for all of this than he'd let himself realize too.

"Glad to hear it's not more serious than that."

She lifted one shoulder and took a deep, unsteady breath. "Nah. It's fine. It's . . . an aborted love affair. Lust affair, really. Happens."

She was trying a little too hard to be casual. It was adorable. And it made him want to touch her. But he wasn't allowed to touch her anymore.

"Yeah, it does."

"So I'm gonna work. And it's fine. I'm fine. You're fine. We're all"—she waved her hand—"fine."

"Obviously."

She pulled the handle on the truck door and pushed it open, stumbling out, muttering something about being fine. So fine. Super fine. Then she headed straight back toward the computer lab.

He let out a long, slow breath, then got out of the truck cab, his boot kicking up a cloud of dust when it hit the driveway. He headed up the path to the main house, and the door opened for him before he got up to it.

Sam was standing there.

"What the hell, man?" Quinn asked, without much growl because he felt a little deflated after all of his personal realizations.

"We're here checking out Longhorn Ranch. We heard it was nice. We might want to invest in it," Sam said.

"Oh, right." Quinn stepped inside and Sam closed the door behind him. "I like how you worked up a story in advance, since you knew I might strangle you to death if you let Lark see you."

Sam shrugged. "She wouldn't necessarily think we were spying on Cade. Maybe we were just taking advantage of vacation time"—he gave his wife, who was standing in the corner of the living room giving Quinn the steely eye, a sidelong glance—"to rekindle our flame."

Jill blushed. Blushed. A forty-whatever-year-old woman, blushing when looking at her husband of twenty-whatever years. It just pissed Quinn off because he was clearly looking at some well-laid people, and he wasn't getting any at all.

Good for Sam and Jill. Really.

Except now he *did* want to growl.

"Yeah, except she's not stupid, and she'd probably think something was up."

"And does it matter?" Jill asked, crossing her arms, the intensity of her death stare growing by the second.

"Yes, Jill, it does. You see, I'm attached to my balls and I like them where they are."

"What did you do?" she asked, her eyes scalding him now.

"Nothing. And I'm not going to do anything."

"Are you going to say you never touched her?" Jill asked.

Quinn looked down at his hands. "Sure. I never touched her. I'm lying, but it's kind of a nice lie. One I wish was true."

For the first time in their years of knowing each other, Quinn thought Sam was going to punch him in the face. "What. The. Hell. Did you do to her?" he asked, teeth gritted.

Quinn didn't especially want to bar brawl with the only person he called a friend, but if Sam was going to start throwing punches, Quinn was going to have to defend himself, because while Sam was more than ten years Quinn's senior, he had no doubt the older man could kick the ever-loving shit out of him.

"I didn't sleep with her," Quinn said. "Calm the hell down."

"She liked you, Quinn," Jill said, her voice low.

"Yeah, and that's why I'm not going to touch her, so you don't have to worry. I don't need you guys to play the part of shoulder angel. I'm an asshole, but even I know when to rethink something."

"But you were going to do something," Sam said.

"But I'm not now."

"I knew you were a dick." This from Jill.

"Yeah, you know, thank you, Jill, I never, not once, said I wasn't a dick. That's common knowledge, in fact. Why do you think it was so easy for Cade Mitchell to paint me as the bad guy? I'm the easiest guy to cast in the role. I get that. But I had a moment of conscience, and I'm not going to do anything with Lark. I don't want to hurt her."

"Are you going to stop going after Cade?" Sam asked.

"Hell no. I still want to hurt him."

"To what end?" Jill asked.

"Honestly, hurting him is the last thing on my agenda. I'd rather figure out a way to get reinstated at the circuit."

"And if you can't?"

"Then I'm going to screw him over. Like he did me. I own up to being a dick when I'm a dick. Cade Mitchell needs to own up to it, or I'm going to burn him. And don't ask me to feel sorry for him because he walks with a limp now."

"Heaven forbid you act like a human being," Jill said.

"I am acting like a human being. Selfish and angry. What's not human about that? I just want back what he took from me."

"And barring that?"

"I'm going to start screwing with his contracts."

"What contracts?" Sam asked.

"They still make most of their money with livestock that goes to the Rodeo Association. I'm not above making sure no one will touch him with a ten-foot pole. He can't ride, but he still makes a damn decent living off the circuit."

"By 'he,' you mean his whole family."

"Collateral damage."

"Lark too?" Jill said softly.

"She'll be fine. She's a smart girl."

"*Girl* being the key word there," Sam said.

"*Girl* being the wrong choice of words," Quinn said. "She's a woman. She's not a child, in spite of what you and her brothers might think. In spite of what she might think. She'll be fine."

"She'll want to kill you."

He shrugged. "Fine. Her personal feelings for me don't matter. All that matters is getting back in the circuit."

"There are other things than that, Quinn," Sam said.

"Not for me. That was my life. And it was taken from me by some jackass having a tantrum. I'll be damned if I let it stand. And I'll be damned if I stand here and justify it to you."

Quinn turned and walked out of the house, inhaling a deep breath of the fresh morning air. It was crisp, an edge of cold clinging to the air even though the sun was shining. It cut through the chill in places, direct sunbeams providing shafts of warmth.

Too bad he was cold all the way through. And he didn't care.

Fine for Sam, standing there with his wife, to say there was more to life. Everything in Quinn's life had been bad. Until ranch work. Until the rodeo.

It had given him purpose, and now that purpose was gone.

Idle hands had been a problem in Quinn's early years, and Cade Mitchell was going to find out that Quinn's idle hands were most definitely the devil's workshop.

Lark managed to make it through the entire day without kissing her boss, talking dirty to her boss or receiving an orgasm from her boss. Considering her recent track record with him, that was no mean feat.

When she walked back into her house and breathed in deep and smelled dinner cooking, she felt absolutely no shame.

Well, no *new* shame, which was pretty good, all things considered.

She felt light. Free. Free of the tyranny of her ridiculous desire for Quinn. Well, not so much free as . . . on parole. It was still there; it was just that she'd made her case clear, and she'd taken a stand instead of letting it all just happen. She'd told him no more, and he'd said he would respect it.

And she'd cried like a baby, but hey, this was big stuff. Her first time doing any of this with a man on the physical plane. Her first time really wanting a man. It was like *Lark's Sexual Awakening, Part II: This Time, It's Not on the Computer.*

So of course it had had impact. New was scary. And

wanting someone made you feel vulnerable. And wanting a man so far beyond her in years and experience hadn't helped. And neither had the fact that he was the man her brother hated more than anything in the entire world.

So yeah, complicated. Emotional. Tears were merited, and not embarrassing, really.

And now she was going to skip that amazing-smelling dinner, grab a gallon of ice cream for her room and bawl her eyes out because she felt like someone had hollowed out her chest with a pumpkin scoop. Which she was sure was also merited and not embarrassing at all.

She hung her purse and coat up on the rack and walked into the kitchen, stopping right outside the door when she heard Cole's voice. She would have walked in or walked away if she hadn't her name. But she did hear it, said in a low, hushed tone. The kind you used when you didn't want people listening, and since she was the object of the sentence—at least she thought she was—she decided she would pause and listen for a second.

And since her conscience was already seared, what the hell was a little more scarring?

"She's not home yet."

"Good." Cade's was the other voice. And they were whispering like a couple of gossiping women in the general store. "So when did she call?"

A different "she," Lark was assuming.

"This morning. I've never actually talked to her before, so that was weird."

"What's up?"

"Nothing, she just . . . she was thinking about coming out here."

"Shit." Cade breathed the word like a prayer.

"I know, but what am I supposed to tell her?"

"Tell her to stay the hell away."

"Oh what grounds?" Cole asked. "This is . . . dammit, Cade, this is hers too."

Lark's mind scrolled through a litany of potential "hers."

Cole's ex-wife? A woman Cole had secretly fathered a baby with? But no, that was too many accidental pregnancies for one man, especially one as responsible as Cole. A woman Cade had knocked up, maybe?

"It isn't hers. Do you know what's hers? That house in Portland."

"The one that got repossessed because dad was a dick who overspent and gambled too much?"

She sucked in a sharp breath, feeling like she'd been punched in the stomach.

"I don't see why she's owed anything of ours. Dad didn't leave anything to her or to her mother. Dad clearly didn't want her involved in our family."

"She is our family, Cade, whether we like it or not. She's our . . . she's our sister."

"Nicole Peterson isn't our sister. She's a stranger, and I don't care if we do have the same father, it doesn't make her a sister. Lark is our sister. Our real sister—and we have to protect her from this."

The world tilted under Lark's feet, and she pitched forward, one hand on the wall, the other on her stomach.

"I agree with you there. That's why I haven't told her."

"If Nicole comes here, there won't be any more protecting her."

Protecting her. They were protecting her. From something huge. From the truth. Except now she'd overheard pieces of it and she knew. She knew that a huge chunk of her life wasn't true. She knew her brothers had let her believe lies.

She took a step into the kitchen without realizing she'd done it, took another step and another.

"What?" She heard herself ask the question, but it sounded like it was from far away.

"When did you get home?" Cade asked.

"I've been standing there long enough to hear you say I'm not home. And also something about having a . . . a sister."

"She's not our sister," Cade said.

"Cole?" Lark asked.

Cole lowered his head, dragging his hand over the back of his neck. "It's a long story, little girl."

"I am not a little girl!" She practically screamed the words. "I am an adult. And I do not deserve to believe lies."

"Lark . . ." Cade's voice was rough, shadows under his eyes. "You deserve to have good memories of dad."

"I don't deserve to have memories that are lies, Cade. I don't deserve to believe things that aren't true. That's not fair. You're making an ass out of me."

"Lark, that is not it," Cade bit out, "and you damn well know it. We've spent our whole lives protecting you—"

"And I've spent my whole life trying not to be a bother to you. Trying to make things easy on you. But I guess all I did with that was teach you that you didn't have to respect me as a human being."

"We respect you," Cade said. "Don't you dare turn it around like we don't. It's because we respect you that . . ."

"That you lied to me."

"We didn't lie to you," Cole said. "We didn't tell you."

"Tell me. Now. Everything. All of it."

"It's better if you don't know," Cade said.

"Really? After I just heard half of it, that's what you're going with? Screw you, Cade, honestly. Don't treat me like a child. Do I ever treat you like a cripple? Have I ever coddled you? Or did I treat you like a human?"

"This isn't not treating you like a human," Cole said. "This . . . this shit? It tore me up, Lark. I didn't exactly want to pass it on to you."

"Because you still think it's your job to protect me. Because you don't think I'm a whole person, you think I'm a child."

"You are a kid, Lark," Cole said, his voice gruff. "When you get to be my age—"

"Bullshit!" she shouted. "You'll treat me like a kid then too." She thought of Quinn, who pretty much was Cole's age and who hadn't, in any way, treated her like a child.

Who had treated her more like a thinking human than either of her brothers ever had.

"You have no idea what this was like for us."

"And I have no idea what it would have been like for me," she said. "I have no idea what it would have been like to find out in a normal way. As normal of a way as I could. Dad has another child?"

"Lark—"

"You still don't want to tell me about it?" They looked at each other, then back down. "Fucking cowards," she spat, then turned to the fridge, grabbed a gallon of ice cream and stalked to her room. She was halfway up the stairs when she realized she'd forgotten a spoon.

She shook her head and laughed, pushing her bedroom door open and slamming it closed again, then throwing herself on her bed, her ice cream clutched against her chest, a block of frozen awful against her skin.

But it wasn't as bad as the pain *inside* of her chest. And maybe it would freeze it out. Numb her. She didn't know what to think. How to process. She was sick. Sick over this idea that her dad had a secret life. Sick over the fact that Cade and Cole had kept it from her. That they'd been content to let her believe lies.

My dad was the best.

She'd said that to Quinn just a few days ago.

And now she'd heard about secret children. Gambling. Houses being repossessed.

How old was Nicole? Was she a child? A cold feeling trickled through her veins. Was she older? Old enough that it meant her father had cheated on her mother?

She curled up into a ball with the ice cream at the center and gave in to her misery. All of it. This new revelation, the anger at her brothers and the loss of Quinn.

She didn't know how long she lay there. A ball of soggy sadness, clutching melting ice cream. Cole and Cade didn't come knocking on her door, and it was a good thing too. She would have thrown said ice cream at their heads.

She pushed into a sitting position and set the ice cream on her nightstand, then looked down at her phone and picked it up, her fingers numb from the cold. She scrolled through her recent calls, then tapped on Quinn's number, pulling up the window for a new text message.

> Do you at least know how to
> text, you dumbass?

She hit SEND before she could think better of it. It only took a second to get the response.

> A little bit.

> Know how to sext?

His response came quick. I didn't think we were doing this.

> Maybe I changed my mind.
> What are you wearing, big boy?

There was a pause, and then Quinn's next message came in. Been drinking?

> Nope.

> Calling.

> No.

And then her phone rang.

She punched the green button and lifted it to her ear. "Hello?"

"What are you doing?"

"I don't know," she said, standing up. "I don't know. I . . . I . . ."

"Come here."

"It's late."

"Now," he said, the command impossible to deny.

"I'm on my way."

* * *

Quinn was awake now. He'd been ready to fall asleep after a long day of work, and trying not to think about Lark and the fact that he'd determined never to touch her again.

Sure, it was early, but it was tiring walking around with a hard-on that could cut glass. And he'd been ready to work out his frustrations with his right hand. He hadn't had to help himself this much since he'd been a teenager. But damn, Lark Mitchell made him feel like a horny sixteen-year-old.

Then she'd texted him. And offered to sext with him. Well, that was something he'd never done before.

He wasn't about to start now either. If he was going to have her, he wasn't doing it with this kind of distance between them again. He wasn't coming on his sheets again, or going unsatisfied again. If she wanted him, she was going to have to have him, in the flesh.

He paced the length of his living room, in front of the windows. It was dark outside, the lights from inside creating a reflection that obscured the view and only let him see himself. Pacing. Like a man who was thoroughly hooked by a woman. Like a man who was caught by the balls.

Basically, he was acting like what he was.

How had this happened? How had he gone from intending to seduce this geeky, awkward girl to feeling like he was the one who would die if he didn't have the woman? It was ridiculous.

Headlights pierced through his reflection in the window, aiming straight for his heart, which jolted like it had been hit.

She was here. And he was shaking inside.

What the hell was his problem?

She was. She was his problem. And he was about to solve it.

The knock on the door was hardly that of the bold, brazen woman who filled his imagination. It was hesitant. Soft. If he hadn't been expecting it, he might not have heard it.

He went to the door and saw Lark standing there,

clutching a tub of ice cream. Her eyes were red, her nose was red, her hair hanging loose and tangled around her face. She was in the same clothes she'd worn at work today. The only difference between then and now was how thoroughly rumpled she looked. How miserable.

She took a deep breath, her shoulders rising and falling with the action. Her breasts probably did too, and he would have been more interested in that. But her breasts were covered by the ice cream.

"Can I come in?"

"Of course." He moved back from the door and she walked in slowly, dark eyes wide, searching the room.

"There are no ninjas hiding behind my furniture and preparing to ambush you, so stop looking so nervous."

She looked at him, a crease between her eyebrows. "I was more afraid you were going to ambush me. And a little afraid you wouldn't, considering our talk earlier."

"What's going on? A meaner man might call you a tease, you know."

"I'm not meaning to be. I'm not teasing. I'm confused."

"There's nothing confusing about sexual attraction. If you're attracted, you want sex. It's that simple. The complication comes with emotions."

"I agree."

"That's why I don't deal in emotion." A disclaimer, because, true to at least one of his words, he didn't want to hurt her. He was about to be, he had a feeling, steadfastly untrue to some of his other words. Especially of the "I won't touch her" variety.

He would make a note to keep sharp objects away from Jill next time he saw her. Or to keep tonight from her for as long as possible. Maybe forever. There was really no need for her to be in his business, after all.

"Right. Well. Can I put this . . . Is there a place for it?" She held out her ice cream.

"The freezer? Unless you want to eat it."

"Could we?"

"Gimme the tub, and tell me what's going on."

He took the bucket from her and headed into the kitchen, setting it on the counter and opening the lid. It was chocolate dairy soup.

"How long has this been out?" he asked.

She looked a little dazed. "What time is it?"

"Eight."

"Two hours?"

He turned and shoved it into the freezer and slammed the door closed, then turned back to Lark, his hands planted on the island countertop. "What's going on, Lark?"

"I've spent my whole life being good, Quinn. Not causing any trouble because my sainted"—she laughed bitterly—"brothers were doing their best to raise me and that was trouble enough on its own without me being rebellious. So I've been good. I've been trying to honor memories that might not even be real. I've been trying to be something I thought I was supposed to be, but now . . . who am I supposed to be?"

"Whoever you want," he said.

Silence hung between them, thick and heavy. Then she lifted her head. "I want to make a mistake, Quinn." She started pacing, her hands clenched into fists at her sides. "A big one. I want to do something that's bad for me, without caring. I want to do it because I want to. Because they're allowed to. They're allowed to do whatever they want, and I've always just tried to be . . . good. I'm tired of it. I thought . . . I thought honor and family was what the Mitchells were, but I don't even know the Mitchells."

Quinn knew there was something deep happening with Lark right now. Something bigger than the two of them. Something that had broken a fragile, tenuous thing deep inside of her.

And he would be a bastard to do anything to her under the circumstances.

Too bad he *was* a bastard. Too bad for her anyway. Because she might regret it. He sure as hell would not.

"I want you to be my mistake," she said, meeting his eyes, licking her lips. "I know you'll be one. But . . . but I never thought . . . a man like you . . . I'll get to look back and say 'I made that mistake.' Because . . . damn, Quinn." She sucked in a breath and looked him over. "You're going to be the most fun a girl ever had screwing up."

He chuckled, the sound strangled even to his own ears. "That's pretty flattering."

"I'm not trying to insult you, but . . . but you said that you just wanted to . . . to . . ."

"To fuck you."

"Yes, you said that. Which . . . let's face it, most people would say I was making a mistake taking you up on that. But right now . . . it's what I want. I don't really care if you were the one who put the spike under Cade's saddle"—she tilted her chin up, her eyes glittering—"because this has nothing to do with him. Nothing to do with anyone but . . . but us. I want you. I think that's pretty clear. I think it's been clear from the moment we met. I wasn't resisting for me. I wasn't resisting because I was afraid of getting hurt. Or because I was afraid at all. I was resisting because I didn't want to betray him. It had nothing to do with *me*. And I'm so tired of that."

Lark felt like she was going to rattle apart. Her teeth were chattering, and it had nothing to do with the ice cream she'd been clinging to.

She was scared. She was excited. The whole world was dropping away beneath her feet, piece by piece, and she had no idea what she would stand on when it all dissolved.

Tonight, she could cling to Quinn. And later she would have to figure out a way to stand on her own, but for tonight . . . for tonight she could have him. She could live.

It was Cade who had told her she had to get out there and experience life. But he'd been all talk. He hadn't really meant it. He'd been shielding her. Lying to her. And maybe his intentions had been good, but in the end it just showed how little they thought of her ability to cope.

And it showed that she was living for things that didn't really exist. Being good to meet the ideal of a family that wasn't real. A father who hadn't been who she'd thought. A life that wasn't what she'd thought.

But tonight . . . tonight, it wouldn't matter. Because tonight, nothing but what she wanted mattered. And Quinn was what she wanted. Even if she was scared as hell.

He was a lot of man, with a lot more experience than her. Although that was probably a plus. She was sure he knew all the right things to do. Well, she knew for a fact he did, because she'd already been on the receiving end of his skill. If he could make her feel as good as he had that night in his truck, just think how good he could make her feel with actual sex.

Sex was supposed to be the best thing since sliced bread, as evidenced by the fact that people were always acting dumb to get it, and even destroying marriages to have it when they really craved it. People would destroy a lot in the name of sexual satisfaction. And it apparently ran in her family, so her acting a little idiotic to get laid really wasn't all that surprising.

Quinn extended his hand, touched her cheek. It was a gesture that had almost become familiar. But even though it had an air of familiarity to it, it sent a shiver of excitement straight down to her stomach.

"Ready to go to bed, baby?" he asked, his eyes dark, almost black, glittering in the light from the kitchen.

"Yes," she said, her voice barely a whisper.

"You're sure?"

She nodded. "I'm sure. I made the decision. For me. It's what I want." She crossed her arms beneath her breasts. "And you don't have the right to question me."

"I like it when you talk like that."

"Do you?"

"Yep. That's fine when we're out here. But when we get into the bedroom, I'm in charge."

Excitement pulsed through her, increasing her heart rate, making her breasts ache, her nipples tighten. The idea of taking orders—naked orders—from Quinn was a lot more thrilling than she ever would have imagined.

She could only nod. Her throat was too tight for her to get a word through. And her heart was pounding so hard in her head that everything sounded fuzzy. Distant.

She tried to breathe deep and easy, slow and steady, to keep from hyperventilating—or worse, from forgetting to breathe altogether.

"This way," he said, tilting his head to the side, toward the staircase. He didn't touch her. He just turned and started up the stairs. She wondered why.

Maybe this was his way of being sure. Being certain he wasn't leading her. Because without him grabbing her hand, she had to be the one to propel herself forward. Had to make the journey entirely on her own steam.

He sure made a girl have to be actually proactive, rather than just saying she wanted to be, only to be picked up by big strong arms that confirmed her decision.

She was sort of hoping for the big strong arms. But then, she imagined this was really what she needed.

For a second, her feet seemed rooted to the spot, but then they started moving, started moving her toward Quinn, toward Quinn's bedroom.

She followed him down the long hall to a large closed door. It was dark wood, natural, with imperfections and dents. Heavy-looking. She had no idea why she was musing about the door, except it seemed a lot safer than musing about what was behind the door. Or musing about the man who was standing at her side, his hand on the knob, ready to open said door.

He pushed it open, revealing a big bed. There was other stuff too, but she was mainly focused on the bed. It had a big wooden frame, but much more importantly, a huge mattress covered in a deep brown suede-looking comforter, with a massive stack of pillows partially concealing the headboard.

"Nice. Nice stuff . . ."

He turned then and tugged her into his arms, pulling her hard against his chest. Then he was still, studying her face, making no further movements. It was simply a paused motion, not a rest, like he was a big cat, ready to make a move, to pounce at any moment.

Then he lifted his hand, slowly, tracing the line of her lip with his thumb, from the center to the edge and back in again, all the way to the other corner of her mouth. Something about that soft touch over her lip, the way it echoed through her body, made her want to melt into him.

So she did, because she couldn't resist anymore. Not for a second.

She pressed her face against his chest and inhaled his scent. Like hay, dust and sweat. A familiar combination of smells to her, but somehow, on Quinn's skin, it seemed different. New. Masculine and enticing. On other guys, she would have called it horse stink, but not on this one.

She inhaled again. No. On him it was sweet and musky. But she wasn't close enough to him. She didn't want his shirt between them. She didn't want her shirt between them. Suddenly, the nerves were fizzling out, overcome by the crackle of attraction as it overwhelmed them, replaced them.

She lifted her chin and pressed a kiss to the hollow of his throat, nuzzling him with her nose, before moving a little lower, kissing him again, where the collar of his shirt gapped, just above the first button.

Then she slowly lifted her hands and worked the button through the hole in the faded red fabric. She kissed him again, where she'd just revealed more of his skin. Then she went to the next button and repeated the action. And again. And again.

Until her lips were hovering just above his belt buckle. Until she was on her knees in front of him, painfully aware of the bulge in his jeans, just in front of her. Aware of the fact that she was in the position to return the favor of what he'd done for her in his truck.

She'd actually fantasized about doing that before. Because in her mind it had seemed like a very powerful thing. To have a man at your mercy like that. To be the one to make him lose his mind, just with your mouth, with your skill.

But now that she was there, she realized she had no skills.

But it didn't stop her from wanting him. From wanting to try it.

And she owed him.

She kissed his stomach, his belt buckle cold against her chin, his skin hot beneath her lips. His muscles jumped at the contact, his breath a sharp hiss.

Then she pulled the buckle from the hole in the leather and worked the belt through the other side, leaving it hanging open while she pulled at the snap on his jeans, then pulled the zipper down slowly.

He had on a dark pair of underwear, stretched tight over the ridge of his erection. She took a breath and moved her hand over his length, feeling the weight and thickness of him. Even with a layer of fabric over his skin, he was hot.

She looked up and her eyes met his. He was watching her, the lines in his face more pronounced than usual, his jaw clenched tight.

"Do you like this?" she asked.

He was either angry at her or he was trying to hang on to his control. She really couldn't tell which, though she assumed, and hoped, it was the second one.

"I can't talk right now," he said through clenched teeth. "I'm trying to keep the top of my head from blowing off."

"I'm assuming that's good."

"If you stop I'm gonna have to run outside and throw myself in a water trough."

"Okay then," she said. She bit her lip and pulled the waistband of his underwear out, doing her best to make sure she didn't hang it up on any of his body parts, and down. She just had to make sure she liked it. She'd never seen a naked man in person.

And then there he was. All of him. Thick and much larger than she'd anticipated. And much, much more enticing than she could have possibly imagined.

She almost wept with relief. It wasn't strange, or off-putting, or unattractive. Quite the contrary. He was perfection. Sexy, large perfection.

She curled her fingers around him, struck by how soft

his skin was. How hard he was. How hot. This was what she'd been missing during their phone call. She squeezed him gently, marveling at how her touch made him respond. How every muscle, from his abs to his pecs, shifted as she gave his shaft attention.

This part of it, of having a man, this man, at her mercy, was just like she'd fantasized about. And it made her wonder about, crave, the rest of her fantasy. She leaned in and flicked her tongue over the head of his erection. A quick taste. A test.

She held him tight while she angled her head forward, taking him as deeply into her mouth as she could.

His hands came up to her head, fingers sifting deep in her hair, tugging hard, holding her to him. He curled his fingers tighter, the motion sending a shock of pain through her, but she didn't mind. This was her fantasy. He was losing it. Because of her.

She lifted her head and slid her tongue down his length, until the fabric of his jeans impeded her progress.

"These are in the way," he said, his voice a growl. He shrugged his shirt off, then pushed his pants to the floor.

And finally, he was the one who was naked, while she was fully clothed.

Good Lord. She couldn't have imagined him any more beautifully and wonderfully made than he was. Sculpted body, a male member that was, frankly, one of the most impressive she'd seen, even with sketchy Internet searches in her past. Tan skin, the perfect amount of body hair. And the tattoo, the horse moving with each shift of his arm muscle, the physical representation of Quinn's wildness. His rage.

He moved to the bed, sat on the edge of it, his dark eyes trained on her. "Take your clothes off."

"Now?"

He looked down, then back up. "Seems appropriate to dis-attire for the occasion, don't you think?"

"Yeah." She'd been basically naked in front of him before. So there was no reason to be nervous now. None at all.

She gripped the hem of her shirt and tugged it up over her head, knowing her hair would look insane after she did it. She threw her top on the ground and then quickly dispensed with her pants, leaving her bra and underwear on.

"Come here," Quinn said.

She obeyed. Because she could do that at least. She felt hideously out of her element, but if he gave orders, she could follow them.

He put his hand on her stomach and curved his other arm around her back, his palm over her butt. He pulled her gently to him, his eyes fixed on her breasts. "You're so beautiful," he said, the hand that had been resting on her stomach drifting upward, cupping her breast, still covered by her bra. "I'm not even going to pretend to try and look at your face right now. Not because your face isn't beautiful; it is. But because I spend so many hours of the day trying not to think about your breasts. Trying to keep my eyes on your eyes and not let them drift down. So right now, I'm going to indulge myself. I hope you aren't offended."

She shook her head.

"Good," he said. He leaned in and kissed her skin where it met her bra cup, sliding his tongue along the line between flesh and fabric. "Take it off," he said, his tone harsh.

She complied, her fingers unsteady as she worked the clasp and shrugged it off, letting it fall to the floor.

A low growl rumbled in his chest as he looked at her. "I've been dreaming about you like this. Since that night. Dreaming about seeing you in the light. You keep me up at night."

"Me?" she asked, the word choked.

"Yes. You. You keep me awake, and hard. You make it impossible to sleep. Do you know what I've had to do to get any rest?"

"What?" she asked.

"Since you weren't here, I had to fantasize about you."

"You mean you . . . thought about me and . . . and . . ."

"Touched myself?"

Her face got hot. "Yes."

"I did."

"And you really thought about me? Because . . . because you know you could have thought about anyone. You could have put Gisele Bündchen in there if you wanted to."

"I didn't want to. I only wanted you."

"That's . . . especially flattering, since we're talking fantasy, and that's an endless pool."

"Who have you been fantasizing about, Lark?"

"Bradley Cooper."

He leaned in and bit her. Lightly, just a scrape of his teeth over her collarbone, but the warning was clear. "Lark," he said, "tell the truth."

"Richard Armitage."

"Say it was me."

"There's this guy that works at the general store . . ."

"Say it was me, Lark Mitchell. Tell me I'm the only man you were thinking about. Tell me I'm all you've thought about since you met me."

"That insecure?" she asked, her voice harsh.

"No, but I'll feel like an ass. Because you're sure as hell the only woman I've thought about. From the moment I met you."

"It was you, Quinn."

"Good girl." He leaned forward again, this time rewarding her with the slow, leisurely slide of his tongue over her nipple. "Tell me you want me." His lips brushed against the tightened bud, promised more pleasure.

But only if she obeyed.

"I want you," she said.

He sucked her deep into his mouth, pleasure hitting her deep and hard, like an arrow.

"Now the rest," he said, kissing the hollow between her breasts. "Take it all off."

She gripped the sides of her panties while he kept doing wicked things with his mouth, and dragged them down her legs, kicking them to the side.

He put one hand between her thighs, his middle finger moving through her slick folds, then pushing deep inside her, before sliding out, working the slickness from inside of her over her clit.

A short cry escaped her lips, and she braced herself on his shoulder while his lips teased her breasts and he continued toying with her with his hand, adding a second finger to the first, the slight stinging sensation that accompanied the pleasure keeping her from going over the edge completely.

He raised his head and wrapped his arm around her neck, tugging her down and kissing her, deep and desperate. "Later," he said, breathing hard. "Later we'll spend hours at this. But right now? Now I just need you. Need to come with you. Need to come in you."

"Oh . . . I . . ."

"Condoms," he said, shifting and leaning toward his nightstand, opening the drawer and producing a black box. It was unopened, which she found both unsurprising, considering what he'd said to her about not wanting other women, and immensely comforting.

He tore at the packaging and produced a little plastic packet, which he separated from a strip and handed to her. Oh. Right. She was supposed to know what to do with this. Because she wasn't supposed to be all virginal and stuff.

She turned it in her hands and gripped the perforated tab, opening it easily enough and pulling the condom out of the package. She turned the condom over, making sure she had the right end up, then scooted toward Quinn, ignoring the tightness in her stomach, a ball of fear that had rolled in and steamrolled some of her desire.

She gripped his shaft and put the condom over the head of his penis, rolling it down over his length to the base, in a smoother motion than she'd imagined she might manage.

And Quinn was kissing her again, and the ball deflated a bit, warmth and languor taking its place. When he kissed her, things seemed so easy. And it made her want him so much.

He pushed her back onto the bed, onto all those plush pillows, every inch of his hot, hard-muscled body pressed against hers. She wrapped her arms around his neck, curled one leg over the back of his calf and held him to her, kissing him until she was dizzy from lack of oxygen.

His hands skimmed over her curves, over all of her exposed skin, not ignoring any part of her. He made her feel special. Made her feel like every bit of her was something to be savored, treasured.

And, stupidly, she felt tears prick her eyes. Emotion, intense and huge, swelled in her chest, crowding out her heart, making it feel like it was being squeezed tight.

He moved his hand to her butt and shifted his weight so that he was settled between her thighs, the blunt head of his arousal pressing against the entrance to her body.

And suddenly, all of the arousal scurried away and hid, leaving nothing more than a naked ball of panic. She tensed as he pushed into her, searing pain assaulting her, so much worse, so much more than she'd imagined.

"Owowowshitshitshitow." She curled her fingernails into his shoulders and held on tight, tensing every muscle in her body.

Quinn froze. The look on his face would have been funny if she weren't dealing with a feeling of pain, a slug of emotion and a strong sense of being invaded.

"Lark . . ."

"I didn't know it would hurt this bad," she said, the last word wobbly and pathetic.

A million emotions flashed through Quinn's dark eyes, but the most off-putting, and the most hysterical, had to be the pure terror she saw there. She hadn't expected a little hymen could frighten such a big strong man, but it seemed that it did.

"Baby . . ." He leaned down and kissed her face. "Do you want to stop?" he asked, his voice ragged.

She shook her head. "No." She shifted. "It's not as bad now."

"Well, damn, that's about the least complimentary thing I've ever heard during sex. 'Not as bad now.'"

"I'm sorry."

"Don't apologize to me," he said. "Not now anyway."

He shifted and went in deeper, another flash of pain accompanying the motion. She held on to him, moved her hips up and took him inside the rest of the way. It still burned, her body stretching to accommodate him.

"Just hold still," she said, closing her eyes, waiting for her body to get used to him. And while she did, he kissed her shoulder, her neck, her face, her lips. And her arousal started to build again.

Eventually, the pain passed. And it was replaced by need. For him. For release.

"Are you okay?" he asked.

"Yes."

"Are you hurt?" She shook her head. He withdrew from her slowly and she locked her legs around his, trying to hold herself to him.

"I'm fine," she said.

"I'm not going anywhere." He thrust back into her, and this time it didn't hurt at all. This time she just felt full, in the very best way, and closer to him than she'd ever felt to anyone before. "Good?"

"Very."

"That's an improvement."

He established a rhythm, slow and gentle at first, but one that picked up as they went further. A rhythm that started to falter and fray as Quinn's breathing got harder, as his muscles tightened.

"You feel so good," he said, his face buried in her neck, his hands holding tight to her hips.

"You too," she said. And she wasn't lying.

She was so close to the edge, each of his thrusts pushing her closer. She arched against him, her breasts rubbing against his chest, her clit pushing against his pelvis, sending streaks of heat through her body.

"I can't . . ." he said, "I can't . . ."

"Don't stop," she said.

He lowered his head, sucking her nipple into his mouth as he thrust into her, pushing her over the edge, the tension that had been growing inside of her fraying, breaking. She was falling and she didn't care. Surrounded by pleasure, drowning in it, in a wave so intense it overtook everything in her. Everything around.

The world had truly fallen away. But she was in Quinn's arms. And nothing else mattered.

CHAPTER

Thirteen

For the first time in his life, Quinn was struck by the deficit of curse words in the English language. There weren't enough of them. He'd thought through them all, in varying combinations, ten or eleven times since his head had cleared.

Since the roar of blood in his ears had dissipated and his heart rate had returned to normal, the aftereffects of his orgasm slowly slipped into the ether, dragging all good feelings with them.

He had just gotten the dirtiest revenge a man could have. He'd seduced his enemy's younger sister. His enemy's younger sister who, up until a few moments ago, had been a virgin.

And he hadn't meant to.

Well, he had, but it hadn't been for the reasons he'd set out to seduce her. He'd decided not to seduce her for revenge, and yet he still couldn't shake the feeling that he'd used her. Taken advantage of her. He'd slept with . . . lots of women. He'd never bothered to count. But he'd never, ever in his life slept with a virgin, and he was too damn old to be stumbling across one now.

But then, that was the problem, or part of it. She was way too young. And way, way too innocent. Much more innocent than he'd ever guessed at. Obviously she wasn't overly experienced, but he had not, under any circumstances, expected a woman who looked like her and who clearly enjoyed physical touch as much as she did to be a virgin. It made no sense in his mind.

His mind that was now working again. Which meant he had no excuse to lie here with her curled up against him and not say anything. And not even dispose of the condom. But he was afraid if he tried to stand up, he would just fall over.

She shifted, kissing his chest, and he felt it with all the impact of a bullet. A little show of affection he didn't deserve. Not after that.

"Are you okay?" he asked, because it was the most important thing. The look of pain, of fear, on her face when he'd been inside of her had been the single most horrifying moment of his life. And he had felt, in that moment, every inch the villain he'd ever been accused of being.

Funny, he'd always thought he already was. Bad blood. Beyond redemption. Unable to sink any lower.

Turned out, there had been a lower. It had been that moment. And it had most especially been the following moment when he'd decided to keep going. To stay inside of her. To chase his pleasure rather than pulling out, wrapping her in his shirt and running out of the room.

"Yeah," she said, her voice all dreamy and sleepy. Content. Something else, along with her virginity, that he didn't deserve. For her to not be screaming at him. For her to not throw something at his head.

"I've got to go and . . ." Why was it hard to say he had to go and throw out the used condom? Why did he suddenly not want to say the word "condom" in front of her when she'd just rolled one onto his cock fifteen minutes ago?

He cleared his throat and rolled away from her, tugging the condom off so she wouldn't have to see. Then he turned back and looked at her. And saw a smear of red on his bedspread. His eyes followed that to her inner thighs, where there was more blood. More evidence of what he'd done to her.

"Shit," he breathed. He forgot about the condom and sat down on the edge of the bed. "I hurt you."

"You didn't. Well, no, you did, that's why I cussed. But it's fine. It's . . . supposed to hurt, right?"

"I don't know."

"What do you mean you don't know? Aren't you, like . . . an expert?"

"A virgin expert?"

"An expert on sex and women and stuff."

"I've never . . . I don't . . . I've never been with a virgin before." And for some reason, just then when he said them, the words sent a shot of pure satisfaction through him. He was the only man who'd ever been with her. The only man who'd ever touched her, made her come.

And he should not be taking any pleasure in that. But he was. He couldn't help it. It was a deep, primitive beast that lived inside of him that he'd never known was there until this moment. He'd always enjoyed a woman's experience. Mixed with his own, it made for some serious fun in the bedroom.

Women who knew he was a rough guy, women who wanted that and knew all the right ways to work with the tools at their disposal, so to speak.

But Lark had no experience. She didn't have tricks. And she'd just given him the best, and worst, sex of his life.

The best because being with her, in her, had been damn near transcendent. The worst because he had emerged from it feeling evil and a little bit dirty. And he'd made her bleed.

"Just a second." He walked into the bathroom and paced the length of it before realizing he was still holding the condom in his hand, which he wrapped in toilet paper and chucked into the trash before resuming pacing.

He braced his hands on the sink and looked in the mirror. Bad idea. All he saw was his own hated face. Dark eyes, dark skin, features that looked nothing like those of anyone in his family. Evidence that he didn't belong written all over him from the moment he was born.

Even deeper was the evidence of what was inside of him. Evidence that spilled out in times like this. Had he really not known she was a virgin? Or had it just been convenient to ignore it?

And why was it such a big deal? He wasn't the kind of guy who should even think it was a big deal, and yet . . . it mattered. Because everyone remembered their first. Even he did. He probably remembered it better than most of the encounters that had come since, because the first time was so important.

And her memory would be of clinging to his shoulders, every muscle in her body tight with pain while some great rutting bull tore the hell out of her.

Romantic. Sexy.

He doubted this was what she'd meant when she'd said she wanted to look back on him as a mistake she'd made.

And then some jackass cowboy scarred me for life and ruined sex for me forever.

Damn.

He walked over to the big raised tub and turned the faucet on. It was situated in front of a window, facing the mountains behind the house. A view of the world from in the tub. He didn't much care about the world right now. The only thing that seemed to matter was the woman back in his bedroom.

He went back in there and saw her, still lying sprawled on the bed, the blood on her thighs screaming at him, a condemnation.

He moved to her, scooped her up into his arms, holding her against his chest. She flailed a little bit, her eyes wide. "What are you doing?"

"Taking care of you," he said.

The bath was half full now. He set her down and leaned in to test the water with his hand. Warm. Perfect.

He scooped her up again and stepped into the tub, setting them both down in it, her bottom fitted snugly between his legs, his arms wrapped around her chest.

"Seriously . . . what are you doing?"

He pulled a washcloth off the side of the tub. "You bled," he said, the words sticking in his throat.

"I didn't really notice."

"I did."

He dipped the cloth in the water and put it between her thighs, moving it over her skin slowly. As if washing it away would make it better. Would make it like he hadn't done it. Like it hadn't happened. If only actions were undone as easily as blood washed away.

He leaned forward and pressed his forehead against her shoulder. She was so beautiful. Far too beautiful for him. He didn't like how looking at her like this made him feel. All pale, smooth and beautiful, her glossy brown hair curling in the moist air. She made him feel like touching her would spoil all that beauty.

Like she was a priceless artifact and the more he handled her, the more he would corrode her loveliness, damage her color and shine. His fingers, his very touch, like acid.

Neither of them spoke as he continued to hold her, the warm water surrounding them. He should release her. He didn't want to. But he would have to.

He sat with her until the tub filled to the top and he had to turn the water off. Until the water got tepid.

Then he scooped her up again and dried her off, taking her back into the bedroom and setting her on the bed.

"A girl could get used to this," she said, her voice sleepy.

He went to his closet and found a big long-sleeved shirt, then threw it to her. She tugged it over her head and pulled her knees up to her chest. "Thank you. I forgot to bring anything. Except for the ice cream. Which we could still eat later."

"Aren't you tired?"

She yawned. "Very. And I think maybe you liquefied my bones." She poked at her arm. "I'm not sure I can walk."

"You'll heal," he said. And he hoped it was true. In every way possible.

She laughed. "I know." She didn't make a move to get under the covers. She just sat there, her hair damp, looking warm and far too inviting.

"Get in bed, Lark."

She obeyed, sliding beneath the covers and flashing an enticing amount of leg while she did it. His body stood at attention, and he wanted to punch himself for it.

She smiled at him. She damn well smiled at him. Like he was a pleasant sight. Like she was happy to see him.

"You're still naked," she said.

He looked down, at himself and his reawakening erection. "Yeah, well." He bent down and picked his jeans up, tugging them on, tucking in all pertinent members and zipping his pants. "Not now."

"Why not?"

"You need sleep, baby."

"I'm pretty good, actually. You suddenly got it into your head that I was desperately tired, and you're a stud, Quinn, don't get me wrong, but it's not like we just ran a marathon."

"You need sleep," he said again. And he had to get out of the room before he was tempted to touch her again.

She narrowed her eyes. "You're making that face."

"What face?"

"There's this face that Cole makes when he's going to make me do something I don't want. Something that's for my own good."

"I'm not your brother."

"Nooo . . . clearly. So why the face?"

"Good night, Lark. I'm going to go and sleep in another room," he said.

"The hell you are!"

"This was a mistake."

"Yes, Quinn, it was a mistake. I know good and well it was a mistake. In fact, I think I'm the one who went into it saying it was going to be my personal gigantic, sexy, amazing mistake!"

"And now it's been made. It's done."

"I am not done making you, Mr. Mistake," she said. "I want to have you more than once."

"This isn't what I bargained for," he said.

"Were you a virgin? Did you not know how sex is?"

"You know I wasn't."

"Then how could it have surprised you? Or is it just that because *I* was a virgin, I wasn't any good? Because I'm not as experienced as your little . . . buckle-bunny skanks."

"Jealousy?"

"Yeah. And?"

"Look . . ."

"No good statement ever has started with 'look.' Unless it was 'Look, a puppy!' or 'Look, a unicorn!' When you say it like you just did, though, you can guarantee I'm going to want to kick you in the balls."

"Lark," he bit out, "I would never have touched you if I would have known you were a virgin. I am way too old for you as it is. And adding that . . ."

"Wait, what?"

"I wouldn't have slept with you if I would have known you were a virgin."

"That doesn't make any sense," she said. "The only person my virginity should matter to at all is me. And news flash, I was well aware of my status."

"Well, I wasn't."

"And . . ."

"I don't want to hurt you. And you might think you know about sex—"

"I do know about sex. I had a cybersex . . . fling with a guy about six months ago. We talked dirty. I got off. I wasn't hurt."

"It seems the cybersex left your hymen intact," he said through gritted teeth, his heart pounding so hard and fast he felt lightheaded. "So for the sake of argument, let's say it didn't count."

"Why do you get to say my sex didn't count?" He gave her his hardest stare, and she shrank back a bit. "Okay, it wasn't actual sex. But I'm just saying, I'm not totally inexperienced."

"You are. You were. And you have no idea what the ramifications might be to something like this."

"What . . . like if we end up in a horror movie I'll be the first to be killed because I'm no longer the virgin of the group?"

"Lark, be serious."

"Are *you* serious, Quinn? Are you honestly serious?"

"Yes, I am, I'm trying to protect you, and—"

"Hold. The eff. On. Did you just say you're trying to protect me?"

"Yes."

"What is wrong with . . . every man everywhere? At least every man I know. Stop protecting me from life. Do you want to protect every woman from your big bad penis?"

"That isn't—"

"No. You don't. So stop trying to protect me from it! I am not a thing for you to coddle and protect. I am a human being. You men can go ride on a bucking freaking bronco and travel the country and screw everything in Daisy Dukes, but I'm not allowed to know about my family. I'm not allowed to have sex. One flipping time. I thought you at least respected me. I thought you realized that I wasn't a child."

"This isn't about not respecting you—"

"How could it be about anything else? You're basically saying I made the wrong decision and had you had all the information, you would have made a different one for me. Disrespectful."

"Fine, if it's not about you, then what about me? Maybe I didn't want the responsibility of being your first. Did you think of that?"

"I—"

"Isn't that my choice?" he asked.

"I . . . What . . . I don't really see how it matters."

"It does matter," he said. "It does. I would have changed the way I did things. I would have taken my time. I wouldn't have hurt you like that."

"It was just a little pain. It's nothing."

"It was something, because I hated hurting you."

"Well, I think it was basically unavoidable."

He crossed his arms over his chest. "And I think it was avoidable. Because like it or not, I do know more about sex than you."

"And you're an expert in devirginization?"

"No, I've never been with a virgin before, and for good reason. I'm a bad bet. I'm not ever going to do the love and commitment thing."

"That's fine. I don't want it. Not from you. You're my mistake, remember?"

"Well then, Ms. Mitchell, what do you want? Because you seem to have it all figured out."

"I do," she said, craning her neck, looking like a little heiress. In a baggy T-shirt with stringy hair.

"And it is?"

"We have an affair. Physical only. And in the end we part ways several orgasms richer. How does that sound to you?"

"And what about Cade?"

She bit her lip. "I don't care."

"Do you want to keep it a secret from him?"

"He's a pretty great secret keeper himself. It seems like I'm entitled to a few. Plus, it's not my brother's business who I want to have a strictly physical affair with. It's not like I'm going to bring you home for dinner."

This was all getting tangled. Cade knowing Quinn was sleeping with his sister would be a hell of a way to goad him. He'd thought so almost from the get-go. But that was when the sister had been more abstract. Now that he knew Lark, and most especially now that he'd been with her, he didn't want to bring her into it.

And wasn't that unexpected? A conscience he didn't know he possessed had kicked into effect. Sure, it was on a low hum, behind the drive for revenge and absolution, but it was there.

"He doesn't have to know," Quinn said.

Of course, in the end, it wouldn't really matter. He was

intent on taking Cade down if he had to, regardless of his
personal relationship to the man's sister. No matter how he
played this, Lark was going to end up getting hurt.

"No," she said. "He doesn't have to know. But I want this,
Quinn. I want it for me."

It was too easy to say yes, and anything that came naturally to him was probably the wrong choice. He'd learned a
few things in life, among them that being good was hard,
and being bad felt good. Until the next morning when you
woke up with a hangover or ended up in jail.

That alone should have been enough of a reason for him
to say no. For him to turn and walk away and go sleep in a
different bedroom.

She was too young. She was too inexperienced. And no
matter how he played it, she was going to get hurt. Better
he pull the plug now than later. Better he stop things before
they went too far.

They already had.

He looked at the blood on his comforter and swallowed
a lump rising in his throat. There wasn't really any fixing
it. And she was looking at him like he was the solution to
something. A solution she needed badly.

"Let's get one thing very straight," he said, speaking
before he thought his words through. "I'm not going to fix
any of the problems in your life. You sleeping with me? It's
not going to make anything easier. It's not going to give you
anything but memories. Hell, it might even make your life
harder in the end, because that seems to be the effect I have
on people."

"Does that mean you want to have an affair with me?"

Quinn looked at Lark, his heart raging, his body aching.
He unzipped his jeans, shoved them down his hips and got
into bed with her.

Want didn't come into it. There was an element of need
that ran through all of this, something that seemed to be
driving him, pushing him past that sudden, reemerging conscience and into Lark's bed. Well, his bed. With Lark in it.

She smiled, and it was like the sun breaking through the

clouds. He didn't deserve that smile. He didn't deserve this moment, or any of the moments that would come after it. But he was going to take them.

Because it was so easy for him to be bad. And it was so hard to be good.

She curled herself around him, smooth legs tangling with his, warm breath fanning over his chest.

"Quinn," she said.

"Yes?"

"Don't ever try to protect me from me again."

He hesitated for a moment, then leaned down and kissed her hair. He let out a long breath. "All right, baby. But who's going to protect you from me?"

"You're not as scary as you think."

Except she didn't know. Not really. She didn't know the real manner of man she was letting hold her in his arms. Hard drinking, hard fighting. The man who had been rejected by every person who, by genetics or the fact that they'd raised him, should have at least grown an attachment to him.

"When you say things like that, it only makes me sure you need to be protected."

"And you're the one to do it?"

"I'm not sure the lamb should be asking if the big bad wolf can protect her. Can he? Sure. Should you trust him? No."

"Mmm . . . big bad Quinn. Why am I not scared of you?"

"I haven't bitten you yet," he said, only half joking. "Don't you realize that I'm the guy you've been warned about all your life?"

"Probably," she said. "But I went after you. I seduced you."

"You seduced me?"

She raised her eyebrows. "Don't sound so surprised. You'll wound my pride."

"You were a virgin."

"And so?"

"I'm older than you."

Her lips stretched into a wide grin. "Hot."

"Excuse me?"

"Older men," she said. "Rawr."

"I'm not an older man. I'm thirty-four."

"You're lots older than me, baby."

"You're just a lot younger than me."

Her smile broadened. "Yeah, do you think that's hot?"

He tensed. "No."

"Why not? I think it's hot that you're older."

"Because it's not . . . I don't . . ."

"Because it's not okay to think it's hot that I'm younger? And that I was a virgin? That I picked you to be the first man to ever touch me like you did? To ever let you inside of me?"

He was getting hard. Damn that woman. "No, it's not okay."

"I thought you were bad. I thought you were a bad, bad boy. But you've never even debauched a virgin before. And now that you have, you're sweating bullets and getting ready to go to confession or something."

"Sleep, Lark."

"I want to have sex again."

And now he was sporting a crowbar between his legs. "No."

"Why not?"

"You're probably really sore."

She wiggled against him, nipples hot on his arm, the thatch of curls between her legs brushing his thigh. And he pulled back like she was burning him. "I don't feel sore."

"Woman, you don't—"

"Are you about to tell me I don't know if I'm sore?" She gave him a look that could have burned him through a wall.

He arched his brow and put his hand between her legs, stroking her gently. A sweet, sexy sound escaped her lips, a smile curving them upward. He slipped a finger inside of her and she winced. "See?"

"I like it," she said.

"And would you like it about this size?" He took her hand and wrapped it around his cock.

"Probably not," she said, squeezing him.

"So wait then, until you will. I know you're bristly about being told what to do, or told you don't know about something, but at least trust that, while I'm not quite the defiler you thought I might be, I know a few things about sex. I don't want to hurt you again."

"You win this time, Parker."

"Oh no, I don't consider this a win." He moved his hand around to her back and held her close. "But it is the right thing to do." The one right thing in a list of wrong choices.

"I'm sleepy anyway. And pissed."

"What are you pissed about?"

"Cole," she said, "and Cade." She yawned, her eyes fluttering closed. "In the past couple hours I've screamed down my brothers, cried till I wanted to throw up, and lost my virginity. You're right, Quinn. I am tired. So tired."

He pulled her in close and stroked her hair. "Then sleep."

And then she was. And he was left there with a raging hard-on and a pain in his chest that wouldn't go away.

"Did she answer her phone?"

"No."

Cade put his face in his hands, then started pacing the kitchen. As fast as his leg would let him. He felt particularly horrible, in every way.

His stupid body was failing him, at thirty-one, and he'd gone and failed his sister. He was one giant fail today.

"I don't even know when she left," Cole said, sitting down at the kitchen table. "I looked out the window last night and her car was gone. And it's still gone. I called down at every hotel."

"Did you call Longhorn Ranch?"

"They aren't listed in the damned phone book," Cole said.

"Did you google it?"

"Yes. I did. That number doesn't get you the ranch in Silver Creek; it gets you some corporate office."

"She always has her phone," Cade said.

"Yeah, and I think she has it now. I just think she's opting not to speak to us."

"That's not like her either. She usually lingers and growls."

"I think this isn't like anything else, Cade. I think we screwed up. And I think she's really angry, not just regular angry."

"You know who screwed up," Cade said, pacing and trying not to wince when his foot made contact with the slate floor, "is dad. He's the one who messed everything up. He's the one who did this. He's the one who put us in this position. First by cheating, second by dying. This is his fault."

"It's not his fault he died."

"The affair. The . . . kid, is still his fault."

"She's not a kid. She's twenty-five."

"Yeah, older than Lark. And how is she going to feel when she finds that out? All she has of Mom are vague memories. She had the most of dad. And now what she believed is gone. It's ruined."

"It doesn't have to be," Cole said slowly.

"It wasn't for you?"

"I've let it. I don't know if that's fair. I've made some pretty big mistakes. I married the wrong woman the first time around. I know you've made mistakes. Does that make everything we've ever done a mistake?"

"Getting philosophical? Let's make one thing clear: If you ever cheated on Kelsey, I would disown you so fast your head would spin," Cade said. "I don't care if you cured world hunger while your dick was in that other woman, and it was the magical power of her brilliant vagina that led you to the discovery. You would be dead to me."

"Good to know. I'd never cheat on her, though."

"I know. But I'm just saying. I'm saying that it *does* matter that much. It does to me. And I knew it would for Lark. And that's why . . . that's why I didn't want her to know."

"Yeah, and now she's Lord knows where doing Lord knows what, so there was clearly a flaw in the plan."

"As long as she's safe. Maybe she's at a friend's," Cade said, sure, even as he said it, that she wasn't.

"Does she have friends? Not being condescending, but does she? Away from the computer, I mean."

"I don't know. And if she does, I have no idea where to look." That was surely a big-brother fail. But then, this entire thing was a big-brother fail, so where was the surprise in that?

"Well, damn. You mean we have to trust her to get her ass home all by herself?"

Cade ground his teeth together, a muscle in his cheek twitching. "I guess so."

"Trust and respect, I guess?"

"Yeah. Trust and respect," Cade said. "Forced on me by my lack of foresight. I would have put a tracking device on her car if I would have been thinking ahead."

"I think you missed the entire point of why she's pissed at us."

"No, I didn't. I'd make sure I didn't get caught. She wouldn't know."

"You're a dumbass."

Jill took a long, slow breath of the air, of the hay and warmth, dust and pine, and smiled. Things were starting to feel . . . different. Not fixed, maybe, but like she and Sam were building something new. Learning about each other again. Or maybe about who they'd become, for the first time.

Sam came out from the cabin, came to stand behind her. She was so aware of him, in a way she hadn't been for years. She could feel the heat from his body, could feel his presence.

He walked up to her, wrapped his arms around her, resting his hands on her stomach, his chin on her head. "Good morning."

"Good morning," she said.

"I hope you slept well."

"Better than I have in a long time. You?"

"You wore me out."

She blushed. She'd been doing that a lot lately. Sam wasn't shy about saying things to her that were definitely not for anyone else's ears. He hadn't always been like this.

Her sweet ma'am-ing, hat-tipping cowboy husband would
have never dreamed of saying the F-word in her presence
before. Oh, maybe if he smashed his thumb with a hammer
while he was out in the garage. But not during sex. Not
purposefully.

He did now, though. Often. Just thinking about it made
her warm.

"I deleted the emails," she said.

"What?" he asked, his voice rumbling against her back.

"I deleted those emails. I don't need to keep them. I'm
sorry that I did."

"I'm not."

"Oh, really?"

She felt his nod. "It made me wake up. It made me realize that if I didn't make you feel the way a man should make
you feel . . . someone else would. And it would be my own
damn fault if you had to look somewhere else."

"It would never have gone that far."

"But you deserve more than what I was giving you. And
I . . . I know things aren't fixed yet. I know we have to put
all this, the talking and the sex, into practice in the real
world. I know we have to keep doing it. Right now it feels
easy. It's like falling in love again, except . . . I was already
in love. It's better, actually, than the falling. It's going
deeper. Discovering something new about the most important thing in your life. I know later . . . it might not always
feel this easy. But we still have to. I still have to."

She swallowed past the lump in her throat and leaned her
head back, resting it on his chest. "I was so afraid that if we
talked, we would find out how much we'd changed. And I
was afraid if we did that . . . we might have to wake up and
realize that we weren't the ones for each other anymore.
That we would see that we were hopelessly mismatched. I
was right, Sam, we've changed. Because twenty years makes
you change. And it should. But if I met you now, not knowing you at all, I would still fall in love with you."

"I don't know if you'd fall in love with me . . . Into bed,
maybe."

She laughed. "Definitely that. It would have been a lot like when we actually met. I think we fell into bed pretty quickly then too."

"That's true."

She turned to face him, his arms still around her. "We've changed, but you're still the only man I want to be with. I'm choosing you. I think I was afraid that if we ever got to this moment, this one where we talked, where we were honest, where we admitted we were less than happy, that . . . that I might not. And that you might not choose me."

"I do," he said, pressing his forehead against hers. "Now and always."

"I love you."

"I love you too."

She bit her lip. "Do you think Quinn is going to leave Lark alone?"

"Knowing him? No. I knew the minute I found out he'd hired her he didn't have any kind of good intentions. And it's not because I don't like him . . ."

"I don't."

"I know. But I do. He's had it rough. It doesn't give him license to use her, but it's a fact. He goes about things in his own way. He doesn't listen to me."

"Then what good are you?" she asked, only kind of teasing.

"I've kept him from getting killed. And he hasn't been arrested since I've known him either, so maybe I've done some good."

"Yeah, well, I just hope he doesn't hurt her. She's a sweet girl. A lot sweeter than he is."

"Reminds me of a couple I know," he said, kissing her on the cheek. "A sweet girl and a cowboy who doesn't deserve her."

Lark stepped onto the first floor with one foot, the other lingering on the last stair, and froze. She didn't want to run into any of the other ranch workers. She didn't really want to sneak up on Quinn. And she didn't want him to sneak up on her.

Last night had been . . . amazing. Incredible. So many adjectives.

It had also been transformative. Which she was aware was a virgin thing. This idea that she was different somehow because she'd slept with someone.

But as silly as it might seem, it was the truth. She felt like there'd been this whole section of herself that had been pushed down, shoved way deep inside of herself. She'd had tastes of it. Little bursts of it during her online liaisons. But now it was like the floodgates had opened and she was just so fully aware.

Of every temptation a man's body presented, and why. Of just how intoxicating it was to have masculine hands on every inch of her skin. Of why she ached deep inside when she was turned on. Of all the places on her body that could be used to give her pleasure.

She shivered and put her other foot down on the hardwood floor, wrapping her arms around herself. She was wearing yesterday's clothes and yesterday's makeup. And her hair had seen better days.

It had seen better days prior to the tumbling she'd received the night before. And prior to sleeping on it for five hours. At this moment in time it looked more than a little bit like a potential habitat for baby rodents.

"Good morning."

She jumped and scrambled back to the step. "Hi." She leaned against the wall and put one hand on her hip.

"You okay?" Quinn walked out of the kitchen, a cup of coffee in his hand.

"I'm fine. You startled me is all."

"You're jumpy."

"Yeah. And? You were sneaky. Do we need to go over sneaky again?"

He shook his head. "Not for my benefit. Though I fail to see how walking out of my kitchen and into the living room qualifies as being sneaky. And I brought you coffee."

"Sweet nectar of life." She stepped down from the stairs again and reached out for the mug. And he drew it back, just out of her reach, her hands following the trajectory. She froze when she nearly touched his chest. "What are you doing?"

"Not yet."

"Coffee tease."

"Kiss me." He pulled it back farther and she followed the motion, her lips a whisper from his. "Lark. If you want the coffee, you have to kiss me."

Heat suffused her cheeks, then flooded through the rest of her body. He wanted a kiss. From her. "If you insist."

She pecked him on the cheek.

He growled, the glint in his eye dangerous and sexy. "Not good enough."

"You're changing the rules," she said.

"When did you start thinking I was the kind of man who played by the rules?"

"Good point." And because rebellion would only hurt her, and because he smelled like soap and skin and Quinn, and that was a combination she couldn't resist, she leaned in and pressed her lips to his.

"Mmm," she said, reaching out and snatching the cup from his hand. "Good morning, indeed."

"I made breakfast."

"Oooh."

"Come with me."

"I did that last night," she said, feeling way too proud of her use of double entendre as she followed him into the kitchen and sat at a little square table that was positioned by the window.

"I see what you did there." He picked up a plate of waffles from the counter and brought it, along with two other plates and a jug of syrup, to the table. He sat across from her, the expression on his face odd.

"What?" she asked, pulling three waffles off the stack and putting them on her plate, putting syrup between each one.

"I've never had breakfast with a woman before."

"Really?" She picked up the fork that had already been sitting on the table, waiting for her, and cut a bite off of her waffle stack, shoving it into her mouth. "How is that possible? And wow, these are good."

"Because breakfast comes after sex. And after sex, I leave."

"And I didn't let you last night."

"No. You didn't. You tempted me back into bed."

"That makes me feel like a wicked siren. I kind of like it. Lark Mitchell, scarlet woman. Enticing men to make her waffles. Not quite enticing men to their doom on the rocks, but hey, it's still pretty good."

"I think this is why I don't normally have breakfast with women," he said, taking a bite of his own waffle.

"Oh, really . . . Why specifically?"

"Because then I have to talk to them. Although I actually like talking to you. I don't think I could have talked to those other women. But then, maybe I could have. Maybe they weren't all airheads. Maybe they were just playing a part."

"We all kind of do that, right?"

Quinn shifted in his chair. Lord knew he did that. He'd played the rough, simple bad boy for all the women he'd slept with in the past. And they, for all he knew, had just been playing the part of dumb buckle bunny for the evening. A chance to be stupid and have fun.

Boy, didn't he bring out the best in people? And himself. He was an ass.

Not that that was a huge surprise.

"I guess so. What's your role?"

"Um . . . I don't know that I have one anymore. I think I left it on your bedroom floor. With my panties."

"Yeah, you never did tell me why."

"I wanted you?" she said, her mouth full of waffle. She was so damn cute. And since when had he been interested in cute women?

Vampish. Sexy. Sexual. Yes, all those things—but cute?

Well, except all of those descriptive words could be used for her. It's just that she was cute too.

"You've wanted me since you met me," he said, leaning back in his chair. "What I want to know is what brought you here last night, clutching a tub of ice cream like it was a magical talisman."

"I . . ." She leaned forward and put her elbows on the table. "It's bad."

"What happened?"

"I got into a fight with my brothers, who are massive idiots and deserved every bit of my rage. I basically told them to go to hell, and I came here to make sure I was headed in that direction too."

"I see. And what was the fight about?"

She let out a long breath, her nostrils flaring a little bit and why the *hell* was he noticing that? More to the point, why did it fascinate him?

"I . . . The stupid thing is that I didn't even get all the details. Cade, who is . . . just . . . such an asshole, didn't want me to find out because he didn't think I could deal."

"Well, he's just crazy, because clearly, fleeing into the night with a gallon of ice cream and giving your virginity to your brother's mortal enemy is dealing just fine."

"Har. Har. You're heavily concerned with this virginity thing, aren't you?"

"Don't change the subject on me, Mitchell."

"We're putting a bookmark in this portion of the conversation and we will return to it later."

He shrugged. "If you insist."

"I do."

"What did you fight about?"

"Specifically about them not trusting me. About them choosing to lie to me to protect me, which I think is condescending as hell."

"Okay, and what did they lie to you about?"

She blinked, furiously, and to his horror, a tear slid down her cheek. "They were . . . trying to hide the fact that my father . . . had another daughter."

"Another daughter? One not with your mother, obviously."

"Obviously," she bit out. "And they wouldn't give me any more details. I overheard them talking and . . . she wants to come and visit us, but Cade didn't want her to. Because heaven forbid my life be spoiled by reality."

"Reality is overrated," he said. "But secrets . . . especially the kind that everyone knows but no one will talk about, those are worse. Because you feel them. I was the kid your half sister is. The one no one wanted to talk about. Of course, since it was my mother who had me, there was no hiding me."

"I don't want secrets. It . . . it sucks, Quinn. I don't want to think that my dad cheated on my mom. I don't want to face the idea that he knew he had another child and somehow, even though he took care of us, and loved us, he was able to justify never seeing her. Who wants to deal with that? Who wants to know it? But if it's true, then I don't deserve to believe something different. To have memories that aren't even real. That isn't fair. It makes me feel like an idiot. They think they were protecting me. But how is letting someone believe a lie protecting them?"

"They thought they were doing the right thing."

"Well, maybe. But now I just feel like . . . I was telling you about how great my parents were. How wonderful my father was. And I feel like the biggest fool on the planet because it was all such a lie. What I thought. Who he was. How could the man I remember ignore a child for . . . for . . . I don't even know how old she is."

"Maybe you should go and talk to them."

"I tried, but Cade is digging in and insisting I don't want to know, even while I'm standing there telling him I do."

"Maybe he wishes he didn't know." Quinn wasn't particularly in touch with his emotions, but if there was one thing he did know about, it was being the subject of a secret. It was having everyone know your secret shame and whisper about it behind your back.

So he knew. He knew just how destructive secrets could be. How the wrong revelation at the wrong time could destroy a family. And why a man who had other children would sometimes close the door in the face of his son, a son who so desperately needed someone to accept him, to save the life he'd built on lies.

Quinn knew all of that.

"Maybe," she said, tugging on a lock of dark hair.

"And maybe you should go home and talk to them." Why the hell was he prescribing her a moment of kumbaya and hand-holding? It didn't make any sense. None at all. He should be enjoying the family discord, except one thing kept him from total enjoyment: Lark.

She was hurt. And he didn't like it.

"I'm not going home," she said. "I have work to do."

"I'm the boss. I can send you home."

"You agreed to give me a scorching affair."

"Did I?"

"Getting into bed with me last night signified a nonverbal agreement to conduct a scorching affair with me, as I had suggested only a moment before."

"Is this a . . . binding . . . nonverbal agreement?"

"Yes. Binding. I didn't write contract law."

He crossed his arms. "I didn't sign anything."

"You spooned me. All night. That's as good as a signature. Any lawyer would take my case."

"So I'm now contractually obligated to engage in sex with you," he said.

"Scorching sex. In various locations."

"They can't get too varied—I have fifteen teenage boys coming to stay at this facility at the end of the week."

"Then we only have a few days to be varied."

He stabbed his waffle with his fork. "How long do you see this affair lasting?"

"How long are you staying here?"

"A few weeks, I expect." But she would be done with him before he left. About the time she realized what he was willing to do in order to get Cade to clear his name. She might be mad at her brother now, but Quinn doubted she would appreciate him putting her family into dire financial straits.

"Then . . . until then?"

"Now we come back to the bookmark," he said.

"Do we?"

"Yes. This is sex for me. I already told you that, but at the time, I didn't realize how little experience you had."

"I have experience."

"I have blood on my bedspread and a lingering trauma that beg to differ."

"I mean, I've . . . Okay, I was a virgin, obvs, but it's not like I had no experience."

"What are we talking here? Second . . . third base?"

"What are the bases, anyway? I always wondered. Second is boob action and third is like . . . is it oral, or a hand job? Or anything south of the belt line, so to speak?"

"Tell me about your experience." Weirdly, he wanted to knock the guy who had given her her "experience" in the teeth. He liked being the only guy. There, he'd admitted it. He was an asshole, so it shouldn't be that big of a surprise.

"Well, there was this guy. Aaron. Underscore. 234."

"Wait, what?"

"That was his name. Handle. Whatever."

"His handle? What was he, a trucker?"

"A recruit. In our clan. For zombie killing."

"Wait, what? You didn't know him in real life?"

She looked down at her lap. "Not exactly."

"And how did you . . . gain experience with him?"

She bit her lip, her brown eyes far too wide and far too innocent. "This is the, um . . . cybersex . . . I mentioned last night."

"Oh, really?"

"Don't sound all scandalized. You and I had phone sex."

"True, we did. But he's the only experience you've had?"

"So what if he is?" she said, craning her neck and looking down her nose at him before taking another bite of waffle.

"I find that very interesting."

"Well, 'cuz you're a man. Men are predictable about things like this," she said around a mouthful of waffle.

"So I've heard."

"It's boring," she sniffed.

"I know, baby, I know I bore you to orgasm."

"Ha. Ha."

"So," he said, setting his fork down, "what do you do with cybersex? I'm a Luddite, remember? Did you send pictures?"

"Oh. No, I would have died. We just . . . told each other what we looked like and . . . and went from there."

"I need an example," he said, shifting in his chair, embarrassed by the fact that he was actually getting hard anticipating her giving him some examples.

"You know . . . you don't need an example."

"I do, Lark. I find myself very jealous that this guy was on the receiving end of your dirty-talk skills."

"You do not," she said.

"My masculine pride demands satisfaction."

"Liar."

"Tell me."

Her cheeks turned red and she gnawed on a piece of waffle that was dangling from the end of her fork, then set it back onto her plate. "I might have lied to him."

"What about?"

"Well, I told him I'd done it before. Lots. 'Cuz I'm hot. And then I told him I had on a thong. Which I didn't. I don't own a thong."

"You should get one."

"Shush. I am telling a story. Anyway, then it was the usual, 'my cock is so hard for you, baby,' etcetera."

"Typical."

"Right?" Her blush deepened, even while her tone stayed casual.

"And you got off with him?"

She looked down. "Yeah. It was easy. He said to imagine him doing certain things to me, and it was up to me how to . . . to . . ."

"Touch yourself."

"Yes," she said, looking at him now, her eyes a little defiant. "So there. I have experience."

"Sorry, that doesn't count."

"What? That's not fair, you can't say my experience doesn't count. I have it. And what's more, it was purely physical. Virtual. Whatever. It was only for sex. I used him. He was very sad when I was done with him, but when I was bored with him, I was bored with him. I feel no emotional attachment to him whatsoever."

"You don't ache for him when your fingers stroke your . . . keyboard?"

"No," she bit out. "Not in the least. So go ahead and make your point, but recognize that I have a fork sitting near me and I will stab the fleshy part of your hand with it if you get too proprietary and . . . bleah, brotherly."

"Fleshy?" he looked down at his hand and pinched the place between his thumb and forefinger. "That is not fleshy."

"Missing the point."

"Actually, you're missing the point, and making mine really easily. You don't know as much about sex as you think you do. You were a virgin last night. You've had sex once. Sex tends to make virgins a little bit crazy. Even I remember that."

She rested her chin in her hands. "What was your first time like?"

"Off topic. But it made me a little emotional, and I never am. Which means I'm a bit concerned about you."

"How old were you?"

"Fifteen."

"Dear Lord." She straightened, looking appropriately horrified. "You're a slut."

"Yeah, kind of."

"Well, I'm twenty-two, so I think I'm a little more mature than a . . . Ew, you were too young."

"I'm inclined to agree with you. I was seduced by an older woman. Who may not have known how old I was."

"Quinn Parker, you are a bad boy."

"I told you that. You seemed all right with ignoring it. Or maybe you like it."

"I kinda like it, I won't lie."

"But you don't see the reality of it. You see the fantasy. And for women I've taken to hotel rooms for one night? The fantasy is fine. I've done that—I need you to know that. I've spent a couple hours at a time with women I barely knew, screwed them, left, never thought of them again. I'm that kind of guy. I don't do romance. I don't do relationships."

"What's this?" she asked, looking around the kitchen.

"Waffles," he said. "And that's it. I'm not going to fall in love with you, and that has nothing to do with you. It's me."

"I appreciate your honesty."

"I know it's important to you."

"It is."

"I'm not going to protect you. I'm not going to lie to you. But I'm giving you a disclaimer. I need you to know that what I said to you, what I reminded you of last night, is still true."

"Well, Quinn," she said, leaning back in her chair, arms over the back of it, her breasts thrust forward into prominence, "I thank you for the warning. No love, no marriage. I get it. And you keep reminding me of what you told me. Well, has it occurred to you that maybe I don't want love or marriage? I don't, Quinn. Not now, not with you."

"Then what do you want?"

She stood up and leaned over the table, her hair falling forward and shielding them from the outside world, her lips a whisper from his, dark eyes so deep he wanted to get lost in them. "I just want to fuck you."

CHAPTER

Fifteen

Quinn Parker had never been accused of being a gentleman. But he knew that there were certain ways you treated a lady. And when a lady asked for something as nicely as Lark just had, he knew it was downright ungentlemanly to turn her down.

So he did what any gentleman in that situation would do. He hauled her onto his lap and started kissing her. Deep and long, his tongue sliding against hers. He speared his fingers into her hair and came up against a nest of tangles, but he didn't care.

Because he was kissing Lark. And no matter how bad of an idea it was, he couldn't bring himself to stop. Couldn't find any motivation to.

She wanted him. He sure as hell wanted her. And he was going to have her.

He said a brief prayer of thanks, one he had a passing concern might be blasphemous, for the condom he'd put in his wallet, and for the fact that he had his wallet in his back pocket already. Because he didn't want to haul her upstairs and hunt for protection. He didn't want a bed. He didn't want to wait. He wanted whatever surface they could find here, and he wanted it now.

"You need to invest in skirts," he said, shifting them both so that she was lying back on the table and he was over her, between her parted thighs. "Think how much easier that would be."

"We're in the kitchen," she said, her eyes round.

"Did I not get an order for varied locations? I thought I was contractually obligated."

"It's the daytime."

"And I'll get to see you." He unsnapped her pants and tugged them down, moving himself out of the way when the position of his body started to impede his progress. "Are you sore?" he asked.

"No. But you weren't willing to take my word for it last night."

"Apparently I'm selective about these things." He reached into his back pocket for his wallet and pulled out a condom, tearing the top off, freeing himself from his jeans and rolling the condom onto his length. "My chivalry just ran out."

He put his hand between her legs and pushed a finger inside of her. She was slick, ready for him already. He added a second finger, just to be certain. The last thing he wanted was an outpouring of screaming and swearing again.

Well, actually, that would be fine, if it wasn't pained screaming and swearing.

"Ready?"

"Yes, Quinn. Yes, please."

That was almost too much for him. Enough to make him lose it then and there, before he even got in. He gritted his teeth and pushed inside of her.

Damn it. She was so tight. So hot. He didn't know how he was going to survive this. Somehow, in the few hours since they'd made love, he'd forgotten how it was. He'd forgotten just how intense it had been.

He'd forgotten that this little virgin had given him the best sex of his entire life. He'd thought he'd made that up. He'd thought, in the bright light of day, it couldn't be possible.

Because honestly, it had been awkward. And it had scared at least five years off of his life when she'd obviously been in so much pain. And the blood had scared off maybe three more.

So bearing all that in mind, he hadn't really believed it was possible that she was the best he'd ever had.

But she was.

She arched beneath him and he realized his error in not taking her top off. He didn't have access to her breasts. Those perfect pink breasts. But he didn't want to struggle with her top right now either, because that would mean breaking his rhythm, and that, honestly, might kill him.

Slender legs wrapped around his hips, pulled him in harder. "Good?" he asked.

"Yes," she said, her voice a whimper. She hadn't cussed at him. She hadn't said "Ow."

He pushed deeper into her and she let out a short, sharp sound.

"Good," she said, as if knowing what his next question would be. "So good."

He increased his pace, watching Lark, her eyes closed tight, her head thrashing back and forth, her body arching into him, moving up to meet him with each thrust. The sight alone about did him in.

And then he felt a wave go through her body, her internal muscles tightening around his cock, stealing every chance he had at rational thought, stealing all of his control, and pushing him over the edge into the abyss.

He grunted, an actual grunt, like an animal, as his orgasm thundered through him like a stampede. He hadn't been able to hold it back. Hadn't been able to hold anything back because, for some reason, Lark Mitchell made him lose his mind.

As the haze faded, pleasure receding into the background, he had a concept of how much of an ass he looked like. Standing there at the table with his pants undone, inside a half-dressed woman, with his front door unlocked.

He looked like a man who hadn't been able to wait. A man who had been half out of his mind. And that's what he was.

Sobering. Like a bucket of ice water over the head.

He looked down at Lark, who was flushed, her lips deep pink, swollen. She looked dazed, which made him feel a little bit smug, but she also looked a little nervous, which made him feel like a terrible person. A defiler of innocents.

Damn that newly discovered conscience.

"Just a second," he said, dashing for the half bath just off the kitchen to dispose of the condom before straightening his jeans and doing his belt back up. When he went back to Lark, she was dressing, tugging her pants on, doing a kind of one-legged hop as she did.

"Lark—"

There was a knock on the door that was closer to the punch of a battering ram than a polite request for entry.

"Lark," he started again, and the battering ram slammed against his door again. "Just a second," he called. "Stay here."

She nodded, straightening her clothes and smoothing her hair with unsteady fingers. She still looked recently kissed, and thanks to the high color in her cheeks, pretty recently full-on tumbled, but he wasn't going to tell her that.

He went to the door and jerked it open. "What?"

If the realization from a moment ago had been a bucket of ice water over the head, this was a block of ice thrown into his face. It wasn't employees on his doorstep, or a religious faction with tracts. It was two very large, very suspicious-looking men who he happened to know were related to the woman he'd just defiled—that was the word he'd settled on earlier—on his kitchen table.

And in the split second it took him to register who they were, he could see the flash go off in Cade's eyes. And suspicion turned to the desire to commit cold-blooded murder.

"What the hell are you doing here?" Cade growled, advancing on Quinn, not waiting to be invited in.

And that was all the time it took for the flashbulb to go off in Cole's head. And then Quinn had two men looking at him like they wanted to kill him.

"I live here," Quinn said. "And I'm not sure what makes you think you're the one with the right to just walk in."

"You know good and well why," Cade growled. Yes, the other man had a limp, but he also had a brother standing behind him who was just as big and just as angry. "You're Longhorn?"

"What do you think, Sherlock?" he asked. If he was going to die, he wasn't doing it meekly.

"Where is my sister?" Cade bit out.

Quinn hadn't expected Cade to move so quickly, considering his limp, but it turned out he was pretty damn fast, and before Quinn could respond Cade had him by the back of the neck, ready to introduce his head to the ground if Quinn made a wrong move.

Cade was lean—Quinn probably outweighed him by a good twenty pounds, thanks to muscle mass—but Cole was a house, and between the two of them? It was better to avoid bloodshed.

"I swear it, Quinn, I don't care very much about my life at the moment, and that puts you in a damn dangerous place," Cade said, his voice a low growl. "So if I were you, I'd start talking. Where. The hell. Is my sister?"

"She's right here, asshole, what are you doing?" Lark came out of the kitchen just then. The damn woman was trying to get him killed.

Cade released his hold on him and looked at her, and Quinn could feel the other man thinking, putting all the pieces together.

Shit.

"What are you doing here?" Cade asked.

"I work here," she said. "And obviously, you already figured that out, or you wouldn't be here."

"I hoped to God it wasn't true," Cade said. "You work for him?"

"Yes, for him," she said, her voice trembling, arms

crossed beneath her breasts, chin thrust upward. "Looks like we're both good at keeping secrets. Oops."

Cole's lip twisted up into a snarl. "You bratty little hypocrite," he said. "You were keeping this from us? And you have the nerve to get all up on my ass for not telling you about Dad?"

"Totally different. One only needed to affect *my* life and *my* choices; the other was something that concerned me, and was hurting someone else so you could protect me. It's different."

"How is it different?" Cole asked, advancing on her.

"I didn't know I took a job with Quinn when I first signed. I didn't know who Longhorn Properties was either. Surprise, it was him, but I'd signed the contract already."

It was a nice stay of execution, the three of them going over fine details. Quinn wasn't complaining. He wasn't looking forward to what was going to happen when Cade's very slow deductive reasoning skills took him to the obvious point of conclusion.

"And you didn't think to ask me for help?"

"I didn't *need* help. I had a job. So look at it from my perspective. Either I break the contract and I owe him money, or I work like I'm supposed to and he owes me money. And, I might add, if I owed him, it's money I don't have, so it would have been you paying him. I walked into an impossible situation and I did the best I could."

Cade crossed his arms over his chest. "What the hell do you call the situation we've been in? Im-damn-possible. Sometimes you make a bad choice. And since you should know that, I expect better, more adult behavior than what you treated us to last night. Act like a baby and I'll damn well continue to treat you like one."

As Lark looked between him and her brother, Quinn called himself a villain a thousand times over. Because she looked so torn. So anguished. So angry. And it was his fault. If he'd never touched her, at least she would only be defensive over her position as his employee. Not over the fact that they'd had sex no more than ten minutes ago.

And then the attention was back on him.

"Where did you stay last night?" Cole asked, his voice suddenly turned to ice, the question directed at Lark, his eyes resting on Quinn.

Quinn looked at Lark and tried to send a quick, telepathic plea for her not to get too defiant. She didn't get the message.

She looked at her brother directly, her eyes glittering. With rage. With tears. With determination. "Here."

Quinn expected Cade to question her on what that meant, since they'd been standing there talking for the past few minutes. So the impact of Cade's knuckles on his jaw was unexpected. Unexpected enough that he lost his balance and fell into the wall, the side of his head striking the corner of the doorway.

"Shit." He held on to the side of his face and felt around inside his mouth with his tongue for missing teeth. Thankfully, there weren't any, but he couldn't see straight.

"Did you touch my sister?" Cade grabbed him by the shirt collar and slammed him against the wall. He was still too dazed to fight back. "You sick fucker. Did you touch my sister? It wasn't enough for you to mess me up, but you had to . . . For what? Because you're pissed that you got caught cheating?"

He wanted to be defensive. He wanted to get mad and defend . . . his honor? He didn't have any. But hers, maybe. The thing was, that was what had happened. He'd been pissed and he'd plotted a way to get back at Cade, and even though that wasn't why he'd slept with Lark in the end, the result was the same. He was still standing here, with Cade's knuckle print on his face, having divided their family.

And yeah, his head hurt like hell. But Lark was going to be hurt too. That was the part he couldn't reconcile. The part that made his gut ache.

But it was Cade's fault. In the end, it was Cade's fault. And he'd be damned if he thought of it differently. To hell with standing here and taking punches. He wasn't the one laying down false accusations. He wasn't the one ruining a man's life because of his own stupid grudge against someone for not being friendly enough.

Yeah, Cade was like everyone else. He'd looked at him, and he'd seen the bad blood.

"I didn't do anything to you," he ground out. "I wouldn't waste my time trying to beat you by sabotaging you."

"So show me who did it, Parker. Who on the circuit? Everyone else is my friend."

"Or everyone else bothers to fake it and pretend they like you. It's a competition. Grow up, dumbass, none of us were friends. I just didn't play games."

"You're wrong about that. We are all friends. We just didn't like you. Now I'm only going to ask you one more time before we kick the ever-loving shit out of you: What did you do to my sister?"

"Stop it," Lark said. "I mean really, stop it. You insulting . . . horrible . . . Go away."

"Lark, did he hurt you?" Cole asked.

"Get out," Lark said.

"Us?"

"Yes, you," Lark said, directing her anger at her brothers. Just how he'd hoped.

No. This isn't the plan anymore.

Does it matter? It's what's happening.

"How could you do this?" Cade asked, the question directed at Lark. "How could you work for this bastard, come hide out with him just because you got mad at us? How the hell can you stand there and ask me to get out? I sacrificed for you. I feel more like a parent than your brother and the whole time you were . . . Shit, I don't even want to know."

"Did you ever stop and think maybe this isn't about you, Cade?"

"How can it not be? You go around trying to tell us how smart you are, and I can only assume you're either stupid or you don't know who this guy really is."

Silence fell between them, thick with anger. Lark's cheeks were pink, tears pooling in her eyes. Quinn didn't know if she was going to dissolve or explode.

She didn't do either.

"Sure I do," Lark said, hands on her hips, her tone strangely calm. "I know exactly who he is. Quinn Parker, former rich boy, ex-con turned rodeo rider currently barred from the circuit. Occasional bouts of assholeishness followed by moments of shocking decency. Good with his hands."

Damn. He was going to get killed. She was going to get him killed.

"Anything else you want to know?" Lark asked.

Cade looked like he was going to throw up. Or hit something. "Did he . . . Did you?"

"Is that your business?" she asked.

"You did. You *fucked* him," he spat, his voice laced with venom. "Even though you know what he did to me, you let him put his hands on you."

And just like that, Quinn saw red. "Back off, Mitchell," he growled. "If you want to be pissed at me, that's fine, but you have no right to come in here and start yelling at her. You have no right to talk to her like that."

"Where the hell do you get off telling me what I have the right to do, Parker? I'm her brother—who are you?"

And Quinn made the decision that, as days went, this was an okay one to die. "I'm her lover."

Yeah. Shit. Getting your nose broken hurt. It wasn't his first time getting his nose broken, but it had been a long time. The impact was so intense he saw stars, and very little else, because his eyes were watering like a son of a gun and his knees shook, giving out beneath him.

Back in his bar-brawling days, he'd done a lot better. And it had hurt less. Maybe because he was usually drunk when he got into those fights. Now he was eight years too sober to be taking hits to the face.

"Out!" Lark screamed.

He heard Lark shouting through his haze of unholy pain. Finally his vision started clearing, and he stood back up, wiping the blood off of his face with the back of his arm.

"Not without you." Cole or Cade, he couldn't hear the difference in the pain haze.

"Are you going to pick me up and carry me out? Because I don't think you can do that. I am an adult, you're on Quinn's property and you just assaulted him. I will call the cops on you, Cade, I swear it. Please don't make me."

"Lark . . ." Cade said, his voice choked.

"I'm serious. I would rather keep it between you and me. But if you don't get the hell out right now, I'm not afraid to escalate it."

He looked up and saw Cade walk out. Cole stood for a while and looked at Lark, who had a tear tracking down her cheek.

"Door's open if you want to come home," Cole said. "But you have to come alone."

Cole turned away and slammed the front door shut, and Lark's hand was on his arm.

"Are you okay?"

"Broken nose," Quinn said, suddenly a little bit embarrassed that he hadn't put in a better showing for Lark. But the alternative had been punching her brother, and then she would have been mad at him and not them. "Not the first time. But I feel like I should be asking you if you're okay."

"I can't believe he did that to you. I can't . . . What were they doing coming here to defend my virtue?"

"You *did* have virtue."

"They don't know that."

"Honey, I'm sure they did. How many dates have you been on recently?"

"You haven't taken me on a date. You've taken me on a table, though."

"Yeah, well"—he wiped at the blood running down his face again—"I'm still imagining they had a fair idea. Which, whether you like it or not, makes you the innocent party and me the guilty one. Plus, I think Cade would cheerfully slit my throat in a dark alley regardless of my relationship with you, so this just gave him a really handy excuse to go on a hate rampage with my face."

"Maybe you should get a tissue. Or a drop cloth. You're

sort of having your own personal plague of blood coming out of your nose."

He looked down at his arm and winced. "Yeah."

"He's an ass." She brushed a tear from her cheek, her shoulders shaking.

"Hey." He put his hand on her cheek. "Are you okay?"

"No," she said, her voice thick. "I'm not. I wanted to . . . have this and not have them know. I wanted to make a grand gesture without actually having to face any consequences for it."

"You could have gone with them."

She shook her head. "No. I couldn't. But I have to . . . I have to make my own decisions. My own mistakes. They have to let me someday. Today's a good day to start."

"Fair enough," he said, his chest tightening when she said the word "mistakes."

"I can't believe he did that to you," she said, wiping a tear from her cheek.

"Okay, I don't like your brother, let's get that straight right now."

"It wasn't unclear to me, ever, how you felt about Cade," she said.

"Yeah, well. I'm making sure you know. I don't like him. But in his position? I probably would have done the same thing."

"Really?"

"Yeah. And my sisters are older."

"So you're all sexist asshats who think women can't make their own decisions?"

"No. We're brothers. We're protective. Right or wrong. Double standard or not."

"It's not fair."

"Fair doesn't come into it. It's all gut-level emotion, which isn't exactly logical."

"You haven't really talked a lot about your siblings," she said.

"I didn't know we were sharing personal stuff," he said.

"Uh . . . my brother just got all up in your grill, and you

know my dirtiest family secret. Do you need any more? Cade used to wet the bed; it's true. Oh, and because of some old debts that I'm now certain are connected to my dad, we've been struggling financially."

"Really?"

"Well, we have money, but getting enough cash flow to keep the ranch going has been tough. The only thing bailing our asses out are the new contracts Cade helped get us for providing stock to the Rodeo Association. There. I shared. I shared dirty personal stuff. Spill your secrets, Parker."

He tried not to let that thought linger in his mind, tried not to weigh the significance of it. Of what it could mean for him. Of how he could use it.

He looked at Lark instead. At the sincerity on her face. At the concern in her eyes. Even while she was in her own personal hell, she was worried about him.

"Follow me to the bathroom so I can mop my blood up and I'll tell you." He blinked, and a pain shot through the bone in his nose up to his forehead. Then he started toward the bathroom.

Lark closed the lid on the toilet and sat, watching him as he stood at the sink and cleaned the blood off of his arms.

"How many brothers?"

"Two," he said. "Sisters. All older. All blond. Pale." He looked up at the mirror, at his busted-up face and brown eyes. "They all have blue eyes too," he added.

"So you don't belong."

"No. And I know why."

"Your dad."

"Yes, the man who fathered me. I don't actually have a dad. Not the man I was raised to call that, and not the man whose genes I share. It's funny, because I still consider my mother's husband to be my dad. He's who I think of when I hear the word."

"Have you met your real father?"

He nodded slowly, still looking in the mirror. "For about thirty seconds."

The front door to the modest track house had opened to

reveal a shocked-looking man. A man with eyes that matched his own.

"He told me to go away," Quinn said. "Because his real family couldn't find out about me." He looked down at the sink, at the bloody water running down the drain. "That's the story of my life, really. I was a bomb. Talking about me too much, or in the case of my real father, acknowledging me at all, would have blown up people's lives. My mother's husband pretended not to know so that he didn't cause a scandal. My mother pretended I didn't exist. That she'd never had her moment of insanity. I'm this thing they made that doesn't fit anywhere in their lives."

She stood up and walked behind him, reaching around his body and putting her hands beneath the water. Then she put her palm on his forearm and slid it over his skin, over the blood that was still there.

"You fit, Quinn. You fit with me." She moved her hand to his jaw and removed the blood there too. "You fit in me."

"Not at first."

"Well, you do now. Turn and face me." He did. She grabbed a hand towel from the rack by the sink and wet it, smoothing it over his face. "I've never gotten to take care of anyone before. Everyone's always taking care of me."

This felt weird. Wrong. Because it felt so right. Because it made his heart feel like it was too big for his chest. Like he could stand there, in the tiny bathroom, forever, with his face bleeding and Lark Mitchell taking care of him.

It didn't feel like a couple of weeks. It didn't feel temporary.

But it was. Nothing would change that fact.

"Well," he said. "No one ever took care of me, so . . ." He cleared his throat. "I kind of like it."

"Yeah, well, don't make a habit of this."

"I used to," he said. "Make a habit of getting the shit beat out of me."

"What changed?"

"The rodeo. I got serious about it. I won't say I stopped being a drunk jackass the minute I got into the circuit, but it started easing then. Having a goal gave me a purpose."

He winced. "I was a better fighter then, or maybe alcohol just made me think I was. Ten foot tall and bulletproof. I miss the feeling a little bit today."

"We could go get a drink."

"Nah. I can't."

"Off the ranch," she said.

He shook his head, for some reason a little embarrassed to make his next admission. "I don't drink anymore. At all."

"Really?"

"Yeah, I . . . I don't know if I was an alcoholic; I wasn't drinking all day. But I was more prone to being an ass when I was drunk, and I got drunk pretty much every night. That started early on. I got a DUI when I was sixteen. Kinda kept up with the drinking through my early twenties. In bars, so I would say, 'Yeah, well, I'm not drinking alone,' like that made it okay. Then one day I was hungover before a big ride. I fell off the damn horse and into the dirt almost before he was out of the gate. I didn't feel so bulletproof right then. I looked like a fool. I felt like one. I lost the event. I never drank again. Eight years sober."

"The circuit really changed you."

"Yes, it did. For the better. Being without it seems to be bringing out the worst in me."

Lark's hands shook while she kept dabbing at the blood on Quinn's face. She was so angry. So beyond angry that Cade had hit him. That Quinn hadn't fought back. Even while knowing she would have been mad at Quinn if he had fought back.

"And in Cade," she said.

"He thinks I stole what he loves," Quinn said, his dark eyes intent on hers. She didn't know if he meant the rodeo or her.

"But you didn't," she said. Either way, it was true. Because she was going to be left without Quinn in a few weeks, and she didn't believe that Quinn had done anything to hurt Cade.

Not the man she knew. The man who had been consumed
with guilt after taking her virginity. The man who cared so
much about her satisfaction. The man who'd drawn her a
bath and cleaned up her blood. Like she was doing for
him now.

The man who had been rejected by everyone who was
supposed to love him.

That man wasn't perfect, but she had no trouble believing
him now when he said he hadn't done anything to Cade.

Which was why, as much as it hurt to know she'd made
Cade feel betrayed, she'd stayed. Because he didn't deserve
their hate. He didn't deserve the consequences he was living.
As much as she ached to go with her brothers, too much of
her was with Quinn. Walking away was impossible. It
shouldn't be, but it was.

"You're so sure?" he asked.

"My brother just beat the sassy out of you with his fists,
and you didn't do anything about it."

"Fighting is stupid."

"And so is cheating. So is cheating when the cost is going
to be worth so much more than the gain. You're not a stupid
man, are you, Quinn?"

He leaned in, and she looked at his nose. At the purplish
bruising spreading from the bridge and down beneath his
eyes. "I might be. I think this . . . us . . . it's probably kind
of stupid."

"Well, thanks," she said, her next stroke of the washcloth
over his skin a little bit too hard. "Should I be glad to be
your moment of stupidity?"

"I'm your big mistake, aren't I?"

"Fair enough. And next time, please don't let my brother
use your face as a punching bag."

"Next time?"

"Well, you know, yeah. Can you imagine how dead you
would be if he'd caught us on the table?"

Quinn laughed, a humorless sound. "The authorities
would be scouring the woods for bits of my bones."

"They're so stupid. Like I didn't have a choice. Like I

didn't drive here myself." She knew it wasn't that simple. She knew they thought that Quinn had nearly killed Cade, and in the beginning, she had too.

But not now.

She'd known it, deep down, probably since that night in his truck. Because he just wasn't the villain he'd been made out to be. Sure, he was rough, but he wasn't the bad guy in the story. She just knew.

Maybe . . . maybe she could make them see.

"Lark, you're going to have to make up with them eventually."

"Like when you leave?"

He shrugged. "If you want to leave it that long."

A wave of embarrassment hit her. "Sorry, I realize you didn't offer to let me stay here, and that's sort of what all this . . . sounds like. Like I'm inviting myself."

"Hey, I wouldn't complain about having you here. But we will have a bunch of teenage boys staying, so it just can't be too obvious you're sleeping with me."

"Setting a good moral example?"

He snorted, then winced. "Hell no. I'm incapable of that. But it would go one of two ways. Either they'd see you were with me and leave you alone for fear I'd squash their heads like grapes if they touched you, or they would see that you were a woman engaging in a sexual relationship and decide you were game for them."

"Oh."

"In which case they'd find their hoodlum asses sent back to where they came from. I can take a lot. If they want to cuss and yell and generally be horrible snots for a while, fine. But if they disrespect any of the women here—you or anyone else—it's over."

Her heart tightened, and her certainty in her decision—about Quinn, about staying with him—intensified.

"I've come to a conclusion," she said, standing back and assessing him. She'd gotten his face clean, but his nose was swollen, and he had bruising spidering out from there and along his jaw.

"What's that?"

"Now that I've seen so much of it, I'm convinced."

"Of what, darlin'?"

"Quinn Parker, I don't think you have a drop of bad blood in you."

Something changed in his eyes. For a moment he looked lost, sad. Then it disappeared, replaced instead by that sort of steady, emotionless void that was always in Quinn's eyes.

"I wish that were true, but it's not."

"You've never done anything to hurt me."

He laughed, and it chilled her down to her bones. "Baby, I'm hurting you right now. Every minute you spend with me is saving up more and more hurt to cash in when I leave. I've already messed things up with Cole and Cade."

"They messed it up themselves. I get that there's no way Cade is going to be thrilled that I'm with you, but if he just got to know you . . ."

"I'm having sex with you, and he's perfectly aware of that, which means any chance he had of liking me is over."

"That's stupid. Cade's had sex with, like . . . a million women."

"Double standard, like I said . . . It's a brother thing. I'm sure he would even agree, but I'm sure he wouldn't care either."

She started to unbutton his shirt. "You have blood on this. It'll stain. And you really seem to understand him for someone who considers him a mortal enemy."

"I have a feeling we're a lot alike. Don't repeat that. Ever."

"Both boneheaded dumbasses?" she said, pushing the shirt off of his shoulders and throwing it onto the ground.

"I told you I was stupid." He bent down and kissed her lips. "You make me stupid, Lark."

"How hard did you hit your head?"

"Hard," he said. "You're going to have to stay with me and make sure I don't fall asleep. If I sleep I'll slip into a coma and die."

"Liar."

"Come back upstairs with me." His voice was rough and

sexy and his face was swollen and misshapen. And she wanted to go upstairs with him. Wanted to start the day again, in Quinn's arms, without all this crap with Cole and Cade.

Because very suddenly she wasn't high on adrenaline. And she wasn't even angry. She was just tired. And sad and confused. Every tear she'd already shed threatened to build into an endless stream of them.

She forced a smile. "I can never resist a man with a flattened nose."

"If I would have known that, I would have had your brother hit me weeks ago."

"Quinn, I was just being nice. You look like a raccoon." He laughed and she went up on her toes and kissed the tip of his nose. "I'll totally still bang you, though."

"Thank God he didn't kick me in the balls." He swept Lark up into his arms and she flailed, putting one palm on the wall.

"Hey! What are you doing? You're bruised and beaten. Put me down."

"He only hit my face. My body's fine."

"I'll say." He looked at her and she smiled, some of the sadness easing. "You going to show me how fine?"

"Yes, ma'am."

"My knees are weak."

Quinn took them out of the bathroom and started up the stairs. "Good thing I'm carrying you, then."

"Just don't drop me." Her eyes clashed with his and she tightened her hold on his neck. And she suddenly didn't feel like that was part of the joke.

Please, Quinn, please don't drop me.

Unfortunately, even in his strong arms, she was afraid she was already falling.

Sixteen

Lark knew she couldn't stay away from home forever. For one thing, she only had one pair of clothes. And her panties were honestly missing. They were somewhere in Quinn's room. She was starting to get scared they'd gotten put in his laundry.

There was something intimate about laundry mixing. About her panties tumbling around with his Fruit of the Looms.

Not that there was anything less intimate about rolling around naked in his bed all morning. Which they had. Saddle sore didn't begin to cover it. But it was freaking worth it.

Sadly, she couldn't stay in bed with Quinn forever. There were already other employees on the premises, and she didn't relish the idea of one of them catching them like this. Which meant she needed clothes. Sometime at around ten that morning, the third time Quinn had taken her to heaven and back, he'd told her she definitely needed to stay, and that they would be as discreet as they needed to be, but he wanted her in his bed.

She had not been about to argue with that.

But that meant she was headed back to Elk Haven—

without Quinn, because she didn't want her brothers to shoot him and mount him on a wall.

She was a little too attached to him to let that happen. Which was another problem, because this was a temporary affair. She knew it. Had known it from moment one. Quinn had never lied to her about that.

But for some reason her stupid female emotions were drawing hearts, flowers and "Mrs. Quinn Parker" all over that memo.

She was a mother-effin' cliché.

She put her car in park and hesitated before turning the engine off. She didn't want to go inside. She didn't want to face her brothers like this. They'd been mad at each other before, but this felt different. It *was* different.

This felt like permanent rift material. It made her feel sick to her stomach.

She walked up the porch, her steps heavy on the wood, then stopped at the front door. It was strange, but she almost felt the urge to knock. To get into her own house.

"Stupid." She pushed the door open and walked into the front room. Cade was standing there, leaning against the counter that held the computer they used to check in guests. Great. The person she was most hoping to avoid.

Because just looking at him made her feel guilty and sad and angry, all at the same time.

His eyes widened.

"What?" she asked. "I freaking live here." She slammed the door shut and headed up the stairs.

"Hey, wait a second."

"No."

"Why are you here?" he asked, his tone accusing.

"Just getting my things."

"Your things?" He walked to the stairs and gripped the ends of the handrails, looking up at her. "What do you mean you're getting your things?"

"What do you think it means?" she shot back, wanting to yell at him and cry at the same time. "I'm going to Quinn's. I'm going to stay there."

"Are you serious, Lark?" he shouted. "Are you that stupid?" Heavy footsteps were now following her up the stairs.

She stopped and turned. "Seriously, Cade? Insulting my intelligence. Again? That's what all of this is about. Well, half of it. And all you're doing is reinforcing my convictions."

"He's using you," Cade said.

"What? For sex? Because I *do* know that. I know I'm not going to marry the guy, and if you dare get pissed at me about that, I will cry bullshit, because you aren't a virgin and you aren't married."

"He's using you to get . . . to get back at me."

"How? How does him sleeping with me affect you?"

"I would always be pissed at the guy who was sleeping with you, but this . . . Do you not see how damned affected I am, Lark Mitchell? I can't believe that . . . animal somehow convinced you to let him put his hands all over you, when he just about killed me . . . How do you not see it?"

Her heart was hammering hard, the beat echoing in her head. "I don't think he did it, Cade," she said, her voice choking out partway through the sentence.

"What?"

"Have you ever thought, for a second, that you could be wrong?" she asked.

"No, Lark, I haven't. No other guy on the circuit would have done it. I'm friends with them. This is why I can't believe it. He is an antisocial jackass. He doesn't have any friends. He's got a crew, but they don't mix with us. I couldn't pick any of them out of a lineup. The only time Parker ever went out in a group with us, he ended up bar brawling."

"And the other guys weren't involved?"

"What does that have to do with anything?"

"Who threw the first punch?"

Cade shrugged. "He was at the center of it. That's all that matters."

"No, that's not all that matters. What do the other cowboys say to him? How do other people treat him? You don't have any evidence, Cade. You never did. No one did. It's all just about not liking him, and I can't get behind that."

Cade shook his head, his expression dark. "Lark, some people just cause trouble wherever they go. It's like he's . . ."

"Bad blood?" she asked.

"Yeah."

"I've called you an asshole a lot of times, Cade, but I've never really meant it. But now I do. You are an asshole. You aren't even willing to think, for a second, that he didn't do this to you, and you're willing to let him lose his whole life over it. Because you just don't *like* him? That's BS. High school garbage. And you're better than that. You want me to grow up? You first."

She turned away from him and stomped up to her room, flinging the door open and grabbing her Rainbow Brite duffel bag from the back of her closet, flinging her clothes into it. She didn't have anything sexy, or she might have paid closer attention to her things.

"Actually . . ." She turned on her computer. Oh, her computer. She would miss it. Actually, weirdly, she hadn't missed her clan as much as she'd thought she would. How long had it been since she'd checked her email? Two days?

Why didn't she care that much?

Maybe because life had suddenly gotten more interesting. Maybe because she had Quinn.

She logged in to the computer and grabbed her phone out of her purse, doing a quick search for her early correspondence about Longhorn and pulling up the email that had his address.

One lingerie website and a mortal wound to her bank account balance later, she had some sexy winging its way to Longhorn Ranch of Silver Creek, care of Quinn Parker. Rush delivery.

Because they didn't have all that much time.

She swallowed the lump in her throat and went back to packing. Then she zipped her bag up and slung it over her shoulder, and nearly ran into her sister-in-law.

"What's up, babycakes?" Kelsey asked.

"Kelsey, you just about scared a year off my life."

"And you're actively scaring years off mine. What's going on?"

"I'm staying at Longhorn for a while." She lifted her chin, feeling all defiant.

"This is the guy who hurt Cade, Lark. The reason he can't walk right. The reason he can't ride . . . That's not like you. This isn't like you."

"He didn't. Kelsey, he wouldn't."

"Some guys are really good at making up stories, honey. Trust me, I was with one for a long time. A guy who would try to play off me catching him in bed with another woman as 'not what it looks like.'"

"But that's not Quinn. He's been really honest with me. He has. He told me what our relationship was. It's physical, and that's all. And I get that me having a purely sexual relationship makes Cole and Cade want to burn out the portion of their memory that holds that information with a branding iron, but I wouldn't have told them." She put down her duffel bag and examined Rainbow Brite's hair with an unnecessary attention to detail. "But he also told me, from day one, that he didn't sabotage Cade's ride, and I believe him. And what if that's true, Kels? What if he didn't, and Cade is just being angry and he's directing it at the wrong person? Including him in all of this for no reason?"

"But . . . He's so convinced . . ."

"Yeah, and I was too. Until I got to know Quinn."

"Okay, so for a second here, I'm going to let the Cade thing go and just . . . I have a sister thing to do. Because Cole and Cade won't. Are you using condoms?"

Lark's face burned. "Yes. Gosh."

"He's not doing anything to hurt you?"

"No!"

"Not asking you to do things you don't like?"

"No. I'm getting everything I want out of the relationship." *Lies.* "And I mean, yeah, I like the guy, but he's not going to break my heart or anything."

"The first guy is a hard guy to get over, Lark. And my

first was a lame teenage guy who probably thought a clitoris was a type of salamander."

Lark let out a harsh breath. "Yes, and Quinn is a multiorgasmic god of bedroom gymnastics. I get that. I get that it will be hard to give up."

"Well, yeah. That's why I married your brother. I found a good thing and kept it."

Lark scrunched her eyes closed and frowned. "TMI."

"You deserve it for what you put Cole through today, and I'm not finished. When it's that good, it makes you feel a lot of things. You're going to feel a connection with him; it's only natural. And I'm just afraid you're going to get hurt."

"Well . . . yeah, maybe I will, but I'll get over it, right? It's . . . Everyone has to go through a crazy and turbulent love affair at some point."

"I guess, but most of us don't go into it knowing they'll fail."

"Really, Kelsey? Don't TMI me, but you knew you were going to marry Cole the first time you—"

"Oh, hell no. I just wanted his body."

"See?"

"But Lark, I *did* marry him. And it *is* what I wanted eventually. And when I thought things weren't going to work out, it devastated me."

"Well, the difference is that you love Cole, and I don't . . . love Quinn." She blinked against the strange feeling in her chest, the one that made her feel like what she'd just said was a lie.

"I didn't love him at first; I fell into it. Without my own permission. Thanks in part to the sex. I'm just worried about you, that's all."

"I'm not going to confuse orgasms with love. I promise. We're not in a complicated situation like you and Cole."

"Really? Really, Lark? Because I think your brother punched your boyfriend in the face today because he believes he's partly responsible for his life-altering injury. Is that not complicated?"

She sighed. "Fine. It's complicated. Right now, though,

I'm picking Quinn." She picked her bag up from the bed. "It's been two days since I checked my email. I haven't gamed in a week. I rode a horse. I . . . I feel like me, but better. And it's because of him. I want that for as long as I can have it."

"I understand," Kelsey said, looking down at her hands, twisting her wedding ring in a circle. "I really do. But please be careful. And keep using condoms."

"Thanks, Kels." She gave her sister-in-law a hug and walked out of her bedroom, down the stairs, saying a prayer of thanks that Cade wasn't out there still.

Then she got in her car and headed back to Quinn's. And when she got there, she didn't feel like she had to knock.

"The boys are coming today."

Lark opened one eye and found herself staring at a denim-clad thigh. Then she looked up and saw Quinn standing there, arms folded over his chest, looking down at where she was still curled up in his bed.

"Oh." She scrambled into a sitting position and pushed her hair off of her face. "What time is it?"

"Ten."

"Ten? FFS, Parker, I should have been working an hour ago!" She slid out of bed, holding the sheet up over her boobs as she started digging through her duffel bag for clothes.

"I kept you up late."

"Doesn't matter, I have a job here, and I need to make sure everything is running perfectly for your snot-nosed hoodlums when they get here."

"Be nice."

She looked up at him and quirked a brow. "Did you just tell me to be nice?"

"Yeah. They're just hoodlums. They're old enough to wipe their own noses. And they'll really be learning that here. That they have to wipe their noses, make their beds and work for their food. Life blows, and no one's entitled to bypass labor via laziness and crime."

"Well, I have to double-check that your vile, soon-to-be-self-sufficient hoodlums can't search for kinky crap on the Web."

"I thought you had that done."

"Just a precaution. I'm even more acquainted than you are with what men will do for a flash of boob."

"Entire countries have fallen for the pursuit of boob flashes."

"And boob flashing happens a lot for Mardi Gras beads. Does that mean they're all-powerful?"

"The key to world peace or total destruction."

"Note to self: Buy Mardi Gras beads. Take over the world. Bypass Quinn's hard-work edict."

"You're going to be a bad influence, aren't you?"

She dropped the sheet and shook her shoulders. "Maybe. Eeek!" She found herself flat on her back on the bed with Quinn on top of her, his eyes hungry.

"Distracting woman," he said, raising his hand and cupping her breast, his thumb sliding over her nipple.

"It proves my point, though," she said, breathless, wanting him again.

"Does it?"

"They're getting me out of work."

"I didn't realize you were going to use your breasts. I thought you were going to use Mardi Gras beads and the breasts of other women."

"Whatever works."

He rolled to the side. "I really do have to go tie up all the last-minute details. And I need to also not be having sex when social workers and the like roll in."

"Fine, fine." She got up and turned back toward her bag, and Quinn slapped her rear with a resounding smack. "Hey!"

"You liked it."

She smiled. "Yeah, I did." She rummaged around, finding a pair of Dalek undies that read EXTERMINATE. She laughed as she tugged them on and turned to face Quinn again.

His eyes widened. "Is that a threat?"

She swayed her hips from side to side. "I dunno. Want to take your chances?"

"You're wicked this morning, Mitchell."

"And you're a pansy-ass this morning, Parker. Afraid of my panties."

"Your panties are threatening my bits."

"Nothing bitty down there," she said, tugging her jeans on. "Not even a little."

"You flatter me."

"Not flattery. The truth."

She put her bra on and earned a cranky grunt from Quinn, then pulled her T-shirt over her head and earned a glare. "You were the one who said you couldn't be caught with your pants down when social services showed up, Quinn."

"I did, didn't I?"

"Regretting it?"

"Hell. Yes."

"Eat your heart out, baby."

"Or I could just eat out—"

"Quinn!"

"Breakfast. We could eat breakfast out."

"What about the social workers?"

"We've got a couple hours."

She crossed her arms. "And you're choosing an outing over sex?"

"A date, Lark. Because you're right. I've taken you on a table, but not a date. And that needs to change."

Quinn felt like the fox escorting a hen to prom. And that's pretty much how everyone in the diner looked at him when he walked in with Lark's fingers laced through his.

It was hard to say what had possessed him to ask her for a date. Except that he didn't want to be the guy who just slept with her and kept her hidden. He wanted casual—hell, he needed it—but he didn't want it to seem so much like he was just using her for sex.

Because that's what his original plan had been. To seduce her to get revenge, to drive a wedge between her and Cade. And then he'd changed his mind, but it had all turned out just as bad. So he wanted it to seem less like that, to feel less like that.

Pancakes to salve his conscience. Though he suspected it would take more than that.

"Table for two," Lark said. She smiled shyly at the hostess, all proud to be with him, like he was worthy of her pride.

He wasn't.

And the citizens of Silver Creek seemed to know it. Sure,

they didn't know he had issues with her brother. But they saw young, beautiful, innocent Lark Mitchell with the kind of guy every good girl's mama had warned them about. A rough older cowboy who had no business being with such a nice girl.

The thing was, Lark hadn't had a mama long enough to take the warning, and everyone in here knew that too. Which was probably why they were watching so closely. Ready to step in if need be.

Small towns were certainly more curse than blessing half the time.

The hostess raised an eyebrow. "Right this way."

All eyes, from the counter to the little tables by the window, followed them back through the restaurant. Thankfully, they got a seat in the back, away from the über-locals who were earning nods and waves from Lark as they passed.

The hostess handed them their menus and sat them in a booth with red vinyl seats.

"Your server will be with you in a moment," she said, giving him the steely eye as she walked back toward the front of the house.

"Is it just me, or is everyone eyeballing me?" he asked.

"Curiosity. Much like to Cole and Cade, I'm a child to all these people."

"I'm not from a small town, but I'm from an insular social group, so I get how all that works on one level. Still, some of these men look like they might try to hurt me."

"They won't. They might call Cole and tell him his baby sister was out with some no-good, dusty cowboy, but they won't personally do anything. Unless Cole asks them to."

"Cole is a pillar of the community, huh?"

"More or less."

"Hey, Lark." The waitress that had approached the table was looking at Lark with disapproving brown eyes.

"Amber. I didn't think you did breakfast."

"I don't usually. I'm picking up extra shifts."

"Oh . . . So . . . have you . . ."

"Talked to Cade recently?" She looked pointedly at

Quinn, and he nearly shrank beneath that laser-sharp gaze. Amber was a tough girl, that much was obvious. "Yeah. A couple days ago."

"I'd like the two-egg breakfast with sausage instead of judgment on the side," Lark said, handing Amber her menu.

"I'll have the same," Quinn said. "But can you substitute the nonjudgmental sausage for bacon?"

"Coffee with that?"

"Are you going to spit in it?" Quinn asked.

"I don't make promises I can't keep."

"Coffee," Lark said, her expression defiant now. "We want coffee."

Amber turned and headed back toward the kitchen, and Quinn considered praying over his food for the first time in years.

"What's her deal?" he asked. "Besides everyone's general overprotective deal."

"Amber is Cade's best friend. She's bound to be unhappy with me."

"I see. Yeah, I think 'unhappy' is an understatement."

"Fine for her. She can judge me. I judge her and Cade, who are so dependent on each other—platonically, mind you—that they can't have functional adult relationships with anyone else. Yeah, *I* can recognize that. Which means it's a bit screwed up."

"It makes sense, then. That she's looking at me like she wants to cut me."

"I'm sure Cade told an unflattering story. And I fought with him when I went to the house to get my stuff. He makes me so mad!"

"We can talk about other things. Talking about Cade makes my face hurt."

"Okay, so let's talk about other things, then."

"Your move. I'm not good at this dating thing."

"Liar," she said, her cheeks coloring. "I'm sure you're really good at it."

"Because I'm good in bed?"

She turned a deeper rose, and he had to fight to keep

himself from leaning over and kissing her where her blush stained her face. "Yeah."

"That's just sex. That's not dating. I'm not all that experienced with dating."

"Then why are we on one now?" she asked.

"Because. It doesn't feel right to keep you in bed all the time. Because you deserve to go out. To have something from me other than just what happens in bed. Even if that something is just sausage."

"You gave me sausage last night," Lark said, wiggling her brows.

"Granted. But I thought I'd give you literal sausage this morning as a goodwill gesture."

It was a poor offering, considering what he'd done to her life, to her relationship with her family. But it was pretty much the best he had to offer.

"Oh . . . well . . . I think this is pretty much my first real date."

"Lark Mitchell, you are a scarlet woman."

"Well, you know, I warned you."

He laughed, and he felt it. Really felt it. With Lark, feelings seemed to come easy. Feelings that went beyond anger and resentment. It was a hell of a thing. "You did."

Amber brought their meals to the table, and Quinn was shocked that they were hot, given the waves of frost coming off of the waitress. He was tempted to be offended. But he couldn't manage it.

It was too good of a reminder. Of everything his being with Lark was costing her.

You're only here for a few more weeks. Then it's ending. And you're leaving her with a hell of a mess. Because you're a bastard who dropped an innocent girl into the middle of your feud.

He ignored the sinking feeling that accompanied the thought. He knew exactly what it was—a little bit of fun. It just felt different because of her age. Because she'd been a virgin. Because she was so damn weird and funny. And because she made him laugh a lot, when very little else did.

"And I warned you," he said, the words slipping out. For him. For her.

She blinked rapidly, her fork frozen in front of her lips, and then she nodded slowly. "Yeah. I know you did."

"Okay."

"Okay." She put a bite of egg in her mouth. "But also, you don't usually have breakfast with women. And you've had it with me a bunch."

"It's just breakfast, baby," he said, looking down at his plate and picking up a strip of bacon. And ignoring the slowly intensifying feeling that after Lark, he would never really enjoy eating breakfast again.

The boys were here. All fifteen of them. Some of them complete with parole officers, some with social workers. Some with concerned parents. It was a mixed bag. There were boys like Nathan, closed-off, unreadable, with a rap sheet that put Quinn's to shame.

And there were boys like Mike, who hadn't been arrested yet but whose parents feared he would go down that road.

And there was Jake. The angriest of the bunch. No parole officer but a social worker, and, going by what he'd read before they'd arrived, no parents in the picture. Just an ever-rotating string of foster homes and group homes, everyone trying to find something to do with him, no one quite managing it.

Quinn surveyed the group and watched as his staff interacted with them. Or tried to. Some of them were very resistant to interaction. And Quinn related. This all looked like supreme dumbassery to kids in their position. He knew. He'd been one.

Angry at the world, desperate to fight against it.

Wow, Parker. You were one? Or you are one?

Since when was he insightful? He didn't do insightful. He closed down his train of thought and stood back, his arms crossed.

And then Jake caught his eye, and Quinn could swear the boy paled. "You're Quinn Parker," he said.

"Yeah," Quinn said, taking a step forward. "I am."

"What are you doing here?"

"I own here," Quinn said.

"Oh."

"You know me from?"

"The rodeo. I . . . did some work, volunteer shit, when I was with this one family a couple years ago."

"Volunteer shit, eh?"

Jake crossed his arms, his stance mirroring Quinn's. "Yeah."

"Well, I'll probably work you a damn sight harder than they did."

"You think?"

"Nah. I know. I'm gonna work you so hard you won't have the energy to get into any trouble."

"Energy is all I got," Jake said.

"Well, that's good. Because I've got a lot of work."

From her position in the computer lab, Lark watched the interplay between Quinn and one of the boys. She hadn't met any of them yet, but she'd seen them. An angry, surly bunch, and the wiry little guy Quinn was with looked the stormiest.

He was also closely copying the way Quinn stood as Quinn spoke to the small group that was outside, digging a trench for an underground drip-line system. He was making good on his promise to put the boys to work, that was for sure.

And they didn't hate him for it. Oh, she'd heard them cussing at him when she'd passed by earlier, but right now they were doing it.

Quinn would be such a good father.

The thought, so wistful, so filled with longing, sent a streak of terror through her. Because she wasn't supposed to think of Quinn's potential as a baby daddy. Not ever. Not even a little bit.

But something in her, some hideous, traitorous part, insisted on picturing Quinn with his shirt off, his horse tattoo on full display, cradling a tiny baby in his big hands. Of Quinn finding a new chance at a father-son relationship with a child of his own.

No. No no no. Stop it, you predictable virgin!

She couldn't be seeing visions of a white-picket-fenced future. She couldn't be. She knew better. She knew things weren't going to be that way with Quinn. She knew it. She really did. In a few weeks he was going to leave.

And just thinking about it made her feel like she was going to choke on the sob that was building in her throat.

How had she gone from hating him to needing him in the space of just a couple of weeks? How had she gotten to the point where she'd compromised—possibly forever—the most important relationships in her life for him?

"Stupidity," she said, up against the window, the word bouncing back to her. "That's what it is. It's bloody stupid stupidity."

She blew out a breath and left a spray of fog on the glass, then turned back to the computer lab. She was all set for her first monitored session. Some of the boys really didn't know how to use computers, so they were going to need a lot of help getting started.

But she was ready, and excited to be a part of offering them something beyond the life they knew.

And really looking forward to thinking about something that wasn't Quinn leaving, Quinn's babies or having Quinn's babies.

Half the boys, the ones not currently engaged in manual labor, filed in, followed by a couple of the male staff members. Lark made quick intros and got everyone set up at a computer, then passed out papers with their personal log-in information.

She wandered around and helped with menial questions, then went to stand at the back, sitting on the counter and keeping an eye on the Web surfing and all of its content.

She turned and started when she saw Sam standing in the doorway. It jarred her to see him outside of Elk Haven. To see him here.

She walked over to him, and he looked at her, wide-eyed as she approached. "Hi," she said, keeping her voice low. "Can I help you with something?"

From her conversations with Jill, she knew that they had kids, but she hadn't heard anything about one of their children being in trouble.

"Oh, no . . . I . . . I, uh . . . was looking for Quinn Parker."

"He's outside. Making them work. I can show you?"

"Uh . . . sure."

She mouthed *Back in five* to Dave, then led Sam through the lobby area of the building and out the side door, then across the lawn to where Quinn was standing with the boys.

Quinn lifted his head and froze. "Hey, Sam," he said.

"You know Sam?" she asked. "He was staying at Elk Haven."

"Yeah, I know."

"What do you mean you know?"

The boys had stopped working and were watching the three of them. "Boys," Quinn said, "this is Sam. He's going to make sure you don't slack."

"I am?"

"Just for the next ten minutes or so. You should be able to handle it."

Sam shrugged. "Sure I can. But can they?"

"Don't break them, Sam." Quinn turned to her then. "Come here for just a second."

She followed him toward the house, her heart pounding, her hands shaking, and she couldn't for the life of her understand just why she was so nervous. Except something was weird, and she was sure it was something she wasn't going to like.

She stopped when they rounded a corner on the bark-laden path and the boys disappeared from view. "What's up?"

"Sam works for me."

"Oh?"

"Yeah. So . . . that's why I know him, and it's why he's here."

"For how long?" she asked, trying to process the meaning of the revelation.

"Years. I've known Sam since I was a punk kid."

She felt numb. Starting at her fingertips, moving to her lips. "And it wasn't a coincidence that he was with his wife at Elk Haven, was it?"

"No."

"Damn it, Quinn," she said, tears stinging her eyes. "Couldn't you have lied? A little?"

"No. Not to you. I was already hiding it."

"What was he doing there? And please, don't say he was poisoning the water supply or something heinous, because I will . . . I . . ."

"He was spying on Cade."

"Why?" she asked.

"To see if his injury was real," Quinn said, his face drawn, the lines more pronounced around his mouth.

"You could have asked me," she said. "It's real."

"I know. But no one else was looking to see who might have caused the accident. No one else ever wondered who sabotaged the ride. So I had to go in and ask questions. I was the only suspect, so I had to see if I could find another one."

"And now what?" she asked. "Now that you know it's real?"

"I still need to get back in there, Lark. No matter what, I need to make sure I get back to the circuit. I can't spend the rest of my life like this. Drifting. With nothing. Being nothing. I can't do it."

"What do you need?"

"I need him to recant his story."

"And if he won't?"

"I need him to."

"So, you tell me, Quinn . . . is that what you're using me for? Is that why I'm here?"

"No. And yes. It's complicated."

"Damn it, Quinn!" she shouted, shaking now. "Is that why I'm here?"

"It's why you're here. But it's not why I'm sleeping with you. Obviously I didn't contract you to come here at random. I thought I could use you to get information about your brother. I thought I could use your position at the ranch as an annoyance to him at minimum. And I thought seducing you might be the way to accomplish that. Or that . . . if you saw something in me he might change his stance."

"Brilliant. Brilliant plan. You banging me on every available surface in your house totally made my brother your best friend. Oh, wait, no, it made my brother punch you in your face. On what planet was this a good idea?"

"I told you, that's not why I'm sleeping with you. Because it was a terrible idea. The better I got to know you, the less I liked myself for what I'd been planning to do, and I already like myself a damn small amount, Lark." He took his hat off and pushed his hands through his hair. "And I told myself that seducing you . . . that it was wrong. That I couldn't do it. And I wasn't going to. But then you came knocking on my door with your ice cream, and your body, and those eyes . . . baby, I didn't seduce you. You seduced me."

"I was a virgin," she sniffed. "Virgins don't seduce. You . . . took me. You brute."

"Your story has changed."

"I'm pissed at you now."

"Enough that you want to leave?"

The way he was looking at her, those dark eyes, eyes that didn't match anyone in his family's, filled with . . . regret, made it hard to think about leaving him. It wasn't hard to be mad at him. He deserved for her to be mad at him.

He deserved for her to be relationship-ending mad at him. But the thing was, she just wasn't. Maybe because he'd told her. And he didn't have to. Because he'd stood right there and told her the whole story.

"Why are you sleeping with me?"

"Because I can't resist you," he said. "Because, no matter

how much my conscience burns—which, it's news to me I have one, by the way—I can't stop myself. I see you, and I want you. I think of you, and my body is on fire like that." He snapped his fingers to emphasize the point. "Lark, I want you in Superman underwear and out of them. And what we have, it has nothing to do with Cade. Yeah, it started that way. But that's not why we ended up together."

Her throat tightened, her stomach aching. Because they hadn't ended up together. They were sleeping together, having lots of great sex, but that wasn't ending up together. It wasn't feelings, love and forever. It wasn't wedding bells and babies.

She thought back to that day at Tyler's wedding. It had hurt, but she'd known, even then, that she hadn't wanted wedding bells and babies.

She wanted them now, though. Not in the general sense. In a very specific one. She wanted to walk down the aisle toward Quinn. She wanted to have his babies. She was a sad, predictable, lovelorn idiot.

And Kelsey was right. She'd been lying to herself, all this time. She'd thought she was fine with losing Quinn after a few weeks, thought she was accepting their affair for what it was. But deep down . . . deep down, she'd always wanted more. And secretly believed there would be.

Because she loved this big rough idiot. This man who had never fit in anywhere. Who had been the worst, and then been content to let people go on believing the worst, even after he'd semi-reformed. This man who was driven by anger. A man her brother hated.

A man who would probably never love her back.

She couldn't have made this any harder on herself if she'd tried.

"Quinn," she said, her lips dry, numb. "I . . . What are you going to do?"

"What do you mean?"

"To Cade. To get back in."

"Whatever I have to do."

"I don't want you to hurt my family." Even as she said that, she had an image of Cade's fist slamming into Quinn's jaw. "I love Cade," she said.

"I want one thing," he said. "That's to get back into the circuit. I don't want to hurt your family. But I will do what I have to do to get my place back."

"And where do I fit?"

"You're . . . you're not a part of it."

"I am, though, Quinn. I am."

He put his hat back on, his expression blank. "Then maybe you should go on home. I'll pay you. For the rest of your contract. I really didn't mean . . . Well, I decided not to tangle you up in this, even if it was too late by the time I decided it. So I'm letting you go now."

He turned away from her and walked down the path, back toward the boys, and she just stood there, her fingertips icy, the world unsteady beneath her feet.

Then she walked back toward the house. She walked in through the front door and saw a box sitting on the sideboard in the entry with a stack of envelopes on it.

It was from the lingerie company. To Longhorn Ranch, care of Quinn Parker. She put the envelopes on the table and picked up the box, then opened it and looked inside at the neatly folded thongs, bras and negligees, wrapped in tissue paper.

She picked up the box and carried it up the stairs to Quinn's room, then sat on the bed, staring down at all the frilly, lacy things.

When she'd ordered those, she'd felt so brave. So different. She'd felt like changing herself from the ground up, or at least changing her underwear to match the woman she felt like she was becoming.

She still liked *Doctor Who*, but the underwear was starting to seem silly. Maybe not for daywear. But for the times when she was with her lover. So funny, because change and instability had always terrified her, and now she felt like she was running toward change. Toward the new Lark.

Quinn wanted to get revenge on Cade. That was simpli-

fied, and she knew it. Quinn was willing to do whatever he
had to in order to get himself back on the circuit, and at first,
hurting Cade had been an added bonus to the whole thing.

She couldn't ignore that. Quinn might be innocent of the
accusations made against him, but Quinn wasn't innocent.
He was a man who got things done by whatever means necessary. He didn't just want his life back—he wanted to punish her family in the process.

He wasn't a sure bet. He wasn't safe. He'd already dragged
her out into the sun and put her on horseback. He'd been her
first real sexual experience. He'd made her step away from
the keyboard, stop looking at life through a screen.

He made her want touch. Skin. His lips, his hands, his
body. Virtual would never be enough again.

But she had a feeling any man who wasn't Quinn wouldn't
be enough either.

This was all scary. It would be easier to go home. To
return these slutty undies to sender and get back in her comfort zone. Shooting zombies and curling up in bed alone,
instead of making love, laughing and falling asleep in
Quinn's arms.

She could go back to staying away from the sun. To having nothing more than typical sibling conflict with her
brothers.

She could go back to the bedroom that had become her
pen. The thing that kept her safe from life's dangers, while
simultaneously keeping her from any of life's most incredible treasures.

She could stick to cotton panties and never, ever, ever try
on a thong.

Safety. It would be a run back to safety.

Lark pulled a pair of black, exceedingly sheer underwear
from the box. She stood slowly, watching them dangle from
her fingertips.

Then she whipped her shirt over her head, took her bra
off, tugged her pants down and put them on.

She wiggled. Good Lord, that was weird. Her butt was
bare, and the little band of fabric that ran between her cheeks

left her feeling more exposed than if she were naked. And also gave her the vague feeling of having a wedgie.

There was nothing safe about thongs. She and her comfort zone had officially parted ways.

Lark bent down and tugged a sheer black camisole from the box and slipped it on, looking at herself in the full-length mirror that hung on the wall. She looked . . . not like her.

At least not like she imagined herself. She looked like a woman. Not like a girl who would hide in her room and play games in order to keep the world from intruding.

She looked like the kind of woman who would face her relationship difficulties head-on. And who knew some seriously naughty sex moves. Who knew what she wanted.

She wanted Quinn. But with Quinn came a whole massive bag of issues and the potential for serious heartbreak.

"Well, be realistic," she said to her reflection. "If you left now, it's not like you wouldn't be heartbroken."

No, she would be broken. In every way. Cade and Cole might never forgive her. Ever. And that was a reality she hadn't been willing to face before this moment. Because they'd always been there, so imagining a time when they wouldn't be . . . it was too painful. But remembering the way Cade had looked at her the last time she'd seen him . . .

She might have broken that relationship past the point of fixing.

And when Quinn left, who would she have? No one. She would be alone. Alone, and she wouldn't have the man she loved.

Oh, yeah, love. She already loved him.

There was no reason to run, because there was no reason to run to. Because if she ran, she would be running from her feelings. Running scared. She'd been scared all of her life. Of being alone, of being unloved. She was facing the possibility of both of those things now.

Of being without her brothers. Being without Quinn.

Unless she stood her ground and fought.

She was tired of being scared.

Tonight she was going to give him a serious show.

It was time to be brave.

Quinn had avoided the house for as long as possible. Now he had to go in and see how empty it felt.

He'd never had a woman live with him before. Somehow, he and Lark had been living together, even if it hadn't been for long. And now he knew the house was going to feel hollowed out. Because she would be gone, and he deserved it.

He pushed the front door in and bypassed the kitchen, walking straight up the stairs, taking his hat and shirt off as he went, not caring where they landed.

His bed was going to feel big and empty tonight. He knew it. It was stupid, because he'd never liked sharing a bed. Not after the sex was over. He didn't do the limbs-tangled-up, listening-to-each-other-breathe thing.

At least, he hadn't before Lark.

That little geek was doing a number on him. At least she had been. He should be thankful it was over.

He opened his bedroom door and froze.

Because the little geek wasn't gone. She was in his room, on his bed, looking like anything but a little geek.

She was perched on the edge of the mattress, clad in black lingerie, enticing hints of pale skin beneath the dark fabric sending a rush of blood straight down below his belt buckle.

Her hair was messy, tumbled over her shoulders, and there was a fire in her dark eyes that he could feel burning through him, into him.

"Hey there, Parker. I was starting to think you weren't going to show up."

It was Lark. She might look different, but she was the same. He couldn't even explain the flood of relief that hit him.

That she was here. That she was her.

"I had work to finish. I don't know about you."

"My boss told me I could leave." She put her hands

behind her and leaned back, thrusting her breasts into prominence. He could make out the faint shadow of her nipples beneath the thin fabric.

Lark in lingerie was threatening to bust his zipper. His cock was so hard it hurt. She was sexy enough in the crazy panties she normally wore. She was sexy without trying. And apparently when she threw effort behind her sexy, she was downright deadly to his health.

"Your boss is an idiot."

"Yeah, no argument." She stood up and he groaned, couldn't stop himself. The faint shadow of dark hair visible through those tiny panties was enough to send him to his knees. "Are you still planning on getting revenge on my brother? Say there's nothing that can be done about the circuit. He won't reverse his statement. Will you seek revenge, or do you just want vindication?"

He swallowed, his throat so dry it nearly stuck closed. "I won't give up," he said. "I'll keep pushing. And pushing. If I have to make his life hell, make it so I'm not worth sticking to his guns quite so hard, I'm prepared to do it. I'm prepared to ruin him."

"He's ruined already, Quinn. As much as it hurts you to have lost the rodeo, it hurts him too."

"But there's no other option for him. If I had caused his injuries, I would deserve to share the same fate he does, but for the first time in my life I'm an innocent bystander."

"I believe you," she said. "And that's why I'm still here. My brother is wrong. But so are you. I don't want you to . . . I don't want you to keep pursuing it all this way."

"I don't have another choice, Lark. And even if that means you walking out the door, even if it means me never touching you again, when I want you so much I ache, that's the way it has to be."

"You can't choose me over your revenge?"

"I don't have a damn thing to give you, baby."

"You're more than the rodeo, Quinn," she said.

"I'm really not. And that's why I can't give up on this. It's why I can't choose you over revenge."

"Fine," she said. "Because I'm not going to ask you to."

"What?"

"Shocking, right? I was shocked too. I was all ready to go, and then these came in the mail. I ordered them. For you. For me, because I was tired of being embarrassed about what I was wearing to bed. You bear my eccentricities like a champ, Quinn, but god of the sack that you are, I felt you were owed recompense." She turned. "A thong. I bought a thong."

"Shit." He hadn't meant to say that out loud. But she had the most perfect ass ever, and it basically wiped out his vocabulary to see it on display like this.

She turned to face him. "It's definitely worth it."

"Stop . . . for a second, because . . . you want to be with me?"

"Yes."

"You aren't giving me an ultimatum?"

"Quinn Parker, I wish that you could let it go. I wish you thought you were enough without the rodeo. I wish you didn't feel like you needed this. But I'm choosing to stay with you, my choice."

"Why? Because I can't give you anything but . . . pain."

"And multiple orgasms. And companionship. And the feeling that I can make choices and not be so afraid of every little thing. Not be so afraid to leave my room. Do you know why I didn't ride horses anymore, Quinn?"

"Why?" he asked, his throat hoarse.

"I'm allergic to them, for a start." She cleared her throat. "And because my mom used to ride them with me. And I was afraid of it hurting. Doing it again. Coupled with the fact that a part of me is always afraid something catastrophic will happen to me. She died in an accident on the ranch. She was the bravest, toughest woman I ever knew, and she died, Quinn. Part of me, I think, has always thought she wouldn't have died if she just hadn't had to do everything. If she could have lived a little more quietly. So I've lived quietly. I've lived inside. I've lived over the computer. When I took a chance with you, I said it was because I was tired of trying to be good. But it's more than trying to be good. It's trying to be safe. And I'm over it. I don't want safe. I want you."

She walked up to him and pressed her breasts against him. He put his hand on her lower back, held her to him. "Lark . . . I'm a bad bet."

"I know," she said.

"You should have gone."

"Maybe."

"But I'm glad you stayed."

"Me too." She put her hands, so soft, so warm, on his chest. She bent her head down and kissed him, just above his nipple. "I made a big choice when I stayed, Quinn. Not tonight, but when Cole and Cade first came. It's possible I made a big sacrifice."

That hurt. Having to see how his actions had injured her. To know that his stupid revenge had had a part in compromising her relationship with her brothers. It made it hard to even look at her.

But he couldn't look away either.

"I'm not sure I deserved that." He sifted his fingers through her hair. "I can't promise you anything."

"You keep saying that."

"It's true."

"Let's just not talk about tomorrow, then. Can you do that?"

He swallowed hard. "Yes." He wanted it. He wanted to freeze time on this moment. To keep things from moving to their inevitable conclusion. The conclusion had already been waylaid. He'd been given an extension on time with Lark that he didn't deserve.

She was offering him something incredible, and he was offering her nothing. Nothing but more sex while he changed absolutely nothing about his plans.

He shut all that out. He shut everything out but Lark in her lingerie. Lingerie she'd ordered for him. She was his. That thought, it ran so far beneath the skin; created a feeling so bone deep he couldn't deny it. It was so possessive, so proprietary, and it shocked him. Disgusted him. And yet it didn't make it go away.

He didn't deserve to have her. Didn't deserve anything she'd given him. And yet he reveled in the fact that he *did* have her. That she was staying. That he was the only man who'd ever touched her.

The only man who'd ever been inside her.

That he was the man she'd chosen, even if she'd chosen him knowing he'd be a mistake.

"You're mine," he said, his voice a growl as he pulled her more tightly against him. "Only mine."

"Yes," she said.

He lowered his head and traced the edge of her camisole with his tongue, before tugging the top down and revealing her breasts. "The best part about things like this is taking them off," he said. He ran the flat of his tongue over her nipple, then blew lightly against her skin, watching it tighten, watching goose bumps break out over her pale skin. "You are so beautiful."

"I never thought so," she said.

"No?"

"Not before you. But you make me feel beautiful. You make me believe it."

"Oh, you'd better believe it. You make me so hard. I haven't felt so on edge . . . I was going to say since I was a teenager, but not even then. I've never wanted a woman more than I want you. You make me forget them."

"Who?"

"The other women. I don't even want to remember. Your skin is the only taste I want on my tongue."

"Bringing up other women during sex is sort of dangerous there, Quinn."

"I'm sorry," he said, kissing her breast. "But as I said you were only mine, I wished that I was only yours."

She wrapped her arms around him. "It's good enough that you're mine now." She slid her hand down his chest, fingers skimming his abs, moving down lower and covering his erection, her touch burning him even through his jeans. "You're mine."

"Yes," he said, because he could say nothing else. It was true. She held him in the palm of her hand in every way.

She moved her hand slowly, squeezing him, her eyes intent on his. "I love this," she said. "I could never get tired of it."

"The feeling is mutual."

She blinked, leaning in and burying her face against his neck, her lips warm on his skin. "I'm glad."

She moved away from him and got into bed. He followed, kissing her, deep, long. Until they were lying together, her body half on top of his, her hands roaming over him. There was something perfect about it. About kissing her when they were both half naked, just kissing and touching, not in a hurry to take it further.

It was a step he'd skipped in his sexual discovery, and it was one she'd skipped in hers, thanks to him.

But it didn't take long for the fire to burn too hot, the flames beneath his skin too intense. He needed release. He needed more. He needed her.

As if on cue, she put her hands on his belt and undid the buckle, working on his jeans next. He tugged them down while she took the rest of her naughty lingerie off. And then they were skin to skin.

She kissed his jaw, his neck, his chest, her tongue tracing a line down his stomach and to his shaft.

"Lark." He grabbed a fistful of her hair, pleasure shooting through him, pushing him to the brink. "Too good," he said.

"Mmm . . . good."

"Not fair," he said.

"Why no— Whoa!" He gripped her hips and hauled her up, adjusting her so her thighs were on either side of his head and he had her right where he wanted.

"Equal opportunity," he said, sliding his tongue along her slick flesh.

She moaned, sending a vibration from her lips over his

shaft. It was all perfect. Lark's mouth on him, and her, the taste of her, coating his tongue. And every time he pleasured her right, she made a little sound that added to his own pleasure.

He slipped a finger inside of her and she lifted her head, a shocked gasp on her lips. He didn't even mind that she'd stopped. He was too focused on her now. On how tight and hot she was. On every sound she made. On the way she moved her hips, trying to show him her rhythm. On how perfect she was.

She stiffened, her muscles spasming around his finger. But the best part was when she said his name. A prayer and a curse all rolled into one.

He changed their positions, resting between her thighs, kissing her lips as he reached into the nightstand drawer for protection.

"I don't think I have the energy to come again," she said.

"You will."

He rolled the condom on and slid inside her welcoming body, gritting his teeth as pleasure overwhelmed him. Raw, intense. He was already close to the edge, and this was almost too much to take.

But he'd promised her another orgasm, and he was going to deliver. Then she curled her fingers around his neck and whispered in his ear.

"Yes, Quinn. Like that. Oh, yes."

And there was no more tactical thought. No more measured thrusts. It was nothing but a blind, furious race to the finish as he lost himself in her body. He was surrounded by her. Her scent, her warmth. Lark.

He had a dim moment of thankfulness when he felt her arch beneath him, felt her give in to another climax, as his own roared through his ears like a hurricane, consuming him completely.

When it was over, she was holding him, her hands moving over his hair, like she was soothing him.

And he rolled to the side, the condom necessitating his withdrawal from her body, but he didn't get up. He just stayed with her, his arms wrapped around her, one leg tangled through hers.

She kissed his shoulder, fingers now tracing circles over his biceps. "Tell me about the horse." He looked down and followed the line of her hands as she continued to move her fingers over his skin.

"Because of the rodeo."

"But he's not just a rodeo horse. He's like a warhorse. He's angry."

He cleared his throat. He didn't think much about the tattoo. It was just there. Another thing he'd done to his body, in a long list of things, that had either been stupid or a waste. He liked to pretend it hadn't meant anything. But it had. Even then.

"I got it right after I went to find my dad. It was stupid."

"You're the horse."

"Yeah, and no dick jokes please."

"Because that's where I was going with this very serious conversation."

"Nah, I know. But I'm allergic to sincerity." Especially when it was about him. About old wounds. Anger was easier. That was why the horse was angry. To remind him to be mad. Mad at his dad. Mad at the world. It was easier than feeling anything else.

"Did you ever think about letting the anger go?" she asked.

"How?"

"I don't know, Quinn. But maybe someday . . . maybe someday you'll be able to feel something else that will be big enough to push it all out."

He looked down at Lark and he felt something bloom in his chest. Something warm, incredible. And terrifying. Really terrifying. Something that had the power to do just what she'd said.

Unless the anger won. With him, why would he ever think anything else could happen? Bad blood. And just like always, all that anger, everything that was wrong inside of him, would poison the people around him.

Would poison Lark.

The idea grabbed him around his heart and squeezed tight.

"Not me, baby," he said, a response to her statement— and also a plea. That she would remember what he was capable of. That she wouldn't want more. More than he could give.

"Probably not, while you're hanging on to it so tight," she said, her voice getting sleepy. "You'll have to let go."

He looked down and her eyes were closed. And he held tight to her.

Let go? The anger was his drive. It always had been. And it wasn't that simple anymore.

It was a part of him now. Integral. It was the thing that fueled him. The thing that sustained him. No, nothing better would ever be able to grow inside of him. It would be choked out the minute it appeared.

He had to hold on to it. But for now, he would hold on to her too.

"Uh-oh," Jill said, leaning back on the bed and looking at Sam. "He told her?"

"Yeah, he did. And she's still here."

"Really?"

"As far as I know he told her everything, and last I talked to him he said he told her to go home, and he expected her to have done it. But I saw her car parked over by the barn. She's still here."

"That's because she loves him," Jill said. "It's harder to fall out of love than you think."

"And it's more work to stay in it than you think too," he said. He sat on the edge of the bed and kissed her on the lips. "Not an insult."

"I get that. I disagree, though."

"Really?"

"I was never out of love with you, Sam. I just forgot to take the time to feel it."

"I forgot to take the time to show it."

"You've been showing me admirably these last couple of weeks."

He pulled her into his arms, against his body. It felt right. Only Sam had ever felt right like this. And she didn't know why she'd let herself forget. Why she'd let herself take it for granted. She'd never been passive, not in the early days of their relationship. But somehow, she'd stopped telling him what she needed.

They'd both retreated to their own corners, little balls of hurt, and neither of them had bothered to communicate. Neither of them had even tried.

Thank God they were trying now.

"I love you," he said, like he'd said every day since they'd first started reconciling.

"I love you too," she said. "My heart kind of breaks for these boys. Especially Jake."

"I know," he said.

She bit her lip. "He doesn't have anyone."

"I don't know if I like where this is going."

"Why not?"

"Because I just found you again. I just stopped being consumed with other things. I don't really want to add a high-maintenance kid to the mix."

She didn't like what he'd just said, but at least he'd said it. A few weeks ago she would have gotten a grunt. A non-response that told her nothing and left her feeling ignored at best.

"I don't either. But I don't want to leave him alone. And he . . . he calls to me."

"Jill . . . he's not a puppy. He's a teenage boy who's had brushes with the law."

"I know," she said. "But you could handle him."

"Colton and Callie were good. I never had to deal with teenage rebellion."

"That we knew of."

"What I don't know won't make me go after a boy with a shotgun," Sam said.

"True."

"Just tell me, are you wanting to take him on as a project because you don't like only having me?"

Her heart squeezed tight. "No. And I know I kind of earned that. I know I spent too long pouring it all into the kids, and none into you . . ."

"No," he said. "I mean, maybe sometimes I felt that way. But you're a good mom. And you can't take all the blame for what happened with us."

"No worries," she said. "I wasn't going to. Okay, the timing isn't great. But he's sixteen. No one else is going to take him. And think how much support Colton and Callie still need. He's going to need that too. He isn't going to have it. He's never really had it and that kills me."

Sam sighed, heavy, defeated. "This is what I love about you," he said.

"What is?"

"Your heart. I mean, and your body."

"Oh . . . Sam, please. I'm not exactly a spring chicken."

"Don't care. I don't have any use for spring chickens. Give me a woman who knows what she's doing and is comfortable in her skin. That's real sex appeal. That, and the way you care about people."

"But you don't like the way I want to care."

"Not really. But it's hard for me to imagine right now, babe."

"I like that," she said, letting her hand drift across his chest.

"What?"

"'Babe.' It's hot."

"Are you trying to seduce me?" he asked.

"Would it work?"

"Yes."

She laughed, warmth blooming in her stomach. She felt like a teenager with a crush. Or a forty-three-year-old woman with a crush on her husband. Even disagreeing, she felt that way.

"It's a big thing, I know," she said. "And I don't expect you to just be able to give me an answer immediately."

"I know," he said. "But the thing is, I don't want to think about it, because I have a feeling you're right. That he needs to be taken care of. That he needs someone. And right now, I feel too selfish. I don't want it to be me because I just want to spend my days wrapped in your arms."

"Yeah, but at some point we go back to real life, right?" He nodded slowly. "Yes."

"And we have jobs and friends, and we can't spend all day wrapped in each other. But that's the challenge, Sam. To remember to want all that even with all of these other things going on. To not repeat the same mistakes."

He cupped her face and kissed her lips. "I don't ever want to work you around my life again. Life has to work itself around you. You're my priority. In fact"—Sam released his hold on her and got out of bed, then went over to the chair his jacket was sitting on—"I wrote some stuff down."

"Sam, what did you do?"

"You'll see." He pulled a folded piece of paper out of the pocket. "I've failed you a lot, Jill, these last few years. There are things I didn't say, and I should have just said them. But I took for granted that you knew. That somehow you could read how much I cared, even when I wasn't saying it. Or showing it."

"I wasn't either . . . I—"

"No. This is my time to eat dirt and grovel," he said. "And to make some new vows. I vowed to love you on our wedding day, and I do. To stay with you through sickness and in health, and I have. Richer and poorer, we've done that too. But there are a lot of little things that I never thought to promise. Things I should have promised, because maybe if I had, I would have been a better husband for all these years."

Jill sat up, her heart pounding hard, tears stinging her eyes. "You're going to make me cry."

"I might make me cry," he said, clearing his throat, "but I'll try not to." He unfolded the paper, his hands shaking. "Jill, I promise not just to love you, but to tell you I love you. I promise to give you romance, not just sex. I promise to tell you how beautiful I think you are, every time the thought comes into my head, which is a lot. I promise to remember that you come first. That nothing is as important as you. To remember that if you weren't in my life, there would be no meaning. I promise to stop taking you for granted. To cherish your every smile, and hurt whenever you shed a tear. I promise to make the next twenty-three years better than the first twenty-three."

She launched herself off of the bed and into his arms, not even bothering to fight the tears. "Sam," she whispered, her face buried in his neck, "these past twenty-three years have been wonderful, and I let myself grow resentful when I should have just told you what I needed. You don't shoulder the blame. I have a share in it. And I have a share in making this better going forward." She stepped back and looked into his eyes. "I promise to tell you I love you. I promise to give you good sex, and not just a cranky afterthought with the lights off. I promise to tell you what I need, instead of making you guess. I promise to wear sexy underwear sometimes."

"I like where this is going," he said, his voice rough.

"I don't want to forget again."

"I won't let you." He tipped her chin up and kissed her. "I won't let me either. And . . . I promise, I will think about Jake. I feel possessive and selfish right now."

"Which is hot, by the way."

"You think I'm hot?"

"Oh, baby."

"Anyway, I feel possessive, but the thing is, you're right. There will always be real life, and the key isn't pushing it away, it's learning how to prioritize us even when it's trying to intrude."

"Listen to us having reasonable discourse."

"Nice, right?" He scooped her up in his arms, walked them back to the bed and deposited them both in the center of it. "Now, if these walls are thin, people might be hearing us having something else."

"Promises, promises."

"I'll make good on all of my promises." He kissed her, deep and long. "You can count on that."

The next week was problematic. Because the ax was closer to falling on their relationship, and Lark had only fallen more in love with Quinn.

Because she slept in his arms every night, ate breakfast with him every morning. She even watched TV on the couch with him, curled up against him, her head resting on his chest. And he held her hand when they walked places on the ranch.

He suddenly didn't seem to care so much about keeping them a secret. But then, the boys had proven that they responded well to him. Despite a bit of grumbling, Quinn was a big hero to all of them. As was Sam.

Guys who were tough, worked hard and had money and success—and all without serving jail time. Well, without serving jail time recently.

Lark put her elbow on the table and took another bite of her dinner and listened to everyone talk. The staff and all the boys were sharing dinner tonight. Except Jill and Sam, who were eating in their cabin.

"Did I tell you guys about the time I got arrested for robbing a convenience store?" Quinn asked.

"You robbed a store?" This came from Mike.

"Yep. I grabbed the cash drawer while the cashier's back was turned," Quinn said. "Do you know why?"

"Why?" Jake asked.

"Because I was an asshole. I thought life owed me something, I don't know what. So I was walking around with a chip on my shoulder just begging to be put in my place. And I did get put in my place. Jail. Which is a terrible thing, by the way, for those of you who haven't been."

"And how did you get here?" Jake asked, looking down at his plate. "I mean . . . I'm curious how you went from that to . . . you own all this and you were in the rodeo."

"Hard work. And more than that, finding a goal that I was working toward. But this is the second part of my cautionary tale. I did a lot of stupid things when I was young, and some of you have done things just as stupid. Some of you haven't yet, but you're headed that way. I don't ride in the rodeo anymore," Quinn said. "I'm barred from it. Because I was accused of something. Something I didn't do. But when you look into my past, I have legal evidence that says I'm the kind of guy who wouldn't hesitate to break the law to benefit himself. The prejudice follows you. And it burns worse when it's prejudice you've earned."

Mike shrugged. "So I've been arrested. You're saying I'll always have a harder time?"

"Maybe, but not as hard as if you kept being stupid. You have time to turn it around. But the choices you make now will affect you, I'm not going to lie about that. Also think hard about getting tattoos."

"Too late for that too," Mike said.

"Yeah, well, for me too."

"But you look like you do okay," Mike said, looking around.

"Yeah, I do okay."

And with that, Lark was officially done for. As if she

hadn't been already. It hurt. To love him so much. Especially when she knew he loved himself so little.

Quinn didn't think he meant a thing without the rodeo. He'd attached all of his value to it. And he had so much to give with just him. Without the fame, without the acclaim. But he didn't see it. And she didn't know how to make him.

Except by taking him as he was. Even with all the rough edges and the self-loathing and the plans for getting revenge on her family. And that was a lot to take. But wrapped up in all that somewhere was Quinn Parker. Her lover, the man she wanted to spend the rest of her life with.

She felt like she was doing battle against the chains that were wrapped around his wrists. Manacles that held him back and kept him from moving forward.

"Eat up," Quinn said. "Because you're all on cleanup crew tonight."

This was met with a slew of swearing and the show of several middle fingers. Quinn never got on them about that stuff, as long as they did what he and the other staffers asked. It was one thing she admired about him.

He didn't ask for blind obedience or for them to be happy about doing the work, so long as they did it. He wasn't trying to protect them from things they'd already seen. Wasn't trying to smooth every rough edge. Quinn had his own rough edges, and she loved those too. They were part of what made him who he was.

When the table was cleared and the boys were in the kitchen with Kevin and Maggie, Quinn took her hand in his and pulled her in for a kiss.

"I've been wanting to do that all night," he said.

"And I've been wanting you to do it," she said.

"Want to take a walk with me?"

"Are you leading me down the garden path, sir?"

"Is that fancy talk for leading you into the woods so I can take your panties off?"

She laughed. "Yes."

"Then hell yeah, I'm leading you down that garden path."

"Lead faster." He led her out of the mess hall and into the warm evening. Lark breathed in deeply, the sweet scent of pending summer filling her lungs. "Beautiful," she said.

"Yeah. I'll be kind of sad to leave it."

"Then don't," she said.

He stopped walking and turned to face her. "I have to. When I get reinstated, I'll be traveling again, competing."

"And if you don't?"

"Not an option."

"Why not?"

"Because I . . . It's not what I want, Lark."

"And in life you're guaranteed to get everything you want?" she asked, reaching out and taking his other hand in hers. "Quinn, what if you never get back into the circuit?"

"I have to."

"But what if you don't?"

"I can't even think about that."

"Why?" she asked. "Would it be so bad? Does it matter so much?"

"It's everything I am, Lark. Everything good that I am. I know how I am, and without a goal . . . without a goal and without people watching . . . what keeps me from becoming what I was? A drunk petty criminal with nothing to offer life."

"You would never be that again. Did you listen to yourself talking to those boys?"

"Talk is easy," he said, his voice rough.

"It's not just talk, though, Quinn, it's your life. It's what you've lived."

"It doesn't look like a lot to me."

"Really? You're a dumbass, do you know that?"

"Oh, really?" He leaned toward her. "Tell me about what a dumbass I am, little girl."

She pulled him toward her, planting a kiss on his lips. "Don't 'little girl' me. I might be younger than you, and I might be less experienced in . . . everything. But I'm a lot less screwed up than you are."

"You think?"

"Yes. And you know what I see? I see a man who has a lot of money, a lot of appeal and a lot to offer the world. But I also see a man who can't make use of any of his resources to their fullest extent because he's too busy licking his wounds."

"Is that what you think? What do you know about any of it?"

"A lot, Quinn. I know a lot. I know what it's like to lose people you love, and damn it, I even lost the memory of the father I loved. The way I knew him . . . none of it's true. It hurts. It sucks."

"At least they wanted you."

"Yeah. I'm not going to say you don't have a uniquely sucky situation, but that doesn't mean you get to be all damaged for the rest of your life."

He shrugged. "I'm over it."

"Liar." She caught herself poking her index finger into his chest, and she couldn't be bothered to stop. "You are not over it. You're controlled by it."

He wrapped his hand around her arm and pulled her up against him. "Says the girl who showed up at my house for sex because she was pissed at her brothers."

She looked up at him, her dark eyes glittering. "And because I wanted you."

"Still, I'd be careful not to fall down off my high horse there, darlin'. You're pretty controlled by the crap you've been through too."

"I was," she said. "But not so much now."

He leaned in closer, his nose nearly touching hers. "Really?"

"I already told you, I used to be afraid of my shadow. Afraid to put a foot out of line."

"And you think I'm afraid?"

She pulled out of his hold. "Yeah, I do." She put her hands on his face. "I think you're afraid that you aren't good enough."

"Baby, you really think I have an ego problem?"

"I do."

He shook his head and pulled away. "And here I thought we were getting to know each other. I guess not."

"Yeah, Quinn, I guess not. I thought we were sharing things with each other, but . . . we're not really, are we?"

"Just in the biblical sense. But that's all this was ever going to be."

Pain stabbed her, sharp and hot. And it was stupid, because she knew, she had known, from the beginning that this wouldn't be forever. But hearing Quinn say it stole her chance to live in denial about it.

She let out a heavy breath. "I'm tired. I'm going to go to bed."

"Fine. I'm going to go make the rounds and make sure everything is set for the night."

"Great."

Lark headed back toward the house and climbed the stairs. It was funny how she hadn't even thought of taking another bed, or going home. She was upset at Quinn, but she wasn't going to play games.

She didn't want to sleep without him, so she wouldn't.

She turned the lights off, took her clothes off and got into bed naked, curled into a tight little ball facing away from the door.

She didn't know how long she lay there alone, replaying the conversation with Quinn over and over and trying not to cry.

She heard the bedroom door open and Quinn's heavy sigh, but she didn't have the energy to say anything. She hardly had the energy to move. His clothes hit the floor with a muffled sound, and then he climbed into bed behind her, wrapping his arms around her and pulling her against his body.

And she let him. Feeling his heart beat heavy against her back, his hand warm on her stomach. Then he kissed her shoulder and whispered in her ear. "I'm sorry, baby."

She nodded silently and put her hand over his. Then she finally drifted off to sleep.

* * *

"What the hell is he doing?"

Lark watched as Quinn mounted a horse in a small chute that was just off of the ranch's main arena. The boys were lined up outside the fence, their eyes glued to him.

"A demonstration," Jill said, moving to stand by Lark.

"What kind of demonstration?"

"The kind that makes me glad my husband only assists bronc riders."

"Oh."

Sam released the door on the chute and the horse bolted out. And Lark's heart climbed into her throat while she watched Quinn keeping time with the horse's movements as it did its level best to throw him off and into the dirt.

But Quinn hardly looked rattled. He was one with the animal. He didn't fight the movements; he embraced them. She'd never seen a man ride quite like that.

"He's so good," she said.

"He is," Jill said. "And I wanted to say . . . I'm sorry about everything. About being at the ranch. I really didn't know you were working for Quinn. I wasn't trying to trick you any of the times we talked."

"I know," Lark said.

A bell rang and Quinn dismounted, then went after the horse, herding him back through to the chute.

"He made the ride," Jill said, a smile on her face. "And you should also know that Quinn hasn't always been my favorite guy in the world. I've spent a lot of time resenting him for having Sam on the road. And I was more than a little PO'd by our romantic getaway at Elk Haven being just another assignment from the boss."

Sam looked back at Jill just then, and his smile could only be described as smitten.

"It seems to be working out, though," Lark said. "Better than it was?"

"Yes," Jill said. "See? Things work out, even when you don't think they will."

Lark blew out a breath. "Well, I cling to that hope."

"Trouble in paradise?"

"It's hardly paradise. I'm not really sure exactly what it is we have going."

"And you want more?" Jill asked.

"Yes." Lark curled her hands around the fence, the cold metal stinging her skin. "But I don't know if it's possible."

"You fell in love with him, didn't you?"

Lark looked down. "I'm so predictable."

"Yeah, well, if it helps, I fell in love with a bad-news cowboy too." Jill put her hands on her hips and looked over at Sam. "And he's caused me a lot of trouble. But he's given me more joy than anything or anyone else in life, so it kind of evens out."

"I don't want to get my heart broken," Lark said.

"Sam's broken my heart a couple of times," Jill said slowly, "and I think I've broken his too. When you love someone with everything, that's the risk you take. Though a few heartbreaks could have been avoided if we'd just stopped being so wrapped up in ourselves and our own issues for about five minutes and looked at the other person."

Lark followed Jill's line of sight over to Sam, who was standing next to Jake and Quinn's horse, letting the kid deal with getting the animal ready to be put back in his corral.

"I don't think Quinn can," Lark said. "He's so hurt. And I don't think he can see past any of that."

"And here I just thought he was a jerk."

"Ugh. No. I wish." Lark took a deep breath. "He's not a jerk. He tries to pretend he is. He's like a dog licking his paw. Huddled in the corner, growling and too stupid to let anyone come and put a bandage on him so he doesn't get an infection that spreads to his brain and makes him act like a total asshole. Actually, it's too late to stop the infection."

Jill laughed. "Descriptive."

"See, he's not an asshole, it's just—"

"The wounds."

"Yeah." Lark bit her lip and looked at the ground. "I was so mad at him when we first met. All I could think about were Cade's injuries. And how he might have caused them. I missed how hurt Quinn was because he didn't walk with a limp. But I see it now."

"He hides it well. I've known him for years, and I just wrote him off."

"That's what everyone's done. But in fairness, I think he was daring people to do it. I think he's daring me to do it."

"Are you going to let him win?"

"No. I'm not going to let him scare me off. I might scare him off, though."

Jill shifted her weight from one foot to the other. "Well, if he gets scared, then it's his loss."

"Hey, Quinn, can I talk to you for a second?"

Quinn turned and saw Jake walking away from Sam and toward him. "Sure. What's up?"

"I just wanted to . . . ask why you don't ride in the circuit anymore."

"I told you guys I got booted."

"Because you got blamed for something you didn't do. What was it?"

"You follow the rodeo, right? I mean, you knew who I was. You used to work with the horses."

"I helped, yeah. So . . . I guess I kind of follow it."

Quinn took his hat off and rested it on the fence post. "You know Cade Mitchell, then. You remember his accident?"

Jake paled. "Yeah, I remember. I was there that day."

"It was a hell of a thing. Not something you want to see happen to anyone, even if you don't like the guy."

"They blamed that on you?"

Quinn nodded once. "Yeah. Because out of everyone there, I'm the one with the past. I'm the one who wasted my time as a kid getting into trouble, and I'm the one . . . I'm the one who walked into the circuit expecting to be rejected. So I was a jerk to everybody. I didn't make a single friend who would stand up for me. I pushed everyone away."

"Like I do," Jake said.

"Yeah. Like you do."

"What do you do when you feel like you're too far gone to come back?" Jake asked. "Like you've already made the worst mistake you could ever make and there's nothing you can do to fix it."

"That's called rock bottom, kid. That's when you start climbing out of the hole."

Jake looked down. "How?"

"Sometimes it's just not being too stubborn to ask for a hand up." Quinn ignored the pressure in his chest, and the image in his head of Lark standing over him with her hand held out to him. "Why don't you go help Sam clean the tack?"

Jake smiled, the first time he'd seen the boy look happy. "Okay."

Quinn let out a breath and leaned against the fence, putting his hat back on his head. Weird how much he would miss this place when he was gone. How much he would miss the woman he'd found here.

But staying wasn't an option. It never had been. He had one goal, and one goal only. Nothing could be allowed to get in the way. He had one more option, and then he was going to start chipping away at the Mitchell empire until Cade had no choice but to give in.

Cade walked toward the door and cursed his leg the whole way. "I'm coming," he said, wishing faster were an option tonight. It just wasn't. That was the most frustrating thing: when what he wanted to make happen with his mind couldn't be matched with his body.

That had never been him before. Whatever he'd wanted, he'd done it. But now . . . now he felt like he couldn't do a damn thing. Three years, and his body still felt like it belonged to someone else.

He wrenched the door open and froze, pondering getting the shotgun as he stared down Quinn Parker.

"What do you want?"

"To talk to you."

"Do you want my blessing to keep defiling my sister? Because I can't give you that. But I can give you a 'go to hell.'"

"I'm actually kind of surprised you haven't come to drag her back by her hair," Quinn said.

He'd thought about it. He'd dreamed about it. Storming that bastard's house and bringing Lark home. Fixing whatever was wrong with her head that made her think he was an okay guy to be with.

But what was the point? He couldn't make her stay. He couldn't make her care that the asshole had nearly killed him. If she didn't care, what more was there to say?

"Well, she's an adult," Cade bit out. "I can't force her. But I don't have to accept it either."

"Well, that's fine. I didn't come here for that. I didn't even come here to talk about her," Quinn said, leaning against the support beam on the covered porch. "I want to give you one more chance to clear my name."

"And why would I do that?"

"If you aren't interested in the truth, maybe you'll do it to keep things running smoothly at the ranch. Maybe you'll consider the personal connection I have."

"I knew it. You're using her." Cade's blood had just about reached the boiling point. Leg pain or no leg pain, his fist connecting with Quinn's jaw seemed like a good idea. Followed up by kicking the bastard in the ribs, stomping him. Just like the horse had done to him. So he would know even a fraction of his pain.

"I didn't have to use her. She's told me a lot of her own free will."

"Out. Off my property right now, or I can't promise you they won't be looking for your body tomorrow." Rage poured through Cade, unreasonable, uncontrollable. But when he pictured this man, the man who had ruined his career, with his hands all over his sister, murder was the nicest thing on his mind.

"One more chance, Mitchell. One more, and I pull the rug out from under you."

"You think you have connections I don't?"

"In this instance?" Quinn nodded. "Yeah, I know I do. And I know where you're weak."

"I'm not clearing a name that doesn't deserve it. Do what you need to do, but I'm not giving you your place back in the circuit. If they ever hinted at reinstating you, I would fight it until I ran out of breath, and if you think I'm bluffing, watch me get out of bed in the morning. How long it takes. How I look like an old man. Then you'll know how serious I am."

Quinn raised an eyebrow and tipped his hat. "Then you'll hear from me soon."

He turned and walked back down the porch and to his truck. Cade watched him drive away, and he wondered how in the hell life could get so screwed up.

It had been bad enough for Quinn Parker to take the rodeo from him. For him to take his ability to ride from him.

But now he was tearing apart his family too.

Quinn got off the phone with his buddy who dealt with the livestock contracts for the circuit. One well-placed word, and they could get the Mitchells cut loose from their horses being used in competition.

It was shameless, and he knew it. He didn't have a lot of friends, but Steve was one, and Quinn knew he could count on him to do this favor with minimal questions asked. He also knew it would be a pretty big blow to the Mitchells.

Because he knew, from Lark's own mouth, that the injection of revenue they got from competitions was the thing keeping them from sinking.

If he had to go down, Cade would come down with him.

He'd done it. He was every inch the bastard he'd always thought. That he'd always believed. The vision of Lark's face sent a sharp stab of pain through his body. How would she handle it? What would it mean for her?

How had it all gotten tangled like this?

In the end, though, of course he'd chosen to do it. No matter how it affected Lark. Because that was who he was.

And she should know. She should know whose house she was in. Whose bed she'd been sharing. She thought she knew, but she didn't. That was the thing. She was lying to herself. She thought she knew who he was, and even though he'd told her the way things really were, and she said she believed him, she didn't really.

He had to make her see it. He had to make her understand.

He walked up the stairs and hoped he'd find Lark in their room—his room. It wasn't their room. They'd been sleeping in it together, but it wasn't theirs. None of this was theirs. It was his. And she had her life, her life with her brothers.

The life he was uprooting.

Because that was the brand of bastard he was.

He threw open the bedroom door and found it empty. He could hear water running in the bathroom, and he walked through and inside. Lark was in the shower, the glass door steamed up, obscuring the details of her. All he could see was her shape. Pale skin and sweet curves.

She was swaying back and forth beneath the water, her arms above her head, in her hair, scrubbing while she moved to a song that seemed to be only in her head.

"Lark," he said, his voice echoing in the room, competing with the shower spray.

"Hi," she said, not opening the door. "You should come in."

"Not now."

"But, Quinn, I'm lonely. And I need someone to wash my . . . back."

For some reason her words, the familiarity of them, the request to help with something he knew damn well she could do by herself and had done by herself before him, sent a shaft of pain through him.

"You don't need me to do that."

"Oh." She stopped swaying, lowering her arms slowly.

"I went to see Cade today."

"Why?"

He was glad the glass was between them. He was glad she couldn't see his face.

"To tell him that if he didn't clear my name, I was going to ruin him. And happily. I told him basically what I already told you."

"And he said?"

"He won't do it."

Silence fell between them, the shower on the tile the only sound now. "What did you do, Quinn?"

"I made some calls. Elk Haven is set to lose its contracts with the Rodeo Association."

"What? How? Why?"

"Because Steve is a friend of mine. Because I told him the situation, and he's prepared to stick his neck out for me on the basis of the fact that Elk Haven might not be able to fulfill its word because of Cade's injuries."

"Quinn . . . if that happens . . . I don't know how they're going to keep the ranch going. We needed that money."

"And you told me," he said, his voice rough. "And I used it. I told you, Lark, I told you who I was. I told you I had bad blood. And you . . . you're just a simple little virgin who believed you could reform a bad boy. Whatever you told me, whatever you told yourself, that's the truth of it."

The water shut off, and Lark pushed the shower door open, emerging completely naked and not even trying to hide herself. "Is that what you think? That I wanted to reform you?"

"Isn't it?" he asked.

"You stupid asshole," she said. "I didn't want to reform you. I wanted you to see what I saw. Because if you did . . . Quinn, if you saw the man I see . . . you wouldn't need this so bad."

"Honey, you're just looking at life through freshly fucked glasses. It's not me, it's you. You think you see something that's not there."

"No, that's where you're wrong." She took a step to him and she put her arms around him, heat and moisture from her skin seeping through his clothes. "You're trying to push me away so that I don't look and see who you are. So that you don't have to look and see who you are. But I see you, Quinn."

"Not clearly." His heart was pounding hard, and he was trying, trying with everything in him, to find the strength to pull away. Because he had no right to touch her. Not again. Not after what he'd done.

He was hurting her. Even while he was hurting her she was giving to him. Touching him like he was a man who was worth something. Like he was a man who could understand softness, who could understand tender emotion.

She was wrong. But he didn't want her to be. For a moment, just a moment, he wanted to be the man Lark thought he could be.

He wanted to fold himself into her embrace and be worthy of it.

The sudden feeling of being absolutely ashamed filled him, washed through him. He felt like nothing. A man with an empty chest and arms that were full of a woman he didn't deserve. A woman he should never have touched.

"Oh, I see you."

No. He wanted to say it. Wanted to scream the denial. He'd come up here to confess his sins and make her see, and now he wanted to hide the monster he'd presented to her because when she saw, when she finally saw, she would turn away from him in complete disgust.

He would. If he didn't have to live in this body, he would have peeled his own skin off and escaped years ago.

But you can't escape your soul. It's rotten no matter what.

She started working the buttons on his shirt. "I need you," she said.

"No, Lark." He shook his head. "Did you hear anything I just said?"

"Shut up, Quinn," she said. She leaned in and kissed his neck.

"You can't need me."

"Then you need me."

And he couldn't argue with that. He let her undo the buttons on his shirt, let her kiss him like she was gasping and he was air. Let her undo his belt buckle and push his jeans to the floor.

Then he followed her out into the bedroom, and he didn't protest when she pulled him onto the bed with her.

She stopped kissing him for a second, her eyes locked with his, her hands on his cheeks. "You need me," she said again.

He was shaking with his need for her. Couldn't deny it. But couldn't bring himself to say it either. For her. For him.

So he just let her keep kissing him, pouring into the deep, empty spaces inside of him. And he took it, let her try to fill him, even though he knew she could spend all of her life trying and never have an impact on the emptiness.

And he would leave her empty too. Everything spent on a man who would take and take and never be satisfied.

She parted her thighs for him and he groaned, rubbing his cock over her slick folds. He shuddered, pressing his forehead against her chest. "I can't wait," he said.

She reached over and grabbed a condom out of the drawer and tore it open, reaching down between them and rolling it onto his length. After she removed her hand he gripped himself and made sure the protection was on as well as it should be. The last thing she needed was a lasting consequence from him.

As if you'll leave her without any scars.

He pushed the voice away and pushed into her, the feeling of completeness, of homecoming, so overwhelming it tugged the breath from his lungs.

For a moment, he felt so satisfied, so complete, he just wanted to stay there, joined to her, forever. He'd never felt so at peace. Had never felt as comfortable in his own body as he was when he was pressed up against hers.

But then she flexed her hips, her internal muscles tightening around him, and his need slipped its leash, roaring through him like a lion, demanding satisfaction.

And he could do nothing but chase it. He thrust into her, deep and hard, and she moaned, fingernails digging into his skin, her breath hot on his neck.

He was lost. In her. Her scent, the feel of her around him, against him, soft and yielding, the perfect answer to his hardness. Strong where he was weak. Vulnerable where he had no give.

She was perfect for him. His perfect fit.

He let that thought spur him on, push him home. He felt her reach her peak, and he raced her over the edge, pleasure pouring through him, washing over him. Like a baptism by fire.

He lay against her, that last thought echoing through him. She was perfect for him.

"I love you, Quinn."

For a second, those words filled him with a joy that was so big, so terrible, he thought it would crush his insides.

And on the heels of the joy came the hard, cold bite of reality.

She was perfect for him, because she had so much to give. Because she was beautiful, lovely inside and out, unlike anyone else he'd ever known. Because she looked at him and saw a man with nothing as worth something. Because she tried to see beyond the bad that had been born into him.

But he wasn't perfect for her. Because no matter how badly she wanted to see a good man, it didn't make him one.

He moved away from her, his heart pounding, his body still burning from the high of the orgasm, from the high of those three words. Words he was sure he'd never heard directed at him in his life.

And now they were ringing in his head like a damn church bell. A call to salvation he couldn't answer.

"Get out, Lark," he said, stumbling away from the bed and going back into the bathroom to get rid of the condom and collect his clothes.

"What?" She followed him, standing in the doorway, her body flushed from her orgasm. "What did you just say? I said I love you and you actually said—"

"Go."

"Quinn, I told you that I wasn't going to make you choose. I told you I would take you like you are."

"Are you stupid? I'm serious. Are you stupid that you would take the *nothing* I can give you? Lark Mitchell, you could have the whole world, and you just want to take my sick, twisted piece of it. Why would you want so little?"

"No, Quinn, the entire world is open to you and you choose to live in a sick, twisted place and act like a trapped, scared little boy. *That* is stupid. I'm standing here holding the door open telling you to walk out, and you're in the corner telling me you're trapped. Why do *you* want so little?"

She turned away and he bent down and picked up his jeans, tugging them on and following her out into the bedroom.

"There's no more to me than this, Lark. I'm an asshole. My own family couldn't deal with me. None of my parents wanted me. I had one home, and it was in the rodeo. It's the only point in my life I ever managed to stay out of trouble, and without it? Without it I'm that same worthless nothing that I was before. I don't love women, I sleep with them, and when I'm done, I never think about them again. You're not going to be any different."

Lark felt like she'd been slapped. Quinn was looking at her with eyes so full of blank rage, rage that seemed to turn inward, not toward her, that he looked like a stranger. The lines on his face were hard, every muscle in his body rigid. Even the horse looked angrier, Quinn's biceps straining, tension coursing through him.

"I don't believe that," she said. Her voice came out a strangled whisper, her throat so tight she could hardly breathe, let alone speak.

"You don't want to believe any of this, I know. But you made me into a man that I'm not. You lied to yourself. I told you the truth, Lark. You were convenient, honey. And I won't deny, it wasn't just proximity. It was a hell of a lot of fun to get your brother so worked up. But this wasn't more than that, and I never told you it was."

A tear ran down her cheek, and she was too horrified by it to brush it away. So she ignored it, let it fall. And let the next one fall. And the next.

"You held me last night," she said. "You didn't even ask for sex—you just held me."

He shrugged his shoulders, his Adam's apple bobbing up and down. "Guess I'm not as horny for you as I was in the beginning."

She could hear him saying all these things. The words coming out of his mouth so ugly, with a grain of truth in them that landed in her sensitive, insecure places, rubbing her raw. But if she really listened, listened to the desperation running beneath the words, she could hear the truth.

"You big coward," she said.

"What?"

"Quinn Parker, you are the biggest pansy I have ever known. You play so tough, you play so bad, but you are a scared, hurt little boy, and that's all." She took a deep breath. "Do you know why I see the scared? Because I know scared. Because I never had a real date or a real boyfriend, because I was too scared. Because I didn't go to college, or get a job away from home, because I was scared. Oh, Quinn, I know scared. But I'm not scared anymore."

"You don't know what you're talking about."

"No, Quinn, in this instance, I know exactly what I'm talking about. Before you, I was afraid of everything. But now . . . now I love you. And you're rejecting me. And it hurts like a son of a bitch, I'm not going to lie. But I'm not backing down. I'm not afraid to say it. Because I would rather take chances. I would rather ride horses up to your ridge, and spend a day away from the computer. I would rather be with the man I want, and have something that I desire with my entire being, than experience a watered-down version of desire with an Internet connection and no risk."

She took a deep breath and looked at him, at his face, frozen, hard. She continued. "You think you're nothing without the rodeo, but I think you're using that. You feel like you're missing something, and it's easier to pretend it's that.

But I think even with the rodeo you're worried you don't
mean anything. That you don't have anything. And the truth
is? You don't. As long as you reject anyone who wants to
care about you, as long as you refuse to care back, you're
going to be empty inside. You have to love people. You have
to let them love you. Even if it's not me, Quinn, let someone
love you."

He took a deep breath, his chest pitching up and down.
"No one loves me, Lark. Not for very long. You might think
you love me now, but it's not going to last. It never does.
There's one place in this world for me . . . and I don't care
if you don't get that, or understand it. Because I do. And I
have to get back to it. Nothing else matters. You don't
matter."

Lark felt like he'd wrapped his hand around her heart
and crushed it into a ball. "Oh, Quinn." She closed her eyes
and felt another tear fall.

And she knew he was right. That Kelsey was right. She'd
lied to herself. Told herself she only needed temporary. Told
herself she would be fine if she didn't get him in the end.
Told herself she believed him when he said that sex was all
it would ever be.

Deep down in her heart, she'd believed he would love
her. That he would see. She'd believed, in the truest part of
herself, that he would be the man she would marry one day.
The father of her babies.

And right now, he was standing there tearing that dream,
that beautiful, untouched, half-realized dream, into tiny
little pieces. Glitter around her feet. Sparkling, lovely even
in its brokenness.

"I need to pack," she said.

"Fine." He walked over to the closet and pulled a shirt
out, tugging it over his head. "I won't run into you again.
I'll mail you your check."

"Don't," she said, but before the word was out he'd
slammed the door behind him.

She looked down at her bag, still filled with her clothes.
She'd never unpacked. She'd just sort of lived out of her

duffel. Because he'd never told her to put her things away anywhere. Because he'd never wanted her to stay.

A sob wrenched through her, and she pulled out the pile of lacy underthings and threw them on the bed, spreading them out over the comforter. She didn't need them anymore. And he could keep them, and remember. Remember that she hadn't even had the chance to wear all of them for him yet.

She bent down again and found another thong, slinging it over one of the posts on the bed. And then she saw them— the Superman panties she'd been wearing during their illicit phone call.

She picked them up and traced the *S*. Just like Quinn had told her to imagine he'd done.

She threw them onto his pillow. Then she pulled on jeans and a shirt, zipped her bag shut and slung it over her shoulder. She surveyed her handiwork. She wasn't leaving like she'd never been here. She'd be damned if she would leave him without a reminder. If she'd let him forget.

So let him deal with that.

She wiped another tear away and walked out of his room, closing the door behind her. She went down the stairs and out of the house, heading toward her car. And she refused to look back.

She'd spent too much of her life looking back. Being sad. Being scared. That wasn't her anymore.

Quinn could stay behind and embrace all that fear, but that wasn't her anymore.

Quinn had changed her. Too bad he'd also left a Quinn-shaped hole inside of her.

Lark walked up the steps and into her house, every step heavy. She refused to feel ashamed. She refused to feel guilty. But she still kind of did.

She heard footsteps coming from the kitchen and looked up. Cade was standing there with a beer in his hand.

And her resolve broke. "Oh, Cade," she said, throwing her arms around him, tears streaming down her cheeks. "Please don't make me feel stupid. Please don't tell me you warned me."

He wrapped his arms around her. "No. I won't. Lark, I won't."

They stood like that for a while, then he pulled away, his arm still around her shoulders. "You know, I was all ready to be really pissed at you."

She nodded and wiped the tears from her face. "I don't blame you."

"I'm not, though," he said. "Come sit down."

She let him lead her to the couch and she sat, her knees drawn up to her chest. "I left. Obviously."

"Yeah, you did. Finally get sick of him?"

"He got sick of me."

"He's a damned idiot."

"I . . . I just . . ."

"You're not the first person to be stupid over sex. You won't be the last. Hell, I've been stupid over it plenty of times. And I can't hold it against you. Even though part of me wishes I could."

Her teeth chattered. "Yeah, well, I wish it were just sex."

He stiffened next to her. "You aren't . . . I mean you used . . ."

"Not pregnant," she said. "Just in love."

"How did you manage to fall in love with a guy like that?"

She looked down at her hands. "Because I know for a fact he's not a guy like that. I know you don't believe me. I know you don't. He doesn't either, if it helps."

"Nothing helps. He hurt you."

"And you really aren't mad at me?"

"No." He shifted. "Like I said, you're hardly the first person to make an ass of yourself for love. Cole made a way bigger ass out of himself than you did. Seriously. Shawna?"

"True."

"But look, he found Kelsey later. And everything is . . . well, it's not my thing, but he's happy. You'll be happy again someday too."

"Why isn't it your thing, Cade?"

"I'm not the kind of guy who's up for something like that. I'm more of a temporary man. Itchy feet."

"Cade, I think you have the same problem Quinn has. You don't really see yourself." Lark leaned her head back against the couch. "Listen to me; I'm full of advice tonight."

"Yeah, me too. We could write a book and fill it with our wisdom." Cade put his hands behind his head. "You can talk about your incredible insight into psychologically damaged men after one love affair, and I'll talk about moving on and finding functional relationships. I'll write most of it from a hotel the next town over while in bed with a woman whose name I don't know."

"Sounds legit."

"As much as most self-help books."

Silence fell between them, and Lark leaned forward, elbows resting on her knees. "Tell me about Dad."

"Now?"

"My heart's broken, Cadence," she said. "Might as well throw another brick on the pile. You can't break it more. And you can't protect me from the truth either. That's how all this started."

Cade ran a hand over his face. "I know. But I wanted to. I wish you knew."

"I do. I got . . . I got upset because I felt like . . . like I believed this silly story. Like you were laughing at me, maybe."

"No. Never that. Nothing about this is funny. But when I found out about Dad . . . I was sixteen. And I wished that I could unknow it. You have no idea how much. I just wanted to spare you from that."

"So . . . it was a long time ago. She's . . . How old is she?"

"I think probably twenty-five now."

"So she's older than me." Lark looked down at her hands, expecting more misery. But it didn't come. It was just a kind of cold, sick calm. Acceptance. "It just sucks."

"I know."

"It's not her fault, though."

He nodded. "I know that too."

Lark let out a slow breath. "So . . . so maybe instead of protecting me, and protecting the guy who made the mistake—and who is dead, by the way—we protect the sister who's here?"

Cade smiled, slow, sad and more genuine than any smile she'd seen on his face in a while. "What was I protecting you from? You're a lot more grown-up than I am."

She stood up. "I'm glad you think so. Now, if you could please ignore the very teenage angst coming from my bedroom and think of me fondly as an adult. Look the other way if you hear me crying like a child."

"I can't promise that."

"Why not?"

"Because if I think you need me, I'm going to be there."

She sighed. "So annoying. And I love you for it."

"I love you too."

"That's the first time it's been said back to me all day."
Cade winced. "Yeah, I know, right?"

"Do you want me to kill him? I have to offer. But you
know, I'd do it anyway. That he hurt you is just a bonus."

She shook her head. "I appreciate the offer. I really do.
But he has to live with his issues. I think that's punishment
enough."

Why the hell had he quit drinking? He couldn't remember
now. Not now, when he felt like his entrails had been pulled
out and exposed. When he felt scrubbed raw inside, his eyes
so dry and gritty it was laughable. Especially when he was
pretty sure he wanted to cry but that he'd lost the ability to
do it.

If he got drunk, he could probably cry. Probably release
the hideous pressure that was building in his chest. Yeah,
he could wail like a drunken idiot. An emotionally crippled,
drunken idiot. He could curl up on his bed with all those
panties Lark had left him and bawl his eyes out.

But he wasn't going to. Because he had to work today.
Because he wasn't going to let the boys down when he'd
promised them more riding demonstrations. Because Lark
would be pissed if he drank because of her. Because she would
be really pissed if he let the boys down.

And he would be pissed at himself. So drinking in the
middle of the day was out of the question. Damn it.

"Quinn . . ."

Quinn turned around and saw Jake standing by the fence,
his hand gripping the top rail like it was his support system.

"Yeah?"

He wasn't in the mood to deal with teenage issues. Even

the admittedly real issues these guys were dealing with. He had his own issues, and they were eclipsing everything and everyone at the moment.

He couldn't say that, but it was true.

"I need to talk to you."

Great. "Sure. What's up?"

"You said that stuff about rock bottom. And I talked to Sam for a while . . . and . . . and I have something to tell you."

"Okay," he said, privately wishing he could just tune out whatever talk the kid thought was so important.

"I told you that I used to help at the rodeo. And I did. That day, the day of Cade Mitchell's accident, I got approached by a guy. I didn't know his name. He wasn't one of the riders, and he sure as hell wasn't you. He asked me if I would do something for him. He offered me a lot of money. Like . . . it was a lot. To me anyway. He said if, when I was inspecting the gear on Cade's horse, I would put a spike under the saddle, I'd get paid. So I did it." He shook his head. "I didn't mean for him to get hurt. He was just . . . I guess he was just supposed to lose, and I thought, it sucks for him to lose, but I needed the money. But if I could take anything back . . . any of the dumb shit I've done . . . that would be the one thing." He shook his head. "I need to put it right. That's . . . that's why I chose to come here. There were a few options open to me and I saw this one and . . . I knew I had to see you because . . . I have to fix this."

Quinn felt like he'd been punched in the head again. "You did it?" he asked, his heart pounding, his palms slick with sweat.

He couldn't believe it. Couldn't believe that his ticket back was here. That it had just been handed to him.

"Yes," Jake said. "And I'll testify before the board or . . . court. Whatever you need. I don't really want to get arrested, but I understand that . . . whether I meant to hurt him or not, I did."

"If he presses charges, you could go to jail," Quinn said, reiterating the point.

"I know."

"And you're still ready to confess?"

"You made all this happen," Jake said, "because you got it together and worked hard. Because you hit rock bottom and took a hand up. And I'm taking something from you by not doing the same. I don't want to do that anymore."

And right then, Quinn realized something. He hadn't hit rock bottom before. Not truly. Not before today.

Because when a hand had been reached down to him, when help and salvation was within his grasp, he'd turned away.

He looked down at the boy. So young. So much braver than he was. "You'll really confess?"

"Yes. I have dreams about it. About how it looked when he fell. When his boot got caught and . . . and how he got dragged around like a rag doll. That was my fault. I did that. I've done . . . things. Stolen stuff and vandalized . . . stuff. But I never did anything to people. I never wanted to hurt anyone."

The things that hit Quinn surprised him. Concern for Jake. Because the kid could get in major trouble. Because this was something he had to live with. A consequence Quinn had been spared. He'd never hurt anyone seriously, even when he'd been at his worst.

"And I'll be reinstated." He said that last part out loud. To try to make himself feel that. To make himself feel elation, excitement. Some sense of accomplishment. Vindication. It was here. He had it. Right in his hands.

And he didn't feel anything. Nothing but this strange, hollow ache that permeated everything. All of him.

He didn't feel a drive to punish Jake. To pursue the man who'd put Jake up to it. He didn't feel a damn thing.

It didn't change when he called his lawyer. Didn't change when he got his notice of appointment to stand before the board. For Jake to go and confess.

It didn't change, four days later, when he got the call telling him he was absolved. That he was cleared to compete in the circuit again, since he was innocent of any wrongdoing in the incident involving Cade Mitchell.

He walked into the barn and sat down in front of the stall. Why couldn't he feel anything? Why didn't he care?

The words of the chairman still echoed in his head.

You're cleared to begin competition at the beginning of next season . . .

No apology. But he hadn't expected that. Never in a million years. But the speed at which they'd disbarred him had been amazing. Still, with Jake's confession, his knowledge of details Quinn certainly hadn't been privy to, plus a deposit slip showing the money he'd been paid going into a personal account the day of the accident, they'd had enough reasonable doubt that they'd felt obligated to allow him back.

And he was waiting now. Waiting to feel like everything in his life was back the way it should be. Waiting to feel . . .

He didn't even know. He didn't know what he'd thought he would feel. Satisfied. Whole. Like he was someone. Someone more than a bastard forced on a man too dignified to turn him out onto the streets. A bastard who put an irrevocable crack in a marriage.

A bastard who had never fit. Who had never been wanted.

He knew what he'd been expecting. He'd been expecting to get reinstated and find the kind of satisfaction he'd felt when he'd first started riding. Purpose, a sense of focus that had pulled him out of the fog he'd been living in.

But it wasn't working now.

And he didn't know why. It had been enough. It had been enough before Lark.

He closed his eyes and put his head down. Yeah. It had been enough because he'd been so used to the emptiness inside of him that it had made him feel full.

Lark had brought him something bigger than purpose. Something richer than drive. She'd brought something into his life no one else in his life ever had.

I love you.

No one else had ever said that. No one else had ever felt it. No one else had ever given him love. And Lark had done it regardless of his actions. When he'd been too angry to let go of revenge, too afraid to give her the words in return. Even though he wasn't some famous bronco rider. She'd loved him regardless of his position.

She'd loved him even with all the broken pieces inside of him. She hadn't waited for him to change before offering it. Hadn't held it up out of reach.

She'd held out her hand, her love, to him where he was at, at the bottom of that pit. That rock-bottom hole he'd been living in for so long.

And he'd turned her down. A dying man in the desert refusing water.

He was a fool. And he was a coward.

It had been easier to want the rodeo, because at the end, even if he didn't have the circuit, it wouldn't destroy him. But acknowledging his love for Lark . . . and damn, but he loved her . . . if he lost it, it would destroy him. Utterly. Completely.

Except he was a dumbass. He'd thought he could stop it. That if he sent her away, if he didn't let himself think it, if he didn't acknowledge that the feeling of peace, of being full, was love, he would be protected from it.

Even now, with his heart cracked open and bleeding, with the loss of Lark so real and painful, he was afraid of what it would mean to say the words. To want a future with her.

From the time he was a kid, he'd been made to feel like he wasn't good enough. And the biggest lie he'd ever told himself was that he didn't care. That he didn't need to fit. That he didn't want to fit.

That he didn't want the love that had been denied him.

Well, he didn't want his mother's love. He didn't want love from either of the men he could call father. Not now.

But he wanted Lark's love. And he was sure that he wasn't worthy of it. That was his real fear. That he would reach his hand out, and find she was still out of his reach. That no amount of wanting her, of wanting to be the man she deserved, would make him good enough.

Not even with the rodeo. Not even if he gave her every bit of his bruised and damaged heart.

But he would ask for it anyway. Because his pride could go to hell.

He had lived afraid, and he had lived angry. But as he sat there with the ground hard under his butt and his chest feeling empty, he realized that until Lark, he'd never actually lived.

Lark didn't mean to eavesdrop, but it was hard not to. Especially when everyone was talking in hushed and grave tones like they didn't want to be listened to. That made it all the more interesting.

Jill and Sam were there, and so was Jake. They were all talking to Cade.

"Lark!"

She took the last step off the stairs and into the living room. "Yeah?"

"Do you do that a lot?" Cade asked.

"No." She hesitated. "More lately than normal."

"Come here."

She did. She looked from Jill to Jake to Sam and back to Cade. They all looked like they'd just buried a family pet.

"Jake came because he had something to tell me," Cade said.

"Oh?"

Jake stood up and took a deep breath. "I was the one who put the spike under his saddle. I was the one who caused . . . everything."

Lark felt like she'd been hit in the stomach. All the air was knocked out of her, all the thoughts wiped from her head. "What? Jake . . . why?"

"Not because I had anything against him," Jake said, looking back at Cade. "I got offered a lot of money to do it. Which is . . . I'm not excusing it. Or justifying it. I just . . . I'm sorry." Jake's face crumpled, and so did Lark's heart.

Jill got up from the couch and put her arm around him, and Sam stood too, just near him, offering support.

Jake composed himself and turned back to Cade. "If you wanna press charges, I understand."

Cade stood up, his movements labored, possibly a little more than normal. Possibly on purpose.

She got it now. They weren't burying a pet, but Cade was having to bury a hatchet she knew he hadn't wanted to let go of. "I don't think that's necessary," Cade said. "From my point of view, you were a kid. A dumbass kid, but a kid. And I used to be one of those too . . . So. If you know who asked you to do it, though . . . if you could remember . . ."

"I didn't get his name. He was a guy in jeans. Belt buckle. Expensive hat and boots. He wasn't a rider."

"All right. But if you ever do remember . . . he's the one I'd press charges against. Not you."

They all shook hands, and Jill and Sam led Jake from the house, leaving her and Cade alone.

"He did it," she said.

"Yeah."

"Not Quinn," she said.

Cade shook his head. "That's how it looks."

Lark's heart splintered. Again. How did a heart break again in the space of a few days? This heartbreak business was balls. "I knew it," she said, nodding. "I did."

"I know you did. Which just underlines the fact that he's an idiot."

She laughed, a nervous, sad, elated laugh. One born from feeling too much emotion at one time. "Oh, really?"

"Yes. Really. Because you believed him. No one else did. And look what he did to you. I still think he's an asshole.

And I don't take back the punch to the jaw. I would have done that no matter what."

"'Cuz he stole my virtue?"

Cade made a face. "Stop with that. I do not need details. Or any more reason to want to go after him with a branding iron."

"After years of dealing with your innuendos, I think I've earned the right. It's my turn, Cade. My turn to make you uncomfortable. My one solace in this moment."

His lip curled. "Find a new solace, please. This one is going to ruin my life."

There was a knock on the front door, and Cade went to answer it. Then he froze when he swung it open.

"What the hell do you want?"

Lark froze too, because she knew, without even looking, that it could only be one person. Because only one person could earn such a frosty reception from her brother. The only person she wanted desperately to hide from, from here to eternity.

And, perversely, the only person she wanted more than her next breath.

"You know what I want."

Quinn. It was Quinn, and he was here. And he wanted . . .

He wanted to make sure he was reinstated. That he was no longer barred from competition. She was such a stupid girl. For a half second, she'd been convinced that what he wanted was her. But that wasn't true.

She'd never been what he wanted, not really. Not deep down. She'd been a nice diversion, but she wasn't enough for him. Wasn't enough to bring him out of the pit he seemed determined to live in.

"Jake's been here already, and I don't see what I have to do with you and the board at this point," Cade said, barring the way.

"I got reinstated two days ago," Quinn said. "Jake's confession made it pretty immediate. But you know what? I don't give a damn. Not about any of it. That's not why I'm here."

Lark looked up, all the way and past Cade, her eyes locking with Quinn's.

Quinn pushed his way into the house, apparently no longer caring about manners, decorum or her brother's mean right hook.

"Lark."

"What do you want?" she asked, breathless, hurting.

"You," he said, his voice thin, strained. "Always you." He advanced on her, tugged her into his arms and kissed her lips, pouring emotion, pain and longing into it. And she felt it, answered it with all of the emotion, the love, inside of her.

When they parted, they were both breathing hard, Quinn's eyes intent on hers, dark and glittering with emotion.

"Well." They both looked back at Cade, who was standing there, staring. He put his hands in his pockets. "Uh . . . well . . . this is awkward."

"Go away, Cade," she said, her voice cracking.

He assessed them both, then nodded slowly. "My pleasure." He walked out the front door, closing it behind him.

"Was it really that easy?" Quinn asked.

"No," Lark said. "He's going to give you hell later, then Cole's going to give it to you twice. And first, I'm going to give it to you. What are you doing here? Why are you kissing me? Like you have a right to put your mouth on mine when you told me that you didn't want me to love you. When you told me that you didn't want me."

He shook his head. "I don't have the right." His voice was rough, shredded. "I don't have the right to touch you. To want you. To love you. You deserve someone so much better than me, Lark. And you could find him, easily. But the one thing you won't find is a man who wants you more than I do. Is a man who will love you more than I do. I have nothing to give you. Nothing but my baggage, nothing but my heart, such as it is. But I will do everything, everything in my power, everything out of it, to make myself worthy of you. To make you happy. If you would have me . . . Lark,

I feel like I shouldn't even ask. But I want to ask. I need to ask. I need you to be with me. Forever."

"Quinn . . . I don't . . . I don't even know . . . What the hell am I supposed to say?"

"Say you love me still." He held her hands in his, tight, against his chest. "That I didn't shake it out of you with my stupidity."

"Of course I love you, you moron."

He pulled her in and kissed her hard, kissed her until she was dizzy. "I'm so glad to hear you say that."

"But hang on," she said. "You have a story to tell me, Quinn Parker, because when last I left you, you told me you didn't want this."

"And you told me I was scared. Guess who was right."

"Well, me, obviously."

He kissed her nose. "Obviously." Then he pulled her in close and just held her, held her so tight she could feel his heart beating. "Lark, it's so much easier to pretend you know you're unworthy of love than to ask for it again, to want it again, and have it denied you. It's easier to want something like the rodeo than to want a person, a woman, so much it consumes you inside. I was terrified to love you, and in some ways I still am. But you're all my missing pieces. Parts of me I've been searching for all of my life."

She pulled away from him and looked into his eyes. "Me?"

"Yes, you. You are my bravery. Without you, I've always been afraid. You are my hope. Without you, I was just sitting in darkness. You are my peace, Lark. Without you, I was never at rest. You are the piece of my soul I thought I was simply born without. When the fact of the matter is, you were just there, waiting for me to find you. And I was looking in the wrong places."

She tried to blink back the tears that were blurring her view of his face. His perfect, wonderful face. "Quinn . . . you were always complete. Even without me. You've always been enough."

"I've been angry," he said. "So angry, for most of my life.

Angry at my parents for making me feel so ashamed of who I was and how I was born. Angry at your brother. Angry at the world. And I blamed other things, other people, for the parts of me that felt wrong. But it was me. It was my anger. It was my fear. It drove out everything good. I used my anger, for most of my life. I let it drive me, let it push me, and that worked in competition. But when I didn't have the circuit anymore, it felt a lot more like what it was. Unhappiness. Rage."

"But you can go back to riding now," she said. "You can compete again."

"Yes, and do you know what I felt when I found that out?"

"What?"

"Nothing. I can't lie to myself anymore. I can't pretend that's happiness. I can't pretend it's life. I can't pretend it matters. Not when I've been with you. Not when I've seen what life can really be like. That? It's all a shadow compared to what you bring to me."

"Me?" she asked again, apparently stuck on repeat. "But you're . . . so sexy. And amazing. And older."

"Seriously? Again with that?"

"I still think it's hot. But . . . but I'm a computer geek who was recently a virgin, and who barely lived life away from the screen before you. And somehow . . . I'm the one who brings life to you? You brought it to me, Quinn. You made me brave."

"Lark Mitchell, how can you question, for one moment, everything you bring to me? You are brave, with or without me. You're diabolical—leaving your underwear in my bed was plain evil. You're weird, and beautiful, and you make me laugh, and I can't remember when I did that and meant it before you came into my life." He smiled. "There, I thought of something else you are."

"What?"

"My laughter."

"Stop it," she said, a tear sliding down her cheek. "You're making me melt. I will be melted. You don't want a melted girlfriend."

"I don't know that I want a girlfriend at all."

"What?"

"I want something a lot more permanent than that. I'd really like a wife, and I've never wanted one of those before. But I want to keep you forever, and that seems about the most societally acceptable way to go about it, something else I've never cared about before."

"A wife?"

"Scary?"

"Yeah. But . . . but . . . wonderful. And right. But you have to understand something first."

"What?"

"I never needed you to change. I never needed you to be more. I never needed anything more from you but you being Quinn Parker. You say I'm all these things for you, that I fill all these empty places, but don't you know you do that for me too? Don't you know? I was scared of my own shadow before I met you. Afraid to want. Afraid to love. I feel like you broke the cage I was locked in. Like you set me free, like you helped me find . . . me." She cupped his face, looked into his eyes. "You are enough. Shame on your family for not knowing it. Shame on them for making you feel like less, because they were too afraid, too selfish, to see what a gift they had in you. They made you feel like you were wrong, because they were angry at themselves and you were the easiest way to express that."

"You think?"

"Yes. Also, I think I'm a damn good amateur psychologist. I should be charging you by the hour."

He smiled, a lopsided, genuine grin. "I can afford you."

"Yes, that's right, you can." She paused for a second. "Speaking of affording . . . can my brothers still afford the ranch?"

"You're just asking me that now?"

"Stupid as it is, I love you no matter what. Whether you ride on the circuit, whether you've carried out your vengeance . . . no matter what."

"Well, they can still afford the ranch, because I told my

buddy to leave the contracts be. I actually put a stop to it after you left. Before I found out Jake was the one who put the spike under Cade's saddle."

She shook her head. "Big bad Quinn Parker . . . making good decisions and thinking of others. Your street cred is ruined."

"Don't let it get around."

"You better go straight to the tattoo parlor and get a unicorn horn and glitter added to your tattoo."

"No."

"But you aren't angry anymore," she said, smiling at him. "You aren't, are you?"

"I'm not. But I'm not getting a unicorn tattoo. You get one if you want."

"Me? A tattoo?"

"Could be pretty damn sexy. Although you don't need anything extra to be sexy."

She raised her eyebrows. "Not even lingerie?"

"I like the lingerie, but you don't need it."

"Dalek undies will do?"

"Baby, anything will do, as long as I have you."

"Even if I'm threatening to exterminate your bits?"

He kissed her lips. "You won't really do it."

"I know. They're too valuable to me."

"I hope the man attached to the bits is valuable too."

"I know I already told you how much," she said, pushing his hat off of his head and onto the floor, weaving her fingers through his hair, "but I'll say it again until you believe it. Until you know that every drop of your blood is good."

Quinn closed his eyes and rested his forehead against Lark's, an intense burst of happiness tearing through him. He'd never felt anything like it. Had never felt so complete. So whole.

Had never simply felt like being, just breathing in air, was enough.

But he did now. With Lark's arms around him, he did.

"I love you," he said.

"I love you too."

He put his hands on her hips, to keep her near him, to keep himself from falling at her feet. "I've never had a place in this world," he said. "I've spent all my life searching."

"The search is done, Parker. You have a place. In my heart."

He closed his eyes, a wave of emotion threatening to wash him away. "There is no other place I'd rather be."

"I'm glad to hear it."

He just held her, felt her warmth, her body. Just her. The woman he loved. The woman who brought him peace. "This is the closest thing to perfect I've ever had in my life."

"What would make it perfect?" she asked.

"If Cade Mitchell wasn't going to be my brother-in-law."

She laughed. "I didn't say yes, you know."

"Then say yes."

"Me saying yes to you is how we got into this mess in the first place. The work contract?"

"That's true. I was thinking of the other times you said yes."

Her cheeks turned pink and she cleared her throat. "Yeah, well, there was that too."

"Face it, Lark, good things happen when you say yes to me."

"Fine, then . . . yes."

"Yes to what?"

She smiled, and his whole world got brighter. "Yes to forever."

Epilogue

"Today is insane," Lark said, looking around at the barbecue that was set up in the covered arena in honor of the first class to "graduate" from the program at Longhorn.

There were parents, foster parents, parole officers, family and friends. An eclectic group, but considering the group, it seemed right.

"Yeah," Quinn said, surveying the pandemonium, "it is. But it's pretty awesome too."

"I've never seen them happier."

"It's amazing what a little direction can do. More than that, it's amazing what love can do." He looked at Lark, at the diamond ring glittering on her left hand. He'd asked her properly after the clumsy, ringless proposal in her house five months ago.

He'd even gotten her brothers' blessing. Or he'd at least gotten their promise not to punch him in the face again.

"Love is pretty kick-ass," she said, beaming at him.

"Yeah." He managed to look away from her, at everyone scattered around the ranch. At Jill and Sam, who had never looked happier, standing there with Jake, who finally had a home. "Love is pretty kick-ass, all right." He took a deep breath and made a decision, then and there. "What do you think about moving the wedding up?"

"To when?"

"Summer."

"But that's the middle of the next competition season."

He took another deep breath and looked down at Lark, at the woman who'd become his world over the past few months. The woman who had managed to glue all the broken pieces in him back together. She'd rebuilt him. Made him better. She'd made something that had been the biggest thing in his life seem so very small now. "I don't think I'm going to compete again," he said slowly. "At least not this year."

"But . . . but . . ."

"I've been thinking a lot about it. And the timing doesn't feel right. Everything is going so well here. And I just . . . I don't feel like I need it, Lark. I used to think that if I couldn't compete . . . there wouldn't be anything for me. But that's the furthest thing from the truth. Everything in my life right now is more important than the circuit. You're more important."

"Quinn, I don't want you to give this up for me."

"You'll still love me if I'm not a big rodeo star, right? You aren't a secret buckle bunny, are you?"

"Maybe. Maybe I am."

"I don't believe it."

"I have secrets. Secrets only my browser history knows."

"Mysterious," he said, kissing the top of her head. "I like that. It's sexy."

"Yes, well. I try."

"I just feel like my priorities have changed. I was this guy willing to do anything to get back into the rodeo. Now . . . my life is full, Lark."

She blinked rapidly, her eyes glittering. "That's so good to hear. And you know I'm all about marrying you sooner. Even if you're not a big rodeo star. But I just need to be sure it's what you want, and not what you think will make me happy, because as long as I have you, there is no unhappy, Quinn."

"That's just how I feel. What I do . . . it just doesn't matter as much, not when I've got you. I might go back someday. But for now I think I want to stay here. And do this. Run the ranch. Be with you. Keep you near your family. This feels like my home to me. The first one I've ever had. I always felt out of place in my parents' house. And I just sort of drifted everywhere else. But this place, with you? This is home. I'm not in a big hurry to leave it."

"Welcome home, Quinn Parker." Lark hugged him, that way that only she could, the way that made him feel like his heart was going to shatter into a million pieces, then re-form, stronger and bigger than ever. "You are an amazing man, do you know that?"

When he'd first met Lark, he was nothing. A man with no home, no family and bad blood. Now he had her. A place to call home. And he knew he wasn't worthless. Because Lark loved him.

He leaned down and kissed the top of her head. "Thanks to you, I actually do."

Keep reading for a special
preview of the next Silver Creek
romance from Maisey Yates

UNBROKEN

"It's bad form to get drunk at your sister's wedding, right?"

"Since when has that ever stopped you, Cade?"

Amber Jameson leaned back in the folding chair and then checked to make sure the little purple bow tied to the back hadn't fallen off and onto the grass. She'd spent too many damn hours tying those things on yesterday.

They were finicky. Finicky flipping ribbons. Almost as finicky as the bride, who, while cute as a button under normal circumstances, had had a bridezilla flare-up during the decorating yesterday and had gone around micromanaging said ribbon tying.

And placement.

She'd demanded ribbon curls in lengths that were impossible for mere mortals to achieve. If Lark weren't the little sister Amber had always wanted, she would never have gone along with all of it. Not without attacking her with the scissors she was using to curl ribbons, at least.

But then, Lark's life had been short on frills. Being raised by two brothers and a dad. So Amber supposed she was entitled.

But then, Amber's life had been short on this kind of thing too, and she didn't feel at all yearny for it. Nope. Marriage and men and bleah. Not her thing. Not these days.

"It doesn't usually," Cade said, leaning back in his chair so that they were sitting at the same angle. "But I thought, since this is for Lark, maybe I should behave."

She looked at her friend's profile. Strong, handsome. Square jaw, roughened with dark stubble. Brown eyes that always had a glint of naughty in them. And today he was wearing a suit jacket and a tie, along with a black cowboy hat.

Damn, damn, *damn*, he was fine. Sometimes it hit her. Like a shit-ton of bricks, that her best friend was the best-looking guy in a five-hundred-mile radius. Or possibly the world. And it made her feel . . . things she didn't want to feel.

Then he turned to face her head on and offered her his very best smart-ass Cade smile, and the moment faded out as soon as it had hit. Like driving on one of Silver Creek's fir-lined highways and seeing a sunbeam peek through the trees. A brilliant shaft of light that colored the world gold for just a moment before racing back behind the dark green branches. Just a glimpse, an impression of something she didn't want to explore.

Like, ever.

"When did she grow up?" Amber asked, looking over at the dance floor where Lark was currently holding on to her new husband, both of them swaying to the music without displaying any particular dancing skills. Quinn was a rough-and-tumble-cowboy type, though he seemed to have a little more rhythm than his new bride. "It makes me feel old," she continued. "Like an old cliché. Sitting here at her reception looking at this grown-up woman in a wedding gown and thinking . . . how is she not eight years old still?"

"Imagine how I feel," Cade said, his voice rough.

"Yeah, I know."

The Mitchells were a part of Amber's cobbled-together family. She didn't have a lot in the way of people who loved her, so when she found people who were willing to accept her, she clung to them as best she could.

In her younger years, that clinging amounted to some very poor decisions, but she'd matured past that. Especially after she'd realized that her grandma and grandpa weren't going to just ship her straight back into the system. That they were going to let her stay in Silver Creek.

That she could stay with them, in their home.

Since then, she'd built herself a solid foundation for her life. And Cade was the cornerstone. Had been since she was fourteen years old. She would never, ever do anything to jeopardize that.

Though, there was nothing wrong with infrequent, secret ogling.

"Are you having empty-nest syndrome, Mitchell?" she asked, nudging him with her elbow.

"Me? Oh, hell no. This nest isn't getting emptier. Maddy runs around like hell on pudgy feet. That little beast cut holes in one of my work shirts the other day with those little plastic-handled scissors. And now Cole and Kelsey have the other baby coming in January. Nope, it's just filling up over here."

"But Lark's gone."

"She's been gone. She's been shacking up with that asshole I now call a brother-in-law for a year."

She patted his thigh and didn't notice how hard and hot and muscular it was beneath those thin dress pants. "I know. But now it's official."

"Yep."

"Emotions don't bite, Cade. Don't run from your feels," she said dryly.

"That's pretty rich coming from you, missy."

She made a face at him and earned a smile. "I don't have to take advice to give it. I'm emotionally stunted and I know it."

"That's why we get along so well."

"I thought it was because I'm such a good pool player," she said, lifting her beer from the table and taking a long drink.

"That's not it. I'm a lot better than you are."

"Uh-huh."

"What do you think?" he asked. "Wanna dance?"

She eyed Cade. More specifically his leg. The one she hadn't just patted. "Um . . . really?"

He lifted a shoulder. "Okay, maybe not." The grooves around his mouth deepened and Amber felt an answering chasm deepen around her heart.

She hated that he couldn't dance anymore. Hated that the man she knew as being so totally vital and energetic was hobbled because of a rodeo accident four years ago.

For a long time they'd all blamed Quinn, Lark's husband, but they found out they'd been mistaken. Hard for Cade to process, as evidenced by the fact that he frequently referred to his new brother-in-law as an asshole.

They were getting there, but they weren't exactly best friends yet.

The dude-bonding process was not yet complete.

Now they didn't know quite who to blame, except for a poor kid who'd been paid to sabotage the ride. The spike he'd put beneath Cade's horse's saddle had only been intended to end the ride faster, not send Cade to the hospital and cause life-changing, career-ending injuries. Getting hung up on your horse was never a good thing, but when the horse was that spooked? You didn't walk away. You got carted away on a stretcher.

Quinn got to move on from it all. His name was cleared. He was reinstated into competitions. And the question of who'd sabotaged Cade was left unanswered.

And Cade would never be fixed. Even if they did find out who was behind it, Cade wouldn't magically be healed, damage undone by justice. That hurt her. Always. Every day.

Because whenever she had a problem, Cade was there. He was always trying to fix things for her. Had been since they were in high school. But there was no fixing this for him. And she'd give her own leg to do it. So he could go back to doing what he loved.

She only used her legs to wait tables and help around her grandparents' ranch.

She didn't do anything like Cade. Watching him ride? It had always sent a flash of light down her spine. A spark that lit her up everywhere and sent tingles to places.

It was art with him. Athletic grace, and sheer masculine willpower. Straining muscles, gritted teeth, dirt, sweat and mud flying in the air.

Yeah, that flipped her switches like whoa.

Cade Mitchell on the back of a bucking horse was a truly orgasmic experience.

When he was through with a ride, he always shook. From his hands down to his boots. Adrenaline, he said. She shook too, though, and it wasn't always that.

He scared the hell out of her. Watching his accident during the Vegas championships, on TV in her living room, had been the single most painful moment of her life.

Her best friend, her family, dragged around the arena like a rag doll, white as death and knocking on that door.

In those moments, she'd gotten a look at life without Cade. And it had been a yawning vacuum of empty cold. She'd always known he was important. Right then, she'd realized just how much.

Ironically, she would still give it all to get him back in the saddle, so to speak. Because he loved it. Even though she knew that after that accident she'd sweat off three pounds during those precious seconds he was on the back of one of those beasts.

Small price to pay for allowing him to have his passion. For giving him back the ability to dance, however badly, so they could go out on that wooden floor together on his sister's wedding day.

But there was no going out on the dance floor for Cade. So they sat at the table and drank beer until the sky turned purple and the candles, strung over the tables in mason jars, lit everything with a pale yellow glow.

"Last dance," Amber said, knowing that Quinn and Lark

would be leaving soon. Off on their honeymoon. "Wanna get out of here?" she asked.

"Are you hitting on me?"

"Hay-ell yeah. What do people come to weddings for but to hook up? Certainly not to see their BFF's little sister tie the knot with a ridiculously handsome cowboy."

"You think he's handsome?" Cade asked, eyes narrowed.

She looked back at Quinn and Lark, who were still twined around each other like vines. "Uh, yeah. Have you checked that tat he has on his shoulder? Meow."

"Hey, he's my sister's husband," he said, grimacing slightly when he said the words.

"Don't worry, I'm out of the game."

"I thought we were gonna hook up."

"Did I say hook up? I meant 'let's get out of here so I can whup your ass at pool.' How about that?"

"Sounds like more fun anyway."

More fun than watching his little sister ride off into the sunset with a guy that Cade still had a tough time with in some ways. He didn't say that, but Amber could read Cade's subtext pretty well. Most often, said subtext was: *cheeseburger* or *breasts*. But every so often it was a real, deep emotion that he was never, ever going to show to the public.

Or even to himself.

Which was when she made sure she was on hand to help him out.

"Yep. I'll even buy you a beer because you look so damn pertty," she said, tweaking his hat.

"Well, shucks," he said, that lopsided grin tilting to the left, tilting her stomach along with it. "Let's get on with it . . . Can you play pool in that dress?" he asked, indicating her very abnormal and feminine attire.

"If you can play in a tie."

He reached up and grabbed the knot at the base of his throat and loosened it. "I think I can handle it."

"But can you handle me?" she asked, quirking her brow.

"I guess we'll see."

* * *

The Saloon, so named because it had been around since that was the usual name for a place where drinking and carousing occurred, was packed. Not so much because it was a Sunday night but because there was no other nightlife in Silver Creek. Nothing beyond a music festival that ran through the summer and attracted mainly the gray-hairs who lived in town only seasonally.

Not that Cade needed much of a nightlife. Not considering he hadn't done any real "going out" since his accident. Not considering that, even if he did, he couldn't dance.

He didn't know why he'd asked Amber to dance at Lark's wedding.

Ah, shit. Lark was married. That made him feel . . . well, it made him feel. And that was just something he hadn't been prepared for.

But she was his baby sister, and damn it, no matter how unsentimental he wanted to be about it, he and Cole had practically raised her. Which really made Amber's words closer to the truth than he wanted to admit.

He had empty-nest syndrome. A thirty-two-year-old single man with commitment issues . . . and empty-nest syndrome. As if he wasn't enough of a dysfunctional gimp-bag already.

He wandered up to the bar behind Amber and settled in next to her, his forearms resting on the wooden surface. Scarred from years of use and misuse. Bottles broken in brawls and Lord knew what else.

There was a story on the menus about a shootout between a sheriff and an outlaw that had resulted in the outlaw giving up the ghost on that very bar top.

The Saloon was filled with history. And Cade had spent too many nights in it over the past four years. Just soaking in the alcohol haze and absorbing the hormones of those more up to the challenge of getting laid than he was.

He'd become pathetic. And he didn't have it in him to change it.

"Two Buds, please," Amber said, leaning over the counter and catching the bartender's attention a lot quicker than Cade would have.

"I wanted a hard cider," he said. In truth, he would really like to have something that would knock him on his ass, but he tried to save the pitiful drunk trick for the privacy of his own home. In case he got maudlin.

"Too bad," she said.

He was glad she was here. Because there was nothing she hadn't been there for. Every hard thing he'd ever had to cope with. Finding out about his father's affair, his mother's death, his father's death . . . his accident. Lark's wedding.

Amber Jameson had been there for every-damn-thing.

"Beer me," he said, once she had the bottles in hand.

"Try again. I don't speak frat bro."

"Amber," he said, giving her his very best plaintive look.

"Fine. I pity you. Drown your sorrows in the way society has dictated men ought. Much healthier than expressing genuine emotion."

"Can I interest you in a friendly game of pool wherein I use your sad, pathetic skills at stick handling to make me feel more like a man?"

She arched a brow. "Sure, honey, if you think hitting balls into a pocket will make you feel more like a man."

"I do," he said, getting up from the bar and heading to the table.

Amber picked up a cue and started chalking the end. "Your balls are mine, Mitchell," she said, the light in her eyes utterly wicked.

"Whose balls haven't been yours?"

That taunt didn't come from Cade's mouth, and it had him on edge instantly.

Mike Steele. Standard, grade-A douche who worked at the mill. They'd all gone to high school together, but he'd never been too big of an ass. He was drunk tonight, though, and hanging out with two other guys from high school who fell on the wrong side of the douche spectrum.

And for some reason, they were interested in letting their asswipe flags fly.

Cade opened his mouth to tell them to back down but Amber had already whirled around, the end of the pool cue smacking sharply on the floor, the tip held up by her face.

"Can I help you, Mike?" she asked.

"Just saying, is all," he said, his words slurred.

"Maybe you should just say a little clearer," she said, "because I didn't quite take your meaning."

"He's just sayin'," douche number two said, "you're like the town mare. We've all had a ride."

Cade saw red. Death and destruction flashed before his eyes, but Amber barely blinked.

"Come on now," Amber said, her tone completely cool, "official rules say there's no score if the cowboy can't stay on for a full eight seconds. And if I recall right . . . you didn't."

"You stupid slut . . ."

And then Cade did step in, his fist connecting with the side of the other man's jaw. And damn it felt good. He hadn't punched anyone since . . . well, since he'd broken his brother-in-law's nose a year ago.

He was worried the other two goons might round on him, but they were too drunk to maintain a thought that went in a straight line, so they didn't seem to key in to the fact that Cade had just laid their buddy out flat.

"Hey!" Allen, the bartender shouted. "Cade, could you not bust faces in my bar?"

"Tell these assholes not to run their misogynistic mouths in your bar." He looked around at all the people who were staring at him, agape. "Yeah. Ten-dollar word, I just raised the IQ of the entire room," Cade shouted.

"Oh, Cade, for heaven's sake," Amber said. "Knock it off."

"He said . . ."

"Like I haven't heard it before?"

"I'm not going to listen to it."

"There's no point. And I don't need you to step in and

save me. I just wanted to play pool. Now you punched him
and we have to go so he doesn't call the cops on you."

"I know the cops."

"So what? Now I'm a spectacle, so thanks."

"Are you . . . are you pissed at me for punching a guy
who called you a . . ."

"Yes! I am pissed at you! Outside," she said. "Now."

They walked out the swinging front door of the bar and
into the dirt and gravel parking lot. Dust hung in the air,
clinging to the smell of hose water and hay and mingling
together to create its own unique scent of summer.

"What did I do? He was the one . . ."

She turned to face him, her cheeks red, her brown eyes
glittering. "He's not worth it. He's got half a brain and a tiny
peen. And all you needed to do was just let it go. I don't
need attention called to shit like that, Cade."

"What do you mean 'shit like that'? As in, it happens
frequently?"

"Yes."

"I've never . . ."

"Because they're normally too sober to do it in front of
you. Why do you think I have no friends other than you?"

"Because I'm all you need?" he asked, knowing full well
that wasn't true.

"Because I came into town with a bang, no pun intended,
seventeen years ago and no one can forget it. Because a lot
of the guys from high school I . . . And now as far as the
women are concerned, I'm that skank their husband screwed
under the bleachers during free period."

The blood was pounding in his ears, his heart racing. "I
don't think of you that way."

"I know. But I didn't have sex with your husband."

A laugh rushed out of him, awkward and angry. "Obviously that will never be a problem I have with you. And it's
not like you slept with their husbands after they were
married."

"Granted. But it doesn't seem to matter."

"Who cares about that high school BS anyway?"

"Everyone," she said. "Everyone but you. Which is why we're friends."

"I did a lot of stupid things in high school. Nobody gives me crap."

"That's because you were never naked with them. Guys are dumb about that stuff," she said, the lines around her mouth curving downward. "Anyway, it doesn't matter, Cade."

"It does."

"No. It doesn't. And don't go punching people for me anymore."

"Come on . . . you liked it a little."

The previously noted grooves at the corners of her lips turned up a bit. "Fine. A little bit. But only because he so had it coming."

"He really did."

"I wonder if any of your former flames are going to come up and accuse you of being a manwhore."

"Nah," he said, "they won't. But only because they don't want anyone to know they slept with me. That guy's just pissed 'cuz he's not going there again."

"I'm going to go ahead and take that as a compliment."

"I would never mean it as anything else."

"I know," she said looking down at her thumbnail. "I'm not the same person I was then."

"Sure you are. You're just more emotionally well-adjusted."

That earned him a smile. "Is that what you call this? Shooting pool, drinking beer, bar fights?"

"If it's not well-adjusted, then we're both screwed."

"I think we're screwed."

"Good thing we're screwed together, then." He slung his arm over her shoulder and they started walking back to her truck, the gravel shifting underneath his boots with each step.

"I guess so." She pulled away from him and rounded to the driver's side, climbing up inside the cab and turning the engine over.

He got in after her, slowly. Pissed that just climbing into a truck made him conscious of his limitations. Made him see the bad kind of stars, not the orgasmic kind, lightning bolts of pain shooting up his thigh and crawling up his back, stabbing right at the center of his spine.

He settled into the seat and let out a long breath. For a second there he'd felt ten feet tall and bulletproof. Punching that jackass in the face.

He didn't want to know what that said about him. But maybe it didn't matter, since he was back to feeling roughly six feet three and vulnerable to being trampled on by a horse.

Which he was.

He held on to the handle just above the passenger window and leaned out, shutting the heavy truck door.

"Do you feel like a man now?" she asked, maneuvering the truck out of the lot and onto the cracked two-lane road that led back to Elk Haven Stables.

"I'm riding bitch in your Ford, how much of a man could I possibly feel like?"

"Would you like me to throw you a raw steak when we get back to your place?"

"No. Tuck me in and read me a bedtime story."

"Aw, poor baby." She leaned over and put her hand on his thigh. Second time that night. Weird, but he seemed to be keeping a ticker on "number of times her fingers caressed him" that evening.

"She's married and off on her honeymoon," he said, resting his elbow out the truck window.

"Yeah. What do you think they're doing right now?"

He whipped his head around to face her. "Playing Scrabble."

"Is that what the kids are calling it these days?"

He had no frickin' idea what the kids were calling it these days. He hadn't had it for four years. Four. *Years.* He half expected the League of Players to come and confiscate his dick after so much time off.

He grimaced. His thoughts had taken an unsanctioned turn. He didn't like to think about his celibacy. His sister on her honeymoon was honestly preferable.

"Word games. In flannel pajamas," he growled.

"Fine, Cade, whatever works for you." She cleared her throat. "I bet Quinn got a triple-word score."

"No!" he said. "I punched a guy for you, don't torment me."

"You deserve it. You've given her enough hell."

"I have not," he said. "I've been a steadying and wonderful influence. Godlike, in many ways."

"In what way?"

"I have to think of examples."

"No, I believe you."

"She turned out in spite of me," he said, letting out a heavy breath. "I'm well aware of that. Kind of amazing that Cole and I were able to turn her into a functional human being. Or maybe she just did . . . anyway."

"Either way, you should be proud."

"Damn. I am an empty-nester."

"As you pointed out, you still have Cole."

"Oh, yes." Never mind that living in his older brother's domain was suffocating as hell. Cole was a great guy, but when it came to the ranch, which they all owned equal stake in, he could be a control freak.

And Cade had usually been happy to be in the backseat on decisions, because he liked to be a silent investor, so to speak. He'd put money into the ranch from his wins on the circuit, reaped profit in return, had had a place to crash at when he was home and mainly got to live on the road.

Now he was home. All the time. And having a brother who thought of himself as his boss didn't really do a lot to help with their sibling rivalry.

Cade had been fine for a while, playing the dumbass and in general drifting along with whatever Cole said.

But now that this was starting to look like it was going to be his life . . . like he was never getting back in the saddle in a serious way . . . well, now he was starting to realize he was going to have to make a new success for himself.

Otherwise his glory days would be perpetually behind him. And never in front of him. Ever again.

What a nice thought that was.

"I only drank half a beer and I'm starting to get philosophical and shit," he said.

"Uh-oh, better get you home, then. I wouldn't want to embarrass either of us by being present for this."

"You really are a good friend," he said.

She looked at him and smiled. "The best."

"Pretty much the only one I have."

"Because you're surly."

"Am I?" he asked.

"You just punched a guy in the face for offending you, so yeah, I'd say."

"I think it was noble of me," he said.

"Noble and godlike in one conversation. If this is your version of being a sad drunk then I'd hate to be exposed to your ego when you're feeling sober and upbeat."

"You'll be around me in that state tomorrow. Because now I owe you a game of pool."

"I don't know, I think I owe you for defending my honor. I didn't need it defended, but nonetheless, I appreciate you risking bruised knuckles for me."

"Anything for you," he said. "You know that."

"Oooh, dangerous promise, Cade Mitchell. You never know what I might ask of you."

"I've known you for seventeen years and you haven't shocked me yet."

"That smacks of a challenge," she said, giving him an impish smile. "You know I can't resist a challenge.